RULES
OF
COMMAND

C. A. MOBLEY

BERKLEY BOOKS, NEW YORK

RULES OF COMMAND

A Berkley Book / published by arrangement with
the author

PRINTING HISTORY
Berkley edition / October 1998

The Penguin Putnam Inc. World Wide Web site address is
http://www.penguinputnam.com

ISBN: 0-425-16746-1

BERKLEY®
Berkley Books are published by The Berkley Publishing Group,
a member of Penguin Putnam Inc., 375 Hudson Street, New York, New
York 10014.
BERKLEY and the "B" logo
are trademarks belonging to Berkley Publishing Corporation.

PRINTED IN THE UNITED STATES OF AMERICA

10 9 8 7 6 5 4 3 2 1

"Torpedo!"

The sonarman's shrill voice echoed inside the cramped MIUW van. Bailey turned and was jerked back by the cord that connected her headset to the console. She untangled it from the console joystick and got as close as she could to the sonar console.

"Where?" she demanded.

The sonarman pointed at an oddly unstable signature on his screen. "There—it's not U.S., not Soviet—nothing I've seen before. But look at that—and here—active sonar pings on passive." He reached up and cranked the speaker overhead to full volume. Sure enough, she could hear it now. The light, caressing quivers of sound that were characteristic of a fire control sonar. She turned back to Boston. "Tell *Jouett*—now."

"Captain." The sonarman broke in. "Ma'am this one isn't headed anywhere near the *Jouett.*" He pointed at a second set of lines on his display. "That merchant—that's the target. . . . "

RULES OF COMMAND

Don't miss C. A. Mobley's first electrifying novel, introducing National Security Agent Jerusha Bailey in a one-on-one battle with a German U-boat commander. . .

RITES OF WAR

Berkley Books by C. A. Mobley

RULES OF COMMAND
RITES OF WAR

My thanks to the rest of the team: Jake Elwell, brilliant agent and trusted friend, for tolerating my occasional mutinies and letting me steal his last name for the book. There really *is* an Uncle Billy. George Wieser, who frisked me for weapons during my last trip to New York. Tom Colgan, the world's best editor—naval aviation's loss is my gain. Laura Blumenberg, the newest star in Berkley's publicity department. And Joe Sullivan, the copy editor who caught me thinking in Marine when I was writing in Army.

Lynnette Spratley and Linda Coffman, who heard the story first. Doug Clegg and Andrew Harper, who talked me through the hard parts. Mom and Dad, to whom the real thanks are due for good genes.

Most of all, my family: Heather, Daniel, and Ron. Your patience, tolerance, ideas and proofreading made the difference. Thank you.

My e-mail address is: CAMMobley@aol.com. Two Ms. Spelling counts.

Snail mail address is:

C.A. Mobley
c/o Tom Colgan
375 Hudson Street
New York, NY 10014

Drop me a line.

Warriors, when irretrievably trapped will be fearless, in inextricable position will be resolute, when deeply penetrated will consolidate, and without other alternatives will fight. ... On the day orders are given, the seated warriors' tears moisten their collars, and the prostrate ones' tears streak down their cheeks. And when they are launched into inextricable positions, the valor of great heroes will arise.

Sun Tzu, *The Art of War* (514–513 B.C.)

Direct all the armies' legions as if exercising authority over one person. Direct them onto missions without explanation. Direct them into hazardous situations without revealing other prospects. Launched into annihilative places, they will survive. Trapped in lethal places, they will then live. Only troops perilously caught will have for victory sought.

Sun Tzu, *The Art of War* (514–513 B.C.)

Concerns in commanding armies are: scheming in impenetrability and being impartial in supervision; having the capability to subjugate the eyes and ears of warriors and soldiers, making them suppress their senses; modifying their assignments and adapting their plans, making the people suppress their judgment; modifying their campsites and winding their routes, making the people unable to think; leading them on joint operations as if climbing to a high spot and removing their ladder; leading them into deep penetration of other lords' lands and pulling their trigger; herding them as a flock of sheep, being herded to and fro without ascertaining the destination. ...

Sun Tzu, *The Art of War* (514–513 B.C.)

1

FIFTEEN MILES OUTSIDE THE GULF OF PANAMA: 23 SEPTEMBER 2003

NIRU 3

T'sing Lin was running out of air. The metallic taste tainting the last dregs of precious oxygen, the tightness in his chest, and the urge to breath faster were warnings he'd come to recognize.

It wasn't right. One hour for transit and attack maneuvers, ten minutes for the final approach, then thirty minutes for recovery. Two hours of air. More than enough if everything had gone well.

It hadn't, of course. The objective had been three thousand yards away from the briefed position, steaming north instead of west. By the time T'sing Lin had puzzled out the sonar anomalies and compared his contacts to the mission profile, he'd wasted fifteen precious minutes. It had taken him another ten minutes in an expanding search pattern to locate the contact, set up for the final approach, and slam the *niru* into the hull of the merchant ship. Now, vectoring back to the recovery location, not entirely sure that his grease-penciled track plot was accurate, and still dazed from the full-speed impact against the objective, T'sing Lin was beginning to suspect that he was lost.

But if the *niru*—the arrow, in the Manchu dynasty vernacular—missed the training target, it would simply claim another victim, one who already had so much to pay for. T'sing Lin would die now, rather than at the time and place the Chinese Navy would decree. And his failure would simply compound his dishonor, not absolve it.

He took shallow breaths, forced himself not to pant, and tried to slow his pulse by sheer willpower. There was no reason to panic, none at all. This was simply one more mission, the last in the six-month training course. A short period, but longer than any deployment he'd made to date with the Chinese Navy.

Too long. And not long enough. He steered his thoughts away from that train of thought, focused on a calm and peaceful image. Not now—not with air at a premium. Not with absolution, the all-forgiving Tao of redemption, within his grasp.

Twenty minutes of air left, according to the clock mounted on the console. He could hear it click quietly, the hands methodically creeping around the dial to mark the passage of the minutes. An irrational flash of resentment at it, that it could move without worrying about oxygen use.

Indeed, if one ignored the needs of the human inside, the *niru* had a combat radius of well over fifty miles. Four massive banks of batteries connected in series, a compact, powerful electric motor to drive a highly efficient propeller, all the propulsion and sensor equipment fitted neatly inside an advanced torpedo design. The warhead took up another three cubic feet in the blunt, rounded nose of the *niru*. The piloting compartment was wedged in between the batteries and the explosives.

Nineteen minutes.

T'sing Lin checked the gyro, deflected the *niru* slightly to the west, using the smallest movements possible. Successfully navigating an intricate course within the allotted time—and, he now realized, within the alloted air supply—was the goal of this final training dive. The last mission—except for one that would truly be the last.

He could fail. Purposely. Two of his classmates had already chosen that route, one only last week, preferring the quick bullet in the brain to the terrors of *niru*. The first failure had left T'sing Lin stunned—the second, slightly envious.

Eighteen minutes. T'sing Lin nudged the throttle forward. The reassuring whine of the electric motor overshot the ordered speed, then groaned as the governor dragged it back down.

Yes, the air was definitely getting worse. It was not just one of the waking nightmares that had increasingly plagued his time in the *niru*, one of the visions of cold, hungry deep water swallowing the twenty-foot vessel. It was out there still—he could feel it, the pressure against the hull, the seeping cold that robbed him of thought. Perhaps that was how it would be in the end, that the cold would kill him before the—

No. Do not think about it. Concentrate only on the mission. They do not intend me to die. Not now.

Soon. But not now.

USS *SEAWOLF*

USS *Seawolf* slipped silently through the water, barely more than a black hole in the churning ocean. Three hundred feet above her, the decreasing temperature in the ocean finally leveled off at a frigid forty-four degrees Fahrenheit, and the ocean settled into that stable configuration known as the isothermal layer.

The temperature gradient was of significant interest to *Seawolf*'s commanding officer, Commander Ernest Forester. Below the thermocline, sonar waves would be bent

back up toward the surface before they ever had a
chance to ping off the acoustically quietened hull of his
ship. It was like a black cloak drawn close around his
ship, and he welcomed the silence.

Tracer fire works both ways, and so does the protection of the isothermal layer—remaining below the layer,
as it was known. While no curious sensors located above
them could see the submarine, the *Seawolf* was equally
blind. Still, on balance, safety was preferable to complete knowledge.

Until now.

"We'll have to come shallow, Captain," Lieutenant
Commander Carl Dunning said. "No way we can copy
the broadcast from this depth."

"Tell me something I don't know." Forester studied
the message already decoded from the ELF net. The
communications personnel had already translated the
short combinations of letters into the plain-text message
before him.

FROM: COMMANDER, SUBGRUONE
TO: USS SEAWOLF
QUERY BROADCAST ASAP

Short and to the point—and no more enlightening
than trying to decipher the muted crackling sounds a
school of shrimp made. Why exactly was SubGru willing to risk *Seawolf* being detected? So far, there was
every indication that they'd managed to slip out of harbor unobserved, enter the patrol area, and fulfill their
mission with only the families of the crew members noticing their absence.

Not that staying covert was critical just now for any
particular reason. Their mission was an odd one, all the
more so for its lack of clear objectives. Someone somewhere—who knew who?—in the American intelligence
community had spotted an anomaly just outside the Gulf
of Panama. Forester grimaced, remembering just how

hard he had tried to get more information on this mysterious anomaly. The closest thing to an answer he'd gotten was SubPac's final, exasperated answer. "It's underwater, okay? And it's hinky. Now go find it."

"Well. It's not like we have a choice, is it?" Forester crumpled up the message and tossed it to his XO, who caught it easily with one hand. "Still, they ought to tell us enough to let me exercise some of that command discretion they keep talking about."

"Life in a blue suit," the XO said easily. "When do you want to make this happen?"

"Now would be a good time. There's not a damned thing that would count as a contact of interest out here, although it would sure help if SubPac would tell us exactly what we're supposed to be looking for."

"Maybe they don't know," the XO suggested.

Forester shot him an annoyed look. "That's what worries me most of all."

NIRU 3

Ten minutes.

His chest heaved, trying to draw oxygen out of the stale air inside the *niru*. T'sing Lin fought down panic. The tips of his fingers were blue and numb, and his vision was graying out at the edges.

Why, oh, why, was he here? He knew the answer.

Because he'd stolen an orange from his unit's commissary and had been convicted of felony theft. Because a sailor convicted of a felony while at sea could be executed. Because the *nirus* needed pilots to compensate for the lack of advanced microcircuits for independent guidance circuits. Because the Commander-Admiral had promised him that his wife and son, his parents as well, would die if he did not "volunteer." Too many answers.

And too little air. T'sing Lin squinted at his chart and fought for consciousness.

USS SEAWOLF

"Conn, Sonar! Subsurface contact, bearing 140, range 9,000 yards. Bearing constant, range decreasing!"

Forester swore violently. "What the hell is it?"

"No classification, sir. It's submerged and it's doing fifteen knots. Recommend course two-two-five to avoid."

"Two-two-five," Forester ordered immediately.

"Permission to go active, sir?"

Forester traded a puzzled look with his Exec. "What do you think?"

"Not yet. Not unless there's some indication she's detected us."

"Not likely."

"Not likely there's another submarine out here either."

"I'll be in Sonar." Forester stepped back into the black curtained-off area and crowded in behind the Sonar Supervisor.

The jagged lines tracing down the green screen were fine and discrete, showing only occasional perturbations in frequency. Another line fuzzed around the edges, indicating it was probably a propeller source.

"We're going to clear him by four thousand yards, Captain. At least."

Forester nodded. "But that doesn't answer the more important question—what the hell is it?"

NIRU 3

Three minutes.

His chest was hurting now, demanding that he breath faster, harder, pump oxygen into the starved tissues of his body. He could feel cold sweat trickling down his back. His vision was almost completely gone now, only a small circle of fuzzy light in the center of his field of vision remaining. The fact that he was almost blind seemed unimportant. Most things did now. Dimly, he wondered what really did matter.

Two minutes.

He squinted, forcing the slim, glowing hands of the clock into focus. Divers could hold their breath for two minutes, maybe even three. If he had stayed on course, hadn't missed a turn or a speed change, he would make it to the recovery net streaming out behind the mother ship. Just barely.

USS SEAWOLF

"Trailing exercise," the XO suggested. "Captain, that's the only thing we've seen in the last two months that could possibly count as a contact of interest. It has to be it."

"You think I don't know that?" Forester demanded. "But you saw the message. ASAP, it said."

"I know, it's just that—"

"We grab our traffic and get back down after her. Tell Sonar they damned well better regain contact as soon as we get back down below the layer."

Seawolf rose smartly to communications depth, deployed her trailing antenna, and broadcast her access code and identification to the satellite. Still completely submerged, she picked off the messages waiting for her and headed back down to follow the contact.

NIRU 3

One minute.

He was barely conscious now, panting despite his determined efforts to stay calm. Time, the passage of time—it was critically important, although he could not have said why. The clock in front of him held some particular significance. As the seconds ticked by, he became convinced that it was the clock of heaven, counting off the seconds until the world would be destroyed. He was uncertain as to whether that was something he should be glad about or worry about.

His suspicions were confirmed a few moments later. His entire world shuddered, tilted, then shifted ninety degrees to the right. The chest straps bit into his flesh as the tail of the *niru* jumped up, throwing him toward the console. He pawed ineffectually at the straps, wondering dimly where the release latch was, running his hands repeatedly up and down the length of flat nylon until it disappeared out of reach behind him.

He was upside down now, hanging from the straps, and he wasted a few precious molecules of oxygen to moan. The darkness that had been edging up around his field of vision surged forward, gobbling up the last bits of dim light. He fought it, praying and crying, trying desperately to keep the clock of heaven in view. But the world was ending, there was nothing he could do to prevent it, nothing anyone could do. The noise alone was driving him mad, along with the ceaseless rotation of his world spinning about on all three of its axes, until he no longer could tell whether the straps held him or he held the straps in place.

The noise increased, louder and louder, rhythmic and demanding, as the world was torn apart. At the last second, he screamed as light flooded in, certain that the sun was consuming him.

Light. Light and air. He lost consciousness for a moment, still screaming, while his body fought to suck oxygen in and pump it to the starved tissues. The anoxia receded quickly.

Finally, he was able to focus again. He looked up, barely able to move, into the faces of the crew.

His crew. The one that had strapped him into the *niru*

just two hours ago. Hands behind his back unbuckled the hated straps, peeled them back from his flesh. They came away with a slight sucking sound, leaving bloody strips on his white jumper.

"You did well," a low, resonant voice said calmly. "A little slow on the first leg, but within standards. You are now qualified."

The crew broke into a cheer. T'sing Lin struggled to focus on the face behind the voice, wanting to see yet already knowing who had spoken. There was no mistaking Won Su's voice, especially not for one who'd seen the clock of heaven.

USS *SEAWOLF*

"Where the hell did it go?" Forester asked. *Seawolf* was safely back inside the isothermal layer, searching for the contact. "Furthest-on circle search—now."

"I don't know, sir." The sonarman sounded worried. "I was holding contact on it, that same little shitty propeller going on and on. Look—it spun up, then faded out right after that. It doesn't make any sense. If it was going faster, it ought to be easier to detect. Not go away."

Forester swore quietly.

2

NATIONAL SECURITY AGENCY, WASHINGTON, D.C.: 24 SEPTEMBER

Jerusha Bailey scrolled through the message traffic queued up in her computer. Much of it had to do with events outside her area of responsibility. As Division Head for Western Europe, she paid particular attention to the traffic from those areas.

But not exclusively. The modern world was far more interconnected than her predecessors would have ever dreamed. Political power trickled through the various areas like water through cracked rocks, surfacing in the most unexpected of locations. What at first appeared to be random events often proved to have a connection to other world events—a revolution in Pakistan would spark food shortages in Argentina, inflation in Mexico would decimate the trade balance in France, and so forth and so on. Sorting out those connections and making plans for U.S. policy abroad was the job of Bailey and the other teams of area experts.

She paged through the database quickly, looking for anything out of the ordinary. Europe seemed relatively quiet, with Germany regrouping after their last aggressive onslaught and the rest of Europe hovering around like vultures, picking up concessions and reparations like buzzards.

That's the way it had always been in Europe, a seething cauldron of political tensions fomenting revolutions and insurrections. A relatively small land mass, as political entities went, Europe nonetheless possessed the highest concentration of ethnic nationalities and political systems of any part of the world. Regardless of all attempts to unify it into the European Economic Community, issue a single currency, and otherwise solidify the fractious population into a single entity, there was little hope for real and lasting peace.

Europe seemed quiet for the moment. Oddly quiet, in a way. For the last two years, Bailey had been expecting to see some reaction to the Chinese repossession of Hong Kong, but so far had been unable to discern any connections. There were the usual turmoils in central Europe, the influence of a surging German economy on the Common Market, but both trends were so historically predictable that they hardly warranted comment.

The subject line of one message caught her attention: SUBSURFACE CONTACT, PANAMA. Ever since her first days in the Navy, Bailey had been fascinated with submarines. After her release from active duty and transfer to the Naval Reserve, she'd stayed active in antisubmarine warfare. Now, as Commanding Officer of Mobile Inshore Undersea Warfare Unit 106, she had specific professional responsibilities regarding submarines.

She double-clicked on the message and scanned it rapidly.

A report from a U.S. submarine on special operations off the coast of Panama, with prosecution interrupted by the receipt of an ELF message. She shook her head, continually amazed at the effect of the fog of war.

The fog of war—a German term, coined by the military genius Karl Clausewitz. It was a concept that surfaced repeatedly in military operations. In the U.S., it was known as Murphy's Law: What could go wrong, would.

When the submarine had returned to prosecute the contact, it was gone. And SubPac's critical message, the one that the submarine had interrupted prosecution to download from the satellite? A warning about the tendency of a particular main coolant pump to overheat and smoke. A pump that wasn't even installed on the boat. She grimaced, imagining the sub skipper's mood shortly after receiving that particular message. It wouldn't have been pretty.

But still, this submarine contact off the coast of Panama intrigued her. She toggled over to a different screen, a geographic representation of all the U.S. ships and deployed military assets around the world.

As the names of the ships and their positions quickly painted across her screen, she swore quietly. Coincidence? Probably—but then again, maybe not. The map showed one particular ship just off the coast of Panama, located near the Pacific entrance to the Canal: the USS *Jouett.*

Jouett. *Collins's ship. At least I think she's still there. Surprised that she even got the Executive Officer slot after what happened in the English Channel. Terry must have had a hand in it.*

Terry—that had to be it. Terry Intanglio, her boss and protector inside the NSA, the one who'd both hired her and kept her on after Germany, over the strong objections of her immediate superior, Jim Atchinson. Bailey had been surprised when she'd had a job to come back to after Germany, but Terry had explained that there was little that anyone could do about it. After all, Bailey was a decorated national hero after both leading the U.S. defeat of German forces in the English Channel and exposing the machinations of a renegade faction inside the U.S. military itself. Heads had rolled, several promising military careers had been cut short, and the President himself had pinned the Meritorious Service Medal on her uniform shirt. Evidently, the grant of immunity had been extended to June Collins as well, since the short blond Naval officer who'd fought Bailey every step of the war had been selected soon after for the Executive Officer slot.

But what was the connection here? *Jouett* and Collins in the immediate vicinity of an inexplicable subsurface contact? Or had there been a submarine there at all? She frowned and picked up the phone. If anyone could come up with an alternative explanation, it would be Peter Carlisle.

A few moments later, Carlisle's smiling blond head popped up on the screen of her computer. His eyes were slightly unfocused for a moment, until her image resolved itself on his own screen.

"Jerusha? What's up?"

"Maybe nothing. You got a minute?"

"Sure, shoot."

"In person, I think."

The smile faded into a puzzled look verging on concern. "Serious?"

"I don't know. Call it a hinky feeling. It has to do with some of the players in Germany two years ago." She waited, giving him time to absorb that.

"On my way," he said after a moment's pause.

Pete headed up a section of the electronic-intercept support division, an esoteric collection of acoustic and computer experts who specialized in extracting discrete signals embedded in noise. After her first two weeks at NSA, once it became clear that Atchinson was not going to be leading her fan club, Pete had offered to have Jim's office wired for sound. At the time, she'd thought he was joking. After six months at NSA, watching and being the target of several sophisticated electronic practical jokes, she was no longer sure he had been.

Apart from a warped sense of humor, she and Pete shared one other common interest: the Naval Reserve. Pete had spent five years on active duty as a sonar technician on board a ballistic-missile submarine. When she'd learned he'd maintained his Reserve affiliation, she'd promptly recruited him to fill a vacant billet in her own unit. While Pete had more seniority than she did at NSA, he filled a senior enlisted billet in the unit Bailey commanded.

Minutes later, Carlisle appeared at her door. "What is so secret that you don't want to use taccomm?" he asked, referring to the computer-based tactical communication system. "And, before you ask, I'm not going back to Europe. My fun meter pegged way out last time."

"Collins. She's on *Jouett*." Bailey moved the computer screen around so that he could look at it. "You read that report on the contact down by Panama?"

He nodded. "You know I would have taken a look at it. Based on what the sub sonarman reported, I'd guess it was a real contact."

"That's what I thought. But whose? And is it just coincidence that Collins happens to be in the same area?"

He smiled slightly. "Probably. What, you think there's a worldwide conspiracy to put her in the immediate vicinity of anything that interests you?"

Bailey shrugged. "Maybe not. You don't find it odd that she's down there?"

"No." Carlisle's voice was firm. "I do not. Yes, there was some sort of subsurface contact down there, but I find absolutely no connection with *Jouett*."

"So what kind of submarine?" Bailey asked, dropping the question of Collins and *Jouett*.

"Diesel, probably. I checked known deployments and didn't come up with any candidates. But there are a lot of submarines out there that we can't track. I'm betting diesel based only on how hard she was for the nuke to pick back up. The only nuke in the area aside from ours was a Chinese one in port, and it's a piece of shit. And old Soviet Victor boat—*Seawolf* would have seen her.

Besides, I've got imagery of her tied up at that time."
Noting her surprised look, he said irritably, "Yeah, of
course I checked. I even halfway suspected we'd be
having this conversation, although I didn't know about
Collins and *Jouett*. And before you ask, I've got acoustics, too. So there."

"So now what do you think?" Bailey persisted.
"Knowing Collins is down there?"

"Get off it, Jer. The same thing I thought before—an
unknown diesel submarine in the area. Maybe even Chinese. God knows those little bastards are hard to keep
track of."

Bailey leaned back in her chair and closed her eyes.
The feeling that somehow this was a connection she
should see, a power surge she ought to understand, was
virtually irresistible. China had a long-standing interest
in Panama. Most of the traffic through the Canal was
still going to and from America, but China's takeover
of Hong Kong had expanded her international trade role
far beyond anything the U.S. had anticipated.

And soured many of her relations with the rest of the
world. Especially since China shows no sign of loosening up her human-rights policies. Not that she seems
to care much. China had not even filed a formal protest
over losing most-favored-nation status with the U.S.

"Maybe China's interest in Panama is more that just
friendly," Bailey mused. "Maybe she feels a bit more
comfortable down there with a few submarines around."

"Maybe. But that's a hell of a reach, Jerusha." Carlisle hesitated, then continued slowly. "I can't brief you
on the particulars, but there's nothing in the electronic
intercepts that would indicate forward deployment of an
additional submarine."

Bailey nodded, appreciating his difficulty. Carlisle's
field of expertise was so highly classified and esoteric
that the results were rarely available to other divisions
unless there was a demonstrated need to know. And under the circumstances, there was little reason that the

Division Head for Western Europe would need to know about electronic intercepts around the Panama Canal. He'd stretched the limits of his releasability guidelines just telling her that much.

"Trouble never starts how or where we anticipate it," she said finally. "While Panama isn't exactly in my backyard, this whole thing concerns me. If you find out there's anything you can tell me, let me know."

He nodded. "I will. And I'll keep an open mind about the *Jouett* connection too. You never know."

And that, Bailey thought as she watched him leave the office, was the essence of the problem with U.S. national security policy. One planned for the known problem areas of the world, but in the end one never knew exactly where or how the world would start to come unglued next.

3

GULF OF PANAMA:
25 SEPTEMBER

USS JOUETT

Lieutenant Commander June Collins, *Jouett*'s Executive Officer, made it a habit to tour Combat every night just before turning in. Tonight was no exception—it was 0130 and she could hear her rack calling to her, promising the prospect of four hours of uninterrupted sleep.

Collins shook her head, trying to clear away the dull pounding induced by too little sleep and too much coffee. There were ways to survive mid-watches, methods of coping with the sleep deprivation and distorted circadian rhythms that were the hallmarks of a United States Navy officer. She'd learned to nap when she could during the day, stealing a few precious minutes during chow hours, skipping meals, knowing that the cooks would leave leftovers in the reefers for watch-standers. As a final option, there was always the ubiquitous peanut butter and jelly.

Tonight, she'd been lucky. Pork chops on the menu, a main course that was well suited to prewatch snacking. She could still taste the grease at the back of her mouth, feel the tough, fibrous feel of the meat as her teeth cut through it.

Jouett was steaming within a box just off the coast of Panama, en route to drug-enforcement operations in the Caribbean. Tomorrow at 0900 she would transit the Canal, outchop into the Atlantic, and begin the frustrating and often futile mission of trying to hunt down the myriad small craft that ferried drugs between Central America and the U.S. coast.

Collins nodded to the TAO, Lieutenant Garland Williams, and slid into the console seat next to his. "Any problems?" she asked as she slipped the communications headset on.

"Would have called you if there were, XO," he drawled.

Collins stopped her sharp reply. It wouldn't do any good. Hadn't for the two months that the new Lieutenant had been on board. His remarks consistently carried a subtle undertone of sex, words and phrases fraught with double entendres and insinuations. She'd tried confronting him before. Hurt innocence was something else he did well, although she could see a vicious sort of amusement playing at the corner of his mouth as he protested his innocence, her misunderstanding. All a confrontation would do now would be amuse the rest of the watch section.

She slipped the headset on. Soft voices murmured to her, tracker alley piped into her right ear and surface plot into the left. She nodded—quiet, calm reports of the merchant traffic in the vicinity, an occasional update on a contact approaching. It sounded like she'd be able to get to her rack on time after all.

The Captain was in his cabin, probably asleep, although she could never be certain of that. In her four months on board *Jouett*, he'd repeatedly demonstrated his predilection for roaming the ship at odd hours, apparently taking some pleasure in catching people at their worst. The one time she'd skipped her nightly stint in

Combat, she been awakened four times in the next two hours to answer questions from the watch generated by the Captain's repeated visits. Finally, she'd gotten the hint.

She studied the large-screen display that dominated the forward half of Combat, noting a relatively slow-moving contact that had just popped up. It tracked erratically for a moment, indicating that the Aegis system was correlating the contact from several radars. "What the hell is it doing?"

Williams shrugged. "Who knows? It's commercial air. Course and speed fit."

"Why's the system boggling on it?"

"Atmospherics probably. Ducting or something." Lieutenant Williams yawned, took another sip of coffee, then shot her a pointedly amused look. "Or maybe he's just trying out some aerobatics. Who knows why CommAir does anything? Come on, XO, chill out. This isn't Germany."

"Nor is it the Pentagon," she snapped. "Maybe you were safe and sound behind a desk back there for the last three years, but things are a little different in the real world. You'd know that if you had had normal assignments."

Williams's eyes grew cold. "You've got a problem with my performance, XO?"

She sighed, shook her head. If only it were that simple.

Lieutenant Garland Williams, Annapolis '97, originally headed for the skies as a Naval aviator until a previously unexpected intolerance for high-performance maneuvers washed him out of the flight program. Vertigo, he called it.

Puking was more like it. If his father hadn't been Admiral Garland Williams, he would have been sent home years ago.

But Daddy's influence bought Sonny Boy a cushy job at the Pentagon, followed by redesignation as a surface-warfare officer. Garland Junior was sent to sea to play catch-up, entering the surface-warfare track with his first assignment as a department head on board *Jouett*, an assignment most officers garnered only after two Division Officer tours.

It was a plum for Junior—and a pain in the ass for the rest of the wardroom.

"Keep a close eye on it," she said, ignoring his question. "You don't know what can happen out here."

"It's squawking IFF as Panamanian National Airlines Flight 103," Williams said after glancing at his data console. "Since when were we at war with Panama?"

PANAMANIAN AIRLINES FLIGHT 103

Panamanian President Jose Garcia loosened the seat belt that was cutting into his midriff, and glanced around the spacious cabin of the converted C141 transport plane. The aircraft had started its life as a military cargo vessel for the United States Air Force. Shortly after the Canal had returned to Panamanian control, the United States had had it extensively refurbished, the interior redesigned to accommodate passengers, and divided this forward portion into a first-class cabin. For the last three years, it had been part of the small but growing Panamanian National Airlines.

Most of the other seats in this section were occupied by members of the President's entourage—three bodyguards, his national security advisor, two aides, and a few secretarial personnel. The remaining few seats were left empty for security reasons. A retractable steel-mesh door divided the first-class compartment from the coach section, and normal paying passengers occupied those seats.

No doubt, Garcia reflected, it was no secret that he was on board. Perhaps some of the passengers were wondering, as were the stewardesses, why he had not taken his Presidential aircraft. Why should they be inconvenienced with additional security procedures when the President had other means of transport?

It was a fair question—and one he wished he didn't have to answer. But after the two assassination attempts and threatened coup by the military just two months before, he no longer felt safe trusting the all-military force that crewed his own aircraft. A sad state of affairs, but not an uncommon one in the steamy politics that dominated this portion of the world.

Of all the nations, Panama was particularly susceptible to the whims and vagaries of hot-blooded Latino politics, straddling the border between North America and South, and now in sole control of the only expeditious passage between the Pacific and Atlantic in this part of the world. That his own Administration had lasted so long he took as a tribute to his personal leadership.

That, and successfully weathering the transfer of the Canal to Panamanian control, over not only widespread United States objections but those of his own countrymen as well. More than half of all Panamanians had opposed taking control of the Canal, not so much for the responsibility it imposed on the small nation, but for the resultant loss of dollars and trade that the U.S. military presence pumped into the economy. That those dollars had not been substantially replaced by America's foreign-aid program had been duly noted.

Still, they were making progress—steady progress. A host of Asian nations had been willing to step into the gap left by America's absence, and Garcia had had to pick and choose carefully among those offers of assistance and friendship.

The ones he'd decided to accept—were they a mistake?

He still hadn't decided, not even after eight years of closer ties with the Chinese government. What had started as a small trade delegation had expanded into substantial shipping facilities on either end of the Panama Canal, at Colon on the Pacific side and Balboa, a subdivision of the city of Panama, on the east. Over two hundred Chinese merchant ships now flew the Panamanian flag, and a small military assistance group was a growing presence in both facilities, ostensibly to provide harbor-side security for the Chinese merchants, but more likely to ensure that the Canal was always open.

But the final straw had come last month, when a Chinese trade delegation had announced their intention to conduct routine port visits and goodwill missions with both military warships and nuclear submarines. The first of those submarines was already tied up on the western side of the Canal, and two more were allegedly under way to join it. What had started as a partnership of equals had metamorphosed into something much uglier.

That was the occasion for this flight—and the reason for so many sleepless nights in the past three months. He'd spent days, weeks, every waking moment welding together a coalition of political forces that would finally assert Panama's true independence. And this one mission was the final result. Of all the forces operating inside Panama, the only ones not fully in support were the Panamanian military, long invested with an unreasoning dread of American occupation. So unreasoning that they were willing to accept the assistance of a race as alien and cold-blooded as the Chinese.

Well, no more. In this meeting with China's President, he would make Panama's right to self-determination clear. There would be a discussion, of course, of the possibility of military shipboard visits, but in the end this was one point he would not concede. There would be no more military port visits, most particularly not from the submarines. The one now tied to the pier would be put under way as soon as possible, and the other two would be diverted. Panama would not be intimidated—could not be, not after their long wait to free themselves from American influence.

Garcia felt a flood of confidence and courage as he contemplated his own determination. Yes, it would be good to step out from under the Chinese yoke, to stop this unhealthy relationship before it proceeded any further. He touched the lever on the side of his chair, tilted the seat back, and wondered if it might be possible to catch a nap.

USS JOUETT

As Collins watched, the speed leader in front of the commercial air track wavered, doubled in length, and then splintered into four separate lines radiating out from the contact symbol. The entire contact shivered momentarily, then resolved itself back into what it was supposed to be.

She glanced at the data display to her left. Eight hundred knots now, altitude decreasing steadily. The contact changed course slightly, now headed directly toward *Jouett*. The track supervisor should have been squawking about it as soon as it changed course. "Track supe, XO," she said. "What's going on with 7408?"

"XO, track supe. Noise level just spiked up to ridiculous, XO. The system is—wait, it cleared up. I don't know what it was. Maybe sunspots or something?"

"Sunspots." Possible, she supposed. Electromagnetic shielding kept exterior radiation from reaching the sensitive electronics inside the SPY-1G radar system, but it couldn't do anything about the environment outside the ship. Noise in the search radars degraded the signal, and she'd seen a defense-contractor videotape of some spectacular effects from sunspots.

But never anything quite that well-defined. That hadn't been like any noise spike she'd seen before. And if not the sun, what was dumping energy into the atmosphere?

"It's cleared up now at least," the track supervisor

continued. "I'll put a note in the pass-down log about it, though."

"Is it on a commercial air corridor?" she asked.

"Slightly off—maybe fifteen miles south of it." He was starting to echo the uneasy tone in her voice. "And opening—ma'am, he needs to turn north to reenter the corridor. Like now. Look—I'll put it up on your screen."

A set of narrow red lines blipped up on the screen, delineating the standard commercial air corridor to their north. The errant airliner was moving away from it, and if the contact data was correct, making no attempt to vector back into its assigned airspace.

"All stations, this is the XO. Anyone got anything on this contact?" Beside her, Williams rolled his eyes. She bit back a rebuke.

A chorus of negatives from the surface track supervisor, Sonar, the lookouts, and the SLQ-32 electronic-warfare technicians. The speed leader on the contact wavered again. Collins stood, driven to her feet by the uneasiness seeping up from her gut and tethered to her console by the headset cord. "What are you doing, mister?" she said softly, as though she could reach out and talk directly to the off-course pilot. "Come on, turn north, north, north. . . ."

"Crap, it's—XO, AWG-9 radar indications," one of the electronic-warfare technicians yelped. "Targeting mode. Jesus, it's—TAO, recommend unmask CIWS batteries. Now."

Visions of the USS *Stark* hit by missiles from Iranian P-3 aircraft in the Persian Gulf—no, she wouldn't be sucker punched like that. Never.

"What's happening?" Williams said. He stared at the large-screen display as though he could force it to conform to his version of reality by sheer will alone. "An AWG-9—no, it can't be. That's an off-course airliner, not an F-14! Track supe, check your—"

Collins cut him off. "General Quarters. Now, Mister

Williams. Bridge, XO—hard right rudder to unmask CIWS.''

"Stop it," Williams cried. "You can't—it's not—I'm the TAO!''

The speed leader cracked apart into four distinct lines running close together and almost parallel out from the airliner. She could hear the track supe screaming now, even without the headset. "Jesus, missile separation! XO, vampires inbound. Four—no, it's—oh, shit.''

"Seeker head, seeker head," the EW yelled, his voice cutting through the mounting noise in Combat.

"It's not real!" Williams howled.

"You're relieved. Get out of Combat.''

Williams vaulted up from his seat and tried to pull her headset off. Collins slammed an elbow into his gut and followed it with a closed fist to his groin. Williams screamed, then crumpled to the deck. He clawed at the armrest on his chair, trying to pull himself upright.

Collins turned to look at the weapons console. "Assigning weapons to target. Weapons free now. Take contact with birds.''

"Take contact with birds, aye," the weapons chief replied. She heard the uncertainty in his voice. "XO, that noise earlier—are you sure—?''

"Fire one." She drove one stiff, numb finger down on the button, manually activating the fire-control circuit. "Fire two.''

The hard, shuddering rumble of missile launch momentarily drowned out the voices on her headset. She reached up to cover her ears, operating on sheer instinct and training now.

The four missile contacts on the screen vanished. Too soon to be the missiles—they couldn't have taken them out, couldn't be there yet—the last echoes of the launch were still echoing inside Combat, competing with the incessant gonging of the General Quarters alarm.

The symbols for *Jouett*'s missiles were now on the

screen, arrowing straight toward the commercial air contact.

"Two birds fired," a voice said finally. "Dear sweet God—we just shot at an airliner."

"You tell me what airliner does Mach one-point-two and radiates fire-control radar," Collins demanded. "Tell me."

"None of them," a new voice said. She swiveled in her chair to look up into the face of the Commanding Officer of *Jouett,* Captain Dave Renninger. A look of cold white fury suffused his patrician features. "And you better pray to God that you were right."

FLIGHT 103

The missile slammed into the joint just where the vertical stabilizer connected with the rest of the fuselage. It tore through the thin aluminum outer shell, the continuous expanding-rod forehead of the missile ripping apart the metal as though it were tissue paper. The stronger structural supports lasted no longer, disintegrating into chunks of razor-sharp shrapnel that spattered the passengers in the aft section of the plane against the walls.

In the first microsecond of the impact, Garcia knew something was terribly wrong. The aircraft gave an unhealthy, sickening jolt forward, pitching nose-down at a twenty-five-degree angle almost instantaneously. Every bit of loose gear within the compartment rocketed forward, slamming against the forward bulkhead. For just a second, the aircraft jerked back upward, as if it would find some miraculous way to maintain level flight absent the aft one-third of the fuselage. The massive wings fought for lift, but the wildly unstable aerodynamics won out. The C141 tipped back nose-down and commenced an uncontrolled descent to the ground.

Garcia's face hit the seat back in front of him. Then centrifugal forces jerked him out of his seat and sent him pelting back towards the aft of the compartment. He slammed into the metal grating separating the two compartments, and was held there by the forces of acceleration. Bodies piled up on top of him. The screams of people dying, injured, and crushed were just barely audible over the roar of the air.

By the time the first chunks of flesh hit the bulkhead, the aircraft was already careening down toward the ground in a crazy, death-seeking, erratic spiral. Debris, bodies, and luggage from the open storage compartments trailed behind it, mixing with the aviation fuel pumped out into the air by severed fuel lines. The entire stream ignited into a convection trail of fire, its path following the clumsy spirals and twists of the aircraft's death throes. Black smoke billowed after that, quickly starting to shred and dissipate in what had once been a head wind.

At ten thousand feet above ground, there was sufficient oxygen in the ambient air to support life. The passengers who'd survived, including President Garcia, regained consciousness, slowly at first. By the time the aircraft was five hundred feet above ground, the screaming had resumed. It lasted but a few moments longer.

4

WASHINGTON, D.C.:
25 SEPTEMBER

THE BELTWAY

Jerusha Bailey swung her car out into traffic and headed for work. The sun was not yet up, but traffic was already starting to build on the Beltway. Headlights strung out like a diamond necklace stretched as far as she could see on the other side of the Beltway as the inhabitants of the myriad government facilities located in and around the District of Columbia each tried to beat the traffic in.

The radio spewed its usual patter of dramatized tragedies, weather reports, and traffic updates. Not that the latter would do anyone much good—there were few options other than the Metro for getting into D.C. proper.

''Navy officials are now confirming unofficial reports that the USS *Jouett,* a guided-missile destroyer, fired on and hit a Panamanian National Airlines jet earlier this morning. The scheduled commercial flight was on a normal route between Panama City and Hong Kong. As yet there is no explanation as to why the ship fired at the aircraft or whether there were any American citizens on board.''

Bailey slammed on her breaks as the report concluded, narrowly missing the stopped Mercedes in front of her. She took a deep breath, concentrated on stilling the adrenaline tremor in her hands generated by the near miss.

Jouett again! Now just what the hell—

She eased off the brake as traffic in front of her started moving again.

Collins. An aggressive officer, one who'd never run from a fight even if a tactical retreat was in order. She'd almost gotten them killed doing just that.

And now a blue-on-blue engagement, military euphemism for a harsher word: fratricide. Brother killing brother. It happened in the military, both in exercises and in real life, far more than anyone was willing to admit. Usually it occurred under more demanding operational scenarios. Well, maybe not, she realized, thinking of the USS *Vincennes* and her downing of the Iranian airbus a decade ago.

She gunned the engine, veered off onto the shoulder, and raced for her office.

NATIONAL SECURITY AGENCY, DIRECTOR'S OFFICE

Jim Atchinson carefully laid his pen next to his legal pad and leaned back in the leatherette chair. He laced his fingers across his stomach and smiled at the man opposite him. ''Frankly, I think this would be an excellent opportunity for Bailey.''

Terry Intanglio, Director of NSA, looked startled. ''Why Bailey? Hasn't she been under the gun enough in the last year?''

Atchinson took a moment to look around the small conference room before replying. It was luxurious by government standards, much more comfortable than the small meeting area on his own floor. Up here, genuine wood paneling replaced the two-toned white and green high-gloss institutional paint on his own floor, and the thicker brand of carpet tugged at the rollers of his chair instead of the industrial indoor-outdoor floor covering his own department had. Even the chairs were more comfortable, with marked lumbar support padding and soft, cushy arms.

In one corner of the room, stacks of china cups and saucers graced the top of a credenza. Next to that was a plate of crullers and doughnuts, sent up by the kitchen in anticipation of lengthy morning meetings. The kitchen was always the first to know, right after CNN, Atchinson reflected.

Finally, when he judged enough time had passed to give him the appearance of thoughtfulness, Atchinson shook his head. "You know, I was wrong about Bailey. She did a fine job in that German situation last fall." He paused for a moment to consider how his blatant falsehoods were playing with Intanglio. Seeing his boss nod, he continued. "Before that German affair, you had been talking about giving her a broader range of responsibility. Rounding out her professional education, as it were. This might be just the opportunity."

Intanglio leaned back in his own chair and looked thoughtful. "I hadn't realized you'd changed your opinion of her that much."

Atchinson shrugged. "We all make mistakes. I guess I was wrong about her."

Not like any of you gave me much choice. She was on active duty at the time, the Navy's responsibility. Not mine. And just how the hell am I supposed to treat her when she arrives back here with a presidential pardon in hand as well as a chest full of military commendations, hmm?

"It would get her out of the European Theater altogether," Atchinson continued, fighting down a wave of bitter resentment. "And really, with the high profile she's had since then, it would look like we were sending our best people out there. Give us some good press for once."

"That's worth considering. Okay, I'll give it some thought."

Intanglio watched Atchinson leave, mildly amused at the self-satisfied smile on the other man's face. As though he'd pulled something over on Intanglio, as though his boss didn't understand just exactly what the division chief was trying to achieve. Bailey's success in Germany had rankled on Atchinson, beginning with her insistence on doing her two weeks' active duty while events were heating up in Korea, and ending up with her unraveling the puzzle of events in the English Channel to discover that the Germans were behind the Korean war. That he'd been outsmarted, out-thought, and out-warriored by a mere woman ate visibly at the man.

Still, there was something to what Atchinson said. Sending Bailey to head up the NSA detachment in Panama would give Intanglio another set of eyes on the problem of Panama. Except that it wouldn't happen exactly as Atchinson proposed.

No, they'd send her in under the cover of her Reserve duties, gaining the on-scene intelligence they needed without exposing the Agency to unwanted publicity.

"There's something you forgot, though, buddy," Intanglio said aloud to the empty room. "Just one small thing. The situation is going to shit down there and you're worried about our publicity. And that, my friend, is why you'll never be promoted again. Not as long as I'm here."

5

THE GULF OF PANAMA:
26 SEPTEMBER

USS JOUETT

The ship lingered just outside the twelve-mile limit of
the Panamanian coast, steaming back and forth inside its
small box like a tiger pacing a cage. Commander Renninger's instructions from Third Fleet were explicit—
exercise his freedom-of-navigation rights in international
waters, but do nothing to further provoke the Panamanian government. Conversely, he was also ordered to
maintain an American presence in the area as a sign of
continued U.S. support to the Canal Zone.

For the first twenty-four hours after the shoot-down,
Collins haunted Combat, doggedly playing back the engagement time and time again. She compared her electronic track with the paper track maintained by the
navigator and surface plot in Combat. She watched the
data until her eyes blurred; the white track streaking out
from the coast, designated as commercial air, then suddenly losing altitude and accelerating through Mach 1.2.
She stared at the screen until she could no longer tell
track from the vague glimmers of phosphorescent green

in the screen, desperately searching for some clue as to
the genesis of her mistake.

The intelligence specialist on board kept busy logging
the commercial activity through the western entrance of
the Canal. Twenty-eight Chinese-flagged merchant ships
were now in port, taking advantage of the state-of-the-
art facilities built by their owners. The Chinese port station was almost completely automated, and cargo flowed
through it so quickly that there was constant traffic in
and out of the harbor.

The Canal remained open, and the few ships that still
flew the American flag suffered nothing more egregious
than bureaucratic delays, lost paperwork, and general administrative red tape. The Panamanian government was
making their point—not aggressively, but a point it was.

Finally, Renninger cornered Collins in Combat and
insisted she get some sleep. "You're not doing us any
good here."

"I just keep thinking I might have missed something," she said, her voice hoarse.

He shook his head. "The IFF—that's what you
missed. Anything else, it'll come out in the investigation."

There was an aura of competence that always surrounded large men, Collins thought, studying her captain. Renninger was a case in point. He towered over
her, which required her to cant her neck back uncomfortably to stare up into his furious face. He took a step
closer to her, an intimidation tactic she'd seen work all
too well on his junior officers. She stood her ground,
hands on her hips.

"You panicked." Renninger's voice was cold. "Just
admit it."

Collins' shook her head in denial. "I didn't. You just
saw the last four seconds of the engagement. Prior to
that, it was inbound on threat profile. Under the circumstances, the only option was to shoot."

"The only option you saw, you mean."

"I don't understand."

Renninger hissed a frustrated sigh. "I think you know exactly what I mean. You've got a reputation around here, lady. The Navy isn't all that big. I know what you were like on *Ramage*—and what you did."

Collins's stomach curled up in a knot. Of course he knew—that unspoken knowledge had lain between them ever since she'd started her Executive Officer tour on board *Jouett* four months ago. That she'd been selected for it at all still amazed her. She'd taken it as a sign that the forces in power had deemed she was worthy of a chance to redeem herself, and she hit the decks running for this tour, determined to be the best Executive Officer that ever graced the deck of a destroyer. Or any ship, for that matter. Her selection was all the more sweet after her earlier conviction that she might as well resign then and there from the Navy.

"If you've got any questions about what happened on board *Ramage*—"

He cut her off with a sharp gesture. "I don't have any questions. I know exactly what happened. You mutinied."

"That's not how it looked to me at the time," she said. "You don't understand—you weren't there. We had torpedoes inbound, this Reserve female commander who was on board was making what I thought were some extremely stupid decisions. And she was running from a fight—that submarine wolf pack had both the USS *Weeks* and our allied British forces pinned down in a killing field. And she ran."

"Turned out she was right, though, didn't it?" Renninger said, his voice dripping disgust. "If Bailey hadn't gotten back to the bridge, *Ramage* would be sitting at the bottom of the English Channel with *Weeks*. Wouldn't she?"

Collins nodded slowly. "As I said, at the time—"

"If you ever get a command tour—which I sincerely hope you never do—how would you feel about having

a mutineer assigned as your Executive Officer?'' he
snapped. ''Just makes you feel good about the whole
chain of command, doesn't it? About duty, loyalty—all
those core values we talk about.'' Renninger looked as
though he were about to spit on the deck in disgust. ''I
should have known better than to let you on board this
ship.''

''And what precisely could you have done about it?''
Collins spat out, now goaded beyond all possibility of
self-restraint. ''The Bureau makes the decisions about
who gets the XO slots, not you. The last time I heard,
the Navy didn't give commanding officers veto power
over those decisions.''

''You're right, they don't. I don't know what kind of
political pull you've got to get you special treatment like
that, but it doesn't wash with me. By the time you leave
this ship, you'll have fitness reports that say you ought
to be assigned to a tug for the rest of your life. No, not
even that—nothing that floats. How about duty as a public affairs officer?''

Collins turned pale. ''You won't even give me a
chance.''

He nodded. ''That's right. You've already had one.
And you blew it.''

''I suppose Senator Williams' son would get the same
treatment?'' she flared. Now that Renninger had made
it clear that she had no future on board *Jouett*, there was
nothing to lose. She'd finish out this tour, do the best
job she could, and then retire.

''Senator Williams' son is just another lieutenant as
far as I'm concerned.''

''Yeah, right,'' Collins muttered.

''What was that?'' he snapped.

Collins stiffened to a position of attention. ''Nothing,
Captain,'' she said, her voice cold and formal. ''Is there
anything else?'' She made a small movement, as though
to leave his cabin.

''Now that you mention it . . .'' He thrust a message

at her. "You might as well read this. I could leave you in the dark—hell, I ought to."

Collins took the message and scanned it quickly. It was dated only two hours before, and was a flash-priority "Personal For" message from the Chief of Naval Operations to Commander Renninger.

FROM: CHIEF OF NAVAL OPERATIONS
TO: COMMANDER D. RENNINGER, COMMANDING
     OFFICER, USS JOUETT
SUBJECT: EXECUTIVE OFFICER; RELIEF AS

1. PER YOUR REQUEST DATED 251302Z, YOUR RE-QUEST IS DENIED. LIEUTENANT COMMANDER COLLINS WILL CONTINUE AS EXECUTIVE OFFICER PENDING A COMPLETE INVESTIGATION INTO THE ALLEGED INCIDENT.

2. WHILE NOT REQUIRED, THE FOLLOWING EXPLA-NATION IS PROVIDED: AT THIS TIME, THE UNITED STATES' NATIONAL INTERESTS WILL NOT BE SERVED BY ADMITTING U.S. CULPABILITY IN THIS INCIDENT. RELIEVING LIEUTENANT COMMANDER COLLINS WOULD CONSTITUTE AN ADMISSION THAT WOULD BE DETRIMENTAL TO OUR NA-TIONAL SECURITY POLICY. PENDING FURTHER IN-VESTIGATION, AND AUTHORIZATION, YOU WILL TAKE NO ACTION TO RELIEVE HER.

"So, for better or for worse, you're still the Executive Officer." Renninger's eyes studied her, cold and malevolent. "I don't expect this investigation to take long—the evidence is too clear. We're minus two missiles and they're minus one airbus."

Renninger had a point. As much as it had seemed like the right decision at the time, she *had* been wrong about *Ramage*. Been wrong, and almost lost the ship as a result of it. Bailey had pulled her ass out of the fire, had probably even had something to do with Collins's later assignment to *Jouett*.

Dead bodies floating in the ocean, patchworks of burn marks and white flesh, bellies distended and faces bloated beyond recognition. Fish, sharks, the inevitable decay that started so quickly in water.

She shook her head, tried to drive out the pictures invading her mind. The photographs from the *Vincennes* incident made it all too clear what the aftermath of an airbus disaster looked like. This time, she was the one responsible, the one who had butchered innocent civilians. It would haunt her forever.

But what could she have done differently? There had been no time, no time at all. If she'd waited and the targets had been real missiles, there would be American families mourning their dead instead of Panamanians. USS *Stark* or USS *Vincennes*? Take the first hit on the off chance that you're mistaken, or try to protect the crew entrusted to you? Which came first?

Live with it. That's what she'd end up doing, one way or another, just as she had with *Ramage*. No second-guessing, no excuses. It was the only way she could find to cope with the enormity of the results of her decision.

Collins shook her head, not believing the words on the printed sheet of paper in front of her. "It was the right thing to do."

"So you say. But I believe you've used that line before—and that time you were wrong too."

6

PANAMA CITY, PANAMA:
26 SEPTEMBER

HEADQUARTERS, PANAMANIAN ARMY

Jorge Aguillar, the interim President of Panama, convened his war council in the ancient, stately army headquarters located at the eastern entrance to the Panama Canal. With him were his deputies—those he still trusted, at any rate—as well as the general and titular command of Panamanian forces. As Garcia's logical successor, it was time to reevaluate the deals his predecessor had made, solidify his own power base, and begin the process of building Panama into a world power. Garcia's stodgy provincialism, his continuing paranoia over the power of their trading partners, had frustrated Aguillar for years.

He let them sit around the conference table for a few minutes, savoring their confusion and fear. Despite the reactionaries who occasionally fomented for elections, the continuing presence of U.S. forces in the form of a small Southern Command detachment in Panama, and the pressure the world community increasingly brought to bear on his small country, his word was law within the confines of his national borders. No one knew that better than the men assembled here. It would take but one word, one small gesture to his personal security force that ringed the outer walls, and any one of them would have been executed immediately.

When he judged the silence had gone on long enough to establish the proper mood of cooperation, Aguillar said, "So? Your thoughts, please." He smiled benignly at the men around the table, knowing that they would now embark on the delicate game of trying to guess what it was that their President wished to hear.

"It was the American warship," the general said finally, breaking the silence. "Our radar tapes are clear on that."

Aguillar nodded reflectively. "So the earliest reports are confirmed. The question is, then, how do we proceed?" He looked around the table slowly, deliberately, letting his eyes linger on each one seated there. "You are my advisors, are you not? So advise."

General Martin Bellerosa shook his head solemnly. "Security is becoming more and more of a problem. When it was just the Americans, we could keep track of them." He spread his hands expressively. "A small country, many informants—it was not a problem. Our long experience with the Americans gave us the advantage. But now, now that we own the Canal, we have many others to deal with. Some of them are not so easy to track. They come from closer, more insular societies than our own, and we do not have agents that can pass for friends in their communities, for obvious reasons. You understand."

Aguillar shot him a knowing look. "The Chinese, of course. They would be your primary problem."

The general nodded. "The money they bring in is welcome, I know. But it does complicate matters. With shipping facilities at both ends of the Canal, as well as substantial military garrisons, they could pose a problem. One I am not certain we are equipped to deal with.''

"What have you not told me?" Aguillar asked softly. "Are you incompetent?"

The general stiffened. "Not at all. I'm just suggesting that the problems we face today are more difficult than your predecessor's. And the answers aren't always as easy."

"But there's nothing difficult about this," the Minister for Economics broke in. "You've all seen the evidence. The Americans shot down our airliner. What more do we need to know?"

Aguillar kept his eyes fixed on the general. "You don't believe that?" he asked in a carefully calculated tone of mild astonishment. "That the Americans are at fault?"

"I don't know what to believe. I've worked with them for many years—as have all of you. On acts such as this—well, we would expect to see some justification for it, wouldn't we? How does this possibly advance the American interests in our country, to commit such an act of aggression? What good does it do them?" The general shook his head heavily. "Since I can't answer those questions, I find it difficult to believe the easy and obvious answers—that the Americans are responsible."

"Who else could it possibly be?" the Minister for Economics said, his voice rising in pitch. "Surely you aren't suggesting the Chinese."

The general looked away from Aguillar, and studied the intricately inlaid surface of the table before him. "Not at all. As I said, I know how much money they bring in. It's just that—"

"It wouldn't be impossible for it to be someone else," Aguillar said thoughtfully. "I'm reminded of the incident off the coast of New York, with the TWA airliner. Witnesses still claim they saw a missile shoot it down, but there's been no hard evidence to support that theory. Yet we know how easily handheld weapons could reach to that altitude under the right conditions.''

The general looked back at him, and Aguillar was amused to note a trace of relief on the general's face. ''Just so. Until the Americans are willing to admit responsibility, until they've completed their own investigation, I think it's unwise to jump to conclusions.''

The Minister for Economics shook his head. ''I don't believe this. Your own radar tapes show the missile. Just because the Americans have not admitted it—''

Aguillar cut him off. ''We'll wait then,'' he said, shifting his gaze to the Minister for Economics. ''In the meantime, each of you will prepare a package of recommendations. Develop two sets of plans—one, in the event that the Americans admit responsibility or we obtain more hard evidence of that, and the second if some party or parties unknown are responsible. Include a full range of possibilities, ranging from domestic terrorism to the intervention of our good friends the Chinese. When we decide finally who is responsible, I will tell you what my first action will be.''

His eyes took on a dark, hooded look. ''If the Americans wish our friendship, they will have to earn it. As the Chinese have done.''

7

NATIONAL SECURITY AGENCY: 27 SEPTEMBER

WESTERN EUROPE DIVISION

The note from Jim Atchinson was short and sweet: "See me as soon as you get in." She sighed and slipped her briefcase under the desk. *Jouett*. It had to be. Did Atchinson know about the Collins connection? Probably so—he had an uncanny ability to find her weaknesses, make her look bad, and the fact that Collins was on *Jouett* would give him an opportunity to bring up Germany again.

She pulled the door shut behind her and walked down the passageway towards Atchinson's office. The honeycomb of cubicles and compartments, ranging from unclassified secretarial spaces to those with the most secret vaults and crypto-locks, were starting to fill up as the early morning crowd filtered in. She heard the undercurrent of excitement generated by the shoot-down, caught bits and snatches of conversations as the various divisions and departments went to work on their small parts of the problem.

The best defense was a good offensive.

She knocked once on Atchinson's door, then pushed the door open. "You wanted to see me about Panama?"

The fleeting look of annoyance on Atchinson's face confirmed her hunch. "How did you know?"

She shrugged and slipped into the chair in front of his desk. "Pretty obvious, isn't it?"

"Perhaps. Did Terry talk to you?"

It was her turn to look puzzled. "No. I guess he thought I would want to hear it from you first."

"Well, I take it you have no serious objections then."

Silently, she damned her own deviousness in trying to pretend she knew what his summons was about. Now she'd worked herself into a spot where she understood only half of the conversation, and that was hers.

"It depends," she ventured. "I don't know the details."

"We're sending you in under the cover of your MIUW unit," he said bluntly. "The arrangements have already been worked out with the Navy."

Jerusha stared at him. "You must be joking. Panama will never stand for it, not so soon after the airbus."

"Stand for it—hell, they proposed it. Seems the new President wants a demonstration of our goodwill, just on the off chance that somebody besides that destroyer shot down that airliner. Actually, I think he might be a little grateful. Aguillar and Garcia have been at each other's throats for the last year over this Chinese business."

He leaned back in his chair, crossing his hands across his stomach. "You'll be there to conduct HVV operations—high-value-vessel protection," he continued. "I understand it's a normal MIUW mission, so there's no reason for the Panamanians to be suspicious."

"It's only been eight months since our last deployment," she said.

The MIUW—Mobile Inshore Undersea Warfare—unit was a small, elite Naval command, staffed primarily by Reserve officers and technicians. The unclassified story was that it was comprised of approximately sev-

enty members and maintained a wide range of advanced
surveillance and detection equipment aimed primarily at
intercepting enemy submarines and other forces inside
protected harbors. Insiders—and that most definitely included Jim Atchinson—knew that the Navy drew on a
number of arcane civilian specialties to staff the units.
Like NSA analysts.

During Desert Storm and Desert Shield, several
MIUW units had been deployed inside Kuwait to assume
control of the harbor there as Harbor Defense Commander.

In the years since then, the MIUW units had become
increasingly sophisticated. They were now equipped
with long-range passive sonar arrays that could be laid
on the bottom of the ocean by a small RHIB—rigid-hull
inflatable boat—and terminated back at the RSSC—ra-
dar/sonar surveillance center—van that provided a
comprehensive integrated tactical picture of the area.
Additionally, each unit had several Humvees with radar
mounted on retractable masts that could be deployed at
significant ranges from the van. Data from the remote
radar sites was relayed back to the van via microwave
link. With one MIUW unit in place, a harbor defense
commander could effectively control the movement of
all traffic inside constrained waters.

"They'll probably have heard of me. After Germany,
I mean," she said, reluctantly bringing up the very issued she'd hoped to avoid.

Atchinson nodded. "We've considered that. But actually, it works in our favor this time. We don't want
them entirely comfortable with the situation, and having
you in theater will keep them slightly off balance as to
our intentions."

"Like a sacrificial lamb?"

"I didn't say that. Let's just call it an additional uncertainty factor."

She nodded, and tried to decide what was really going

on. "Who exactly will I be working for? NSA or the Navy?"

"Nominally, you'll be attached to the Navy. However, once you're back on active duty, you'll be given additional reporting instructions to include us as an info addee on any message traffic or intelligence summaries you generate. Naturally, we'll expect some degree of cooperation and responsiveness on your part."

"As long as the Navy makes it official with orders," she said, a little more sharply than she'd intended.

"Just to ensure your own safety, given the political situation, you'll be deployed with a SEAL team to provide perimeter security. We're also assigning a Special Forces team from the Army to the mission as well. Your primary point of contact will be Master Sergeant Billy Elwell, the Special Forces coordinator at the SouthCom detachment in Panama City."

She nodded. The MIUW was well suited to joint operations, and she'd worked with both the Army and SEAL teams on several occasions. While the MIUW possessed its own weapons, primarily pistols and shotguns, it was always something of a relief to leave that to specialists.

"We meet them in-country, or do they deploy with us?"

"In-country." He glanced at his watch. "In fact, the mobilization order for your unit should be released in about two hours."

She stood, feeling a surprising sense of eagerness to get back in the field with her unit. "And just what will NSA ever do if I get promoted and have to leave my billet as commanding officer?" she asked.

Atchinson looked at her somberly, a malicious glint in his eyes. "We have ways of coping with problems. You make a very fine commander. I wouldn't plan on going any higher than that."

8

THE STATE DEPARTMENT, WASHINGTON, D.C.: 27 SEPTEMBER

OFFICE OF SOUTH AMERICAN POLICY

Bradley Jeets twisted uneasily in his chair, trying to keep his boss in view. Undersecretary Doug Turner paced back and forth in his spacious office, his feet scuffing rough tracks into the deep plush carpet. Jeets wished he could do the same. Anything would be better than twisting his spine into unnatural configurations while Turner blasted him. The only consolation he had was that the other three area specialists in the room were experiencing the same discomfort.

As a career civil servant, Bradley was not overly concerned that Turner could fire him. At most, incurring his boss's wrath would result in a transfer to a dreary post elsewhere within the State Department. Not that he'd mind that—not under the circumstances. With only eight months to go until he was eligible for retirement, Bradley Jeets was more concerned with avoiding heart attacks and ulcers than he was with advancing within the ranks of career civil servants.

"Why the hell didn't any of you think of this?"

Turner snarled. He reached the end of his path, turned abruptly, and started back across the room. "It should have been obvious—obvious!"

The silence in response was deafening. Jeets was careful not to flinch or in any other way draw attention to himself. Better that Turner get the anger over with so that they could start looking for solutions. It was always this way with a political appointee, and no more so than in this current Administration.

Turner stopped and whirled on them. "Jeets. You're the area expert. Why didn't you anticipate this?"

Bradley cleared his throat. "We've always had contingency plans for problems in the Canal," he began, stating the obvious, hoping to work through a couple of paragraphs and give Turner a chance to calm down. "Insurrection, riots—ever since we turned the Canal back over to them, there's always been the possibility that—"

"That an American warship would shoot down a commercial flight out of Panama?" Turner demanded.

"Exactly the point," Jeets continued. "How could we anticipate a completely irrational act such as that?"

"At least one person didn't think it was irrational. The officer on that ship that pushed the button. If he didn't, then you can damned well bet—"

"It was a she, sir," Jeets interrupted. "She, not he."

"I don't give a bloody fuck who it was, she—" Turner stopped suddenly. The expression of rage on his face cleared to something slightly less ominous. "What's her name?"

"Lieutenant Commander June Collins," Jeets said, feeling a surge of relief that he'd managed to deflect the tirade off in a different direction. "Career Navy officer—and there's more. She was involved in the *Ramage* affair in the English Channel."

Turner stood motionless, so absolutely still that Jeets wondered if his boss had suffered a cerebral accident of some sort. Turner's face was blank, lips pursed, deep wrinkles cutting furrows in his forehead.

"Collins," Turner said softly. The energy seemed to drain out of him, leaving behind a sense of purpose. He walked over and took a seat behind his desk. He sat silently for a few moments, still lost in thought, then scanned the faces of his subordinates. "You realize what this means?"

He surveyed the blank faces arrayed in front of him. "No, I guess you don't," he said wearily.

"We blame it on PMS?" Jeets suggested, only half kidding. The current Administration had made well known its displeasure with the previous Administrations that had expanded the role of women in the military. Now that women were serving on warships, in ground forces, and in almost every previously forbidden cadre within the military, President Wilson James had almost given up hope of being able to roll back their inroads into combat forces.

Almost—but not quite. Private conversations Jeets had had with his counterparts at the White House suggested that James would not be opposed—might even welcome—a reason to reopen the issue.

"It might work," Jeets said. "Only problem is, we have a precedent. The *Vincennes*—remember, they shot down that Iranian airbus. In that situation, the U.S. decided not to scapegoat the captain of the ship. They left him in command, transferred him off his ship at the normal time, and even gave him a shore command after that."

Turner made a noncommittal noise. "We argue that the circumstances are hardly the same. Different President—that's the most critical factor. And the Panama Canal is clearly a vital national security interest. At that time, the Persian Gulf was not, although it was frontburnered later on. This may be just the angle we need."

Turner stood up. "I'll brief the President this afternoon if I can get on his schedule." The other three men stood as well, each glad that Turner's latest tirade had passed without bloodletting. The door opened to the office just as they were starting to leave. Hank Flashert, the one area specialist notably missing from the meeting, stuck his head in. His face was pale.

"I think you're going to want to see this immediately, sir," Flashert said.

"Something on the Panamanian affair?" Turner asked.

Flashert nodded. "We just received confirmation from the Panamanian government as to the passenger manifest," he said, his words tumbling rapidly over each other. "He was traveling under a pseudonym—that's why we didn't know earlier. But the first rumors were true."

"Who was on there?" Turner demanded, his voice cold.

"President Jose Garcia," Flashert said simply. "The President of Panama is now officially listed as dead."

"Shit," Jeets said with feeling. "He was one of the most stabilizing forces in the area. We can look forward to at least a couple of years of threatened coups and instability while the Panamanians sort things out." He snorted in disgust.

Turner waved him away. "What works against us can also work in our favor," he said calmly. "Garcia was okay, but there were problems with him as well. Now might be an opportunity to show our support for an even more stable political regime."

Stable? He means a puppet government. Jeets felt a welling of outrage, which he quickly suppressed. Eight more months—then he was out of it. After that, his biggest concern would be worrying about what bait would entice the wily catfish inside the Tennessee Valley Authority lake system. Panama would be the name of a hat, not the biggest thorn in his side since he'd joined the State Department.

"We need to get down there immediately," Turner decided. He nodded at Flashert. "You get back down there immediately. Put together the rest of your team—

Jeets, a couple of other idiots like that—I want a list
and an agenda on my desk by the time I return from
seeing the President. I'll be in-country as soon as I can
get free from here." Turner smiled with a disturbing
show of teeth. "Get it right this time, Jeets. Screw this
up, and kiss that retirement good-bye."

As Jeets headed his way back to his small office, he felt
the uneasiness that had surfaced during his initial summons to Turner's office blossom into full-scale paranoia.
No longer was the threat an unstated one. It was indeed
possible that Turner could screw up his retirement, if he
tried hard enough. It wouldn't be easy, but it could be
done.

   Panama. Things had to go right this time. Everything
had to be right. For another eight months.

9

BALBOA AIRPORT, PANAMA:
28 SEPTEMBER

PAN AMERICAN FLIGHT 745

The aircraft circled over Panama for twenty minutes, awaiting clearance to land. Bailey took advantage of the delay to assess the entire area. While a site survey of the area had been done several years previously, the short-notice deployment of this unit had provided no time for a more accurate site survey of the location chosen for the van.

The coastline was spotted with ports and piers, the land itself bisected by the thin ribbon of the Canal that widened into a massive lake in the center of the country. Seven sets of double-doored locks controlled the movement of waterborne traffic into the lake from both oceans, pumping water into the locks to raise the ships 132 feet above sea level. Immediately to the west of the Pacific entrance to the Canal was the port of Balboa, which Panama had leased to China on a twenty-five-year contract.

Bailey studied the array of ships there, noting the pervading sense of orderliness that was a marked departure from most commercial port facilities.

RO-ROs—roll-on, roll-off containers—were neatly queued in long lines, and ground-facilities equipment appeared to be similarly well ordered.

As the aircraft turned to make its final approach to the airstrip, she caught a brief glimpse of the Chinese submarine she'd been briefed on. It was tied up at a pier alone, again the entire location marked by a sense of neatness and order.

She sighed and turned to Carlisle, who was seated next to her. They'd spent part of the twelve-hour flight comparing what they knew about the situation from their NSA files with intelligence briefings they'd received from the Navy. After a full day of manifesting the RSSC van and associated equipment onto a transport aircraft, then loading the people onto the chartered civilian flight, neither had many useful insights.

Although Carlisle had his suspicions that the unit had been deployed at NSA's request, he had not been included in that decision-making loop. Bailey had debated with herself for a moment, then decided not to tell him.

"Nice boat," Carlisle remarked, pointing past her at the Chinese Victor submarine moored to the pier. "Good thing it's a nuke—easier to detect than those diesel bastards."

Bailey nodded. "But more trouble for other reasons, of course. We won't have a chance to catch her on the surface since she won't be snorkeling. And the sustained endurance of a nuclear power plant gives them a hell of a lot more flexibility than the diesel boats ever had."

"All in all, I'd rather be hunting for a nuke," Carlisle said, not disagreeing with her. "More noise."

Bailey sighed. "Well, let's hope it doesn't come down to that. She's still in port."

"Doesn't take that long to get under way, though."

"What do you think about the site location?" Bailey said, changing the subject.

"So far, it looks fine to me." The selected location was on the end of a large commercial pier that extended almost two miles out in the water. While it would be a pain in the ass logistically transporting the crew from the campsite to the site location, the selection promised deeper water and thus better control of the harbor area they were assigned.

"I like it because it's defensible," Carlisle said. "I've always liked working off the end of long piers—that is, if you don't get commercial traffic blocking too much of your field of vision."

"There's that," Bailey agreed. "Some of those merchant ships run in excess of one thousand feet long. Some of them are longer than carriers."

Carlisle whistled softly. "We can forget about radar coverage if we keep the radar on the end of the pier then. Any other high spots around we could mount the Humvee?"

Bailey nodded reluctantly. "There are a couple of possibilities, but I'm not sure I want it that far away from the van. As you said, things are unstable enough down there. I don't like our people spread out over too wide of an area."

Carlisle shot her a sharp glance. "You're expecting trouble? I thought the Panamanians invited us in as a demonstration of their goodwill."

"The Panamanians are still in an uproar over the shoot-down, and with the political turmoil they're bound to experience from the death of their President, there's really no guarantee. That's why it's wise to take sensible precautions."

Carlisle shook his head. "We built the damned thing and we gave it to them. It just doesn't make sense."

"President Carter thought it did," Bailey said neutrally. "If they'd ever been able to reach an agreement on the Panama Canal Treaty, it might have made sense. But as it stands now, there are two different versions of the treaty. Ours requires the Panamanians to guarantee us expeditious access to the Canal for warships. The Panamanian version says we can only take actions to protect the Canal if the Panamanians agree to our doing so. Neither country has ever approved the other's version, and no reasonable compromise has been worked out.''

"Still, the Panama Canal has been back in their hands for years now," Carlisle said. "There've been no problems so far, have there?"

"No. But with the growing Asian presence there, there's every potential for it."

Carlisle shook his head ruefully. "You're paranoid."

Bailey turned and met his eyes with a level stare. "That's what I get paid for."

Fifty yards away, the five-ton truck was jockeying the surveillance van into position at the end of the pier. Sailors swarmed around the ancillary equipment, and the MSP, or Mobile Sensor Platform, was already in position and operating. At Lieutenant Boston's suggestion, they'd left the RHIB back at the foot of the pier to deploy from the small boat ramp there. Carlisle had gone with them to supervise the sonobuoy deployment and pattern placement.

Bailey stood well out of the way, confident that her people could handle it. Besides, her second in command, Lieutenant Boston, was on scene supervising every move. The thin, whippet-like man moved with the grace that had earned him a slot on Annapolis's soccer team all four years at the Naval Academy.

The pier was the largest one she'd ever been on, almost two hundred feet in width. Bollards were spaced evenly down either side. In towards the shore, two massive merchant ships were moored to either side, and cranes were already being positioned to start the flow of RO-ROs off the ship.

A small white car made its way down the pier, pulling up next to Bailey. Two men got out, one attired in a camouflage uniform like her own, except that it had darkened, subdued collar devices instead of the bright metal ones she wore. The second man wore a light-weight tropical business suit.

The other commander approached her, and held out his hand. "Commander Jack Murphy, SEAL Team Three." His fingers crushed around hers. She winced.

"Sorry." He eased off, then withdrew his hand. "Your people are already setting up, I see."

She nodded. "Jerusha Bailey, CO. Have your people done an initial threat clearance on the area?"

Murphy nodded. "Yesterday. We've had the area under surveillance since then, so I doubt there'll be any problems."

"Appreciate that. We'll need to talk out our berthing arrangements, watch bills—that sort of thing." She turned then to the civilian. "And you are—?"

He held out his hand. "Hank Flashert, State Department. Jack said he was coming out to meet you, so I thought I'd tag along and introduce myself. So this is the famous Jerusha Bailey."

Bailey could feel his eyes rubbing over her, studying her carefully. "Not so famous," she said sharply. "We're just here to do a job."

"So I hear."

Something in Flashert's tone made her bristle.

Murphy made a small movement as though to step between the two of them. "It's your first deployment down here, Jerusha, but we've been down here many times. If you're interested in some specific advice on any area, please don't hesitate to ask. I thought after you get your camp set up, a couple of my men might make a tour, check to see that everything's in order." He smiled briefly, his teeth a flash of white against the darkly tanned skin. "For one thing, you'll want to make sure that you keep the pier completely unobstructed. That'll give your people a clear view of anyone trying to make a covert approach."

Bailey nodded. "We always appreciate a second opinion, particularly when it comes from experts," she said carefully. "We have done this before, however. Not on this pier, not in Panama, but I've made a number of deployments with this same group of folks."

Murphy turned slightly away from her to study the people milling about the pier behind them. "All Reservists, yes?"

"If that makes any difference." Bailey's voice was harsher than she'd planned. "They're sailors first, civilians second right now."

"Does that apply to you as well?" Flashert asked.

"Now what's that supposed to mean?" she said, her irritation spilling over. Between Murphy's pointed comments about her camp security and Flashert's vaguely lewd and insinuating comments, she'd run out of patience. "You have something specific on your mind, mister?" She let her voice deepen into the harsh bark she often used with recalcitrant lieutenants.

Flashert looked startled. "Not at all. It's just that we're aware of your civilian occupation, and we were wondering—"

"Just exactly who is 'we'?" Bailey asked harshly. "The State Department?" She turned to Murphy. "Or would that be the Regular Navy, as you people like to be known?"

Murphy's face hardened into a dark scowl. "This isn't the best way to start off our working relationship, Miss Bailey," he said.

"Then perhaps you can tell me exactly what is going on here."

Murphy and Flashert exchanged a silent glance. Finally, Flashert sighed. "We need to be working together on this, people," he said. "The State Department, the Navy, the Reserves—don't bristle at me like that," he added as he noticed Bailey stiffening at the distinction between her people and the active-duty forces. "It wasn't intended to give offense, merely to recognize the difference between the two types of units.''

"Working together to achieve what?" Bailey asked, dismissing the unintended insult. "As I understand it, we're down here as a demonstration of goodwill to provide harbor control security for the Panamanians.''

Murphy nodded and started to speak, but Flashert cut him off. "That's most of it. But you have to understand that there's more to the situation than merely the military aspect. With the shoot-down of the Panamanian airbus, and the disagreements over the provisions of the Panama Canal Treaty, relationships between the two countries are at an extremely delicate state. The fact is, we need the Canal.''

"Then maybe we shouldn't have turned it over in the first place," Bailey said. She was surprised to see Murphy nod in agreement.

"What's done is done," Flashert said. "I suppose you'd both like it if we moved in with military force and took it back." A dark expression flitted across his face. "After fifteen years in Panama, I can tell you that it might not be that easy. Besides, that's simply not the way things are done today. Not any more," he continued. "While there is a very small number of U.S. flag merchant ships traveling through the Canal, the fact remains that at least ninety percent of the cargo that comes through here is headed for the U.S.. Any disruption of those transits has major implications, for our ability to import needed raw goods, but for our export capabilities, as well. It is vital to American national security interests that we have continuing and free access to the Panama Canal. And the best way to do that is through deepening the bonds of our historic friendship with the Panamanian people.''

Bailey and Murphy's eyes met. He shook his head almost imperceptibly, as though warning her to leave this line of discussion for another time. Silently, she acquiesced.

"And that's why you're here, Commander Bailey,''

Flashert continued. "To contribute to that overall national objective, not just to simply exercise your military abilities."

"We'll try to be good ambassadors," she said, her voice calm and professional.

Flashert extended his hand and handed her a card. "My home phone number is listed as well," he said. "Please call me at any time if you feel the need to do so." He turned back to Murphy. "I imagine you two have a lot to discuss. If I can borrow your car and driver for a moment, I'll get back to the office. You know where to reach me."

Murphy nodded. "We're at your disposal, Mr. Flashert. Tell the driver to take you wherever you want, then have him return here." As soon as Flashert left, he turned back to Bailey. "Now. Tell me what you're really doing here. No more games, Bailey. Not with me."

"There's no big secret to this, Commander," she said easily, now determined that he would not provoke her. "Just doing a couple of weeks of goodwill HVV operations."

"Right." His face was unreadable.

"Look, why don't I give you a tour of our gear," she offered. "You've probably seen MIUW units before, but we've got some unique toys on this van."

"Sounds good," he said noncommittally. "Lead on."

Lieutenant Boston saluted as the two approached him, then gestured to the van behind him. "We're just getting ready to energize communications circuits," he said. "Any special instructions?"

Bailey shook her head. "We've got the tactical frequencies for the SEAL command as well as the standard Navy circuits, yes?"

Boston nodded. "All in our communications plan."

"What about radar?" she asked. "The Humvee should be going up just about—yes, there it is." Behind him, a scissors-like assembly was unfolding from the back of a Humvee, slowly straightening out to loft its radar dish thirty feet into the air. "As soon as they get the microwave transmitter aligned, we'll be in business. And the sonobuoys?"

Boston pointed back toward the shore. "The pier is too steep to launch from here, not until we get the floating catwalk they promised us in place. I told them to go ahead and launch from shore—it will be a pain in the ass to manage for a while, but we'll make do. They launched the first sonobuoy fifteen minutes ago." He pointed to the edge of the pier. "There are steel-runged ladders leading down to the water, but it's a good fifty-foot drop. Until we get the catwalk in place, I didn't want to risk it."

"Very well." She turned back to the SEAL commander. "In addition to the normal complement of sonobuoys and antennas to receive their signals, we also carry a fiber-optic array. Our RHIB can deploy it out to a distance of about ten kilometers. It sits on the ocean bottom and gives a long-lasting, self-sustainable sensor asset."

"Unless some ship drags its anchor over it," the commander said. "Have you had that happen before?"

She nodded. "Generally, though, it won't be a problem in a harbor like this. No one anchors out, so there's no reason for a merchant to have anything trailing in the water behind it."

"I understand." Murphy turned back to Lieutenant Boston. "So how long have you been in the Reserves, son?"

Boston bristled. "I've been in the *Navy* for eight years," he said. "We don't make much distinction between active-duty and reserve commands, sir." He looked over at Bailey for support.

Murphy chuckled. "Got them well indoctrinated, don't you?"

"It's not a matter of indoctrination, it's a simple fact," she said calmly. "There's not enough capacity in the active-duty Navy to carry out all of the missions to which we're assigned. Having a fully commissioned Naval command, such as the MIUW, with most of its manpower in the Reserves, is the most cost-effective force-multiplier we've ever come across. We've been doing this job since Vietnam, albeit with substantially different equipment.''

''Lieutenant!'' A high-pitched voice cut through the discussion. Bailey turned back toward the van to see the door open and Carlisle motioning frantically at Boston. ''You might want to see this, sir.''

Boston excused himself and trotted back over to the van. Murphy and Bailey followed at a slower pace. By the time they reached the open steel hatch, the reason for Carlisle's concern was clear. Tracing its way across the sonar scope was a small, ominous-looking blip.

Carlisle himself looked gleeful. ''Contact, Captain,'' he said to Bailey. ''We just put the sonobuoys in the water, and I caught him immediately. Look at those electrical sources—that's a nuclear submarine.''

Murphy scowled. ''The only boat in the area is tied up to the pier five hundred yards away,'' he said firmly. ''If there were another submarine in the area, our intelligence sources would know it.''

Bailey shook her head. ''You ever sneak out of the United States quietly and undetected?'' she asked the commander.

''That's a different matter.''

''Not at all.'' She pointed at the mass of lines squiggling across the paper printout attached to the passive sonar gear. ''That, Commander Murphy, is a submarine. He's about three miles out, making a quiet and virtually undetectable three knots. Are you telling me a submarine can't do that?''

''Not without us knowing it,'' Murphy shot back, his voice adamant. ''There's no way.''

Bailey shook her head. ''You're dead wrong.'' She turned to her lieutenant. ''Call *Jouett*. Tell them what we've got. Get the RHIB back here now for a fresh load of sonobuoys.''

"I'm going with them, Jer," Carlisle said, pushing his chair away from his console. He was halfway to the security door when he stopped suddenly, turned back to her, and said, "I mean, Captain. If it's okay with you."

"Sure, Pete. Go ahead." She stifled a smirk at the rueful expression on his face. It always took them a couple of days back on active duty to fall back into the right roles. And a few days back at NSA afterward before Pete stopped calling her ma'am.

"You two know each other, I take it?" Murphy asked.

She nodded, almost explained, then caught herself. She settled for a polite smile—and no further answers.

For a moment, she felt an eerie sense of déjà vu. Collins on a ship and Bailey ashore—and a submarine between them.

USS JOUETT

The Captain's head snapped around, and his eyes pinned his Exec to the bulkhead with his glare. "What the hell is going on out here?"

"That was Commander Jerusha Bailey," Collins said quietly. "I recognize her unit call sign. The MIUW unit is stationed on the end of the pier. They're reporting a detection on a submarine about one thousand yards astern of us."

"I'm not deaf." Renninger snorted. "Ridiculous."

"I wouldn't be so sure of that," Collins said softly, as though to herself. "Captain, if you have no objections, I'm going to go back to Sonar. Request permission to go active, sir." Her voice was calm.

Renninger shook his head. "You won't find anything in these waters—not this shallow." Although the channel was well dredged for the heavy-draft merchant ships that plied it, it was well outside of preferred sonar parameters. "All you'll get is bottom reverberation. Besides, the water's crawling with merchant traffic. There's too much noise for any acoustics gear out there."

"Probably. But the MIUW has some fairly sophisticated experimental gear," Collins answered. "If Jerusha's right—"

"If Commander Bailey is right," Renninger snapped, "then I'll eat my ball cap."

"I said the same thing a long time ago," Collins said softly. "And for the record, I agree with you. But I've been wrong before, Captain, as you reminded me earlier—and it almost cost me my ship. Are you willing to bet *Jouett* on that?"

Renninger continued to glare at her. Finally, he motioned toward Sonar. "Go ahead."

10

GULF OF PANAMA:
28 SEPTEMBER

SS *OCEANIC GLORY*

For a merchant ship, the bridge of SS *Oceanic Glory* was overmanned. Two officers, in addition to a deck-hand, stood watch, following directions from the master as he guided the tugs and the huge tanker into port. They'd already been assigned a berth at Pier One, and pumping facilities were standing by to off load their cargo of crude oil.

The master of the vessel himself was on the bridge. He paced back and forth, monitoring the civilian pilot's orders, mentally running through the checklist of safety equipment on board.

Why the ship's owners insisted on retaining the American flag, he would never understand. The extensive requirements of the U.S. Coast Guard, which had the authority to stop and inspect the vessel at any time, substantially increased their operating costs. By flagging with another nation, such as Panama or Liberia, one whose safety requirements were considerably less stringent, the owners could have realized a far higher net profit on this vessel.

Oceanic Glory was a Type III merchant with her bridge superstructure located aft on the deck. This configuration made coming into port and approaching a pier more difficult than with other designs, but added to the stability of both living quarters and messing facilities. Almost all of the modern ships were of Type III design.

Consequently, the master had a fine view of the entire deck area of the *Glory*. It was there that he noticed the first signs of trouble.

Under his feet, the deck vibrated reassuringly, the powerful Allis-Chalmers diesel engines driving the ship forward at bare steerageway while the tug shoved her bow in toward the pier.

The master saw the forward part of the bow ripple. Seconds later, the deck quivered under his feet, an ominous grating sound as though they'd gone aground on a sandbar. Impossible in these waters, though—the approaches to the Panama Canal were deep and well dredged, and there was simply no chance that—

A huge fireball erupted on the forward portion of the bow. From waterline to weather deck, roiling flames billowed and curled, too brilliant to look at, throwing searing black smoke off around their edges.

The master let out a cry, and staggered forward on the bridge, moving against the motion of the ship. The bow was pitching up now, and the motion slammed him into the aft bulkhead.

The ship careened crazily to port, still high up at the bow as the explosive force tossed the massive ship around as though it were a toy. The screams of the wounded were barely audible over the noise. Vaguely, the master had some idea of trying to get to the conn, to get control of the ship, back her off of whatever sandbar she'd hit, that last notion lingering in his mind against the creeping darkness.

Long, horizontal cracks streaked down her sides as

the double-hulled construction failed. Tons of fetid heavy black crude poured out, igniting in the super-hot temperatures of the expanding fireball. Within two minutes, the remaining hulk was ringed in fire, listing heavily to port now, with her superstructure only forty feet above the water.

Belowdecks, two damage-control technicians sprawled wounded on the steel grating in after steering. The compartment had been manned during their approach on the pier in case of the loss of manned steering. The first two seconds of the explosion had tossed them around the compartment like rag dolls, finally leaving them wounded and bleeding on what had once been the port bulkhead.

Kiley Blair, the more senior of the two, let out a low moan and tried to crawl forward. His companion, Kevin Adams, lay still and motionless. Blood gushed from an open wound on his head, and his left leg was crumpled under him at an unnatural angle. Kiley tried to crawl towards the ladder, now canted at an unnatural angle across the compartment. Pain shot through his spine, dimming his vision with its overpowering presence. He screamed, fought against the blackness invading his consciousness, and crawled dimly forward. Behind him, Kevin lay unmoving.

Kiley managed to make it to the lowest rung before the transverse crack that had already crossed the keel reached the stern. Just as his hand clung around the slanted rung, an unholy scream of ripping metal filled the compartment. He had time just to glance back at it before tons of warm, salty seawater, blood warm and voracious, filled the compartment.

MIUW 106

Bailey cried out in alarm as the smoke and flames billowed up towards the sky. The tanker's mass made it seem even closer than it was, and she thought she could feel a blast of heat from the conflagration. Burning oil flooded the ocean around the ship, creeping slowly towards the piers.

The MIUW RHIB veered toward the smoke and flames. The fiber-optic array was still coiled on a massive drum in the stern, the thin filament glistening in the sun.

Bailey darted into the van and reached for the communications handset. "Sea Lion One, this is Cayman," she said, using their unclassified circuit call signs.

"Sea Lion One," Carlisle acknowledged, his voice a thin crackle over the circuit. "Altering course toward the tanker in order to assist survivors."

"Stay away from it," Murphy snapped. Bailey turned, surprised to see him standing there, unaware that he'd followed her out to the van. "That oil is spreading— you're liable to get caught in it before you know it."

"We'll keep a close eye on it, ma'am," Carlisle's voice answered. "But we can't just—"

"He's right, you know," Bailey said. "No sailor could stand by and watch someone else die like that."

"I know, dammit, but what can they do?" he said. "This harbor has a disaster force, and they'll be on scene in moments."

"What would you do if you were on that RHIB?" Bailey asked, her voice cold steel. "Would you turn away?"

Unbidden, a vision of the last ship she'd seen burning at sea flashed before her mind. It had been in the English Channel, a British warship that had been the victim of a submarine attack. She hadn't turned away then—nor would she order her people to do so now.

"Sea Lion One, take every precaution—and I mean every, dammit. Keep us advised." She replaced the handset in the receiver and locked her eyes with those of the SEAL commander. "That's the problem with training them," she said levelly. "They end up doing exactly what you would want them to in an emergency."

Murphy nodded. "I have that problem too." He turned to the sailor manning the communications suite at the end of the van. "Do you have that circuit up with my forces?"

"Yes, sir."

"I need to talk to them. With your permission, of course," he added, glancing at Bailey.

"Of course."

Murphy's squad leaders answered the call-up immediately, and the SEALS were soon vectoring out in their own small boats along with the Panama Canal disaster team to the burning tanker. After insuring that an adequate surface plot was being maintained of all the rescue assets, Bailey turned her attention back to the sonar gear located at the other end of the compartment.

"That submarine—how close was he?" she asked.

"Close enough," the sonarman answered. "Well within torpedo range."

"Do we have any air assets yet?" she asked.

Lieutenant Boston shook his head. "The first Panamanian helicopter is not scheduled to deploy for another thirty minutes. I imagine they'll be too busy now to want to work with us."

"Not if they think we've got a submarine that caused this," she snapped. "Let me talk to them."

The Panamanian commander on the other end of the circuit seemed less than completely convinced that the MIUW unit was holding contact on a submarine. He was harried, and she could hear the sounds of his staff moving around him, shouting out orders, making urgent demands for rescue assets to mobilize to the burning tanker.

If only the Navy had seen fit to give them a larger boat, one that was equipped with torpedoes. She raged at her impotence, her inability to do any harm to the submarine that lurked outside the harbor. She had only the RHIB, armed with sonobuoys, and that was—

"Ma'am, the RHIB—the submarine's closing on them," Boston said, his voice high and urgent. "We need to get them back from there."

"Make the call. I want that RHIB back in here—there are plenty of assets on-scene now. There's nothing they can do." Boston nodded, and reached for the mike.

The radar operator turned pale. He started swearing violently.

"What the hell is it?" Boston said, still holding the mike.

"It's the lookout, sir. He's lost sight of the RHIB."

Boston turned pale. "Where is it—near the oil?"

The radar operator shook his head, holding his hands over the earphones that connected him to the surface lookout. "Nowhere near it—he had visual contact, was tracking them with the binoculars. They just disappeared."

"Give me an exact range and bearing," Murphy said immediately. He listened to the information, then related it to the SEAL team that was deploying. Finally, he turned back to her. "I vectored them over to the last position of your RHIB. If you've got men in the water, they'll find them," he said, his voice confident.

Bailey motioned for him to step out of the van. When they were well out of earshot of everyone else, she said, "How good are your intelligence sources down here?"

He shrugged. "Good enough."

"Evidently not." She pointed out towards the last location of the RHIB. "In retrospect, was there any I and W—indications and warnings—about that sort of attack? Any threats made against your people?"

"Just what are you implying?"

"Absolutely nothing—except that there was absolutely no warning that we might expect this kind of aggression. None at all. To the contrary, our briefing—as well as our mission—was billed as a goodwill one. There wasn't even an indication that terrorist activity might be expected. Nor that there would be hostile submarines in the area.''

The SEAL commander's face was cold. ''You expect a schedule of events for real hostilities? That's not how it works in the real world, lady.''

''I expect adequate intelligence support. If there is insufficient information, that fact alone should be advertised. I don't need feel-good briefings that leave us vulnerable to attack. We're supposed to be assigned to a rear support area where there is adequate perimeter defense or in a protected area. My people aren't equipped for this.''

''Then what the hell are you equipped for?'' he said, his voice angry now. ''You convoy up here in your olive-green trucks, wearing forest cammies like you're an operational unit. As far as I can tell, that uniform you've got on has never even been dirtied. And those,'' he said, indicating the bright collar devices she wore, ''are an invitation for a sniper. Do you know just how visible those are at a distance?''

''This is not a front-line combat unit,'' she snapped. ''And if there has been a fatal mishandling of forward-area security defenses, that's your department.''

''If you want predictability, go back to the States,'' he said dismissively. ''The real world is a little more nasty place than you're accustomed to, I suspect.''

''Commander!''

She turned to see Lieutenant Boston motioning at her. ''I'm needed back at the van,'' she said. ''We'll continue this conversation at a later date.'' She stalked off before Murphy could form a harsh reply.

''What is it?'' she said as soon as she was within earshot of Boston.

''It's the SEALs. Our RHIB sank, but they've got the crew.'' Boston's face reflected his relief. ''They should be back pierside in another fifteen minutes.''

''What happened? Did they say?''

Boston nodded. ''They just said there was an equipment casualty. That's all I could get from them—we'll debrief the crew when they get back here. Shit—we've lost the fiber optics, though.''

She nodded. ''I'll want to talk to them myself.''

''Of course.''

Something in Lieutenant Boston's face made her pause. ''What else is it?'' she asked.

He looked troubled. ''Something the surface lookout said just before the RHIB sank. Maybe it's nothing— maybe it isn't.''

''What?''

''He claimed he heard gunshots. Long range, probably a rifle.'' Boston's worried look deepened into real concern. ''Captain, if we've got a sniper out here, we've got serious problems.''

Bailey looked back at the SEAL commander, who had broken into a light jog and was heading towards the shore end of the pier. Two miles would barely break a sweat on that hard, lean form, she suspected, even though he was wearing combat boots.

Just then, a loud noise from the pier one quarter mile south of them caught her attention. She turned to look. It was the pier at which the Chinese submarine was moored, the one she'd seen as they were flying in. There was a flurry of activity around the submarine, with sailors moving rapidly and purposefully.

''Give me your binoculars,'' she ordered. Boston handed them over.

She focused on the submarine, tweaking the binos to bring the picture into focus. The sailors moving about on the pier were indeed Chinese, clad in the universal working jumpers that most submariners wore at sea, festooned with red patches on the left sleeve. She saw a curl of hot air billow out of the open hatch, and sucked in a hard breath. One sailor tossed off one of the two mooring lines attached to the bow.

''They're singling up all lines,'' she said unbelievingly. ''Christ, Boston, I think they're getting under way." She handed the binoculars to him. "Tell me what you think."

He took the binoculars and studied the scene carefully. "You're right," he breathed softly. "Now just why would they get under way right now?"

"There's more going on here than we know about," she said thoughtfully. "But first things first—let's get back to the van and see about our people. Then we'll worry about the rest of it."

Commander Murphy reached the shore end of the pier; he slowed to a walk as he approached his car. His instructions to Hank Flashert had been superfluous—he'd already told the driver to meet him back here at the foot of the pier. The young man leaped out of the driver's seat as Murphy approached.

"Where to, sir?" the young SEAL asked.

Murphy grunted. "They get those men out of the water?"

The SEAL nodded. "Just like you ordered."

"Good. Tell the squad leader to find out if they know anything, then take them back to the MIUW camp." He smiled briefly, a harsh expression.

As the car pulled away from the pier and headed back towards the small compound the SEALs used as a staging area, Murphy settled back on the cheap fabric seat. He closed his eyes, letting his mind wander over the possibilities, damning the screwup in planning that had led to the MIUW unit being deployed here. Without them, things would have been much simpler—and much more clear-cut. Finally, he opened his eyes. "As soon as we get back to the compound, round up the rest of the squad. I want to see them immediately in the briefing room. Code Alpha."

The young SEAL looked startled. "Aye, aye, Captain," he said.

• • •

An hour later, four sailors climbed out of a SEAL Humvee. They were pale, already shaking with shock, even in the warm weather and wrapped in blankets. The SEALs escorting them, to the contrary, looked relaxed and healthy.

"Just four?" Bailey said, cold fear flooding her body. "There were five on the boat crew. A sonar tech—Pete Carlisle. He was with them."

"I'm sorry, ma'am." The SEAL sounded as though he meant it. "We've still got people out looking. I had to leave to take these guys to the base medical clinic. Doc says they'll be fine. But so far . . ."

The unit corpsman bustled up and took charge of the survivors, leading them off to the command tent for another checkup. With an effort, Bailey stilled her mounting anxiety.

"Thank you," she said to the senior man present. "We won't forget this."

The SEAL nodded. "You can return the favor someday," he said, in a tone of voice that let her know that he believed nothing could be further from possible than an MIUW assisting a SEAL team.

She followed the corpsman and survivors into the command tent, and took a seat on a cot next to Boatswain's Mate First Class Bill Storey. "What happened?" she said.

The petty officer still looked shaken. "A lot more than we told them."

"What?" Bailey said, startled. "What do you mean?"

Storey exchanged glances with his other boat crew members before turning back to her. "I told them that we didn't know what happened—that all at once there was a hole in the RHIB and we started taking on water."

"What do you mean?"

Storey looked directly at her, his face grim. "Just before the hole appeared in the RHIB, we heard gunshots. Faint, hard to hear over the noise of the water and the engine, but they were there. And look.'' He threw off the blanket that had been covering him and rolled up his sleeve. An angry, bleeding red furrow creased across his bicep. ''That wasn't an equipment casualty—somebody was shooting at us.''

▌▌

PANAMA:
28 SEPTEMBER

MIUW 106

Bailey stared down at the pier a quarter mile away, watching the activity around the Chinese submarine, now held to the pier by only two mooring lines. Where the hell was Carlisle? Who had been shooting at the MIUW sailors on the RHIB, and why were the Chinese getting under way? None of this made sense—none of it at all. She could conjure up a number of explanations, none of them reassuring. All of them pointed towards an inexorably escalating tactical situation, one she was not prepared to deal with.

She turned to Commander Murphy. He had returned to the MIUW camp to tell her in person that an extended search of the area had yielded no trace of Carlisle. "We need more support services in here—now," she said.

Murphy studied her gravely. "I don't see the need for it," he said finally. "We've got one isolated incident, nothing more."

"And a submarine deployed outside the harbor."

"So you say. Listen, I'll check with the Intel people

at SouthCom—see what I can find out. If anything comes up, I'll let you know right away. If you need us sooner, just call.'' Leaving her alone with the aching hole in her heart, Murphy left.

Bailey turned back toward the submarine and lifted the binoculars to her eyes. A glint of sunlight caught her attention. She focused in, and saw a lone figure standing rigidly upright in the conning tower of the submarine, staring back at her through binoculars. His hair was dark, clipped short, facial bones broad and sharply outlined. His eyes were masked by the twin black barrels of his own binoculars. As she watched, the last line holding the submarine tethered to the pier was cast off, and two remaining sailors scrambled on board. A billow of smoke indicated the approach of a tug, and she shifted her gaze to it. It shifted to the bow of the submarine, its mate taking a position astern.

The distance between the submarine and the pier increased measurably. With a last blast of billowing black smoke, the tugs hauled their lines in from the submarine. The long, dark gray shape moved quietly, silently towards deeper water. The lone figure in its conning tower stared back her way, having hardly moved during the whole process except to make his desires known with a few curt hand motions. He dropped his binoculars finally, and stared at her. She could see bright, intense eyes, almost glistening in the afternoon sun. The expression was grave, almost sorrowful. He turned his back on her and disappeared from view, presumably down into the submarine. Moments later, the water lapped over the exposed weather decks, foamed up around the conning tower, and swallowed the submarine.

A small sound behind her made her turn around.

"Not a good sign." The gravelly voice grated across her ears, sounding as though it came from deep within the man instead of inside his throat. She finally dropped her own binoculars and turned to confront the newcomer.

The man was a few inches taller than she was, well over six feet tall. Short salt-and-pepper hair peeked around the edges of his green utility cap, and the camouflage uniform he wore was a duplicate of her own. The insignia indicated he was Army, though, and she studied with some interest the array of arcane patches and insignia that always adorned Army uniforms. Something about last unit, current unit, and specialty—she'd never managed to completely decipher the significance behind them.

Cold blue eyes met her own, eyes that had seen too much for too many years. The face was impassive, darkly tanned skin indicating that this man was a field soldier, thin lips used to withholding comment.

He allowed her a moment of scrutiny, then lifted his hand in an oddly formal salute. "Master Sergeant Billy Elwell, U.S. Army. I'm the Special Forces liaison from SouthCom."

She returned the salute, then held out her hand. "Glad to have you aboard, Sergeant. You just missed Commander Murphy." Although she couldn't be certain, she thought she saw a slight expression of distaste in his eyes.

"Unfortunate," he murmured politely. "Of course, the SEAL Team is down here on independent operations, as I understand it. I'm surprised the Commander made it by to greet you. Still, maybe I can be of some assistance to your unit. I understand that you had a fatality in connection with the burning tanker," he continued.

"Let's not call it a fatality so fast," she said, more sharply than she intended. "He's only been in the water for an hour—in this water, he could last for days."

The sergeant regarded her, allowing her comments to pass over him without impact. "Not very far off shore, were they?" he observed. He turned back to stare at the sea, shielding his eyes with one hand. "I hope they find him, Commander. It's always hell losing men, especially during peacetime.''

She nodded, suddenly certain that Billy Elwell had lost more than his share of men in the field. There was something about his manner that suggested a rock, a solid, dependable, implacable force when deployed. It was a characteristic missing from Commander Murphy. No matter that the SEAL looked even stronger than the man standing before her. In a contest, she thought that she might bet on the sergeant rather than the commander. For some reason, that made her decide to trust him.

''Look at this,'' she said abruptly. She motioned to Storey, who walked back over, his black face still pale. She gently peeled back the camouflage blouse to reveal the bullet wound.

Nothing in Billy Elwell's face changed, but she could sense the heightened interest in the way he stood. It was something almost imperceptible, a heightened degree of attention, a focusing sensation. ''This happened while you were out there,'' he said. It wasn't a question. ''I wondered about the RHIB.''

''Somebody shot at my sailors,'' Bailey said. She let her anger show in her voice. ''I want to know why—and what the hell is going on down here.''

Billy Elwell studied the wound as though he hadn't heard her. He glanced at the sailor for permission, then gently ran one finger along the side of it, careful not to hurt the man. Finally, he said, ''That will heal up real fine, son. Have your medic take a look at it, but I think you won't have any damage other than a scar. Be stiff and sore for a few days, but nothing permanent.''

Storey nodded. ''Hope so, Sergeant.''

Elwell glanced at Bailey. ''Did you tell Commander Murphy about this?''

''No. I assumed he knew, since his men pulled them out of the water.''

''Ah. And did you tell them, Petty Officer Storey?''

"No, sir. It's not that serious—I just wanted to get back to the unit."

"Don't call me sir, son. Sarge or Sergeant will do." Elwell turned back to Bailey with the air of a man taking charge of a situation. "Ma'am, if you'll take some advice—I think we need to have a look at your arrangements. Security may be more of a problem than we thought."

"Murphy already looked at them," she said, unconsciously leaving out the man's title.

Billy Elwell nodded. "The commander's got more experience with higher-level tactics and such than he does with actual campsite setup. I'd like to have another look, if you don't mind. For one thing, you need to block access to your camp with some physical barriers, particularly if you've got a sniper around." He looked past her, surveying the sailors milling about in stunned silence in the camp. "It'll give your people something to do too—they need that right now. To feel like they're doing something."

"Murphy said—" Bailey broke off the sentence abruptly, remembering how the SEAL had mentioned that they needed a clear field of fire down the pier. "Maybe you're right."

"Maybe your senior enlisted man?" Billy suggested. "That way I wouldn't have to take up as much of your time."

Bailey nodded, aware that she was about to be outflanked, and added tact to the top of the list of things she liked about this strange Army noncom. The sergeant clearly wanted to deal with a peer, someone who would understand the necessity of the suggestions he was going to make. In his mind, he had already dismissed her as an officer, someone who would be more of a hindrance than a help to what he had in mind.

"I'll introduce you to the chief," Bailey said finally. Gunner's Mate Chief Petty Officer Frank Templeton looked to be the naval counterpart of this man, and she had a feeling that they would find they had much in common. Between the two senior enlisted men, the camp would be better arranged than anything she could devise herself.

SEAL HEADQUARTERS, PANAMA

Carlisle regained consciousness slowly. The first thing he noticed was that his hands were tied together in front of him. He was lying on his back on a government cot, stripped naked and under two blankets. Already he could feel the sweat beginning to creep down his forehead. Everything was blurry and out of focus. He squinted, trying to make vague forms and colors resolve themselves into shapes.

He heard a noise, a door opening, and then another shape in the room moved. "So you're awake finally," the voice said. It sounded not at all pleased. "It took you long enough."

Carlisle tried to sit up, and groaned as pain lanced through his head and shoulder. He fell back on his back, that motion hurting even more. "Where am I? My hands."

"In a medical facility," the same voice replied. "You were out on an RHIB—there was an accident. You were delirious for a few hours, and we put you in restraints so you wouldn't hurt yourself. How much do you remember?" The voice had taken on a more urgent note.

Carlisle started to shake his head, then winced as the motion caused new pain. "We were going to Panama," he said, vaguely remembering the details of his deployment. "I remember there was—we were at the airport, and then . . ." His voice trailed off, and he felt a slight sense of panic. The airport—he remembered landing in Panama, but nothing past that. He started to struggle up again, trying to at least regain some control over motion if he couldn't have his memory.

"Not so fast—you suffered a nasty bump on the head, as well as a bit of hypothermia." He felt a hand in the middle of his chest shove him back down to the bed. "You stay put."

"What happened?" Carlisle asked again, the sense that he had to know becoming more and more urgent.

A long silence, then: "Your unit deployed in Panama. You were out in the RHIB planting sonobuoys when there was an accident. A tanker—a lot of fire, oil in the water. You and your crew went in to hunt for survivors. In the process, your own boat was damaged and you got pitched into the water. On the way in, you must have hit your head on something. We can tell you've got a slight concussion, so you're staying here for observation. Your commander will be by to see you later, I'm sure."

"I don't remember. . . ." Carlisle's voice trailed off.

"Not unusual—in fact, that's very common in a head wound. Don't worry about it at all—as soon as the swelling goes down a bit, some of it may come back to you." The voice took on a new note of command. "As soon as you start remembering, I want to know. It's important for your recovery that we know how you're doing."

Carlisle nodded briefly, the motion generating a new wave of nausea. "Man, my head hurts."

"I'll give you something for that." Carlisle felt a cool hand on his shoulder, then warm air touching his body as the blankets were pulled away, the coolness of an alcohol swab, then the slight jab of a hypodermic needle. He turned his eyes toward the person, squinting, and the features swung vaguely into focus. A man, a white man, clad in a camouflage uniform like the one he himself had been wearing.

"You're a Navy corpsman, aren't you?" Carlisle asked. "No drugs—you don't know—the place I work, I can't be knocked out unless you've got security. I can't—" His voice broke as a wave of darkness surged up.

The man nodded. "You're safe here. We know all about NSA," he said reassuringly. "I'll check back in on you in a couple of hours. For now, you need to get some sleep."

Blackness flooded Carlisle's brain, dragging him back down to the dreamless place he'd been in not so long ago. As the last glimmer of consciousness faded, one final thought intruded in his drug-soaked brain.

I have a concussion, he thought. Aren't I supposed to stay awake? They don't give drugs when you've got a concussion.

And why were his hands still tied?

Before he could fully resolve even the beginning of the answer, he felt his lips moving, words spilling out. From far away, he could hear someone asking questions. Odd questions, ones that he answered automatically and completely. Another pinprick, and he was out cold.

12

MIUW 106

Billy Elwell walked fifty feet down the pier, then turned back to look at the MIUW encampment. The collection of green tents huffed slightly in the sea breeze, and two stockpiles of boxes were located too close to the main thoroughfare for safety. He squinted, studying the tents and the approaches to the camp more carefully. A bit more tension on the tent lines . . . need an extra support pole on the corner of the one on the left . . . and just how the hell had they planned on rigging the camouflage netting? Still, not a bad job for a bunch of squids.

He motioned to the driver of the two-ton truck he'd ordered to follow them down the pier. ''Back a little more—there, that's it.'' He touched Chief Templeton lightly on the shoulder, drawing him a few feet to the left. ''See how it blocks the line of sight from that building now?''

Templeton nodded. ''Appreciate your help on this, Billy. This isn't our area of expertise—but you can tell that.''

Elwell nodded. "Takes some time under your belt," he acknowledged. "From what I've seen, what you people do, you do real good. But for this sort of setup, you want a ground pounder like myself."

"So where have you spent most of your time?" Templeton asked. "Down here?"

Elwell shook his head. "Germany. Four tours there, one back Stateside, and a couple in Korea early on. But I get around to a lot of different places when there's a need."

Templeton nodded. "That worries me a little."

"It should." Billy stared at the coastline of Panama, assessing their vulnerability. It was sheer foolishness, forward-deploying a unit like this under these circumstances. Too much could go wrong—too much he couldn't control. It was one thing to do it with an experienced unit, another entirely to take a collection of electronic technicians, computer geeks, and sonar geeks, and put them in the middle of an unstable situation like this. "You got any camouflage netting?" he asked finally, hoping against hope that they did.

Templeton nodded. "Sure. We brought it with us, but I don't know why we'd need it out on the end of the pier here. Doesn't look much like concrete—we brought the jungle pattern."

"Can you get some people to break it out?" He pointed at the trucks, at the clear space between the two of them. "We'll string it between the trucks, to help obscure the direct view. It won't do much to control somebody who's determined to use heavy weapons, but it'll make a sniper's job more difficult. He can't see it, he can't hit it."

Templeton grunted. "I'll get some of my guys right on it."

When he had the sailors working on rigging the camouflage netting, Templeton came back to stand beside Elwell. "So what is this all about?" he asked. "This doesn't look like the mission I was briefed on before I left the States."

Elwell shrugged. "Things have gotten strange down here in the last year or so. You pull out that much U.S. firepower, you create a vacuum. It figures that some-body's going to find a way to fill it." He gestured at the booming coastline and vast shipping complex that crowded up to the very entrance of the Canal. "This is a one-of-a-kind setup. The big problem down here isn't drugs, crime, or illegal immigration—it's the foothold the Asian nations are getting with the people that ought to be our closest neighbors."

"Those Chinese ports, you mean." Templeton looked thoughtful. "I understand they've got bases at either end of the Canal now."

Elwell nodded. "Doesn't take a rocket scientist to fig-ure out what the danger is in that. Especially not with the Chinese involved."

"Don't let the Equal Opportunity people hear you talk like that back home," Templeton said. "The Chinese are some of the smartest people around, from what I hear."

Elwell nodded. "In a lot of things, they are. I'm not talking about individual people here—I'm talking about culture, philosophy, the whole racial-identity sort of thing."

Templeton glanced around nervously. "Hard to even talk about those things these days."

"It is," Elwell acknowledged. "But all the more rea-son for doing it. God's honest truth, the Chinese are just people like you and me. But they're people who've been brought up in a whole different culture, and they've got a whole different tradition of military thought and war-fighting. That's the part that we have to understand. Oth-erwise . . ." He let his voice trail off.

"You think they're really a threat down here?"

Billy turned to face the other man. "Don't you?" He gestured at the port facility. "Look at this. Look how much commerce is trading through here. Put it in terms of money, and start thinking about how much the Chinese control right now. Ever since Hong Kong was turned over to them, they've been even more of a major player in the world. Now, give them a way to control commerce between East and West, and you see the possibilities?'' He shook his head gravely. "I'm not saying that the Chinese are bent on world domination, just that we don't know them well enough to understand what it is they do want. And that's the first step." He pointed up at the hill. "Just like I understand what kind of field position a sniper's going to want."

"I take it you've got some experience in that military occupational specialty?" Templeton said delicately.

Elwell's eyes took on a faraway look. "There are all sorts of career paths in the Army—some we don't talk a lot about," he said finally. "Some we never talk about. Why don't we just leave it at that?"

"So what do you see as the major difference between us and the Chinese?" Templeton said, going back to the earlier subject. "How are they different from, say, the Germans?"

"It's the difference between brute force and strength—hard idea to get your mind around at first. The European tradition of war-fighting is built around Clausewitz—you know the drill. Center of gravity, concentrate your forces, strike at the enemy's center of gravity—it's all about force. The Chinese take a little bit different viewpoint. Instead of Clausewitz, they look to Sun Tzu. It's a whole different way of looking at the problem. Where we look at strength, we see something to counter. The Chinese see strength as something to use against their opponent. They go for the weakness, they look for a way to make you overcommit, they use your own strength against you. That's what's so dangerous about them—they think about warfare in a whole different light than we do. It's like facing an opponent who is skilled in judo, using your own motion and force against you to throw you flat on your back on the mat. That make sense?''

Templeton nodded. ''I wonder if the boss realizes that,'' he said, motioning towards Commander Bailey. ''Smart officer, in a lot of ways.''

Elwell let his eyes linger on the tall, slim Navy officer, watching her talking to her second in command. Her movements were clean, sharp, confident. She wasn't some fragile vessel, some token to equal opportunity within the Navy. From the little he'd seen of her, this was a woman used to command. One who understood its strengths, responsibilities, and would take it as seriously as demanded.

And from what he'd heard of her, he was even more certain of it.

''Like I said, I was in Germany for a long time,'' Elwell said. ''I've heard a lot about your boss.''

Templeton nodded. ''I'm not surprised. She's probably heard a lot about you as well.'' He shot Elwell a sly, sideways glance. ''Like we all have.''

It was Elwell's turn to look mildly surprised. ''Flattering, that.''

Templeton laughed. ''You wouldn't think so, not if you heard all the stories. But from what I've heard, there's only one Billy Elwell in this United States Army. They call you Uncle Billy, right?''

Elwell grimaced slightly. ''Some do,'' he acknowledged.

Templeton clapped his hand on the man's shoulder, and felt the hard muscles tense slightly under his fingers through the camouflage cloth. ''Well, let's just keep it Bill and Frank, okay. One thing I know for sure, Sergeant Elwell—you're a man I want on my side.''

13

PANAMA CITY:
30 SEPTEMBER

U.S. EMBASSY COMPOUND

Doug Turner was stretched out on the leather couch, his arms extended out along the back and one arm. His flight from the U.S. had arrived just two hours ago, and jet lag was taking its toll. Dark circles ringed his eyes, and Hank Flashert had already had first-hand experience with Turner's foul mood.

Turner's peevishness irritated Flashert even more than his superior's presence in Panama. Why the hell had it been necessary for Turner to come down here? He knew nothing of the people involved, even less about the local politics. It would be up to Flashert, with fifteen years under his belt in Panama, to keep Turner from stepping on his dick. And would Turner appreciate it?

Not likely. Flashert's own foul mood, carefully concealed under an air of brisk efficiency, deepened.

"So that's where we are," Flashert concluded, bringing his boss up to date on the events of the last two days. "We still have the MIUW sailor. It's perfectly justifiable, since he still needs medical treatment."

"I see." Turner's words were devoid of inflection, giving Flashert no clue as to how to proceed.

"You did say that you wanted this affair contained," Flashert pointed out. "Events were moving fast—there wasn't time to—"

Turner waved him quiet with a gesture of his hand. "You've explained your reasoning sufficiently, I believe."

An uncomfortable silence settled over the two. The American Ambassador had long since beat a hasty retreat to his private residence, his concern over the embassy and its personnel leaving him little time or desire to inquire into the workings of the State Department officials descending in hordes on his beleaguered building. He'd crossed swords once with Turner early on over the Canal situation, Flashert remembered, and evidently had no desire to do so again. Turner was welcome to whatever blame—or credit—would be attached to the resolving of this situation.

"I should have used the CIA," Turner said finally. "They understand subtlety a bit better than you and the SEALs do. Were they involved, there wouldn't be these untidy loose ends."

Flashert's jaw almost dropped. The CIA. He'd known his boss had contacts in all the various agencies within the government, as did most of the political appointees, but a strong link between the CIA and the State Department was something that was rarely acknowledged, never spoken of.

"What would they have done differently?" Flashert snapped.

Turner stared at him with cold, hooded eyes. "The job would have been completed. Do you really want to know how?"

Numbly, Flashert shook his head. No, he didn't. The whole situation was coming unglued, the lines between black and white becoming increasingly gray. It had seemed straightforward in the beginning—question the

NSA plant sent to Panama under the cover of a Navy operation. But now, Turner seemed prepared to go far beyond that. Flashert gave thanks that he'd withheld the exact manner in which the debriefing was being conducted from Turner. He now suspected Turner had had something a good deal less—coercive—in mind.

"This situation is critical," Turner continued, reading Flashert's mind. "What happens in the Panama Canal will be a model for the same issues all over the world. We've drawn back so much from our foreign commitments that many countries are looking elsewhere for assistance. We have to make them understand that it comes with a price—loss of American goodwill means more than just paying heavy tariffs at ports of entry."

"More incidents?" Flashert asked. "Like the airbus, you mean?"

A still, deadly silence enveloped the room. Turner didn't answer.

"We couldn't have—it was a mistake!" Flashert said, his bewilderment evident. "That wasn't intentional. How can that serve as an example to other nations."

Turner sighed. "Not everything is as obvious as you'd wish," he said cryptically. "You and I know it was unintentional, as do the men and women on that ship. But are the Panamanians certain of that?" He waved one hand around as though taking in the entire surrounding countryside. "If they truly believe that it was a grievous accident, then why are we running into these difficulties? They're not certain—and that's a very desirable state of affairs for us. And my definition of subtle. Are you beginning to understand how this works?"

Flashert tried for a look of bewilderment. "Not exactly."

"If the Panamanians think that this was an act of subtle retaliation for their refusal to agree to Article VI of the treaty, then they may be a little bit more careful about their demands in the future," Turner said slowly, as though speaking to a child. "They're not certain it was an accident—so we use that to our advantage. This game is played on many more levels than you ever considered, Hank.'' Turner stretched, and finally stood. "The sooner you understand how to use the events of the day to your own advantage, the faster you'll progress in the State Department. Subtlety, my friend—subtlety and misdirection. That's at least half the battle.'' He waved a hand at the door. "I have a meeting tomorrow, yes?''

Flashert nodded dumbly. "With representatives from the major military establishments still in Panama,'' he said, still trying to understand how Turner intended to use the airbus shoot-down to his advantage. "They'll all be here.''

"Excellent. In the meantime, we need to resolve this question of the sailor your SEALs have in hand.'' He cocked his head quizzically at Flashert. "I suspect he should be making a complete recovery about now, don't you?''

Flashert turned to leave the room, feeling uncomfortable at having his back exposed to Turner. As he reached the door and his hand touched the knob, Turner asked two final questions. "Those sailors—why would the Panamanians shoot at their RHIB? They're here at the Panamanians' invitation, aren't they?'' He waited.

Flashert turned slowly back to face him. "Probably some separatist terrorist group,'' he said mildly. "You know how those things are down here—so many separate interests and political movements you can barely keep them straight. We may never know, but that would be my best guess.''

"Do you know anything else about it?'' Turner asked.

Flashert felt his stomach coil into a tight knot. How the hell had Turner thought to ask that question? Had he underestimated the political appointee? Too much could go wrong too quickly.

Flashert smiled. "Of course not. Why would we shoot at our own people?''

USS JOUETT

Renninger studied the chief petty officer sitting across the table from him. The senior enlisted man in the Operations Department, Chief deBeers knew more about the guts of the Aegis fire-control system than any other person on board the ship. The chief had just spread out an array of tactical plots and computer printouts on the captain's worktable. "Is this everything they asked for?" Renninger asked.

"Yes, Captain," Chief deBeers said. "Data log entries, snapshots every five seconds of the tactical picture, as well as our JOTS printout. Copies of the duty log, anything else I could think of."

Renninger sighed. "Well, I don't know what else to include. None of this is going to help us any. Any way you look at it, we still shot the airbus down."

"Captain, if I wouldn't be out of line . . ." The chief's voice trailed off as he waited for permission to continue.

Renninger nodded. "Speak up, chief. You know my policy—open door."

The chief fixed his eyes on a point on the far bulkhead. "There's a lot of talk going around the ship. About the airbus. And the XO."

"What kind of talk?" Renninger's voice was sharp. The last thing he needed right now was a loss of confidence in the chain of command, and that's just what he was afraid the chief was leading up to.

"Miss Collins—she's a good officer, sir. Got a couple of rough edges, but that's par for the course for any XO. The shoot-down—well, there's one small discrepancy in the data that has caused some questions. A couple of the junior operators got a hold of it, and the word spread around the ship a bit. Nobody wants to believe we did it—that's the bottom line. But I just thought you ought to know about it."

Renninger nodded, relieved. Better the crew keep

their faith in the unsinkable and unstoppable rightness of their ship than suffer a crisis of confidence. "This data point—what is it?"

The chief shuffled through the computer printouts arrayed on the table, and finally paused and indicated one line of text. "There it is."

Renninger turned the sheet around so that it was face-up to him. It was a printout of the Aegis database, the one that logged all commands entered at each console. It would indicate when a target was designated with a weapon, when the weapon was fired, and the probable results of that. It was a fiendishly accurate system, and had been used more than once for scorekeeping in global war games. He ran his finger down the list of entries just above the one in question, noting the sequence.

Target identified.

Weapon assigned.

Weapons free.

Fire.

His finger stopped at the next line. It should have read "Confirmed kill." Instead, it said "Lost contact," an important distinction in the system.

"Lost contact," he said out loud, saying the words slowly. "That's close enough for a kill, I suppose." He looked across the table at the chief, and saw the same doubts mirrored there. "It does happen, you know. Even the Aegis system isn't perfect. The fact that we lost contact on it indicates it had ceased to occupy that part of the sky, doesn't it?"

The chief nodded. "That's my interpretation. But then again, if all the parameters matched up, you know, it ought to say confirmed kill. That's what's puzzling me, and that's what's gotten the talk started around the ship—the fact that it doesn't. A lot of the crew is hoping that this will show that the whole thing was a mistake and we didn't actually take the bird out."

Renninger shook his head decisively. "Come on,

Chief. You know better than that. We shoot a missile and the target disappears. How much more definitive can you get? The only thing more certain would be a live report from one of those three hundred passengers watching the missile inbound. And that's not likely to happen.''

"I know, Captain, I know. In all probability, it was our missile that took that airbus out." The chief frowned slightly. "Still, it bothers me. Why doesn't it say confirmed kill?''

Renninger pushed the sheaf of papers away, suddenly tired of the discussion. Get used to it, he told himself wryly. It would be the first of many, many questions he would have to answer, and he had the sinking suspicion that many of them would involve this same discrepancy. It would be discussed, analyzed, and finally beaten into the ground for so many years, just as the *Vincennes* incident had been. It was not something he was looking forward to.

The fact that he would probably never be promoted again bothered him far less than the administrative throes of agony the Navy was about to put itself through. He'd had his command at sea, and enjoyed a full eighteen-month tour on board this superb warship. Had he had a choice, this was not the way he would have chosen to end his tour, but life dealt out cards without regard for an officer's dream sheet. He would live with it, as he'd lived with everything else in his Navy career.

"Let the rumors continue," he said finally. "Not that you could stop them if you wanted to. It doesn't do the crew any harm, and this thing is going to drag out forever anyway.''

The chief nodded. "The XO doesn't know about this, sir," he said quietly. He lifted his eyes and looked his captain straight in the face. "Only me, the Ops Boss, and a bunch of the sailors. You know how it is, sometimes things don't roll uphill as fast as they spread through MDI.''

Renninger nodded. Mess Desk Intelligence was one of the most effective communication systems on board. Within the confines of the steel hull, rumors spread faster via the cooks than they did the 1MC announcing system. "Just leave it be—it'll burn itself out in a couple of days," Renninger said.

"Are you going to tell her?" the chief asked bluntly.

Renninger considered snapping the man up short. He was out of line, way out of line. How the Captain ran his wardroom and what his dealings were with his Executive Officer was certainly none of his concern. As he started to form the angry words, he reconsidered. The chief had done him a favor by pointing out the incident, saving him from getting blindsided at the first inquiry. Renninger relented.

"Not right now," Renninger said. "I think we agree, it probably means nothing. No point in getting her hopes up."

The chief nodded. "Aye-aye, sir. I'll let the Ops Boss know, if you like."

"No. I'll speak with him myself this afternoon," Renninger said. Granting the chief a little leeway was one thing, but this matter belonged firmly within the wardroom. "I'd appreciate it if you'd spread the word around the chiefs' mess, though," he added, to take the sting out of his words.

The chief left, taking the massive sheaf of data with him to package for shipping. Renninger would carry it off the ship himself when he left for the State Department conference. He swore quietly as he recalled his upcoming schedule. The last thing he wanted to do right now was leave his ship and go ashore. Not with *Jouett* involved in a shoot-down. And not leaving Collins alone aboard.

He should have relieved her immediately—the very day that it happened. But what had begun as a tactical tragedy had evolved into a political football. His orders were explicit—do nothing with Collins, nothing that would admit any U.S. culpability in the matter. Relieving her as XO of the ship would have done just that.

"Well, Miss Collins, for the time being you're safe. And there's no way around it—I have to go ashore. God knows I can't risk sending you. Not when word gets around about who you are, and Ops is just too junior to handle the firepower. No, it's gotta be me—but you and I are going to have a frank little talk before I leave. While I'm on this ship, you'll know exactly what I expect from you. And I damned well better not see any repeat of this sort of incident. Orders or no, I'll relieve you myself. Right before I toss you overboard."

MIUW 106

Bailey let her hand rest lightly on the rickety railing that ran around the boat platform, and concentrated on keeping her balance by flexing her knees and moving with the motion of the floating dock moored to the massive pier supports. It was a trick she'd learned long ago, to go with the motion of the sea rather than fighting it, concentrating on keeping her center of balance as low as possible. The railing was simply a secondary source of stability.

Not so, she was amused to note, for both Master Sergeant Elwell and Commander Murphy. Both men had both hands firmly clamped to the railing, which rattled and creaked under their grip. The welds that held the stanchions to the dock were none too secure, she suspected, and she resolved to get them back up onto the pier as soon as possible. Tragic enough that they'd lost one man at sea already. She didn't want to see one of them crushed between the dock and the pier stanchions.

"You can't do it, ma'am," Elwell said, raising his voice to be heard slightly over the creaking groans of the floating dock and the slap of waves against aluminum. "It's just too risky."

"Come on," Murphy said. "What is the probability that there'll be another incident?"

"Too damned high, sir," Elwell said, transferring his gaze to the commander. He pointed at the RHIB.

The SEAL commander snorted. "That mark on the sailor's arm—it could have been a rope burn of some sort."

"There's no chance that was a rope burn—no chance at all," Bailey snapped. "I've seen them before."

"And you think I haven't?" Murphy snarled. "Listen, lady, I don't know who your sailors are or why they would lie, but I find a rope burn a damned sight more probable than a sniper attack on an RHIB."

"That's just the point," Elwell put in. "Until we know what happened, there's no point in risking these people."

"Fine," Murphy said. "Instead, you want me to send my SEALs out to chuck these damned sonobuoys into the ocean for them. You'll risk my men, but not theirs. Is that it?"

Both men staggered as the platform took a particularly nasty lurch. Bailey rode it out by leaning into the motion of the dock. "As I see it," she continued while both men were regaining their balance, "it's almost a moot point today. The sun's going down, and I don't think there's any point in any of us running around in small boats after dark. Do you?"

"If we were going to do it—which we're not—then I'd prefer to have it after dark," Murphy said. "If these snipers Mr. Elwell is so worried about are still watching, we'll make a tougher target. I don't see why you need more sonobuoys anyway. You're supposed to have the latest electronic gear, aren't you?"

Bailey nodded. "We do. But they were just starting to lay the fiber-optic array when the boat went down. We lost it along with the RHIB—they're going to be mighty pissed about that," she added. "So, until we can get

another one flown in from the States, we're back to sonobuoys. Doing it the old-fashioned way.''

"I agree you need acoustic coverage out there," Elwell said. "You've got *Jouett* out there with her tail in
the water, but it wouldn't hurt to have some sonobuoys
set for shallow-water operations in place to allow for the
discontinuities in the sound-velocity-profile gradients.''

Murphy looked over at him suspiciously. "Just how
the hell do you know that much about sonar operations,
Sergeant?"

Billy locked eyes with the man, and Bailey watched
as a long, cold stare passed between the two of them.
"I'm afraid I'm not at liberty to say," Billy said softly,
his voice barely audible over the noise of the sea. "But
I do.''

And just how do you know about that scrape on that
kid's arm? Elwell wondered. He didn't tell you—and
neither did his boss. Elwell stopped short of asking the
question, certain it would do no good to expose the
SEAL's gaffe.

"Well, I for one don't even believe that was a submarine out there," Murphy continued. "That makes no
sense at all.''

"I'm going to have SouthCom resolve this," Bailey
said decisively. "There's no point in the three of us
getting into a pissing contest over it. Commander . . .''
She turned to Murphy. "I'd appreciate it if your men
would lay some sonobuoys for us tonight, but I'm not
going to insist on it until I know how our chain of command operates. But be advised that I'm making this a
formal request, and that I deem it essential for surveillance operations in this harbor to have those buoys in
the water no later than ninety minutes from now. After
dark, it's going to be as hard for us to see a submarine
snorkel mask sticking up as it is going to be for this
sniper to see your men. And besides, after dark is our
best opportunity for acoustic detection. If it's a diesel,
it's going to have to come up to snorkel some time.''

"And if it's not?" Murphy countered.

She shrugged, and started toward the ladder that led back up to the pier. "Then we take our chances on detecting a nuke, obviously." She mounted the first rung and looked back at the men still grasping the rickety railing. "Let's continue this discussion topside before one of you falls off."

The two men ignored her, and watched her climb the ladder. Finally, when she was out of earshot, Elwell turned to Murphy. "They've got some pretty advanced gear with them," he said, his eyes boring a hole in the SEAL commander. "You know anything about it? Sir." The last word was obviously an afterthought for courtesy's sake.

"Enough. Do you?"

Elwell shook his head. "Just enough to wonder how concerned the U.S. is about the Panamanians gaining access to it. Concerned enough to wonder if they might have some contingency plans in case the situation here goes to shit. That's what I'm curious about—our role in all of this."

"You ask too many questions, Sergeant. We don't work for SouthCom."

"Perhaps not. But just for informational purposes, you might be interested in knowing that I've done a number of tours with forward-deployed cryptological units. I know what the drill can be. What I'm wondering is exactly what orders you're operating under."

The SEAL commander stiffened, a mistake while standing on the lurching platform. His right foot slipped out from under him, and he had to wrap one arm around the rickety railing to regain his balance. "If you've done time in crypto—well, I wouldn't know anything about that."

"I think you would." Elwell's voice was soft and deadly.

"You're out of line, Sergeant."

Billy moved hand-over-hand along the railing to the rungs that led up to the pier. "Maybe so. If so, I apologize, Commander. But I'm betting that Commander Bailey up there wouldn't have any clue as to what I'm talking about, and that you do. Let me say this—if I have the slightest indication that you're operating under Sanction Alpha, SouthCom is going to be very, very disturbed. Such orders should be cleared through us—this is our area of responsibility, even if the main detachment is pulled back to Florida."

Murphy studied him for a long moment. "If I were, you'd never know it."

Elwell nodded. "Not until it was too late. Just remember—we had this conversation." With that, he started up the ladder without looking back to see if Murphy followed.

U.S. EMBASSY, PANAMA

Murphy moved restlessly about the small office, touching knickknacks on the credenza, pausing to examine a photo on the wall. Most of them pictured Hank Flashert with more important people, shaking their hands and smiling for a staged photo op. Hank sat behind the desk, impatiently tapping his pencil on the spotlessly gleaming wooden surface, waiting for Murphy to get to the point.

"It's Elwell," Murphy said finally. "You'll have to deal with him. I can't."

"I thought you SEALs could deal with anything," Flashert said snidely.

Murphy whirled on him. "Don't give me that crap. We've worked together for too long. You know what the rules are. You deal with the political stuff and leave the tactics and operations to us. But if Elwell gets SouthCom involved in this, we're screwed."

Flashert sighed. "How many times do I have to tell you—it's all arranged. Elwell is there solely for administrative liaison, not as part of the operational staff. I mean, they have to have someone to get their MREs from, don't they?"

"Yeah, well, Elwell sounded like he was a whole lot more involved than that." He glared at Flashert suspiciously. "Are you sure you know what's going on?"

"Do you?" Flashert's voice was cold and harsh. "So far, I've seen nothing but screwups on your part, starting with the issue of this sailor you're holding onto."

"What about him?"

Hank spread his hands out in front of him. "He's recovered, right? So why not return him to his unit?"

"You're the one who said to hold on to him," Murphy snapped. "And just how am I supposed to explain that he's been at the SEAL compound for two days without notifying Commander Bailey?"

"Well, you should have thought of that before you kept him, shouldn't you have? I'm sure if you think hard enough, you'll come up with an answer."

Murphy's eyes narrowed. "It would be better if I didn't have to."

"What are you suggesting?"

Murphy smiled, an expression that made Flashert particularly uneasy. "Nothing. State is the one who authorized Sanction Alpha. And that brings me to another point—just how the hell did Elwell know about that?"

"How should I know? He's military—the Army's had Sanction Alpha granted from time to time, just like all the other services have. There are operational necessities, I understand. . . ."

Murphy looked sullen. "Yes, that's what they always called it. Operational necessity. Those are the words of a man who won't have to carry it out, mister. You try being on the other side, knowing you have to kill your fellow service members before you let them fall into enemy hands. It's one thing to take risks with men who are trained for that sort of thing—another entirely to exercise it on a forward-deployed unit."

"You have a problem with your orders, Commander?" Flashert asked.

"Just with the pricks who give them."

14

GULF OF PANAMA:
1 OCTOBER

USS JOUETT

Renninger stood inside the helo hangar, giving Collins her last-minute instructions before he left. He was still decidedly uneasy about leaving the ship, but could see no way out of the command performance that required his presence ashore. The Ops Boss and the Chief Engineer were standing a respectful distance away, watching them without appearing to do so, trying to pick up any clues that they could.

"Just stay on the track SouthCom laid out for us," Renninger concluded. "No more incidents, understand?"

A look of pain crossed Collins's face, Renninger took some pleasure in noting.

"There won't be, Captain," she said. The expression passed quickly.

He nodded. "There better not be." He shook his head sadly for a moment. "I never thought I'd have this kind of conversation with my Executive Officer. Never." A look of anger crossed his face. "That's the whole point

of having an XO, isn't it? It's the officer you're training
for his or her own command, the one that you can occasionally leave the ship with and feel some degree of
comfort about doing it. I wish that I could say that I felt
that way about you, XO, I truly do. But I don't. I'm sure
you can understand why."

Collins seemed to withdraw into herself, following
some private train of thought. When she spoke, her voice
was calm and professional. "I understand completely,
Captain. If our circumstances were reversed, I'd probably feel just as you do." She attempted a smile. "I can't
say it makes me feel any better, knowing that. But you
have my word on it—I'll do the best I can while you're
gone."

"Let's hope that will be good enough."

Renninger returned her salute, then made his way out
to the SH-60 helicopter already preflighted on the flight
deck. He strapped himself into the backseat, watching
Collins through the small observation window located
next to him. She was talking to Ops and the Engineering
Officer now, looking calm and completely in control of
herself.

For a moment, he regretted his harsh words. But not
much. The Executive Officer billet was supposed to be
a pressure chamber, weeding out those who simply
could not be trusted with the command of one of the
world's most powerful warships. It was a final test, a
last opportunity to cull out those that were lacking in
some necessary ability or character trait. In Collins's
case, as much as he hated the tragedy that had occurred
on his ship, he felt some small degree of relief that
they'd caught her. Caught her before she'd advanced to
a command of her own.

Renninger leaned forward and tapped the pilot on the
shoulder, giving him a thumbs-up.

"Aye, aye, Captain," the pilot's voice said over the
internal communications system. "We'll have you there
in twenty minutes, sir. Just sit back and enjoy the ride.

By the way, we've got a request from the MIUW unit based at the end of Pier 36. They'd like us to spit out a couple of sonobuoys on our way in. Seems they're having a problem with their RHIB.''

Renninger toggled the transmit switch. "Have they made a formal request for us to expend our ordnance on their behalf?''

"Negative—not that I've seen."

The copilot chimed in with another negative report.

Renninger leaned back on the hard upholstered seat. "Then fuck 'em."

U.S. EMBASSY COMPOUND

Jerusha Bailey glanced around the room, trying to take the measure of the men and women assembled there. There were a few familiar faces—the American Ambassador, of course, on whom she had made a courtesy call within hours of arriving in Panama. His aide, who had scheduled the appointment. Master Sergeant Elwell. Commander Murphy. And that was about it. The rest of the assorted officers and civilians perched uncomfortably on formal diplomatic chairs were unfamiliar, a mixed bag of uniforms and specialties.

SouthCom was a joint command, and the detachment remaining in Panama reflected that diversity. Air Force officers sat side by side with Marines, and one Coast Guard officer was even included in the group. Most were commanders or lieutenant colonels, the sole exception being Billy Elwell. She studied his face for a moment, wondering what made him rate a seat in a meeting composed otherwise of high-ranking civilians and officers.

Murphy was a big man, far bulkier than Elwell, who looked like a greyhound standing next to a bull mastiff. But there was an aura of quiet that seemed to surround the Army noncom, a calm confidence radiating out from his presence. Despite the disparity in rank between him and the other members, he handled himself with quiet dignity, replying courteously and thoughtfully to both civilians and military alike. She noted a degree of respect in the body posture of everyone who spoke to him, a quiet acknowledgment of his expertise. Which was exactly what? Once again, the question begged to be answered. She would have to ask somebody besides Murphy—he wasn't likely to admit anything favorable about the other man.

The Ambassador rapped lightly on the top of his desk. "If everyone has coffee, perhaps we could get started?" The Ambassador turned to the man standing next to him. "Allow me to introduce Mr. Doug Turner from the State Department. His visit has been coordinated with the Joint Chiefs of Staff, and we're hoping that this meeting will have us all working towards one coordinated end. Mr. Turner?" The Ambassador gestured politely at him, and Turner stepped forward.

Another tall man. Very senior, too, judging from the way his suit fit. That certainly didn't come off the rack, she thought. And there's something about him—this isn't a common occurrence, coordination between State and the military, yet he looks completely at ease. As though we've already been assigned to his operational control.

Turner surveyed the room, letting his eyes linger on each person individually while waiting for the small murmurs and paper shuffling to die out. "Thank you all for coming on what was relatively short notice," he began. "As the Ambassador said, we're all on the same team. Most of you are senior enough to know that neither diplomatic negotiations nor military force alone provides the best solution to any situation. I want you to know, hear it from me personally, that our coordinated efforts are getting some close attention from the very highest levels." He eyed them all solemnly, then repeated, "The very highest levels. In fact, I expect to be briefing the President personally upon the conclusion of this mission.

"Which brings me to my first point." Turner turned to an aide standing by the door, and the lights dimmed suddenly. A computer-generated picture flashed onto the white screen that had unfurled behind the Ambassador's desk. A map of Panama flashed up on it, with substantial portions of it marked in red. "These are the areas where Asian nations have established industrial bases, manufacturing plants, or shipping facilities." The area surrounding the Panama Canal was largely red. "I'm sure that with all of the experience in this room, you don't need me to spell out what this means. With the forces they have in place right now, the Chinese could completely shut down access to the Panama Canal to all other nations."

He paused and surveyed the room. "How many of you would agree with that?" A murmur of assents followed.

He nodded. "Good—about what I'd expected. Now, we can talk about the mechanics of how they might accomplish that—and, incidentally, how we might prevent it—but the deeper question is why. Why would the Chinese do that? And why would the Panamanians allow it?" The silence that followed that question was unbroken.

"So you can see the dilemma." He tapped lightly with his pointer on the location of the Panama Canal. "The Canal is simply too important to American commerce to permit any nation to deny us access to it. That includes the Panamanians. And as things stand today, there is every possibility that the Panamanians will attempt to do just that. The reason I called you all together is to talk about ways we might prevent that.

"The problem began with the downing of Panamanian Flight 301. With the Panamanian President on board, we can expect a period of substantial instability to start with." He nodded towards the door on the outside world. "Some of you have already experienced that, I understand." His eyes roamed the room and then settled on Bailey. "It seems like the Navy is taking the brunt of the action this time. My condolences on your loss, Commander."

Bailey nodded an acknowledgment, but remained silent.

"We must prepare," Turner said, speaking slowly and distinctly, "to enforce our absolute right to transit the Panama Canal at any time under any circumstances. That is the final objective of all of our efforts. Is that clear?"

"What is our position on the rights of the Panamanians to control their own country?" a voice from the rear said.

Bailey turned to see Sergeant Elwell standing, his hands politely clasped in front of him. His rough, gravelly voice was distinctive. "And how does this fit in with our Wilsonian notions of self-determination?"

Turner appeared a bit taken aback by the questions. Both were politely phrased, respectfully uttered, and quite to the point. Bailey herself had been wondering the same things.

Turner paused for a moment while an aide whispered into his ear. He frowned briefly. Then his face cleared, smoothed over into a professional diplomatic mask of neutrality. "Master Sergeant Elwell, is it?" he said politely. "Good questions—both of them."

"I hope the answers will be just as good," Bailey said, the words coming out of her mouth almost before she could stop them. She heard a quiet intake of breath behind her at her audacity.

Turner turned his gaze towards her. "It seems the Navy is not only an active participant in both of the incidents that bring us here today, but also the most vocal of the military services," he said mildly. "I'll get to both of those points in just a moment. If you would allow me to proceed?" There was a slight bite to the last statement as he asserted his place in the pecking order.

Bailey nodded, then shot a glance towards the rear of the room. Billy Elwell met her gaze with a calm, thoughtful look.

She caught a flicker of motion, then saw the massive oak door behind her open slightly. A civilian stepped into the room, motioning discreetly to the Ambassador. The Ambassador shook his head, and the aide's expression became even more urgent.

"Undersecretary Turner," the Ambassador said, "my apologies, but I must excuse myself for a moment."

Turner nodded politely and turned his attention back to the crowd. "Back to your question, Miss Bailey. I could do some fancy tap dancing, but I'd like to sum it up with an old American phrase—what's good for General Motors is good for the country. The same goes for the rest of the world. When American prospers, it affects beneficially every country within our sphere of influence. When we don't . . ." He shrugged eloquently, as though the conclusion were too obvious to detail.

The door at the rear of the room opened again, and the Ambassador stepped back in. He was pale, obviously shaken, and trying to stay calm. One hand rubbed repetitively at the back of his neck. "Undersecretary—if I might interrupt," the Ambassador said, a slight tremor in his voice. "Effective at two p.m. today, the provisional government of Panama has declared its intention to prevent American flagships and all ships bound to or from U.S. ports of entry from transiting the Panama Canal. They state," he said, glancing at a message in his hand, "that they're willing to enforce this decision with military action if necessary. Until the matter of the airbus matter is resolved, and appropriate reparations are paid, no U.S. bound cargo will transit the Canal."

A deep hush fell over the room. Elwell's gravelly voice spoke up. "I guess the Panamanians just answered my questions."

15

PANAMA:
I OCTOBER

USS JOUETT

Collins paced back and forth on the bridge, stopping at the navigator's table to check their position for the third time in the last fifteen minutes. The senior quartermaster sighed, pointed silently at the round circle that marked their position, and glanced at his GPS indicator again. "On course, on station, ma'am." He withheld the sigh she could tell he wanted to give voice to.

"I know. It's not that I doubt you. But—"

He nodded, offered a small smile. "Always that way when the Captain's gone, isn't it?" he said quietly. "Don't worry, XO—anything goes wrong, if we get even two inches off our track, I'll let you know."

She nodded, grateful for the reassurance.

She paced back and forth on the bridge, scanning the water around her. She could feel the watch-standers' nervousness, heard the tension in the Officer of the Deck's voice as he snapped out an unnecessary order to the port lookout, and knew that there was no point in her presence here. Nothing had changed in the hour since the Captain had left, nothing at all. Still, the weight of her responsibility made her restless, kept her moving constantly in search of anything she might have over-looked. Given her track record, she was not willing to take the slightest chance on something going wrong. Not even a pump breaking down, a position not plotted, or a contact not tracked exactly by the book.

"Roger." The operations specialist charting contact data on the large Plexiglas display looked startled. He turned to Collins. "Ma'am, they'd like you back in Combat, please."

She nodded, and walked briskly through the hatch and down one flight of stairs to Combat. The heavy security door was ajar, as it normally was during at-sea opera-tions. She pushed it open, and stepped into the cool darkness, lit only by overhead red lights and the glow from radar screens and displays.

"What is it?" she asked the TAO.

Williams pointed back towards Sonar. "They think they've got a contact. The same one that the MIUW was reporting."

"A submarine?" she said, then wished she could call the question back. Of course a submarine—she'd just looked around the water surrounding *Jouett* not three minutes ago and there'd been no surface contacts of sig-nificance.

Garland simply nodded. "We're tracking it now."

She walked past him and into the small compartment that housed Sonar. The lights were brighter here, and only three technicians manned consoles. "What have you got?"

The senior sonar technician pointed at the screen. "Passive contact, range about ten thousand yards."

"Anything on active?"

He looked up at her. "We asked Lieutenant Williams for permission to go active and he said no. Do you want a ping?"

She nodded. "Go active."

The ship's hull reverberated with the acoustic energy radiating out from its sonar dome. She watched it trace its expanding circle on the active scope in front of her, pouring five thousand watts of power into the water around them. A few seconds later, a musical chime coincided with a small green phosphorous lozenge lighting up on the active scope.

"Is that it?" she demanded.

The sonar technician shook his head. "Too close—and there's a wreck charted there. No, our contact has got to be further out than that. It was worth a try, but this water is lousy for active returns."

"Not much better for passive," the other technician said. He pointed to two faint lines on his chart. "Tenuous contact—but it's there. Bearing due west, XO. I'd make it a convergent zone contact, although the water is awful shallow for that."

"But you're certain it's a submarine?" she asked, a hard note in her voice now. "Or are you?"

Both men looked up at her, their faces neutral. "If I had to bet, I'd be leaning towards classifying it as a submarine," the older technician said. "But it's not a hard contact—XO, we need to get a helo out on it. That would resolve the problem once and for all."

While the Captain had taken one of the Sea Hawks ashore, the other one was still in the hangar. "Let's do it. Since the MIUW reported that contact yesterday, there's no point in taking any chances." Not with the way things have been going out here.

She walked back into Combat and told Williams to roust the flight crew and inform her when he was ready to set Flight Quarters. He looked up at her askance. "Are you certain you want to do that?"

"Of course I am. Just do it, Lieutenant." She bit back a harsher rebuke, aware that the rest of the watchstanders were listening. Garland's insubordination had gotten out of hand lately, more so now that her relationship with the Captain was rocky. Still, there was no point in airing wardroom grievances in front of the crew. She'd settle this situation once and for all when the Captain returned. "I'll be on the bridge," she said. "Notify me when you're ready to set Flight Quarters."

He nodded. Moments later, on the bridge, she heard the call for the aviation detachment going out over the 1MC. She glanced at her watch, aware that it would take approximately fifteen minutes to get the crew briefed and suited up, and another fifteen to twenty to properly preflight the helicopter. Thirty minutes—a lifetime in the subtle game of ASW. If there were a submarine out there—and if it were ten thousand yards away—it had more than enough time to make a silent, deadly approach on the ship. More than enough time.

She toggled the lever down on the bitch box. "Set Condition 2AS," she said, referring to the special watch-standing teams that would be dispatched during ASW operations. If there was a submarine in the area, she wanted her best eyes and ears in Sonar. She heard that announcement follow shortly.

"Any word from the Captain?" she asked the OOD, fully aware that she'd heard no calls come in from the ground center.

He shook his head. "Not yet. Should we call him?" He held up the cell phone the Captain had left with him.

She paused, undecided, then went back to Combat. "Show me where it is again."

The operations specialist had just finished penciling in the small point designating the hostile contact. "On our port quarter now," he said without looking up. *Jouett* had been executing an east-west track in the Gulf of Panama, the body of water enclosed by the lower half of the S shape of Panama. According to the sonar data, *Jouett* was positioned between the coast of Panama and the submarine. At her current location, *Jouett* was just barely outside the twelve-mile limit of Panama's territorial waters.

She swore quietly, wishing the helo was already airborne. There was nothing a submarine feared more than an ASW helicopter working against it with a pinging deployable sonar dome. One helo and a destroyer—a tough adversary. Two helos would be virtually unavoidable. Now, however, with one helo ashore and the other still in preflight, she had only her passive acoustic towed array and sonar dome as sensors.

But maybe not. She turned to the sonar technician. "Does the MIUW have sonobuoys in the water?"

He nodded. "They deployed them about two hours ago. There should be plenty of time left on them—I think they were set for extended operations. From what I hear, they brought plenty of them with them as well."

"Are we holding contact?"

He looked doubtful. "I haven't tried to dial them up, but I could. We might be out of range."

"How far away are they?"

The sonar technician looked down at the plot and traced one finger along the ocean floor. "About here—just inside the twelve-mile limit."

She nodded, the plan taking shape in her mind. She turned to the TAO, Lieutenant Williams. "Have the OOD head us towards the middle of the MIUW's sonobuoy field. And get the MIUW on tactical—I need to talk to them."

She turned back to the Chief of the Watch. "You understand what I'm doing?" she asked.

He nodded, a smile tugging at the corner of his mouth. "I do. And I like it—this just might work."

MIUW 106

Boston greeted her as she returned to camp from the conference. Given the Panamanians' declaration, continuing the briefing on old information had seemed futile. All of the operational commanders had been anxious to return to their commands, and Turner had eventually bowed to the inevitable. The sergeant she'd already started to think of as part of her unit had left quickly, muttering a partial explanation about some sort of preparation he needed to make.

Bailey went immediately to the RSSC van, and had just stepped inside when the call came in from *Jouett*. She listened to the voice, scratchy over the secure circuit, and frowned as she recognized it. Before Boston could reply, she reached over and took the mike from him.

"Lieutenant Commander Collins," she said, ignoring normal radio protocol. "It's been a long time."

There was a moment of silence, then an all-too-familiar voice returned. "Good afternoon, Commander. Oddly enough, I was just thinking about you."

Bailey smiled slightly. "I imagine you were. Run me through this plan again, if you would."

Over the secure circuit, Collins briefly outlined the scenario. Bailey's analytical mind rifled through the possibilities; then she nodded as she saw the logic behind Collins's plan. "You can't take overt hostile action against it—it's done nothing to indicate you're under attack," Bailey said. "However, I understand your concern—unknown submarine contacts would make me uneasy as well."

"You think they'll buy it?" Collins's voice asked. Bailey gave her points for asking.

"They might. We used the same type of sonobuoys your helo would use, although the submarine won't confuse the active sonobuoy with the frequency from a helo sonar dome. Still, it might make them think that there's a helo in the area. They have no way of knowing you've got one ashore and one still in preflight."

"That's what I'm hoping. The only thing I know for certain about this submarine is that it's not Panamanian. One guess as to who it probably belongs to."

"No bet," Bailey said. "My money's on the Chinese."

"Me too, Commander."

The circuit fell silent for a few uneasy moments. Bailey watched as Boston sketched out *Jouett*'s new track on the surface plot, and then nodded as she saw where it was headed. "At the speed of advance you're making, it should put you inside our pattern—or at least looking like you should be there—in about ten minutes. I'm going to give it five more minutes; then we'll go active on the DICASS buoys. If they start picking up speed, turning into you, or you have any indications that they're targeting you—"

"I know, I know," Collins broke in. "Believe me, we're thinking of that."

Bailey thought for a moment. "Think it through, XO. Once we pull this off, we need to figure out why the submarine's there—and what it's trying to accomplish by announcing its presence. All it had to do to escape detection was to stay well away from you, you know."

Collins's voice was grim. "I know. That's what worries me."

Bailey nodded. "Your Captain will be here in about thirty minutes—he's having lunch with another commander, and then he's coming by for a short tour before he returns to the ship. I'll see if we can locate him, give him a quick update, and send him back out there as soon as he can get a turnaround."

"Aye, aye, Commander. Let's just make sure between the two of us that he's got a ship to come back to."

USS JOUETT

The ship heeled sharply as the OOD ordered the new course toward the sonobuoy field. Collins stayed in Combat, watching their progress in a series of one-minute position marks on the surface plot. Five minute dots on the chart later, she heard it. It was a tinkling sound against the hull, the light caress of a distant active sonar source. Sonar's announcement of contact on the active sonobuoys followed seconds later.

"What about the submarine?" Collins asked.

"I'm certain they heard it, XO. We hold a slight increase in speed—she's running at twelve knots now, changing course to follow us. No indications of hostile acts as yet. And no active sonar from the submarine."

Collins glanced up at the speed indicator located next to the large-screen display. *Jouett* was making sixteen knots through the water, just at the edge of her sonar-detection envelope. Any faster and she'd be blind herself, running from the submarine without any way of knowing whether it was following.

If this was going to work, the submarine should do something within the next few minutes.

The shimmery pings of the sonobuoys were suddenly obliterated by a harsh, ringing stroke of an active sonar. "Sonar!" Collins demanded. "What the—"

"Active sonar, source is the sub that's been following us," Sonar announced, cutting in over her question. "XO, recommend we set up for an urgent attack torpedo down the line of bearing."

Collins thought furiously. "Set up for it," she snapped. "But you keep your hand off the firing key—I repeat, off. No one takes a shot unless I give the order. Do you understand?"

"That's affirmative, XO. On your order only. Wait!" the sonarman said. The few seconds that he was silent seemed like an eternity. Finally, he spoke. "The submarine is turning away from us. She's accelerated to eighteen knots and is on a directly reciprocal course. It worked, XO—it worked."

A few muffled cheers broke out around Combat. She hushed them quickly. "How fast is she leaving?"

"Eighteen knots. At that speed, she's deaf, dumb, and blind."

Collins started to breathe a sigh of relief. "That last ping—that was just to make a point, I think. She wanted to let us know that she had us—that she could take us at any time. So she thinks.''

Collins relayed the tactical information to the MIUW, who had also observed the submarine's turn on their passive sonobuoys. Then Collins secured from urgent attack and ordered *Jouett* back onto her patrol plan. Sonar reported that the submarine executed a depth change, went below the layer, and quietly disappeared off of all their sensors.

16

PANAMA CITY, PANAMA: 1 OCTOBER

CALLE DE RORAIME, PANAMA

Master Sergeant Elwell pulled the aging Volvo sedan to the side of the road and looked across the street at the house. It was built in the traditional Spanish style: white stucco, high surrounding walls, and a red tiled roof. Flowering bougainvillea crept over the walls, not quite entirely masking the viciously sharp shards of cut glass embedded in the top of the wall. A wrought-iron gate coupled with an intercom announcing system at the front completed the security of the house.

There was probably more, he thought, studying the layout. Cameras mounted up under the eaves—he detected a telltale glint of sun on glass. Not too terribly unusual for a wealthy Panamanian family concerned about personal security, or for an off-the-books Special Forces detachment that wanted a base of operations away from the scrutiny of SouthCom.

Not much escaped Billy Elwell. Although most of his tours of duty had been in Germany and Korea, he'd spent enough time with the Army in odd little out-of-

the-way places in Central and South American to have
some friends in Panama. More than once he'd visited
SouthCom headquarters, back when it had been a major
command instead of the decimated skeleton it was now.
Aside from the staff, Elwell had friends—special
friends, who operated in-country and could find out virtually anything he wanted to know.

He put the Volvo in park and considered his next
move. This could be a straightforward game of interser-
vice politics—or something worse. To date, he had just
too little information to decide for sure. But something
about the attack on the MIUW boat and the SEALs'
sudden reversal on deploying sonobuoys for them had
struck him as suspicious.

Suspicious enough to ask around.

Suspicious enough to find those old friends, and to
check out this address.

According to his contacts, it had been rented six
months ago from a wealthy Panamanian merchant who'd
suddenly fled the country to escape prosecution for tax
evasion and money-laundering. The owner was report-
edly hiding out in Bolivia—perhaps with the assistance
of the U.S. government, if Billy's suspicions were true.

Evil loves darkness. So do black operations. He considered this for a moment, then decided on a straightforward approach. Locking the car behind him, he
walked up to the high gate and pressed the intercom
button.

"Que?"

In passable Spanish, Billy asked to speak to Señor el
Commander. There was a pause on the line; then an
American voice broke in. "Who is this?"

"Somebody who knows you're here. That ought to
be enough." Billy waited for an answer. A long silence
followed. He'd learned waiting years ago. There was a
way to do it, and a way not to do it.

Finally, the silence was broken not by a response, but
by the metallic buzzing of the electronic gate latch dis-

engaging. Billy pushed the gate open, stepped through, and swung it shut behind him. He heard the electromagnetic bolt shoot home.

As he walked up the walkway, the door opened. An American, by the look of him, clad in civilian clothes. Light shorts, a tank top. Only the muscles and the close-cropped haircut gave him away. "What do you want?" the man said.

"Listen, we don't have time for games," Billy said reasonably. "Just give me the kid and I'll be gone."

"What kid?"

Billy sighed. "Let me explain something to you very simply. I'm from SouthCom—and so far, I'm one of the few that knows. Not the only one, however. Now, seeing as we're both in Special Forces, we can do this one of two ways. The easy way, which is that you give me the kid and I leave and this goes no further. Or we can do it the hard way, which will do nothing but cause hate and discontent for all of us. And paperwork. You know how that goes."

The man studied him for a moment, buying himself time to think. To speed him along, Billy said encouragingly, "In the Army, we try to get our noncoms to use their own judgment. They're the ones on the scene."

Finally the man nodded. "Wait here."

Again the waiting. Billy stood relaxed, at an angle to the door, trying to decide whether he regretted not bringing a firearm. No, he finally decided. If he needed a weapon against the people that he thought were inside this house, then he was outclassed and needed to come back with a whole squad. Besides, it defeated the whole purpose of the visit.

The door opened and the man reappeared. With him, standing on slightly shaky feet, was a young man clad in an olive-green T-shirt and light khaki swim trunks. "He had a concussion, but he's okay now," the first man said. "He should be fine." He laid one hand on the other man's shoulder. "Go on—the sergeant will take you back to your unit."

Billy stepped forward and closed one hand on the young man's arm just above the elbow. "Come on, son. I'll take you back to Commander Bailey."

The sailor turned to look at him, his eyes slightly unfocused. "Are you with NSA?"

Billy shook his head, hiding the small trill of interest that went through him. NSA—now why exactly did that particular set of initials come to this man's mind? Had he asked about MIUW, the Navy, or any one of a host of other organizations, Billy would not have been surprised. But NSA—he reflected on what he knew of Commander Bailey.

"No, I'm just an Army dogface," Billy said, easing the man down the walkway. As they approached the iron gate, it clicked open. Moments later, they were in the Volvo. Once Billy ensured the man was safely strapped in, he turned his attention to driving back to the pier. He had a feeling that Commander Bailey might have some very interesting answers to the questions that were coming to mind just about now.

MIUW 106

As Bailey explained the details of the tactical situation, Commander Renninger became more and more agitated. Finally, as she described how Collins had made a dash toward the MIUW sonobuoy field, he burst out, "Dammit, I told her—"

Bailey stopped in mid-sentence and placed one hand on his arm. She and Renninger were almost exactly the same height. "I'd like to speak to you outside for just a moment," she said calmly. She tugged lightly on his arm, and motioned to the security watch to open the door.

Once outside, she led him around the edge of the van

and towards the end of the pier. There, they would be safely shielded from prying eyes, something she wouldn't have thought of before Sergeant Elwell's inspection tour of her camp. "What is it with you and your XO?" she said.

"I'm surprised you have to ask that," he said. "Of all people."

Bailey shook her head. "She wasn't my XO. But under the circumstances, I'd say she did a damned fine job. Just what exactly did you tell her before you left?"

Renninger frowned slightly. "I told her not to get us into trouble, and to stay outside the twelve-mile limit. She knows she's treading on thin ice with me—hell, I even tried to find a way to get out of coming ashore to avoid leaving her alone on the ship."

"Why? Think she'll mutiny?" Bailey's voice was sharp. "Let me remind you, the only time she got out of line with me was when she thought she was doing it for the good of the ship. She was a junior lieutenant then, and didn't understand the full tactical implications. Something else you might remember—in the end, she did the right thing. That ship is still alive because of her judgment, and don't you forget it."

"But a submarine—"

She cut him off. "And just how is it her fault that there's a submarine in the area?" she demanded. "Do you think she arranged that somehow? Waited for you to leave the ship and then called the submarine in? Get real, Captain. This scared you, and because you're scared, you're pissed. Collins is a handy scapegoat. But tell me—just what would you have done if your positions had been reversed?"

He thought for a minute, and finally scowled. "I probably wouldn't have thought of running toward the sonobuoy field," he said at last. "That was pretty damned smart—make them think you've got a helo in the area when all your assets are down."

Bailey nodded. She waited.

Finally, Renninger shrugged. "Okay, I was too hard on her. I admit it—she did the right thing. There—are you happy?"

Bailey relaxed. "It doesn't matter if I'm happy, Captain. Like I said—she's not my XO. But if you're going to string her up for negligence and professional misconduct, I don't think this is the time," she said gently. "Of course, it's your ship—not mine."

He shot her a sardonic look. "And hopefully won't be yours ever. I don't intend to be rude, but the circumstances of your last change of command leave a lot to be desired."

Bailey nodded. "I've got no designs on your ship— I've got more than enough to do here, with my civilian job. So," she said, changing the subject, "when will you head back out to *Jouett*?"

"As soon as possible. That seems only reasonable, under the circumstances." He held up a hand as though to forestall her objection. "Don't worry, I'm not going to ream Collins a new asshole. Like you said, she did okay this time." He caught the dark look she shot him. "More than okay," he admitted reluctantly. "I give credit where credit is due, Commander."

Bailey was silent for a moment, then smiled. "It's not easy, being in command. It never is."

He nodded. "You try to think everything through, try to remember how the best men and women you've worked for did it. But in the end, when it comes down to it, you're on your own. Especially at sea. There's nobody else to ask, nobody else around—damn, it's the moment you've trained for for years and years, and when it comes, you still feel like you're not old enough to make the decision. But you have to, so you do the best you can." He shot her an appraising look. "But I guess you know what I'm talking about."

She laughed. "That I do."

He clapped a friendly hand on her shoulder. "If you'll loan me that Humvee and a driver, I'll get back to the airfield. Like I said, I'd like to get back out to *Jouett* as soon as possible.''

''Sure, you want to borrow my Humvee, but you won't let me on your damned ship. How is that for fair?'' she said to break the tension.

Renninger laughed. ''Listen, you get some free time, you come on out. I'll let my XO give you the full tour, how about it?''

She nodded. ''I might take you up on that sometime.''

As she walked Captain Renninger back to her Humvee, another car pulled onto the pier. She watched it, the vulnerability of their situation there sinking in again. But what was also a weakness was a strength—they were at the end of the pier, and had a clear view of anyone approaching them. But they were also isolated from supporting forces. It was, as Elwell would have said, a mixed bag of tricks.

As the car approached, she could make out the details of the interior. There were two people in it, one in uniform and the other—at approximately one quarter of a mile, she recognized the other occupant. She stopped exchanging pleasantries with Renninger in mid-sentence and waited.

Sergeant Elwell pulled the car up beside her. Before he could get out and come around, she was at the passenger-side door, pulling it open. The sailor inside took a shaky step out onto the hot cement. ''Jer?'' he said woozily.

Bailey grabbed him into a tight hug. ''Dammit, Carlisle, if you'd—oh, damn, damn.''

Elwell stopped in front of the car and watched silently. Renninger stepped back, as though unwilling to intrude on the moment. Both were slightly uncomfortable with the public display of emotion between commander and subordinate, though neither one would deny having wanted to do the same thing on occasion.

Finally, Bailey pushed Carlisle away. "Are you okay?"

He nodded. He looked back towards Elwell. "Sarge came and got me." From the slur in his voice, Bailey knew that the rest of the story would have to come from the Army noncom.

She looked at Elwell. "Is he all right?"

Elwell nodded. "Probably could use a checkup at the base hospital, but I suspect what the corpsman told me was true—he had a concussion. He seems to be fine now. Except for one thing."

"What is it?" Bailey demanded. "By God, you should have taken him straight to the hospital. What's wrong with—"

She stopped as Elwell approached, grabbed Carlisle's right arm, and shoved the sleeve back up on his shoulder. He motioned to a pair of angry red marks. "You know what you're looking at?"

Silently, she nodded. The two needle marks stood out in perfect contrast to the pale skin behind them. She looked back at Elwell, hoping her expression wasn't revealing more than she wanted it to.

Elwell lowered his voice. "When I first picked him up, he asked me if I was from NSA." Elwell shook his head, as though puzzling over a tough problem. "I didn't ask any more questions—I didn't figure you'd want me to." He looked at her, his eyes impassive.

With an effort, Bailey regained her composure. "Is he all right?" she asked again, this time with a different meaning.

Elwell caught it and nodded. "As close as I can tell. They have some pretty sophisticated drugs these days. You'll want somebody besides a noncom to figure out what happened."

He related the events of the last hour, concluding with his belief that the SEAL team had actually had custody of Carlisle.

"But why?" she asked, stunned. "The SEALs—
they're on our side."

Elwell shrugged. "There are all sorts of sides, even
within the U.S. military. I'd want to be careful about
who I discussed this with," he concluded. "I sort of
made a promise."

Bailey's mind reeled. Up until now, she'd believed
that the SEALs were her allies—in fact, the force to
which she entrusted the security of her camp and her
people. Now, the SEALs' close attention to the MIUW
camp took on a whole new meaning.

Another thought occurred to her, and she turned pale.
"The RHIB," she said quietly. "Did they—?" She
stopped, unable to voice her suspicion.

Elwell regarded her levelly. "I wouldn't have thought
so, but who's to say? We may never know for sure."

"But why?" Bailey demanded. "What possible sense
does this make?"

"It makes sense to someone. Commander," he continued, motioning towards Renninger with his head,
"how do you feel about him? Can you trust him?"

Two other MIUW sailors darted up then, having recognized Carlisle. Bailey paused before answering, giving
orders to the men to take Carlisle immediately to the
unit corpsman and then to his rack in one of the tents.
After the three had departed, she turned back to Elwell.
"I would have thought I could trust Commander Murphy, but evidently not."

Elwell's voice took on a hard note. "You knew better
after you talked to him, didn't you? What kind of gut
feeling did he give you?"

Bailey nodded slowly, remembering her initial discomfort with the SEAL team CO. Then she looked back
at Renninger. "I feel better about Renninger," she said.
"Better, but not confident. Besides, it's a whole lot more
likely that the commanding officer of a warship is going
to be on the righteous side. I can see how Special Forces

can be used to further a different agenda. Easier for them than a warship.''

Elwell nodded thoughtfully. ''For what it's worth, I agree with you. You're going to have to give this some thought, because sooner or later we'll have to decide who we trust.''

''I don't like this. Not one little bit,'' Bailey said finally. She looked over at Commander Renninger, who was standing patiently out of earshot. He had just glanced at his watch, but was clearly unwilling to intrude on whatever was going on. ''How can we be certain?'' As she asked the question, she realized the logical implication—she'd already included Sergeant Elwell on the short list of people she could trust.

Elwell shrugged. ''We won't know until it comes right down to it, will we? But I can tell you one thing— that's a man who knows how to wait.''

17

GULF OF PANAMA:
1 OCTOBER

SEAHAWK 101

Commander Renninger settled back into the hard seat and listened to the idle chatter of his helo crew. It had taken him another hour to get back to the airport, have the helo preflighted, and get under way to *Jouett*, and that had been pressing the time limits on all safety envelopes. He had a sense of being overwhelmed. Things were moving too fast ashore, the tactical implications and strategic maneuverings of all the military forces and political entities involved moving too quickly to be entirely comprehended. He felt an inchoate longing to be back on board his ship, in the isolated world linked only by radio circuits and weapons ranges to the shore. Even with an XO that he didn't entirely trust, it was a more certain environment than ashore.

"Captain? You might want to take a look at this." The tinny voice of the copilot over the ICS startled him out of his reverie. He leaned forward and looked out of the front windscreen. In the distance, he could see *Jouett*, a stately and impressive sight just above the horizon. As always, her sleek lines inspired a sense of awe in him. She was quiet, majestic, and owned every bit of the water around her. There was a stateliness to her progress that was missing from any other warship he'd ever seen. Perhaps it was just because she was his, but that was enough for him.

But the pilot hadn't been referring to his ship. No, it was entirely something else. This entire area of the ocean was as crowded as he'd ever seen a port. Massive merchants formed awkward, untidy columns, lined up to the horizon in paths waiting to enter the Canal. Just inside the harbor, huge clusters of them were anchored. A light roiling of the air just above their stacks indicated they were still at power.

"How many of them are there?" he asked, knowing that the pilot probably didn't know. "How long has this been going on?"

"They started turning away traffic just before we landed," the copilot answered. "On the way in, I saw the Panamanian patrol craft making approaches on a couple of them. From what I could tell from the ship-to-ship-channel traffic, the Panamanian military is conducting a complete inspection on every ship inbound. Those that have cargo manifested to or from the U.S. are not allowed transit rights. The U.S.-flagged ships—there were two—don't even rate an inspection, just an order to stand off.

"That cluster to the north—Jim, can you get us over there?" the copilot said to the pilot. "They're ships that just left the Canal. Same drill—if they were in the Canal when the order went down, the Panamanians took custody of them as soon as they outchopped. They're supposed to be standing by for inspection as well. Any cargo bound to or from the U.S. will be seized."

"You've gotta be kidding," Renninger said. "They don't have the resources to handle this. Hell, we needed a multinational force in the Gulf to do the same thing."

"They've designated a couple of piers as inspection

points," the copilot continued. "They're taking them in one by one. But I suspect you're right, Captain. This is going to take months and months to sort out."

"We don't have months," Renninger snapped. "And the United States isn't the only one going to be unhappy about this."

"Look at that one," the pilot chimed in, circling the helicopter around to get a view of a massive RO-RO steaming majestically by. "Wonder why she's so special."

"Take us in and let's rig her," Renninger ordered, asking for a flyby and identification of the ship's flag and primary structural features.

"Can do." Without further ado, the helicopter descended, vectoring in to fly at almost eye level with the bridge of the ship. The pilot edged them in close enough that Renninger could make out figures moving around on the bridge, including two uniformed figures who came out on the port bridge wing to stare at his helicopter.

"Type III merchant—RO-RO," the copilot said, and reeled off the structural details of the ship's superstructure. "I make the name as *Lotus Vengeance*. And there's the key to it, Captain—she's flying a Chinese flag."

Renninger was silent as the helicopter crew finished the details of rigging the ship. Finally, he said, "Take us home. I have a feeling there's going to be some mighty interesting message traffic waiting for me on the ship."

Collins met him on the flight deck, waiting for him as he disembarked from the helicopter. He motioned her inside the hangar bay and then down the centerline passageway before speaking. Finally, when they shut the hatch behind them and the noise of the flight deck dropped abruptly, he turned to her.

"For the record, XO, damned fine job on that submarine. As I told Commander Bailey, I wouldn't have thought of that tactic myself.''

Collins looked startled, and a red flush crept up her cheeks. She looked down at the deck. "Thank you, Captain," she said finally. "That means—"

"Enough of that. You only did what any XO would do," he said briskly. "A good XO. But I don't have time to stand around feeding your ego. Tell me what's going on. I saw the merchant ships stacked up outside the Canal.''

Collins nodded and cleared her throat. "The order came out shortly after you left,'' she began, and briefly summarized the same facts he'd heard from the helo pilot. "And there's been no further detection of the submarine,'' she finished. "That's about it.''

Renninger shook his head, puzzled. "What's the response from Third Fleet? Are any contingency plans being put into operation?''

Collins nodded. "Nothing official, but I got an informal heads-up over JOTS that we can expect a major deployment of U.S. forces to the south. Two problems with that, though, as you can probably guess.''

"Let's get into Combat—I want a full briefing there. No point in discussing tactics in the passageway.''

Five minutes later, they both stepped into the frigid air of Combat. Collins led the way over to the JOTS console, and had the operator bring up the wire note she'd referred to. "It's not as good as formal message traffic, but sometimes it's just as accurate.''

Renninger nodded. "You mentioned two problems— let's see if we're thinking of the same two.''

Collins held up one finger. "First, time and distance. It's a good four days' transit down here, more if they have to slow down for resupply ships. With the situation going to crap and so unstable, we're going to want to have our own resupply assets in-theater. That takes time to set up, and we can't rely on the Panamanian government anymore.''

Renninger nodded. ''The smart officer thinks tactics, the brilliant one thinks logistics,'' he noted. ''Go on.''

Collins hesitated. Then she pointed at the last known location of the unknown submarine. ''I don't know how much you'll agree with me on this one, but I'm prepared to analogize this to the Falklands situation. That one submarine—the whole course of the Falklands War was changed by rumors first of a deployed Argentinean diesel boat, and later by the question of whether or not there was a British Swiftsure attack submarine in the area. The mere rumor of the presence of a submarine caused each nation to alter their tactics accordingly. I suspect we can expect to see the same thing down here.''

''The British killed a helluva lot of whales during the Falklands, as well as expending almost all of the sonobuoys they had in their inventory,'' Renninger noted. ''However, it might just be that we're a little bit more capable than our allies.''

Collins's gaze seemed to turn inward. ''I wouldn't know about that, Captain,'' she murmured. ''Some of them are quite competent.''

Renninger frowned as he remembered Collins's first-hand experience with British submarine capabilities. ''You might be right at that. So we have supply problems as well as submarine problems. Speaking of which, how is our own fuel status?''

''Eighty percent fuel, cruising at economical speeds,'' she said crisply. ''The thought occurred to me while you were gone that we might have to make do for a while.''

Renninger nodded once again, impressed by how thoroughly she had thought out their tactical situation. Maybe he had been mistaken about her—hadn't given her a fair chance. After all, he'd never really asked her for her account of the events in the English Channel, just based his judgment of her on what he'd heard from friends and acquaintances. Maybe it was time he gave her a chance to explain.

"What do you recommend, XO?"

She studied the JOTS display for a moment before answering. "That we do exactly what we're doing now, Captain," she said. "That submarine wanted to prove a point to us—well, okay, she proved it. But I see no reason to deviate from our assigned mission. We maintain station down here, cutting holes in the water at five knots, and wait for something to happen."

"And hope we're ready for it," Renninger said grimly.

Collins nodded. "We'll be ready, Captain. I'm certain of it."

18

PANAMA CITY, PANAMA:
1 OCTOBER

THE PRESIDENTIAL PALACE, PANAMA

Won Su stepped disdainfully around the puddles that splattered the walkway to the Presidential Palace. The weather in Panama was one of his chief complaints about being assigned to this mission, although the potential career rewards should have made up for the inconvenience. It wasn't the rain in particular that he objected to—it was the untidy manner in which it occurred every afternoon, violent thunderstorms appearing suddenly on the horizon, sweeping quickly through the capital, then dissipating to leave brilliant azure skies behind again. It was normal weather for this time of the year in the tropics, but its very predictability offended his sense of decorum.

And the aftermath. He gazed around with distaste at the daily carnage of the storm. Leaves littered the cement everywhere, small branches too. How could they not think ahead? Knowing their weather as they did, the Panamanians should have designed this walkway with a slight arc to it to expedite the draining of the water, the restoration of the balance between man-made structures and nature. At his own estate back in China, this oversight would never have been permitted. The damage would have been corrected quickly, efficiently, by a platoon of gardeners kept on standby for just such an occasion.

Nevertheless, one worked with what one had. In some ways, the Panamanian weather was a fitting metaphor for the violent maneuverings that passed for politics in the tropics.

His retinue of assistants and advisors drew in closer around him, carefully maintaining their prescribed distances. That his meandering path up the walkway put some of them in the middle of puddles was not his concern—in many ways, what happened to them was simply irrelevant.

He contemplated the metaphor of weather and military power as he made his stately way towards the building. The delicate power play that had begun with the twenty-five-year leases on port facilities on either end of the Panama Canal was now coming to fruition. In the next few days, the game would have to be played delicately—subtly, at a level the Panamanians would never be able to either understand or appreciate. He sighed, regretting already that understanding the full complexity of his plan would not be part of the Panamanian defeat.

"My friend," President Jorge Aguillar said, stepping forward to greet the Chinese man. He held out his hand, pulled the Chinese man close in another of those excessive displays of emotion that Won Su so abhorred. Yet he tolerated it, as he did so many things here in Panama, for the sake of his country.

"A momentous day, is it not?" Won Su said in slow, correct Spanish. It had taken him nearly a decade to completely master the language, so simple-minded and unfamiliar. The mechanics required to speak Spanish were another thing he disliked—the flapping lips, rolling tongues, consonants and vowels missing the subtle meanings that could be conveyed in Mandarin by a simple change in inflection. The spelling, so rudimentary and crude.

"It is indeed." Aguillar beamed at him. "A new era of friendship—my friends, that is what you are first and foremost." He beamed, and threw an arm across the Chinese man's back. Won Su's advisors drew back slightly in horror. Aguillar pulled him close. "Come, we will make the announcement together."

Won Su demurred politely. It was, he insisted, not necessary to provide such public affirmation of the long and beautiful friendship between Panama and China. The world knew of it—those who mattered. And as the game was played in world politics, it was better to have Panama enjoying this glory alone. A strong, proud people, one that should never have been subjected to decades of American domination.

He saw the point, did he not? That emphasizing Panama's strength and security was best done by Panama alone?

Aguillar continued smiling broadly as he gazed fondly at his new friend. "Of course we understand! But you will certainly be in the official entourage, will you not? Perhaps not participating, but yet there as a demonstration of our friendship."

Won Su hesitated slightly. Aguillar's smile faded, his eyes narrowed. "I would be honored to have you join us on the platform," he said levelly.

Won Su agreed immediately. Aguillar had just conveyed a message of such subtlety that he had not thought it possible: that to refuse this honor would be to insult the Panamanians. He smiled inwardly, delighted at the small gift this day had brought—evidence that the Panamanians might prove far cleverer than he had suspected before.

The ceremonial band played loudly, as they always did. Won Su despaired of ever hearing any indication that the Panamanian musicians understood that music could be played at different volumes. When it finally ended, the discordant cacophony of martial music and sentimental patriotic songs that passed for music in this country, his head was throbbing.

The four officials, each of increasing importance, that introduced each other prior to the Panamanian President speaking, simply added to his discomfort. Finally, Aguillar took the stage. With expansive gestures and facial expressions bordering on hysteria, he outlined the current situation in terms his countrymen could understand. The infamy of the American attack on the unarmed, defenseless Panamanian airliner. The subsequent demands for righteous reparations by his government. Overshadowing it all, the tragic loss of a great man, a great leader—one that Aguillar had been only too willing to assassinate not a month ago—their beloved President. After thirty minutes of increasingly emotional rhetoric, Aguillar finally came to the point. Won Su only hoped that the political analysts in America had not tuned out fifteen minutes earlier.

"Until reparations are paid, and apologies are made, the great nation of Panama will not tolerate the use of its most precious natural resource, a marvel of Panamanian engineering and construction, for the shipment of goods bound to or from the imperialistic nation of the United States. We will not tolerate it."

Much cheering, Won Su noted. All the more strange, since nothing that Aguillar was saying so far was news. The closure had been announced through diplomatic channels, and carried extensively by local broadcast media. Still, it did not take much to arouse the emotions of these people. He sighed, holding his face in a carefully neutral expression.

"Furthermore, we will enforce this demand with our military might," Aguillar thundered. "Let no nation question our determination—challenge our resolve." Aguillar turned theatrically to glare at the lone U.S. representative seated on the stage. Won Su was pleased to note that the other man had not yet mastered the ability to keep a completely straight face.

But even Won Su himself tensed slightly as Aguillar approached the key point in the speech. The idea had been planted slowly, the most delicate of hints sprinkled over the course of several conversations. That it had come to fruition so quickly, so easily, was credit more to the easily swayed nature of the Panamanian than to Won Su's own doing.

Still, looking at the American representative, Aguillar continued. "It is America's fault that this situation stands as it is. Accordingly, as a show of good faith, we request that the American forces now inside our country be assigned to support and assist in this objective. We also ask the American flagships voluntarily abstain from requesting entry into the Canal, thus precluding the necessity for denying those requests."

Aguillar paused to let the full implications of that sink in. Won Su was delighted to note the look of outraged shock on a number of faces.

MIUW 106

Along with most of her unit, Bailey listened to Aguillar's address in simultaneous translation over the Voice of America. As he reached the climax of his tirade, Bailey turned to survey the faces of the other American soldiers and sailors. She saw the same look of astonished disbelief on their faces that she felt on her own.

She turned to stare out at the water. Row upon row of merchant ships queued up waiting for clearance. Her eyes fixed on one ship, noting the Chinese flag. The *Lotus* something—she couldn't quite make out the final word of the name. An oddly configured bright red helo sat on its deck, the tail rotors longer and more massive than she remembered.

She turned to Sergeant Elwell. More and more, the man was becoming a mainstay of the MIUW unit operations. "They can't be serious," she said quietly.

Elwell shook his head. "But they are." He turned slightly to survey the van, the barricade of deuce-and-a-half trucks, and the other gear that went with the MIUW unit. "And guess who they expect to do most of the enforcing."

HMS *DARLING MOIRA*

The Bahamian-flagged dry-cargo ship trudged steadily through the gentle seas in the approach to the Panama Canal. It was well inside the massive natural harbor now, and the water was calm, with long, low swells rising out from the gradually sloping seabed. While industrial pollution in the vicinity of the Panama Canal was becoming an increasing problem, as yet the natural currents and eddies up and down the coast had managed to disperse most of the pollution.

Moira was carrying a cargo of dry wheat transshipped from San Francisco. Following the announcement of the closure of the Panama Canal to American traffic, the captain and his crew had worked hastily to alter their manifest papers. What had once been grain from the heartland of America was now manifested as wheat onloaded in Victoria, British Columbia, Canada.

The Bahamian master glanced at the papers and sighed. In places, the forgery was patently obvious. However, he was counting on the well-known propensity of Panamanian customs officials to supplement their income by other means. In other words, a bribe. It had worked in the past, and he had no doubt that it would be equally effective this time.

Still, the political turmoil involving the area confused and worried him. Access to international waterways was one of the fundamental tenets of freedom of the seas, and Panama's actions boded ill for this passage as well as for the Suez Canal. But he had no doubt that there would be a way to conduct business, even under these conditions. There always was.

"Inspection team approaching," his first mate noted. The Panamanian cutter they'd been told to expect was approaching on the port bow.

"All stop," the master ordered. He listened to the chatter of orders and instructions over the handheld walkie-talkie as his crew prepared to receive the inspection team.

The team made its way quickly to the bridge, and began the formalities of inspecting the *Darling Moira*'s registration papers. Without comment, the master handed them his hastily created manifest.

As the senior officer on the team studied them, the master observed the rest of the team members. He was surprised to note a Chinese civilian with the rest of them. The man had not spoken since their arrival on board, but he could well be a Panamanian. The world got smaller and smaller these days, and finding someone of Chinese descent on a Panamanian inspection team should not have surprised him. Still, since the man had not spoken, he had no way of knowing whether or not he spoke Spanish as a native would.

"We will inspect your cargo," the senior member said finally. He smiled blandly at the master. "All appears to be in order here, of course."

In order *now*, the master thought. He'd observed the man take the registration and cargo manifest to a corner of the bridge, ostensibly to concentrate on the details there, but in reality to palm the thick envelope wedged in between two documents. Five thousand dollars—it appeared to be sufficient. Had it not, he had no doubt that the senior member would have found some niggling discrepancy, something that required a private conversation with the master in his cabin.

How and where the money would be dispersed later

was of no concern to the master. The entire amount would be billed back to the ship's owners and the shipping company as a cost of doing business, either labeled as a fuel cost or a port charge.

The master accompanied the inspection team down into the bowels of the ship, and they commenced a brief survey of the cargo contents. Clearly, this was merely a formality, the more serious business having been taken care of on the bridge. The grain warranted a cursory examination. Then the master invited the inspection team to enjoy coffee and doughnuts in his galley. They all declined, pleading urgent business with the other ships piling up outside the Canal. As the master watched them depart, he mulled how little the business of international trade had changed over the decades. No doubt his predecessors, running the lucrative tobacco-rum-slavery triangle centuries ago, had had to deal with similar costs. He was just glad that this particular obstacle had been overcome so easily.

PANAMANIAN CUTTER

As the team clambered down the access ladder back to their forty-foot patrol craft, they were silent. Once inside the ship, the senior member hastily divided the contents of the envelope between the other officers. It had been tricky, managing to pocket almost half the fat sheaf of bills himself before having to divide it up, but he'd managed it.

"So what now?" his second in command said. He waved the bills he'd been given. "Has she passed inspection?"

The senior member shook his head slowly. He let his fingers curl around the wad of bills stashed in his pocket. "Sadly, I noted some discrepancies in the manifest. Clearly an attempt to conceal his original port." He turned to the Chinese observer. "The *Lotus Glory* is next, yes?"

The Chinese man nodded. "And there you will find everything in order. Absolutely everything," he added with unusual emphasis. He alone from the team had declined to share in the bribe received from *Darling Moira*.

"Let's go then." The senior member turned back to the rest of the team. "We will find everything in order this time."

LOTUS GLORY

"Machinery parts," *Lotus Glory*'s master said. "On-loaded in Hong Kong, and en route to Cuba."

The Panamanian nodded vigorously. "Of course, of course," he murmured.

"We have prepared several containers for your inspection," the Chinese master said. "If you would be so kind to step this way?" He motioned toward the rear of the ship.

"I hardly think that will be necessary," the Panamanian said firmly.

Sixty feet below the waterline, T'sing Lin edged back on the catwalk, away from the sleek, deadly cylinder now poised over the well deck. The metal railing behind him bit hard into his back. He rubbed against it, focusing on the pain to both distract him from what was happening and reassure him that he was still alive.

Two engineers popped open the hatch, exposing the crude pilot's seat positioned in front of rudimentary instruments. T'sing Lin heard Kim Sung emit a hoarse, strangled sound. A moan, perhaps, or the beginning of a scream. T'sing touched his classmate on the arm, and felt the flesh tremble under his fingers.

Would he be courageous when his time came? He and Kim had discussed it often with joking bravado, each

making extravagant claims about their own bravery and
boasting about the damage that they would inflict on
their targets.

But only during the daylight. In the darker hours at
night, when their eventual fates seemed to permeate the
stultified air in their quarters, they'd talked of women,
of their families, of anything except this moment that
governed every second of their existence.

The first engineer glanced at Kim Sung and nodded.
T'sing felt Kim suck in a hard breath, then pull quickly
away from him. In one fluid motion, Kim moved forward, vaulted into the torpedo, and held up his arms to
allow the engineers to coil the straps around his body.

Kim ran through the prechecks quickly, whistling
tunelessly the entire time. Finally, he looked back at the
engineers. "I am ready." These were the first words
Kim had spoken since *Lotus Glory*'s master had announced his selection as the next pilot. They would be
the last as well.

DARLING MOIRA

"That was easy," the first mate said. "Wouldn't have
thought they'd be so stupid about alterations on mani-
fests."

The captain was silent. There was no need to share
every detail of commanding a merchant ship with his
second, not yet. There were things he would learn soon
enough when he became master of his own vessel, when
his own duties required participating in such schemes.
Better to let him keep the modicum of innocence he now
possessed. Not, the master reflected, that under any circumstances could his first mate be called innocent. The
master had been on odd liberties in too many strange
ports with the man to believe that. Still, the machinations
within a shipping company and the responsibilities of
command were something he would have to learn on his

own. He would probably be eligible for his own ship within the next several years if he kept on the course he was now going, and the master planned to have a long, frank conversation with him before he left *Darling Moira* for his own vessel.

"Commence the approach on the Canal," the master ordered, forestalling further conversation. The bridge was fully manned, although an American military ship would have thought it woefully inadequate. There were two officers on deck, plus the navigator, as well as the captain.

Darling Moira swung slowly to starboard, lining up for her approach on the entrance to the Panama Canal. Access was rigidly controlled by a series of shipping lanes, and extra vigilance was warranted with the nearby anchorage crowded with foreign merchant ships waiting to be cleared for transit. Luckily, the weather was still good, and normal caution and prudence should get them safely through it.

The master let the first mate handle the approach, as he had many times before. The ship responded slowly, but the first mate was more than familiar with her maneuverability characteristics, as the large rudder angles he ordered at her slow speeds demonstrated. As she completed her slight course change, *Darling Moira* ended up exactly in the center of the approach transit lane. The master nodded, satisfied. The forty-four-mile stretch of confined waters inside the Canal was normally a harrowing voyage, as it would be today. He'd lost paint several times to the old sea walls, as well as garnered a couple of scrapes and dings. It was to be expected—merely a cost of doing business.

"Five knots," the first mate ordered. *Darling Moira* slowly picked up speed and headed for the Canal.

LOTUS GLORY

The two engineers pulled the safety pins on either side of the deployment mechanism. The torpedo was now firmly cradled in the metallic frame, held there by its own weight and by the gently curved supports that curled around its body. The senior engineer nodded to the other, who activated a small motor at the aft end of the transport mechanism. Its high-pitched whirring cut through the other noises in the bottommost compartment of *Lotus Glory*.

The cradle holding the torpedo crept slowly down the rails, headed for a structure resembling bomb-bay doors located just to the right of the keel. It took four minutes to complete the fifteen-foot journey.

Finally, when the torpedo was positioned directly over the doors, the senior technician nodded. The doors swung open, revealing a small, low compartment just the size of the torpedo. It was half filled with water.

T'sing Lin shivered. Just below, on the other side of the outer doors, was the sea. Should the lock mechanism fail, the seal spring a leak, or any one of a hundred possible accidents occur, the sea would come rushing in without mercy. The only way to preserve the ship would be to dog down the doors to this compartment and leave the men trapped inside to a watery grave.

Yet in ten years of operational use, the lockout mechanism had yet to fail. Stolen from a design built into North Korean Moma AGI merchant vessels, the design reflected the Chinese philosophy that military force was not limited to ships of war. Every vessel that floated, every vehicle that moved on land, could be mobilized for a specific military purpose.

This design also reflected another trait of Asian thought that would have chilled the American military even more. Since the days of World War II, a number of nations had experimented with the idea of kamikaze pilots as pioneered by the Japanese. In addition to their aircraft, the Japanese had used manned torpedoes like this one, equipped with rudimentary sensors capable of seeking out enemy ships when guided by the man inside it: the *niru*.

It was truly an honor to be so called to serve one's country. T'sing Lin had been told that, had believed it when his military commander had freed him from the dank cell that his minor theft had put him in. It was a chance to redeem himself, to cleanse away the dishonor that accompanied the criminal charges pending against him.

That night, Kim would be in glory while T'sing Lin tossed and turned restlessly on the hard, narrow bed in the *Lotus Glory*.

Kim Sung took a deep breath, stilled his mind, and concentrated his thoughts. The mission ahead was one that he'd trained for, spending innumerable hours in simulators and in classrooms studying tactics. The inside of the torpedo was as familiar to him as the engineering spaces were to the men who'd just helped him to deploy. He ran one hand over the sleek inside, giving silent thanks to the men and women who'd built this remarkable weapon.

For a moment, his mind struggled to break free of the iron discipline he'd imposed on it. A child's face repeatedly appeared before his eyes, but he shoved the vision away. A son—his own son, the one that he would never see again.

His child would be provided for, as would his wife. When he became a national hero, his family would want for nothing. He had only to execute this final mission as briefed, pilot this vessel to its destination, and his family's future would be assured more firmly than he ever could have done himself.

The torpedo lurched as the cradle commenced its final

descent into the compartment. There was a dull clang—
the doors closing overhead—then the gurgling murmur
of the sea flooding the compartment. A sudden weight-
lessness as the cradle retracted, leaving the torpedo floating free. He watched the depth gauge, making sure that
he was clear of *Lotus Glory* before activating the small
electric motor aft. The battery-driven propeller gave
forth a reassuring whine as it spun up to speed.

He'd already set the course into the small guidance
system. There was very little to do, except be alert for
malfunctions, and to activate the pinging fire-control sonar as he approached the target. Five minutes—maybe
ten. He tried to clear his mind, to concentrate on the
reassuring sounds he'd heard so often during his training
sessions. And on the mission ahead.

Kim Sung was twenty years old.

NIRU 2

The minutes passed slowly, too slowly. If there was any
fault with the system of kamikaze torpedoes, it was that
they relied on the will of the man piloting them to complete the mission. The Chinese designers, as their Korean predecessors had, had eliminated at least one
temptation. The outer access hatch to the torpedo was
securely locked—from the outside.

Eight minutes later, according to his watch, Kim Sung
activated the pinging sonar. It was a low-power, high-
frequency sonar set, extremely accurate but without an
extended range.

He heard the reassuring return echo, and made a slight
course correction. Already he could hear the dull sound
of the massive propellers beating the water ahead, driving the gigantic merchant vessel through the water. The
sound radiated in through his thin hull, beating in time
with his heart. He took a deep breath, then slipped the

lever forward that would increase the speed of the torpedo.

Kim Sung had less than ninety seconds to live.

MIUW 106

"Torpedo!" The sonarman's shrill voice echoed inside
the cramped MIUW van. Bailey turned, and was jerked
back by the cord that connected her headset to the console. She untangled it from the console joystick and got
as close as she could to the sonar console.

"Where?" she demanded.

The sonarman pointed at an oddly unstable signature
on his screen. "There—it's not U.S., not Soviet—nothing I've seen before. But look at that—and here—active
sonar pings on passive." He reached up and cranked the
speaker overhead to full volume. Sure enough, she could
hear it now. The light, caressing quivers of sound that
were characteristic of a fire-control sonar. She turned
back to Boston. "Tell *Jouett*—now."

"Captain," the sonarman broke in. "Ma'am, this one
isn't headed anywhere near the *Jouett*." He pointed at
a second set of lines on his display. "That merchant—
that's the target."

DARLING MOIRA

The call came over bridge-to-bridge, and the master
picked up the microphone, slightly irritated at being distracted from the task of shepherding his massive ship
through the anchorage. "Say again?" he said irritably.
"Ma'am, please slow down—understand you I can't."
He slipped naturally back into the rhythmic patois of his
native islands. He frowned as she repeated her message,
then turned to the first mate. "A torpedo? Can she be
serious?"

The first mate, concentrating on the water ahead, shook his head. "How could she—they cleared us, did they not? Besides, there's no military vessel within range." He pointed off toward the horizon. The Panamanian customs vessel that had visited them earlier was tied up to the side of a Chinese merchant.

The master shook his head. Whoever the woman was on bridge-to-bridge—he'd caught her name, and dismissed it as soon as he heard her message—she had best clear the circuit before any of the Panamanian officials took notice of her practical joke.

An ominous rumble echoed through the bridge. The master's heart sank. He'd heard that sound only once before, when he was a very young merchant marine sailor. It had been on a dry-cargo ship that had gone aground on an uncharted sandbar. That same scraping, sickly squealing had echoed through that ship then. Now the sound built, reaching ear-splitting proportions. *Darling Moira* heeled violently to port, drawing her crew against the opposite bulkhead. The first mate screamed once, then fell silent as his head hit a stanchion with a sickening crunch. The navigator, trapped behind his plotting table, had nowhere to go. He fetched up against the bulkhead hard, but stayed on his feet and retained consciousness.

The master felt his feet slip out from under him as the ship rocked, and hit the deck on his left hip. His right arm was caught under him, and he felt his forearm give a loud crunch. Pain shot through him, dimming his vision to a red haze. He was aware of sliding, moving, and finally stopping against something metal. He shook his head, trying desperately to clear his vision.

They were aground, they must be. But a sandbar located near the entrance to the Panama Canal? How could such a thing be? It was simply impossible, simply—

The ominous sound he'd heard earlier segued into a violent, glass-shattering blast. The forward portion of the ship exploded into flames and smoke. Metal strakes and steel plating were wrenched into unimaginable shapes by the force of the explosion. The master, who'd managed to haul himself upright with his one good arm, stared out in horror and disbelief at the forward portion of his ship. Where there had once been a clean eight-hundred-foot expanse of carefully maintained deck, there was now perhaps four hundred feet of the ship remaining.

Darling Moira nosed down hard, throwing him from the starboard bulkhead against the forward structure of the bridge. The master heard screaming, the cries of the injured on the bridge. He hung on with his good hand to the railing that ran just beneath the windows, and stared out. Something far more ominous had replaced the smoke and flames billowing from the forward part of the ship, if that were possible. It seemed merely feet away, creeping closer every moment. The sea.

MIUW 106

Bailey jerked down on the pullout rungs that ran up the side of the MIUW van. She clambered up the eleven-foot-tall metal box and stood, face into the wind, and gazed out at the harbor. The stern of a massive dry-cargo ship was now exposed, its propeller windmilling idly twenty feet above the surface of the calm ocean. Around the ship—she squinted, and could make out the name *Darling Moira* on the bow—other ships were belching gouts of black smoke as they prepared to get under way.

A steady stream of tugs was leaving the commercial piers, heading for their client ships. She groaned as she watched one large tanker turn bow into the wind and narrowly miss colliding with a RO-RO. With so many ships in a relatively small area of the ocean, the potential for a mishap was enormous.

One portion of the dry-cargo ship was still floating, the bow pointed improbably up toward the sky. She picked up her binoculars and examined it more closely. Raw fuel oil, its dry cargo, and debris from the explosion clumped in untidy masses on the waves. The grain cargo the ship had been carrying, now saturated with fuel and burning furiously, spread out like a blanket of fire on the water. She saw a few figures struggling in the water, two men clinging to a plank just forward of the burning bow, kicking frantically to clear the area. A tug vectored off toward them, and she lost sight of them behind it as it stopped to take them on.

She had to do something—anything. Just as she was about to order the RHIB out once again to search for survivors, already knowing it would be futile, she saw a flock of Panamanian cutters deploy from the other side of the harbor. She turned back to stare at the conflagration on the water, unable to keep her eyes off it. The need to do something was overwhelming.

Bailey heard footsteps on the hard metal top of the van, and she turned to see Elwell approaching. Something in the man's appearance steadied her.

"I set your security alert team," he said. "Something like this—a good distraction."

She nodded, not taking her eyes off the scene before her. "They'll never get away. All those crews—I'd be running if I were them too."

"You wouldn't. You can't. Not now," Elwell said slowly. "Not with what's at stake."

Bailey looked at him, and her eyes narrowed. "What do you mean by that?"

He gestured out at the burning ship and the others panicking. "Staying alive means keeping your head and thinking things through when everyone else's reacting. It doesn't make a lot of sense for the Panamanians to do this. The Canal is their livelihood—take that away, and they're back to running drugs just like every other country down here. Why would they risk offending a powerful neighbor to the north, the very people who built the damned thing for them?" He shook his head thoughtfully. Then he looked at her. "Do you have any ideas?"

"None that make sense," she answered, absurdly grateful that he'd refocused her away from the tragedy taking place in front of her.

Elwell nodded slowly. "But you should be in a position to know that."

"What do you mean by that?"

Elwell gazed at her levelly. "You work at NSA."

She sighed. "It won't have been much of a secret, I suppose."

Elwell shook his head. "Not after Germany. So, what do you think is happening here?"

She thought hard for a moment, then began slowly. "You're right, it doesn't make any sense for the Panamanians to be behind this. Sure, there's no lost love between some members of the government and the United States, but at least sixty-five percent of the Panamanians opposed returning the Canal to Panamanian control when it happened. That to me says that this is not a country rife with unrest against the United States."

"That agrees with what I know about it," Elwell said. "Go on."

She almost smiled at the implicit order in his voice. There was something about the sergeant's demeanor that made him hard not to obey, even if she was several grades senior. "The shoot-down of the airbus is suspect as well," she continued. She filled him in on what Renninger had told her about the data tapes from the ship, concluding with: "It's not conclusive, of course, but it does make me wonder. Sure, *Jouett* shot two missiles—there's no question about that. Aside from the fact that it's damned difficult to doctor the data tapes, there are over four hundred men and women on that ship who heard it leave the rails." She shook her head dismissively. "No, there's no doubt about the missile shot. It's just a question of the circumstances surrounding it, and whether Collins actually hit it."

"Collins?" Elwell's voice took on a sharp note. "You know the gentleman in question?"

Bailey laughed harshly. "Very well. And it's not a he, it's a she."

For the first time, she saw Elwell's eyes widen slightly. "The same Collins as from the Germany affair," he said wonderingly. "Now just imagine how coincidental that is."

"Everyone at NSA has been trying to convince me it's a coincidence."

Elwell's voice took on a grim note. "They're not Chinese."

Bailey stared hard at him. "Are you suggesting the Chinese engineered this whole episode?"

Elwell shook his head slowly. "I'm not suggesting anything right now, Commander. We're just having a friendly talk up here."

"Assuming that they could do it, it might make sense," she said thoughtfully. "Drive a wedge between the U.S. and Panama, and China's influence in the region becomes all that more important. They've always understood about controlling sea lanes, although they haven't had the power to do it until recently. But back in the earliest days of Sun Tzu, they knew how important constricted passages were." She looked back at him, a new light of respect in her eyes. "There just might be something to this."

He pointed to the burning ship in the harbor. "And maybe not. I think I know what this is supposed to look like—we're supposed to see an outraged Panamanian government taking vengeance on the United States for a horrifying tragedy. All of the elements are in place, all of the players are in the game. I don't know just how or why, but I'm willing to bet that there's more to this than meets the eye. Just like there was in Korea."

Bailey turned back to stare out at the gaggle of merchant ships. Five more were under way now, trailing streamers of black smoke behind them, slowly picking up speed and ignoring the marked inchop and outchop channels. ''There's just one question then.''

''What's that?''

She pointed at a large RO-RO with the name *Lotus Glory* emblazoned on its stern. ''If the Chinese are behind it, how come they're leaving too?''

19

PANAMA CITY, PANAMA:
2 OCTOBER

U.S. EMBASSY

Hank Flashert burst into Turner's office without so much as knocking. The aide looked disheveled, slightly wild-eyed. Without speaking, he went to the TV in the corner of Turner's office and switched it on to CNN.

"What are you doing?" Turner's voice was harsh. "Can't you see I'm working?"

Flashert ignored him. He settled into one of the comfortable chairs in front of the Ambassador's desk and swiveled around to watch the headline news.

"I said, what are you—" Turner's voice broke off as he heard the first words of the broadcast.

"I warned the State Department two days ago," President Aguillar said solemnly. "Every effort was taken to make sure that there was no loss of life. I cannot be blamed if the State Department withholds information from concerned parties."

Flashert swiveled back to look at his boss. "They're already calling."

"The United States has forced me to take the sternest

measures possible.'' Aguillar shook his head and assumed an expression of deep regret. ''I cannot ensure the safety of any ship in the area until the United States admits its complete and sole responsibility for the death of my predecessor and the innocent civilians on board that aircraft. Until such time as reparations are made, we will take the only avenues open to us. While endangering civilian lives is completely abhorrent to this nation, we will target one merchant every day. Without warning. As our airliner was targeted.''

Turner shook his head in dismay. ''I don't have a clue as to what they're—'' His voice broke off suddenly. A fragment of a dinner conversation with Aguillar came to mind. That had to be it—but how could he have known that the little banty rooster was talking about attacks on unarmed merchant ships? What was he supposed to do, pass on every idle rumor as fact? Turner shook his head, his heart sinking.

''No,'' Turner said numbly, ''this can't be.''

Flashert regarded him sardonically. ''I think we're going to need a better answer than that.''

MIUW 106

Elwell followed Bailey down off the top of the van. They went to the small command tent held in place by the deuce-and-a-halves still blocking access to their end of the pier. Bailey offered Elwell a plastic liter bottle of purified water, and slumped down in the chair next to her cot. ''So what do we do now?''

Elwell took two long slugs from the bottle before answering. ''We do something we should have done a couple of days ago.''

''What's that?''

He smiled, an odd expression on his face. ''We play tourist.''

•   •   •

Thirty minutes later, clad in blue jeans and a civilian T-shirt, Jerusha Bailey left the pier in company with Billy Elwell, similarly disguised as a civilian. They walked along the waterway, dodging around towering stacks of containers awaiting transshipment and around moving gantries and cranes. A few dockworkers yelled lewd comments at her, but for the most part the workers ignored them.

"It's been years since I got a good look at the Canal itself," Elwell said as they walked up a major thoroughfare leading to the piers. "Should've done that as soon as I got here."

Bailey kept pace with him easily. "Why is that?"

He shrugged. "Just a feeling I get. I like to know the terrain anywhere I'm assigned. Even if I don't think I'll be needing the knowledge, you never know when it'll come in handy."

"It's easier at sea," she said reflectively. "All you have to worry about is sea state."

Elwell wagged one finger at her. "Not entirely. Out here, you've got solid ground under your feet. At sea, you never know what's below the surface of the ocean. Do you?"

She shook her head thoughtfully. "War at sea operates in all three dimensions. It does on land too, but about the only equivalent you have to submarines is land mines. That's the worst part of it all—submarines." She grimaced, remembering her last encounter with the famed German U-boat ace Karl Merker.

Billy regarded her thoughtfully. "Think in those terms when you try to unravel the political realities going on around here," he said finally. "Me, I'm just a ground-pounder." He pointed up at the first lock in a series that controlled the waterway that was the Panama Canal. "I like to see it, touch it, taste it. You can't do that with politics."

*   *   *

Two hours later, Bailey had had a closer look at the locks and the entrance to the Canal. While nothing had immediately struck her as tactically significant, Elwell was oddly insistent that they take a close look at all the structures near the entrance.

They descended down the steep hill to the pier. Half-way down, Elwell put his hand on Bailey's elbow. "Don't look now, but we're being watched."

Bailey continued her pace down the hill and said, "Where?"

"Off to the left. The dockworkers."

Bailey kept moving, and scanned the area around them. As Elwell had said, a group of burly men clustered under a crane was staring at them. She kept her eyes moving, didn't linger on them, but felt an uneasy prickling at the back of her neck. "Do you think they're going to be a problem?"

"Don't know," Elwell said, his voice casual. "If they are, there's nothing we can do about it now. Just keep moving—act like you have every right in the world to be walking down this dock."

Bailey nodded. As they passed the dockworkers, she heard a noise behind her. Feet on cement, the sound of someone following them. She shot a glance at Elwell.

"Carefully, carefully," he said. "Just keep walking."

Bailey could see the well-lighted entrance to their pier ahead, perhaps a half mile distant. She resisted the temptation to look around behind them. Would the men be armed? It was possible, of course. Guns and weapons within the civilian population were far from unusual in Panama. But then again, it wouldn't have been that strange in Los Angeles either. Or Washington, D.C.

The noise behind them increased, changing from a steady, unruly thump of feet to a clatter.

"Now!" Elwell gave her a shove and started running.

Adrenaline kicked in. In high school, partially because

of her size, but more due to an innate love of exercise, Bailey had been on the track team. She specialized in the longer runs, and had kept up the practice by participating in marathons as an adult. Endurance, not speed, was her forte. Still, she quickly drew abreast of and passed Elwell. While the man was clearly in shape, he wasn't built for speed.

"Stay away from the light. They can't see us, they can't hit us," he said, his breathing even and hard. "I don't think they'll follow us there."

"Come on," she urged.

"Go ahead without me," he said.

"Not a chance." She grabbed him by the elbow and urged him forward. Together, they quickly outdistanced their pursuers. She heard a chorus of angry jeers and shouts behind her, but the dreaded crack of a weapon firing never materialized.

As they passed the iron grating that marked the beginning of the pier proper, they slowed slightly. Bailey risked a glance back. The six men were standing just outside the pool of light, jeering and shouting at them. Even given her limited knowledge of Spanish, she could tell they were swearing.

"Let's get back to the camp," Elwell said, slowing to a trot. He glanced at her. "Now that we're warmed up, we might as well make it an aerobic event."

She fell into step easily beside him, shortening her stride slightly to accommodate him. As they approached the camp, she saw sailors carrying shotguns scampering to security-alert positions. They provided an additional measure of cover for them as they jogged into the camp.

She pulled up to a stop next to the door of the Operations van. "Two miles," she said.

Elwell nodded. "You're in pretty good shape for a commander."

She laughed, almost giddy with the adrenaline flooding her system. "Not bad for an old master sergeant yourself."

Elwell turned and stared back down the pier toward the shore. "Next time, we go to the track."

USS JOUETT

Commander Renninger was deeply worried. Collins could tell it not so much from what he said, but how he said it. His normally short temper was on a hair trigger, and he'd quit eating meals at the mess, preferring to take his meals alone in his quarters. Dark circles were already ringing his eyes, as they were with most of the crew.

"We still don't know what caused it," Renninger said for the second time. He stared hard at Collins. "Do we?"

She shook her head. "According to the sonar technicians, it wasn't a U.S. torpedo. Nor was it Russian. That eliminates about ninety percent of the weapons in the world."

"Well, what about another nationality?"

"Captain, they've been through all the publications, as well as every acoustic intelligence source we have. There's nothing on record that matches the acoustic signature of that torpedo—nothing." She tried to keep her voice calm and professional.

Renninger exploded. "Jesus, what are you trying to tell me? That there's some sort of ghost submarine out there? Which, by the way, we haven't held contact on in a couple of days. That's who shot that torpedo—you can bet on it." He slammed his hand down on the surface plot to emphasize his point. "And with two hundred million dollars worth of warship at our disposal, including some of the most advanced acoustic processing gear around, we can't find it. Is that it?"

"Captain, if you think—" Collins began.

"I don't want more questions, XO. I've had it with

questions.'' He pointed at the large-screen display. A U.S. battle force was still at least fifty-four hours away from arriving in the area. ''I've got the United States Navy's most advanced destroyer and an undetected submarine—and ten warships due in the area in a day and a half. Do you want me to tell the admiral on board that carrier that this area's not safe for his precious bird farm? I'll have to, you know. Unless I can come up with a better answer.''

''The water isn't safe, Captain,'' she said firmly. ''And we can't give them answers we don't have. The facts are simply this—we had a brief detection of a torpedo and then the Bahamian-flagged merchant ship was hit. No submarine detections, no indications or warnings—nothing. So, if you're asking for my professional opinion, yes. That's exactly what you'll have to tell the admiral.''

She met Renninger's furious glare with a calm, level stare.

Finally, her Captain looked away. ''That answer's not good enough.''

''It's the only one we've got.''

''Not good enough, I said. I want some more ideas, not just a summary of what we don't know.''

Collins shook her head, frustrated. She understood what her Captain was asking of her, but she simply had no other data to give him. An idea suddenly occurred to her. ''Captain, perhaps—perhaps there's another source of information,'' she said slowly.

Renninger nodded. ''I thought something would occur to you eventually. What is it?''

''The MIUW. And Commander Bailey.''

''And just what exactly do they have that we don't have on board *Jouett*?'' Renninger said, his voice hard and sarcastic. ''A crystal ball?''

Collins shook her head. ''Something better than that. They've got connections,'' Collins said, pressing on despite his obvious dissatisfaction with her answer. ''This could have something to do with our airbus.''

''Your airbus,'' he corrected. ''Whatever else you've done right out here, you still own that one.''

Collins nodded, unsure of how to proceed. Any arguments she made defending her decision that night would appear self-serving, but the coincidences were just too great to ignore. ''Look at it this way—something anomalous happened that night with the airbus inbound,'' she said. ''And now we've got a new type of torpedo attacking unarmed merchants. I'm not saying that one explains the other, but there might be a link. If Commander Bailey could talk to her people at NSA, she might come up with something. Something that's too classified for either of us to know anything about. It's worth a shot, at least.'' She fell silent and waited for his decision.

After a few moments of silence, Renninger nodded. ''I don't like the idea. I can tell you don't either,'' he said unexpectedly. ''But I'm out of guesses at this point. Okay, call up Commander Bailey. See if she's interested in coming out to *Jouett* for a little look-see at our data. We can put her up on some of the secure circuits, make sure that we download any crypto that she needs to talk to her people. Make it happen, XO.'' Renninger turned and stalked off, still clearly frustrated beyond all endurance.

Make it happen. Well, Captain, I will. And believe me, I don't like this one bit better than you do. And anything's better than not knowing—anything.

MIUW 106

Petty Officer Carlisle held onto the guide line attached to the load of sonobuoys being lowered down to the floating dock. Even in the gentle swells, the dock was unstable. The serrated surface now was slick with seawater and moss, the same variety that grew on the massive pier supports nearby.

Next to the dock, the Special Forces RHIB bobbed uneasily. Ever since the MIUW boat had been lost, the SEALs had been laying sonobuoys for them at twelve-hour intervals. Now, they were ready to head out for the first launch of the day.

Four sonobuoys were strapped together in a cargo sling. Forty feet overhead, two sailors slowly belayed the line around a bollard and played out the rope. Carlisle's line, attached to the bottom of the cargo net, was to hold the load off the pier supports and keep them from smashing into it.

Behind him, the four SEALs were already in their small boat, looking uncommonly relaxed and eager to get under way. Their attitude bothered Carlisle, although it wasn't the first time he'd been concerned about the stability of Special Forces people. In his civilian job at NSA, he'd worked with them closely on several missions, providing advice and mission planning to best utilize the sophisticated electronics that were his specialty.

Carlisle swore as the raft took a sickening launch towards the pier. Sooner or later, it was going to overturn—of that he was certain. Every trip down here brought on a mild case of seasickness after only five minutes' exposure. He turned to the Special Forces men in the boat. "You could give me a hand, you know."

One of them snickered. "Not our job, man. You want us to lay these sonobuoys, you get them down to us. Otherwise . . ." The SEAL shrugged, indicating his lack of concern for the MIUW mission.

The other three men laughed as Carlisle swore again. The load was swinging in, and had missed the last stanchion by only inches.

Finally, the sonobuoys hit the steel deck with a dull thud. Carlisle wrapped his line around one of the dock railings quickly, to prevent them from sliding off into the water. He knelt down beside them, keeping his knees wide apart, and checked the channel assignments. While the sonarmen up above had already preset them in accordance with their channelization assignments, it never hurt to put a second set of eyes on it.

Besides, he had another reason for wanting to take a closer look at these particular sonobuoys. He kept his back to the SEAL team, and shielded the sonobuoys from view while he unscrewed the top of one of them. Inside was a miniature plastic parachute, intended to slow the descent of the sonobuoy when it was deployed from an aircraft. Plenty of room in there—just plenty. He pulled out the small plastic parachute and stuffed it in his pocket. In its place, he substituted one of his special toys. He screwed the top back on firmly, then turned back to the SEALs.

"These are ready to go. You have your deployment positions?" he asked.

One of the SEALs held up a handheld GPS receiver. "Good to within two yards," the SEAL said. "Not that it'll matter much—in the current, these things will be out of position within a few minutes of gettin' deployed." He shrugged. "I don't see much point in putting them out, but the commander says go. It's just a good excuse to get out on the water for a while."

"Well, that's not always fun and games," Carlisle reminded them.

Another of the SEALs snickered at him. "Hell, boy, we're not some sort of wimps. If there'd been SEALs on that boat, nobody would have had to pull us half-drowned out of the water."

Silently, Carlisle passed the sonobuoys one by one to the SEALs. Each one was marked with a sequential number, indicating which geographic position on their list it was to be deployed at. With a final wave of his hand, the senior SEAL on board gunned the engine and sped away from the pier. The wake from the powerful sixty-horse outboard motor splashed back over the dock, soaking Carlisle from the waist down. As the RHIB quickly disappeared from view, he swore silently at the SEALs.

Better get back up—wouldn't want to miss anything. Carlisle climbed quickly up the slippery metal rungs to the top of the pier, then darted for the Operations van. Still soaked, he let himself into the air-conditioned space and went to the sonar console. "I'll take the watch for a while," he told the technician sitting there.

The other man shrugged. "Okay with me—I could use a cup of coffee."

Carlisle slid into the cushioned chair and, after the other sonarman had left, reset the channel assignments on the console. He put his earphones on and selected one for audio input—earphones only. With a pleased sigh, he settled back to listen in on the SEAL mission.

Ninety minutes later, he jerked bolt upright in his chair and stared at the tape recorder. During the previous hour and a half, he'd learned several new dirty jokes, a few more expressions for Panamanians that would not have occurred to him, and the finer points of combat boat driving. All amusing, all worth listening to—but not why he'd planted the transmitter in the sonobuoy.

There was no point in listening further. The SEALs had just deployed the sonobuoy that housed his special device, and he was no longer privy to the conversations within the RHIB. However, he'd heard enough.

Bailey looked at Carlisle quizzically. "You're certain of this?"

Carlisle nodded. "I've got it on tape too," he said smugly. "Just listen."

The voices were somewhat muffled, but clear enough to make out. Bailey listened with a detached air through several dirty jokes. Then Carlisle nodded and said, "Here it comes."

"Little fucker is still gettin' around," a harsh, scratchy voice said.

"For a sailor, he doesn't do so good in the water. I thought he was going to puke when he was down on the floating dock," another one said.

"He damn near puked when he came to," the first voice said. "Smart-ass little shit. 'Course they *all* are over at NSA. Wonder why the boss wanted to talk to him so bad. Bet he'd have been pissed if I put the first round through his head."

A chorus of laughter and derisive hoots followed. "You couldn't," the second voice scoffed.

"Damn straight I could. You've never been through sniper training—what the hell would you know?"

"Big fucking deal. Even I could hit a rubber boat at that range."

"Then you do it next time. Believe me, I could have put one through his head as easily as I hit that boat. Would've saved us a lot of time too—wouldn't have had to fish him out of the water and take care of him afterwards."

"Stupid thing to do."

"Why go to all the trouble of shooting the boat if you're going to pull the men out of the water?"

"Yeah, that's what I think too. But you know the boss. He wants answers."

The voices fell silent for a moment. Bailey raised her head and looked in horror at Carlisle.

"Next time, no more Mr. Nice Guy," the first voice finished. "Here, this one's next."

There was a Rebel yell, followed by an abrupt cessation of the voices, and then the burbling, gurgling sound of water rushing over the sonar transceiver. Carlisle clicked the tape off.

"Call me paranoid, but I think they know about NSA," Carlisle said finally.

Bailey nodded, unable to give voice to the emotions that were roiling inside of her.

Was it possible? It seemed indisputable, based on the evidence of the tape. But why would the SEALs try to sink the MIUW RHIB? What possible benefit could that provide?

"Don't tell anyone about this," she said, already knowing that the caution was unnecessary. "We're a long way from NSA—and a long way from anybody who can get us out of this mess."

Carlisle nodded. "I'm not saying anything. But I'm damned sure not going out in that boat again—not until all those bastards are facing a court-martial." His voice was grim and cold. "What are we going to do about this? NSA's got to know, at least."

Bailey shook her head. "Nothing, right this second. I need to think about this." And to talk to someone, she realized. Someone whose suspicious nature exceeded her own, with more experience in the field in dealing with Special Forces. Clearly she couldn't talk to Commander Murphy—not after what she'd just heard. There was every possibility—indeed probability—that the SEAL commander had ordered the attack on the MIUW boat. No wonder the SEALs had been so quick on the scene to pull Carlisle out of the water, as well as the others. They'd known that the attack was taking place, since they'd executed it themselves—they must have been waiting by the waterfront just for that occasion.

"By the way, who authorized you to plant a bug in the SEAL team's sonobuoys?" she said.

Carlisle shrugged. "It seemed like a little ingenuity was in order," he said quietly. "And if this is true-confession time, then I guess I'd better come clean. It's not the first time I've done it."

"You did the same thing to the last batch of sono-buoys?"

He shook his head. "Not then. Remember when you were running back down the pier with the sergeant?"

She nodded. She remembered that, as they'd approached the camp, she'd seen the security-alert team mobilizing. They'd been in position before she'd even started to run. She felt an incredulous smile tug at her lips. "You didn't."

"I did." Carlisle reached into her pocket and pulled out another of the small devices. "I slipped this into your pocket as you left. Picked up your entire conversation with him." He smiled winningly. "It seemed like a good idea at the time, and it certainly worked out all right in the end, didn't it?"

Bailey swore quietly. "Carlisle, I swear to God, if you ever—"

He held up one hand, placating her. "Don't worry, I'm down to my last two bugs. I won't use them without telling you."

"Those are from NSA, aren't they?" she demanded. "Jesus, you know we're not supposed to—"

"Good thing I did, though, isn't it?" His voice was harder now. He spoke as her equal, which he was at NSA, rather than a subordinate sailor in her MIUW command. It was this strange dichotomy of civilian and sailor that so often threw her for a loop when dealing with Reserves.

Reluctantly, she nodded. "But don't do it again."

What would have happened to Carlisle if Billy Elwell hadn't tracked him down? A cold chill swept through her as she realized the probable answer. But why Carlisle? They must have known that he was employed by NSA. But what else did they want to know from him? She remembered the needle marks she'd seen on his arms when Billy Elwell had returned him to camp, the odd, foggy look in his eyes that had passed after twelve hours. At the time, she had put it down to the concussion, but now she wasn't so certain.

"Those bastards—they drugged me, didn't they?" Carlisle asked quietly. His face was white with fury.

She nodded slowly. "Not a word. Not yet." She had Carlisle make a duplicate copy of the tape. She took one herself, and told him to find a secure hiding place for the other. Ideal spots were limited, given the circumstances, but she thought the wily sonarman would probably find a place.

As she left the command tent, Bailey knew only one thing. She had to find Sergeant Elwell—and fast.

USS JOUETT

Collins scribbled her initials in a corner of the message and handed it back to the radioman. "Can you get that out right away?"

The radioman nodded. "Be out of here in five minutes. Depending on how often they pick up their traffic, that's how fast they'll get it."

Collins frowned. "I think they have a shore termination in the van. Is there any way to check on it?"

Again, the radioman nodded. "I can call the comm station on OTO," he said, referring to the informal operator-to-operator circuit that linked all comm centers. "Ask a few questions."

"Do it. And let me know."

"Aye, aye, XO." The radioman took off for the ship's communication center. Collins looked up at the large-screen display again, her eyes drawn to the battle force heading south. U.S. forces were accustomed to being invincible in whatever waters they invaded. Even now, as they proceeded south, the news that a submarine was in the area was not likely to dissuade them from entering the theater of operations. But as they got closer, as the potential reality of their being torpedoed became more and more imminent, she suspected that there might be some changes in attitude.

"Changes about latitudes and attitudes." The old words of a song popped into her head. She laid down her pen and stared at the screen until the symbols started to blur.

We'll see how concerned you are when you get down

here, she thought. Maybe a little bit more than you are now—maybe not. I just hope to God that Jerusha knows what's going on down here. And that she tells us in time to keep anyone from being killed.

MIUW 106

The ancient ink-jet printer whined uneasily in a corner of the MIUW van. It chugged, and started spitting out a message at its remarkable two-pages-per-minute speed.

Boston glanced back into the communications suite at the noise, and then shrugged. The shore termination setup was a pain in the ass, but at least they got their message traffic quickly. He took four steps back to the other end of the van, and pulled the sheet out of the roller as the DeskJet spat it out. He skimmed the address line, then whistled softly as he saw the content. He turned to the watch supervisor. "Better find Commander Bailey—I think she's going to want to see this."

Bailey had almost exactly the same reaction to the message when he handed it to her. She whistled softly, then pursed her lips. "Wonder what it is that *Jouett*'s so hot to talk about," she said. She looked up from the message and out to the horizon as though she could see the ship itself. "It's worded oddly too—they 'request the pleasure of my presence'?"

Boston shrugged. "I don't know, Captain. Maybe they're just finally admitting that we know a little more about this than they do."

"Or maybe not." Bailey folded the message up and tucked it into her camouflage pocket. As politely as the message was worded, she didn't feel obliged to respond immediately. Besides, leaving the camp right this second didn't sound like a hot idea—not with what she and Carlisle had just learned about the SEAL team. Until she was certain her own people were safe, there was no way she was going out to *Jouett*—no way at all. If they wanted to talk to her so badly, they could come to *her* this time.

It was time for some answers. "Everybody out of the van," Bailey ordered. She waved Lieutenant Boston off as he started to ask a question. "Secure call—no listeners."

Boston nodded, his unvoiced question answered. He rounded up the rest of his watch team and shooed them out of the van. He left last, closing the steel door behind him. Bailey shot home the security lock, then put in the pin that would prevent anyone outside from opening it. She turned to the STU-telephone sitting on the Watch Officer's ledge. She withdrew a crypto-key for it and inserted it in a special access panel, turned it, and waited for an LCD screen to beep its acknowledgment of the secure code she'd entered. She picked it up, got a dial tone, and dialed an all too familiar number.

Atchinson's voice answered immediately.

"Jim? It's Jerusha. Something strange is going on down here." Briefly, she outlined the data-point discrepancies in the destroyer's data tapes, and the conversation she'd overheard on the SEAL RHIB.

Atchinson asked a few questions, then settled for mere grunting as she made point after point. Finally, she finished.

"What do you think?" she said.

There was a long silence. She started tapping her foot impatiently, wishing she'd called Terry Intanglio directly. Atchinson couldn't find his ass with both—

"Jerusha?" Atchinson's voice was cautious. "We're only on a Secret circuit, aren't we?"

"Yes—it will take me some time to round up the key material for a Top Secret circuit."

"Then, there's nothing I can tell you," Atchinson said with finality. "Get the Top Secret crypto and keep us informed. And watch yourself down there—sounds like you could get your ass shot off real easy."

Bailey hung up the phone, more frustrated than relieved. It was easy for him to say, sitting safe and secure in an office building in another country. Sure, there were U.S. forces en route to their location, but what good would that do her now, isolated on the end of the pier with only SEALs for protection? As she undogged the heavy door and let the watch team back inside, she considered her options. There weren't many options—and they were getting fewer by the minute.

A Top Secret circuit. She pulled the message out of her pocket and scribbled down a response for Boston to transmit to *Jouett*: "Not today—maybe tomorrow."

There were simply too many loose ends to nail down before she could comfortably leave the camp, even with Sergeant Elwell around. But it looked like *Jouett* was going to have the pleasure of her company after all. Eventually.

20

USS *JOUETT*

After morning quarters, Collins began her first walk-through of the day. In her years at sea, she had learned that there was no substitute for first-hand observation. Every day she toured the ship completely several times, visiting virtually every compartment on the ship. It not only gave her a chance to observe first-hand the matériel and personnel condition of every department, but also served as an excellent example for her younger officers. As she had learned from her own days as a Division Officer, you learned by watching—not by telling.

She started forward to the missile magazines. All the way forward on the ship and down two ladders, the space was protected by massive watertight doors and a security lock. Access to the missile compartments was limited.

She paused in the passageway outside, listening to the sounds of machinery, blowers and fans, and pumps. The background noise was so much a part of her everyday life that she had to concentrate to hear it, but it was the best indicator that everything was well. While she might not notice the noise itself, any change in the frequency of a component of it would bring half of the crew bolt upright out of a dead sleep.

The sounds she heard, however, were not normal. And not machinery-related either.

Loud voices reached her through the steel doors, strident and angry. She waited for a moment, and when they showed no signs of abating, punched in the security code and shoved open the hatch.

As she stepped over the threshold, she saw a crowd of weapons technicians and gunner's mates gathered around in a circle. One looked up, saw her, and stepped guiltily back from the circle. She shoved her way through the crowd of sailors to the center.

On the deck, Weapons Technician Third Class Avery Harmon was sitting astride Seaman Jim Smith. He had one hand clamped firmly around Smith's neck and the other arm cocked back, ready to deliver a punch. From the condition of Smith's nose, it was evident that an earlier blow had connected.

"What's going on?" she said sharply. Not that it needed an answer—it was all too clear.

Harmon looked up at her, dropped his hand, and bolted to his feet. Smith rose more slowly, his eyes filled with tears from the blow to his nose.

"Nothing, XO," Harmon stammered. His eyes were riveted to the deck.

"Right." She let the silence stretch out uncomfortably, then turned to Smith. "Get up to Medical." She pointed at another sailor. "You go with him. I think his nose is broken."

Smith nodded, and turned to go. He paused for a moment, then turned back to the crew. Without warning, his right foot lashed out and caught Harmon in the groin. The senior weapons technician sank, howling, to the deck. Two first class petty officers stepped in and grabbed both of Smith's arms, staying well back behind him and out of range of his feet.

Collins advanced on him, shoving her own face just inches away from his. "Let him go."

"But XO—"

"Let him go, I said." The other sailors released his arms, keeping their hands up ready to grab him again should he make any movement towards her.

She studied Smith for a moment. "Tough guy, huh? You feel better now?"

Smith nodded sullenly, "He had it coming, XO." One hand strayed up to gingerly touch his battered nose. The sailor winced. "He started it."

"And you started it again after it was over," she shot back. "You two better make up, because you're going to be spending a lot of time together. Standing in line for Captain's Mast. On restriction. Extra duty. You're going to be asshole buddies before I'm through with you." She turned back to the rest of the crowd. "And what are you doing, letting this go on down here?"

The leading petty officer of the Weapons Division stepped forward. "It just started, XO."

"Over what?" She glanced around at the ring of men. They were all staring at the deck, studiously not meeting her eyes. She snorted in disgust. "You find the chief. Have him see me in my compartment immediately. I want some answers, and it doesn't look like I'm going to get them from you people." She fixed the petty officer with a steely glare. "One more incident and you join your two buddies here at Captain's Mast. You're the senior man here—I expect some good order and discipline. That real clear?"

He nodded, and had the decency to look abashed. "Aye, aye, ma'am."

She turned back to Smith. "Now if you're through with these little temper tantrums, I suggest you let your buddy take you to Medical. Unless there's someone else you want to take a shot at?"

Smith started to shake his head, and then winced. "No, XO." His voice was distorted now by his rapidly swelling nose.

"Good." She gestured to the two men on either side of him. "Get him to Doc."

As she left the compartment, she heard the petty officer behind her break into a tirade against the rest of them. She considered standing out in the passageway to listen to it, but then rejected the idea. The Chief would hunt her down soon enough and let her know what had actually happened. But for now, she had the rest of the ship to tour.

The Chief Weapons Technician caught up with her while she was in aft steering examining the auxiliary steering gear. He walked briskly up to her, met her eyes, and said, "XO, do you have a moment?"

She nodded. "Where's your Division Officer?"

The chief hesitated, looking somewhat abashed. "I haven't talked to the lieutenant yet."

"Good reason not to?"

He nodded. "I think so. I'd like to know if you agree with me."

She gestured to two coils of heavy manila line. They were used for additional mooring when rough weather was expected. "Have a seat."

They took seats on the heavy coils facing each other, and she said, "I want the real story. Not what you think I want to hear."

He nodded again. "That's why I came straight to you." He hesitated, looking oddly ill at ease.

"What is it?"

"There's no good way to put this. The fight started over you."

She was taken aback by that, but kept her face neutral and calm. "Go on."

"Harman said you screwed up and shot down that airbus. Smith took exception to it and belted him one.

He got in a shot to the gut, then Harman nailed him in the nose. That's when you walked in.''

She studied him for a moment, wishing that there was some way she could have appreciated what Smith had done, but knowing that good order and discipline within the crew was far more important than her own professional reputation.

"I see," she said finally.

The chief shrugged. "Opinions are divided on the whole thing, XO. The guys take it personally—those are their missiles, you know." He smiled slightly. "Pride in the job and all. They feel like the rest of the ship blames them some for the whole problem."

Now *that* baffled her. "They didn't order the missile shot."

"No, but they *are* their missiles. You see how it goes." The chief hesitated a moment, clearly with something else on his mind. "Permission to speak freely?"

"You're in trouble if you don't, Chief."

He nodded. "I hoped that's how you felt. Part of the problem is the Captain. This whole thing has hit the ship hard. He needs to get on the 1MC, put it all in perspective for them. Explain what happened, show them why we did it. Give them a reason to believe that we didn't just kill three hundred and fifty civilians because of a screwup."

Collins's gut clenched into a hard knot. "Maybe I did," she said softly, almost to herself. "I'm not sure what—"

It was the chief's turn to interrupt. "Get a grip, XO," he said firmly. "You don't have the luxury of feeling sorry for yourself, not in your position."

She looked up to see cold professionalism shining out of his face. "You know what happened," she said. "I blew it—plain and simple, I blew it."

The chief shook his head. "I don't think so. Regardless of what anybody else says, if they'd been TAO right then, they'd have done the same thing. You didn't have any choice, not with what you knew at the time.''

Collins stood abruptly. ''It was a civilian airliner,'' she said harshly. ''I killed three hundred and fifty passengers plus a flight crew of eight. That number includes the President of a country that now seems to view this entire gulf as their own personal shooting gallery. Do you want to explain to me why that's not a screwup?''

The chief stood up as well, taller than she was by almost six inches. He put one hand on her shoulder. ''It was the right decision at the time. Get that in your head, XO, and start believing it. Because if you don't, you're going to cause this ship even more problems. And have a talk with the Captain—he's got to talk to the crew— got to. They have to see you and the Captain as a solid, unified team. You have to believe; because it's your duty to make them believe.''

LOTUS GLORY

T'sing Lin woke slowly, the boundary between waking and sleeping becoming increasingly indistinct these days. The muted hammer of the ship's diesel engines and the creaks and groans as she made her way through the ocean were constants in both his waking life and his dreams. At least while he was asleep he could dream of fresh air, sunlight, and the broad open fields of his home province.

But while sleep gave him respite from the confines of the ship, it did nothing about the prospects of the mission he would be going on shortly. That vision haunted him continually, invading both waking hours and his dreams with increasingly violent and terrifying visions. He opened his eyes, then squinted against the bright glare in the compartment. The other men who occupied this small stateroom were already awake, moving about the cramped quarters with slow, methodical movements.

The one empty bunk, the one Kim had occupied, was stripped bare.

T'sing Lin groaned and slowly shoved himself up into a sitting position, careful not to bump his head on the bunk overhead. He moved his legs out to hang over the edge of the bed. They dangled into space over the bunk below him. The bunks were too close together, even for a small man such as himself.

But they were all small, weren't they? Their physical dimensions had been one of the prerequisites for entry into the *niru* program.

None of the others spoke to him as he shoved himself out of the bed, landing heavily on the steel deck. A sullen glare from one, a sigh of disgust from another. Ever since his outburst last night, he'd become a pariah among the group.

Fei had actually started it. Older than most of the other pilots, and far more pragmatic than most, he'd quietly moved his bedding from an upper bunk to a now-vacant lower one. Shu Tin had objected, claiming it defiled Kim's memory. Sides had been chosen quickly, and T'sing had become the focal point for disagreement when he'd pointed out how very little it all mattered. In a matter of days, they'd all be dead anyway. He might have survived that comment, even though it had indicated his political unreliability, had he not gone on to commit the ultimate sin—questioning the *niru* program itself. Haunted by nightmares of the eventual mission, he'd burst into tears and sobbed over the life he would never have here on Earth.

The others had been stunned—then angry. T'sing had given voice to the fear that each of them felt, and it was unforgivable.

A pariah—how could he have anticipated that? Were they all as devout and holy as they pretended? Or was it merely an act, a way to cope with the sheer horror of the Heavenly Wind program? He'd considered the matter at length, finally decided that since they were all human, they must all have the same reaction, and shared some of his doubts with them, believing that he would draw strength from their reassurances.

That had not been the case. One by one, they'd withdrawn, voiced their disgust at his cowardice, and shut him off from the brotherhood. Now, alone and scared, he was left with only his inner strength and faith to cope with the mission ahead.

The uncertainty added to his anxiety. There was no schedule—none knew who would be chosen next. Rumor had it that their assignments would be decided by lot by the master, but none of them had been able to verify that. Not that they'd tried. For the other men, the assurance of instant translation into the heavens seemed to be enough.

He felt the weight of his own failings increase as he contemplated his family's disgrace were they to learn of his cowardice. It was not enough that he be strapped into the torpedo, guided to its final destination. He must do so with the right attitude, the proper frame of holiness. If they found out—he groaned, barely aware that he'd done so. One of the other men glanced at him. "Ten o'clock—in the dining room." His voice was harsh. None of them had spoken a pleasant word to him since that night. Even more than the loss of any reassurance, he missed the daily interaction with other human beings.

T'sing Lin was alone and scared on the massive Chinese cargo ship.

He was eighteen years old, and doubted he would ever see nineteen.

USS JOUETT

"The morning briefing will commence at 0900 in the wardroom." The 1MC announcement was piped to all compartments in the ship specifically to reach her, Collins knew. The Officer of the Deck was well aware that she was on her morning rounds at the moment.

Collins swore quietly and headed for the ladder that led out of the crew's compartment. She was usually done with rounds by this time, and would have had time to grab a cup of coffee in the wardroom before the brief commenced. The problems with Weapons Division, however, had slowed her down today.

She yanked open the door to the wardroom and stepped in just as the Captain arrived. Their eyes met across the compartment and he gestured roughly to her. "Nice of you to join us, XO."

She nodded, and resisted the urge to explain the delay. It would do no good, and would simply weaken her position with both the Captain and the rest of the wardroom. Silently, she slipped into her chair next to the Captain and accepted a cup of coffee from the wardroom cook.

"Commercial air flights commence again today, with assurances by the Chinese government that all commercial travel lanes will be closely monitored by a coalition of Central and South American military aviation forces," Lieutenant Williams began. He pointedly avoided looking at Collins. "Five neighboring countries are contributing fighter forces to fly escort missions on CommAir. The schedules are posted in Combat, but be aware that there may be some unexpected deviations from it." This time, he did look at her. She seethed, her temperature threatening to spiral out of control, when the Captain nodded gravely in agreement.

"Our problem will be IFF codes," Renninger said. "Any word on whether the Panamanians are going to share them with us or not?"

Lieutenant Williams shook his head. "Not so far. That makes the tracking problem doubly tough. Add to that little mix the issue of our own F-14's. Mexico is denying us overflight rights, as are all the coalition forces. We have to rely on F-14's off of *Eisenhower*. She's currently still one thousand miles north of us and approaching at flank speed.''

The Captain shook his head again. ''I had a 'Personal For' message from SouthCom I need to share with you all,'' he said. He reached into his pocket and pulled out a folded sheet of paper. He unfolded it, glanced at it, and said, ''The gist of it is that the U.S. is sucking up to Panama again. In order to convince them of our good intentions, the remainder of the SouthCom detachment will be leaving the country on a commercial air flight. It's actually a specially chartered flight, and will have nothing but our people on it, but that fact hasn't been advertised. Good old American Airlines to the rescue again.''

''That's the reason for *Eisenhower*'s F-14's?'' Collins asked.

The Captain nodded. ''Of course they won't be flying over Panamanian airspace, but they will be intercepting for escort as soon as it leaves territorial airspace. Now that should be fun—five countries with F-14s in the air in the same restricted airspace.'' He shook his head as though contemplating the possibilities for disaster.

''If there's any intention of retaliation,'' Collins said slowly, ''the SouthCom flight sounds like a prime possibility. We'll need to keep an eye out for that.''

''Agreed,'' Renninger said crisply. ''Make sure all your watch-standers are briefed thoroughly and that we have radio comms at all times with *Eisenhower*. It's going to be easy to get confused, people—be aggressive on identifying and tracking the friendlies.''

A leaden silence settled over the room. Collins could feel the flush creeping up her neck, branding her with a flaming fury of embarrassment. She looked down at the deck, not sure whether to be grateful that nobody had voiced the unspoken—keep the XO from shooting down the friendlies.

21

GULF OF PANAMA:
4 OCTOBER

PRIDE OF KURSK

The Ukrainian RO-RO steamed uncertainly in circles fifteen miles off the Panamanian coast. Her orders from her superiors in Ukraine had been mixed—make expeditious time back to Ukraine, but do not endanger the ship. For the Ukrainian master, accustomed to the more clear-cut orders of the Soviet regime, the situation was fraught with danger. If he attempted the Panama Canal and damaged the ship, his career would be over. Likewise, to steam south on the longer transit around the Cape of Good Hope would add at least a month to his journey. Knowing that his cargo contained critical machinery and computer parts from Japan that were badly needed in Ukraine, a late arrival might well mean no arrival at all.

He paced the bridge, unable to decide. His family had been sea captains for generations, tracing their bond with the seas back to medieval times. Under a wide range of political climates, including a brief period of Ukrainian independence, his family had built ships, sailed ships,

designed ships, and made their living on the Crimean
Peninsula as part of the historic sea trade routes that ran
from fertile Ukraine to the rest of the world. Since the
days of the Peloponnesian Wars, his ancestors had faced
exactly this sort of decision—speed and danger· versus
safety and cargo spoilage. While today that might mean
something different from a load of wheat rotting in the
cargo bay, it was nonetheless critical.

Finally, he reached a decision. Intermixed with the
purely Ukrainian ancestors was a strain of Tatar blood,
the legacy of a Cossack raid on his small village centuries before. It made him bolder than some of his compatriots, slightly more bloodthirsty and inclined to take
risks.

Now, frustrated with delays and determined to get his
cargo home, it rose to the forefront.

"Make preparations for entering the Canal," he ordered, suddenly calm now that the decision had been
reached. A peculiar sense of fatalism overtook him. Perhaps nothing would happen on the transit into the
Canal—nothing at all.

LOTUS GLORY

The men assembled in the small eating compartment, the
others clustering at one end of the compartment, leaving
him alone at his own table. Their leader took note of the
fact as he walked in. Noted it and dismissed it.

"Fei," he said. That one word, nothing more. The
man he'd named grinned broadly, basking in the congratulations of his compadres. It was a call to glory, a
chance to exercise the skills that had been honed in the
murky waters off of China for so many months. It was
his ticket to the heavens, his anointing for a divine mission that would take him that day to glory.

T'sing Lin rose and walked across the compartment
to offer his congratulations as well. Fei, the chosen one,

looked up at him, disdain in his eyes, and then his expression softened. ''You will have your chance,'' he said softly. ''Face it as you should—for the glory of China.''

The raucous celebration escalated.

T'sing Lin tried to join in. He feigned the eagerness and envy that was expected, the absolute surety of divine anointing that the mission called for. Perhaps if he pretended long enough, hard enough, he would begin to feel the fervor that he saw in the others' faces, know the certainty that they all seemed to feel. He smiled, prayed, and hoped.

He followed the others down to the bowels of the ship, through the innumerable close-spaced passageways and narrow, steep shipboard ladders. The others were cheering, singing a victory song as they went, shouting to other members of the crew. Lin saw the faint shadow of pity in other men's faces as they tried to greet the kamikazes politely, saw mirrored in their faces his own doubts. It made him work all the harder to be a part of his group, to escape the no-man's-land in which he was trapped between crew and warrior.

Finally, they reached the torpedo deployment bay. The master had called ahead, and all was ready. Fei was still riding high on the tide of adulation. He reached for his harness eagerly, strapping on the oxygen mask and other accoutrements of their trade. His compadres helped him prepare, each expressing his envy that Fei had earned this honor, vowing to pray harder and more devoutly in order that they might be chosen next. Lin continued to emulate their ebullience.

At the last moment, as Fei stepped down to the torpedo bay, he hesitated. He looked back up at the other five, an odd expression on his face. The others not chosen were still cheering him on. Lin, standing slightly to the back, met Fei's eyes. Lin smiled, gave another rousing cheer.

Fei nodded, now frowning. He looked into the torpedo, then back at his mates. Lin thought he saw Fei's hand start to tremble. When Fei looked back, he ignored his cheering friends and focused on Lin.

Something passed between them, some arcane recognition. T'sing Lin felt the fear penetrate deep into his gut, coiling and knotting around his intestines like a snake. He could see it in Fei's face too, the realization of what he was about to do.

There was no way to back out, not without losing face. That, they'd both been taught since the earliest age, was the most fatal of errors. To live without honor, to have one's fellows know that one had been afraid, had shirked from a duty—that life would not be worth living at all.

Fei had a wife, Lin remembered suddenly. A wife and a son. Did that make a difference for him? Was it their faces that he saw now as he poised at the edge of the torpedo? Fei made a movement as though to force himself down into the torpedo. The cheering around him diminished slightly, then trailed off into a puzzled silence.

"You must go," the master said firmly. He placed his hands on Fei's shoulders and forced him down to the torpedo. "Just as you have practiced—victory will be ours today. And tonight, you will feast with the gods in heaven."

His voice appeared to calm Fei. With a nod, with tears now filling his eyes and with his hands plainly trembling, Fei lowered himself slowly into the seat. He looked back up, his face a mask of anguish, a pleading expression on his face. For a moment, T'sing thought that he would beg, ask not to be put into the dark water in this metal shroud, beg for his life.

Before he had a chance, the mechanics had bolted down the steel hatch of the torpedo. The cheering resumed, no longer contradicted by the look on Fei's face, by his hesitation. The tractor mechanism lowered the torpedo into the bay, and T'sing saw the oily water crowd up around it, covering half of it. Inside, he imagined, the temperature of the torpedo would drop as the water cooled it. Fei would be feeling the slight effects of the water, be running through the checklist inside. T'sing prayed for his friend, wishing him courage now that his fate had been decided.

Finally, the engineering mate shot home the bolt that held the torpedo's cover in place. It scraped across the metal, harsh and clanging, reminding T'sing that there would be no backing down from this mission once inside. One part of his mind calculated coldly—if you must back out, it must be before the bolt goes home. Afterwards, there is no choice, no escape.

The cradling mechanism withdrew, leaving the torpedo alone in the bay. As the well dock hatch slid over the bay, concealing the torpedo, T'sing thought he heard a thin, high wail begin. Before he could be certain, the hatch clanged shut, a dull metallic sound, and sealed off the torpedo.

They heard as much as felt the rush of water into the bay, the opening of the doors that led into the sea, and the final deployment of the torpedo. T'sing imagined himself trapped inside the metal cylinder, his world lit only by the green phosphorescence of the instruments. There was a brief, high-pitched squeal as the torpedo's propeller kicked in. It quickly faded away to nothing.

The master looked around the group of men, now still flushed with their earlier cheering. His eyes focused on T'sing, and a faint frown crossed his face. "Wine," he ordered. "To toast the bravery of Fei. And to each of you, when your turn comes." His eyes were still fixed on T'sing.

T'sing nodded and followed them back to the mess, where tiny thimblefuls of the wine were dispensed. He toasted to Fei, to the men who had gone before, and to his own eventual chance at glory. As he drank the warm, alcoholic liquid, he was ashamed to note that he hoped his turn would not come soon.

USS JOUETT

"Captain, the SouthCom flight should be launching about now," Collins said. "If I might be excused, I'll be in Combat."

Renninger drained the last of his coffee. "I'll go with you."

Why? To make sure I won't shoot them down? The question insinuated itself into her mind, an ugly and painful thought. Would it be this way the rest of her career—assuming she even had one—constantly looking for the small signs of distrust from her superiors? And doubting herself at the same time?

The tinny blat of the 1MC cut through the silence. "Captain to Combat—Captain to Combat."

The room emptied at record speed. The faster, younger officers hung back a moment, allowing the Captain a head start. Collins was hot on his heels as they sped up the ladder and toward Combat.

As the Captain entered Combat, he said, "What is it?"

Lieutenant Williams looked uneasy. "Unidentified sonar contact again, Captain. It's the same signature as last time."

"A torpedo?" Collins broke in.

Williams ignored her.

"Answer the XO's question, TAO," Renninger snapped. "You've got to know I've got the same one."

"Yes, Captain, a torpedo. At least, Sonar thinks it is. That's the only thing that would match up with that acoustic signature."

"Are they holding on active?" Collins asked.

Williams shook his head. "Not yet. The range is too long. Passive only."

"Any idea where it came from?" Collins asked.

"Get back there, XO," Renninger said. "You understand more about ASW than any of us. I want you in

Sonar right now. TAO, where are *Eisenhower*'s fighters?''

"Just off the coast, Captain." Williams flicked the cursor on the screen to the north, and positioned it atop the two friendly aircraft symbols. "SouthCom transport launched four minutes ago. A little earlier than they were supposed to, but—"

"And you didn't think to notify the Captain? Or me?" Collins snapped.

"Sonar, XO," Renninger said firmly. "I'll handle this."

Collins moved quickly, wending her way between the consoles and stepping over a power cord strung across the floor. She pushed into the Sonar compartment and took in the situation at a glance.

"Ma'am," the leading sonarman said, "it's the same contact—not headed for us this time, though."

"Where did it come from?" she demanded. "It can't just materialize out of thin air."

The sonarman shook his head and pointed at the acoustic display. "It doesn't make a whole lot of sense. The only thing in the area is that merchant ship, see?" He pointed at a series of closely spaced discrete lines on the printout. "She left the entrance of the Canal along with the rest of them yesterday, and has been steaming about at bare steerageway."

"Anything unusual about her movements?"

The sonarman nodded. "Here." He pointed at a section of the printout. "You can see where she slowed down past steerageway. Hell, she stopped dead in the water right there."

"How long after that before the torpedo appeared?" She knew from the look on his face that he'd already put the pieces of this particular puzzle together. "You see where I'm going, don't you?"

He shook his head, distracted, staring at the active sonar screen. "About ten minutes. Too long for a normal torpedo shot—hell, XO, you don't think they have torpedo tubes on that merchant ship, do you?"

"Maybe, maybe not. We should have been told about it if they do."

Bailey would know. Would she have told us? Collins shook her head, wondering. Bailey hadn't spoken up about the weapons systems they'd run across in the English Channel. She'd simply given the orders necessary to keep the ship safe without explaining in any more detail.

But she had kept it safe, hadn't she? What if she hadn't been on board *Ramage*? Would she have let the ship sail into harm's way without telling them about the string of mines crisscrossing the English harbor? No, that didn't sound like the Jerusha Bailey Collins knew. And under the current circumstances, if Bailey knew something about this Chinese merchant, Collins was willing to bet Jerusha would tell them.

"Look at it," the sonarman said, breaking into her thoughts. "Jesus, look!"

The contact displayed on the screen was now cycling up past forty-five knots and showed no signs of slowing. Its phosphorescent lozenge on the active sonar screen tracked relentlessly across the round scope towards another contact. She pointed at it. "Who is it?"

"Ukrainian tanker," the sonarman said promptly. "We've been holding her for—"

Collins darted out of Sonar and into Combat. "Captain—we need to talk to that Ukrainian tanker," she said rapidly, her words spilling over each other. "Whatever that is, it's headed directly for it. Bridge-to-bridge maybe—let's try channel sixteen."

The Captain held up one hand. "How do you know? It could be a speedboat, couldn't it?"

Collins stared at him, aghast. "No, it couldn't," she said, her voice firm. "We've seen the signature before—with *Darling Moira*. This is a torpedo, or some sort of underwater weapon." She shook her head, not believing that she was having to argue this point with Renninger. "We call them now—give them a little fighting chance."

Renninger seemed to consider, the moments taking years to pass. Finally, he reached for the bridge-to-bridge microphone. "If anybody speaks English," he said doubtfully. He took a deep breath and began the callup.

PRIDE OF KURSK

The bridge-to-bridge circuit was a continuous babble of foreign voices, accented English, and profanities. The master of *Pride of Kursk* had turned it down to a low volume, not wanting to disturb his concentration as he commenced his approach on the entrance to the Panama Canal. The babble was a background noise. He caught one word: "Kursk." He turned away from the windows that ringed the bridge and frowned.

"What did they say?" he demanded in Ukrainian.

His second officer shrugged. "It was in English, I think."

"I heard '*Kursk*,'" the master insisted. He looked around the bridge, his eyes finally lighting on the navigator. "How much English do you have?" he asked.

The navigator shrugged. "A little. I thought I heard '*Kursk*,' too. But I could have been mistaken."

The master swore quietly. Finally, he reached for the bridge-to-bridge microphone and picked it up. In heavily accented English, he said, "Ship calls, this is *Kursk*. No much English." He paused, struggling to recall the few words that had been drummed into him in the international sailing license classes he'd taken. "Say again," he said finally.

An answer came immediately, in a loud voice stringing together long words. The master stared at the speaker, frustrated and helpless, handicapped by his lack of English. He turned to his second mate. "Pass the word—find our translator," he ordered. "It is probably nothing, but we will make certain."

An uneasy doubt began to gnaw at the pit of his stomach. He shoved it away, his Tatar blood now boiling. Why should they be expected to understand English at every port? It was the port and other ships that should keep translators on board, not *Pride of Kursk*.

Kursk's translator was down in the galley enjoying his third cup of coffee of the morning. He heard the announcement over the 1MC and sighed. With the Canal closed, he thought he would have some time off—more time to spend in the card game going on down in Engineering. It figured, though. As soon as he'd gotten comfortable, that damned Captain would want something from him.

He took one last swallow of the coffee, then carried it over to the tiny galley. He turned on the water, rinsed it out, and placed it in the metal dish drain bolted to the side of the sink.

NIRU I

Fei fought desperately to recover that sense of victory and exaltation he'd felt on board *Lotus Glory*. He could still see the faces of his friends, shining and triumphant, cheering him as he climbed into the torpedo. It had been at that moment, as his foot first touched the metal deck of his weapon, that he'd felt the first plunge of fear. It was as though a camera lens had suddenly gone out of focus. All at once, he saw not the glory, the pride, the victory, but only the cold black water that waited for him. The cheers had no longer seemed a wonderful, exuberant thing. There'd been a darker note behind them, one of death and darkness. Time had seemed to slow down, the pitch of the voices to drop. The world around him had seemed strangely out of kilter, as though it no longer made sense.

He'd started to withdraw, to refuse to enter the torpedo, but momentum and pride had carried him forward. With his friends watching, the men he'd trained with for so many months, he could not appear a coward. Somewhere in the back of his mind he was convinced that there would be a way out, that this was not the end. As the technician had strapped him into the torpedo, carefully fastening the restraining straps just out of his reach, he'd still felt some of that certainty, that the torpedo would hit the other ship, miraculously break apart, and catapult him to safety inside his target. That the torpedo would malfunction, float to the surface, and the *Lotus Glory* would retrieve him. That something would happen, something somehow that would keep him from that last, final awful inevitability.

He'd lost control as the metal hatch clanged shut. With the last trace of outside light shut out and the compartment filled with the eerie glow of his instruments, reality had finally broken through the indoctrination and training that he'd been through. This was the end, this was death. There were no glorious angels appearing to escort him on this last mission, no feeling of divine self-dedication and sacrifice. Instead, there was only gut-wrenching fear, so strong and overpowering that he'd lost control of his bladder as the torpedo was deployed. Now, the small compartment was filled with the stink of urine and fear.

In the end, what choice had he had? He was dying, one way or the other. He'd watched the others deploy, and knew that the torpedo would be his sarcophagus.

There was no way out, not even if the torpedo malfunctioned and floated to the surface. Which it wouldn't. As soon as it lost power, it would sink like a rock to the bottom of the ocean. In the end, that was the vision that kept him going. He had two choices—the first to die trapped and powerless on the bottom of the ocean, slowly suffocating in the stink of urine as his air expired. The second was just barely more palatable—to execute his mission, die as he was intended to do. In the end, he chose quick death over slow suffocation.

The course laid in guided him towards the target, and the rocket's buzzer notified him that he was within range. Numbly, he flicked on the sonar, heard the ghastly, taunting high-pitched shrill of the sonar. The target was where it should be—it had not attempted to evade. He made a minor course correction and bore down on it.

As the seconds clicked slowly by, with his hands frozen to the yoke, he could not help but wonder how it would end. Would he feel the impact? See the sleek nose of the torpedo crumple, peel back as the warhead detonated? Would there be a flash of light, a noise, heat, and fire as the warhead exploded?

Or would the initial shock kill him? He hoped so, and that it would be quick. Of all the nightmarish possibilities that came to mind, the specter of seawater flooding the damaged torpedo, creeping up his chest, to his chin, and finally over his mouth, nose, and head, was the most terrifying. He would hold his breath, he knew, struggling against it. Hold his breath until either unconsciousness or survival reflex forced him to breathe in. He would die strapped into the chair, salt water flooding his lungs, conscious in the last moments as he died slowly from lack of oxygen. Four minutes, perhaps—maybe longer.

He was crying now, tears coursing unnoticed over his cheeks, dripping off his chin, soaking into the coverall he wore. The high-pitched pings of the sonar interactive returns got closer and closer together, accelerating until they outpaced his own frantic heartbeats. He felt his body try to keep up with it, try to keep his heart beating in tempo with it, but it was just too fast.

Soon now—he heard screaming, wondered vaguely where it came from. Suddenly he was cold, so very cold. The screaming and the sonar pings merged into one continuous blast of sound. In the end, he experienced a flash of gratitude. There was a bright flash of an explosion, and he knew that his consciousness was fading. He had one microsecond to realize that he'd hit the target before the exploding warhead shredded his body into a thin gruel.

USS JOUETT

Renninger dropped the bridge-to-bridge microphone and reached for the 1MC. "Attention all hands," he said, his voice now high and urgent. "If anyone speaks Russian or Ukrainian, lay to Combat ASAP. That's Russian or Ukrainian—we need you here now!" He replaced the microphone in its bracket and turned to face Collins.

"It's too late," she said quietly.

"The Tomcats. Call them now," Renninger said. He turned to look at the large-screen display. Five hundred miles away, the air escort for the SouthCom flight was just departing the *Eisenhower*.

"They're not due—" Williams began.

"You heard the Captain," Collins snapped. "Call them now."

Renninger stared at Collins, his face a mask of horrified understanding. Neither of them spoke as they listened to Williams contact the carrier and explain what had just occurred.

"It's all related, isn't it?" Renninger said finally. "I didn't think—XO, it's—"

"Later, maybe we'll know. For now, we have a commercial flight to protect." The corner of her mouth twitched ever so slightly in a conscious effort to put aside the moment she knew must eventually come. "I'll try not to shoot it down."

PRIDE OF KURSK

The translator felt the torpedo hit the ship before the master, but only by a few seconds. The impact traveled rapidly through the steel frame of the ship, rattling strakes and structural beams as it flashed upward and outward from the lower parts of the ship.

The first sound was a low, ominous thud that the translator barely noticed as he placed his now-clean coffee cup in the rack. He had just shut the door when the warhead detonated.

Kursk heeled violently to starboard. The translator catapulted against the galley and slammed into the refrigerator. He was conscious, but just barely. He slid down the door of the refrigerator, leaving a trail of blood from a head wound on it, and crumpled down to the deck. Dimly, he was aware of damage-control alarms ringing, the pounding of feet down the passageways. The deck beneath his cheek was smooth and cool, but oddly unstable. He felt centrifugal force shove him hard against the bulkhead, looked up, and saw the deck tilted at a crazy angle.

While all of the heavy equipment was bolted into place, the restraining racks and straps were insufficient to hold all of the kitchen accoutrements in place. Knives and ladles swung free of their hooks and clattered towards him with sharp points. He tried to cry out, and managed a weak, stifled scream that was not audible above the smashing of glass and cutlery. Debris piled up on him rapidly, poking him with the odd sharp edges that had once been dishware.

With a panic born of desperation, he scrabbled up the deck, clawing as it tilted ever steeper. He reached the hatch to the galley and yanked it open, then crawled into the passageway into the dining area. The deck was now canted at a thirty-degree angle, making walking upright all but impossible. He stayed on his hands and knees as he crossed it and headed for the ladder to the weather decks.

Four decks above, the bridge crew and navigation team fared only slightly better. While they were not trapped below the waterline, the impact had come suddenly and without warning.

The master's instincts were better honed than those of the translator. At the first hitch of the deck beneath his feet, he'd grabbed for the overhead stability bar. Now he hung from it by both hands, his feet barely resting on the slick linoleum beneath him.

His second mate lay on the deck on the port side, his leg crumpled under him at an odd angle. He'd fought to keep his balance as the deck careened wildly, had almost succeeded. But gravity had overcome him, flung him hard against the port bulkhead. The captain had heard the navigator's head hit the plotting table with a dull, sickening crunch. He now lay curled around the radar repeater as though trying to protect the base, blood streaming from his head and pooling only momentarily before running in thin rivulets down towards the second mate.

As the captain hung there, waited for a chance to move, he heard the damage-control klaxon sound. Good—someone belowdecks, perhaps in Engineering, had managed to activate it. At least the noise would wake the off-duty crew, who could assist in the damage control efforts.

Stupid thought, that. The explosion would have thrown them out of their bunks, injuring many of them seriously. While restraining straps were provided in the racks during foul-weather operations, there had been no need of them in the gentle waters of Panama Bay.

Pride of Kursk rocked back violently in the opposite direction just briefly, then settled back into a hard port list. The captain glanced at the inclinometer mounted on the bulkhead and noted that the angle of list was now forty degrees. Deadly instability—in that moment, the captain knew that his ship's wound was fatal. Even if the damage could be fought, and stability restored, too much machinery would have broken free of its welded mounts on the deck. Even the diesel engines—he shuddered, remembering that they were rated only for thirty-five degrees of list, an amount of motion that would be unheard of on the ship in normal conditions.

Abandon ship—they would have to. In the face of the danger, something inside him still protested at the thought of leaving his ship, the one he'd been entrusted with by his people. He howled, knowing there was no other answer. *Pride of Kursk* might remain floating for a while longer, but in the end either fire or flooding would take her to the bottom of the ocean.

He moved hand-over-hand, still supporting his weight on the iron bar, towards the ship's general announcing system. It was almost within reach. Finally, he lunged at it, loosening his hold to one hand on the bar. Suspended like a monkey from it, he held the announcing microphone in his hand.

"This is the captain," he began, amazed that his voice still sounded the same. "Abandon ship—I say again, abandon ship."

22

TWO HUNDRED MILES NORTH OF THE GULF OF PANAMA: 4 OCTOBER

TOMCAT 301

The pilot stared in amazement at his radio as the chatter of tactical data filled him in on what had happened to the merchant ship. He keyed the mike and spoke to his wingman, now located two thousand yards on the other side of the ungainly airliner they were escorting. "Combat spread."

"Roger." Even as he answered, his wingman peeled off and went into a screaming climb, gaining altitude rapidly. The pilot followed him up, putting his own Tomcat in a damned near vertical climb as he headed for the high slot in the traditional fighting formation of the United States Navy.

"What the hell was all that about?" the pilot asked his backseater. "Shit, this was a pucker-factor mission to begin with—now they've got torpedoes in the water? We're next, my friend. You keep an eye glued to that scope."

"You've got it." The RIO's voice was firm. "Now

how about shutting up and flying this thing while I do my job.''

The commercial airliner carrying the SouthCom detachment was cruising at an altitude of 31,000 feet. The two F-14's were now over it, matching its 550 knots of speed. The lead aircraft took position slightly aft, at 37,000 feet. His wingman was below and forward, a mere two thousand feet above the airliner. If anything came at them, they'd see it first. The lookdown-takedown capabilities of the AWG-9 radar on the Tomcat were exceptional.

''Just get us out of here,'' the pilot muttered. He craned his head around and looked at his backseater, whose face was glued to the radarscope. ''How much longer on this course?''

''Another twenty minutes, then we turn north.''

The pilot swore softly. Of all things that made the problem for the enemy easier, it was maintaining speed and altitude.

USS JOUETT

''Fighters in combat spread,'' the operations specialist said. ''Comm air flight tracking due west—range from Panama coast, thirty nautical miles.''

''Not far enough,'' Collins said. She could feel her heartbeat picking up the pace, the sweat starting to prickle under her arms and down her back. She ran one hand through her hair, swept bangs away from her eyes, and stared at the large-screen display. ''Come on, hurry up, you little bastards,'' she muttered. ''Get the hell out of range.''

''Worried about something, XO?'' Garland Williams spoke softly, pitching his voice so that Renninger would not hear him.

She turned to find him staring at her, and watched his lips move, although his voice was audible only in her headset. She glanced around the room, knowing that every other operator with a headset on would hear the exchange. She pulled the mike away from her lips and covered it with her hand. "Just watch the screen, mister," she snapped. "If that's a problem for you, just let me know and I'll get someone up to relieve you."

Williams shook his head. She saw his lips moving, but could not hear him. She slipped her headset back on.

"—won't be necessary, XO. I'm just fine, thank you."

The alarm on the SLQ-32 EW warning set chimed its soft, persistent tone. The electronic-warfare technicians who manned it moved more quickly than she'd ever seen them react before.

"Threat targeting radar, unidentified source," one said immediately. A symbol popped into being on the large-screen display. "No classification, but parameters are consistent with fire-control radar—airborne."

Collins stared in horror at the track. It was located immediately off the coast of Panama, on a course that put it on a dead intercept with the commercial airliner and the two F-14's. "Where did it come from?"

"I've got it too now, XO," the air tracker said over the net. "Estimate intercept on commercial airliner in four mikes. Recommend we take with missiles."

"Weapons, a solution," she said. She watched as the symbol changed shape and color, indicating the computer had calculated a fire-control solution and had assigned a missile to the target. Even burdened with missile-warning labels, the symbol continued its inexorable track across her screen. She picked up the mike for the tactical circuit.

"Tomcat 301, this is *Jouett*. We hold traffic behind you, inbound your location in approximately"—She glanced at the clock—"four mikes. Mach Two and accelerating. Indications of a fire-control radar. Do you copy?"

"*Jouett*, copy all. We're sending the friendly diving to the deck while we sort this out."

Collins watched as the commercial airliner descended rapidly, now approaching 25,000 feet. The Tomcat's tactic was clear—he would skim the airliner along the ocean, hoping that the missile would fail to lock on in the sea clutter and distraction of the waves while he and his wingman tried to counter it. She saw the high aircraft swing around 180 degrees, now nose-on to the incoming missile. The massive AWG-9 radar would surely give them a better targeting solution than the Aegis would, particularly at that range.

"*Jouett*, what the hell are you doing?" The Tomcat pilot's voice was angry.

"Say again your last, Tomcat 301," Collins said, puzzled. "Have you got contact on it?"

"There's not a damned thing here!"

Collins sucked in a hard breath. "We're holding contact. You've got to—"

"If it were here, I'd see it, *Jouett*," the pilot insisted. "You'd better come up with some good evidence to the contrary, or I'm putting my commercial air flight back on flight path."

Collins studied the screen. According to the Aegis data, the target symbol with missile characteristics was rapidly approaching the lead Tomcat. "Does your wingman hold anything?"

"Don't you think he'd see it on Link by now if he did?" Renninger's voice broke in. He stepped into Combat and moved to her side. "What the hell's going on?"

"Tomcat 301, clear the area. Descend immediately to five thousand feet at current speed and maintain escort on commercial airliner," she ordered.

Renninger grabbed the mike from her hands. "Belay my last," he ordered firmly. He glared at Collins as he spoke. "Tomcat flight, resume mission as briefed."

As he replaced the mike in its bracket, he turned to her. "What the hell are you doing?"

She shook her head. "It was inbound on the Tomcats, Captain. The commercial air flight—"

Renninger cut her off. "There was nothing there. Not a possibility in the world there was a missile in the air so close to the Tomcats and they didn't hold contact on it. Between you and that damned Tomcat pilot, I don't know who's more likely to cause another blue-on-blue engagement—you or him."

The atmosphere in Combat seemed deathly still. Collins stared at the large-screen display, trying to understand how it could happen. The Aegis radar was remarkable for its ability to distinguish targets, with a resolution so fine that there was hardly any target that could slip past the invisible net it cast into the skies. Yet twice in the last three days it had shown her ghosts, targets that weren't there. The first time she'd fired. The second time—she shuddered, realizing what she'd almost done. She'd been caught up in the moment, convinced that a missile was inbound on the Tomcats flying within her umbrella of protection, and been determined not to let it happen again.

"XO, you're relieved. Leave Combat immediately." Renninger's voice was cold.

Collins nodded dumbly. She turned and left without comment, and headed for her stateroom.

How could it all have gone wrong so quickly? And why was the Captain so convinced that the hostile missile had actually been a ghost? It wasn't a chance she would have been willing to take—hadn't taken, not until he'd countermanded her orders. She seethed for a moment, the fact of her public humiliation now sinking in.

A colder feeling crept in slowly to replace the anger. What if she had shot? Downed one of the Tomcats, or even the commercial SouthCom jet? She shivered. At least one thing had gone down in flames in the last thirty minutes—her hopes of ever having a career in the Navy.

Forty minutes later, the SouthCom transport was safely out over the open sea.

23

**PANAMA:
5 OCTOBER**

MIUW 106

Carlisle slept exhausted on the sleeping bag spread out over his rack. The air inside the tent was stifling even with the seaward flap rolled in to admit the breezes. His head was pounding and he still felt nauseous. While the unit corpsman had assured him that he would recover from the concussion with no long-term affects, at the moment he felt decidedly less than his best.

The injection spot over the crook of his elbow still throbbed. What had they shot him up with? He sighed, contemplating the lengthy debriefing process he'd go through when he returned to NSA. His memory of most of his stay with the SEALs was a blur of drug-and-concussion-induced haze that defied his best efforts to penetrate.

He took off his uniform jacket and stretched out in his T-shirt on the rack. He shut his eyes for a moment, trying once again to concentrate.

USS JOUETT

Collins walked through Combat and stopped in the middle of the room. After the debacle with the SouthCom transport the day before, she'd almost expected Renninger to bar her from Combat. There'd been that fleeting moment of hope when Renninger had appeared to be convinced that both the sonar contacts and the air contacts were related. Then the Tomcat's report of no contact had destroyed that. Once again, he'd appeared to be convinced that his XO's trigger finger was the problem.

She surveyed the row of green-lit consoles, the backs of the technicians seated in front of them, the odd mixture of green scope light and red overhead lights that protected their night vision. As always, the room was dominated by the reflection from the large-screen display in the forward part of the compartment. She turned to it for a moment, trying to decide what had caught her attention.

There was nothing specific she could pinpoint, but something seemed off, odd, out of place, and strangely off-kilter. It took her a moment, but finally she placed it. It wasn't Combat—it was her.

Before, being in Combat had always brought with it an oddly soothing sensation that she stood at the center of the universe, that simply by watching the scopes, displays, and large-screen displays she had an accurate picture of everything going on in the world around her. Combat created a sense of invulnerability, of all-knowing omniscience, as the destroyer's powerful sensors probed the environment, surface, air, and subsurface, around it. Nothing was hidden, at least not for long. Every pinpoint of data was correlated, analyzed, and marked for display. There were no secrets in the world around them, not for the Aegis destroyer.

The airbus shoot-down and the incident from her last watch had destroyed that feeling. Never again would she feel completely safe in Combat, lulled into security by the massive amounts of data that flashed on the screen and across her console. Now she knew—that the world could hide secrets from the Aegis, that they too were vulnerable.

How could the world have changed so radically without her noticing before? Three hundred or more civilians dead, the threat of a fratricide—there was something wrong with the system—there had to be.

She left the compartment and made her way back to the Data Systems Division office. The chief was sitting at his desk, working his way steadily through a pile of paperwork.

"Help you, XO?" he asked.

She nodded. "I need to talk raw data and processing algorithms. You got a minute?"

"Always for you." He shoved a chair towards her. "Want coffee?"

She shook her head. "Thanks anyway. I'm afraid my nerves are spun up enough as is."

"I wouldn't be surprised." The chief's face was impassive.

"The data tapes—I know we keep track of everything that happens. Where exactly do they tap into the system?"

The chief relaxed slightly. "Way before the data gets to your console. It's raw stuff, precorrelation."

"Can you play it back?"

He nodded. "But the raw data tracks won't be of too much use. You've seen the console in Tracker Alley—it looks like snow falling, almost. So many targets, most of them just dual detections off the same piece of metal." He shook his head and frowned. "Not much use for tactics—there's so much data, it has to be smoothed and correlated before you make any decisions."

"But could you play it back if you needed to?" she pressed.

"If we needed to. If I can ask, ma'am—why? You think it might shed some light on the last two incidents?"

"Maybe." She was aware of his eyes studying her, of an odd gentleness in them. "Maybe not. But I wasn't the only one who saw the contact data go hostile the first time, and I wasn't the only one who saw it the second time. I think there's a problem—no, not with your system," she added as she saw the defensive look start to come over his face. "I'm not implying that. But there is something wrong—there's no way the Aegis system should make that kind of mistake."

"The Aegis isn't infallible, XO. That's why we put people in the loop."

"And neither are people. They operate off what they know, what they see from the screen. I know myself I've rarely had reason to doubt the data I saw on the scope in front of me. It's always been right—always."

"But not this time?"

"But not this time."

He studied her for a moment, then nodded once. "We can play it back," he said. "See if there's anything that looks odd in the precorrelated raw data. I'm not sure it will do us much good."

She stood, shoving the chair back away from her. "How long will it take to set up?"

"Which night do you want? Last night, or the one before?"

She thought about it for a moment, then said, "Last night, I think. I don't want to touch the data tapes for the incident, not when . . ." She let her voice trail off.

The chief nodded once. "Understood, and I agree with you." He stood as well, and walked to the door. "Give me about an hour or so, XO. Where will you be?"

"In my stateroom. If not, have the OOD page me. No," she said, thinking better of it, "I'm not sure I want the whole ship to know what I'm doing. I'll find you in about an hour, okay?''

"Aye, aye, ma'am." He hesitated, then continued. "I hope we find something, XO. I sure do."

She nodded. "Me too, Chief. For more reasons than one."

Next, she went up to SESS, the Signal Exploitation unit, located within the superstructure. In addition to the normal ESM capabilities, the destroyer also possessed an extended-range signal-detection-and-evaluation sensor that monitored many electromagnetic signals that were outside of the normal range. While she wasn't certain what she was looking for, it seemed like another place to start.

"I understand what you're looking for," the cryptological technician in charge of the equipment said. "Believe me, we've got both incidents marked on all of our printouts." He rummaged through a pile of papers on his desk and extracted the relevant sheet. "The only thing I can tell you is that there was a fair amount of sunspot activity during that time." He pointed at two peaks on the graph. "But none of them coincide with the time of the Aegis system problems. If there were problems," he added hastily.

"Sunspots? Tell me about them," Collins demanded.

"Well, I'm assuming you know what sunspots are, XO." He glanced up and saw her nod of confirmation. "They radio broad-spectrum noise—here and here too are the peaks."

She studied the fanfold graph spread out on the desk in front of them. "Would it interfere with the radar?"

"No doubt about it. But not in the way you're looking for. It produces broad-spectrum noise, not a discrete ghost contact. That's just not how it works."

"So we know that there was sunspot activity, but we also know it had nothing to do with the performance of the radar."

"More importantly, we know it had nothing to do with the track-processing logarithm within the Aegis system itself," the technician said relentlessly. "Yes, the radar's going to notice some additional noise. But it's not coherent—it's not going to generate a false contact. Nor can it affect the Aegis system itself—remember, these ships were built specifically to withstand an electromagnetic pulse from a nuclear weapon. While the sunspot puts out a lot of energy, we're shielded against it."

"I see." She thanked him and left.

The odd data point on the printout, the occurrence of sunspots—more and more, it seemed that she was chasing a lost cause. There was only one real reason for the two incidents—or the one incident and the almost-incident. She'd shot first and asked questions later—too late.

Her last stop was the Captain's cabin. She knocked once, waited to hear his grunt granting admission, then pushed the door open. He was seated at his worktable, a pile of message traffic before him.

"Captain, I've found out a few things." She summarized her research activities, including the fact that the chief was rigging the data tape for replay. "I doubt that it will find anything, but I'd like to take a look at it."

He leaned back in his chair, staring at her. "You're really fixated on this, aren't you?"

"With all due respect, I think I've got a right to be interested in this. It's my ass on the line at the Board of Inquiry."

"Mine and yours both. Remember, it's my ship—regardless of how much it may seem yours as Executive Officer. I am solely and completely responsible for everything that occurs." His face looked worn and tired, she noted, as though the weight of what had happened was finally starting to eat at him. She felt a flash of regret at the damage she had done not only to her career, but to his as well. She had never seen him look quite so human before.

"I'm sorry, Captain," she said finally. "For all of it. You've been a good Captain—you deserve a better Executive Officer." She rose and started for the door.

"Wait a minute," he said. She turned. He was studying her carefully. "Sunspots, you said."

She nodded. "The cryptotech said it couldn't have made any difference."

"Still." He appeared to be considering something, and finally arrived at a decision. "That expert you wanted to talk to—Commander Bailey, was it?"

"Yes, Captain. She's still ashore with the MIUW. Her message said it might take her a few days before she could get out here. She might have some ideas on all this."

"Fine. Hell, get hold of her on tactical if you can—maybe she can spare some time for us now."

She nodded, vaguely surprised that he'd finally agreed. "Thank you, sir."

He grunted again. "Don't thank me yet—let's see what this lady knows. Or just as importantly, who she knows."

24

**PANAMA:
5 OCTOBER**

MIUW 106

Lieutenant Boston ripped the paper out of the printer and handed it to her. "Another request from *Jouett*."

She scanned the message quickly, and shrugged. "They can ask all they want, but I'm a little bit busy here." She crumpled it up into a ball and lobbed it into the classified trash bag.

"Captain," the communications specialist said. "Call for you on secure phone."

She crossed the van in a few steps and picked up the receiver. "Commander Bailey."

"Jerusha, this is Terry."

Even through the distortion that always accompanied a secure voice call, she recognized his voice. "Yes, sir." She glanced down at the LCD display on the secure phone. Yes, both sides had their crypto-keys engaged, and the call was secure. "To what do I owe the honor?"

"By now you should have gotten the request from *Jouett* for you to go out there," Intanglio began. "I just want to—"

She took a step back from the telephone set, still clutching the receiver. "Oh, no. No, no, no." She shook her head reflexively, even though she knew Terry could not see the gesture. "No. I'm on active duty right now. I do not—do *not*—leave my unit under less than optimum circumstances just because my civilian boss thinks it's a good idea. I'm sorry, Terry, but you understand the conflict of interest you're placing me in."

She shook her head, marveling at the intricate entanglements that existed between the various government agencies. At the very senior levels, formal governmental boundaries meant little. Yet down on her level, she was expected to know, recognize, and understand the potential conflicts of interest that arose from being employed as a civilian at NSA and being on active duty with the United States Navy. As carefully as she'd thought she'd had it worked out, at least one of the entities involved had decided it didn't want to play by the rules.

"Jerusha, I'm not asking you to run off on your own accord," Intanglio argued. "God knows you can't abandon those people—not with what's going on in Panama right now. All I'm talking about is a quick day trip out to *Jouett*. Take a look at the data, see what occurs to you."

"By now they've already shipped those data tapes back to SouthCom," she argued. "The airbus, you mean, right?"

"It happened again." There was a chilling note of finality in Intanglio's voice. "There's something strange going on out there, and we need an expert eye to take a look at it. Before something else fatal happens. There are other factors at play as well—other sensors. National assets. I can't go into details on this line."

"But why me?" Bailey said, aware that her voice was spiraling up the octaves. "I'm not an expert in electronic warfare or in data tapes. You should know that. You want somebody like—oh." The light finally came on. "It's not really me you're after—it's Carlisle, isn't it?"

"Now, Jerusha—"

"And I'm just going out to run interference for him. That's it, isn't it?"

And just maybe that's why the SEALs wanted to talk to him as well, she thought. Just what the hell does Pete know—and what did he tell them?

There was a long silence, followed by the distorted crackle of a sigh. "I told Atchinson it wouldn't work."

"You're damned right it won't. Carlisle's in the same spot I am. We're on active duty, dammit. You can't just go poking around in every aspect of our lives."

"What did you expect when you came to work for NSA?" The chill in his voice stopped her cold. Had she really been so naive as to think that the National Security Agency, the most secret and powerful of all the intelligence-collection agencies in the United States, would be put off by a mere set of orders issued by the United States Navy recalling her to active duty? Or that they'd understand her duty to the Navy, that she'd be forced into choices they couldn't foresee?

No. What NSA wanted, NSA took. All she could do now was delay matters a bit, figure out some way to keep her unit safe while the intricate power plays at pay grades way above hers took place. "I can't do this on a simple voice request," she said. "And I'm not about to do it based on message traffic from *Jouett*. I'm left hanging out to dry if anything goes wrong."

"Understood." Intanglio's voice was back to normal. Evidently this was an area of high-level politics he understood—covering one's ass. "Before the day's out, you'll see record traffic from the Navy requesting that you and Carlisle conduct an assistance visit on board USS *Jouett*. That good enough?"

"It'll have to be. How much do you know about what happened to him anyway?" She waited for a moment as the silence grew longer. "Terry?"

"We know enough," he said finally. "That's another reason I want him with you at all times. Until we know

exactly what was done to him, and how, we don't know
how much was compromised. Keep an eye on him, Jerusha. We want him back in one piece.''

As she hung up the phone, Bailey turned back to look
at the rest of the watch team. No one appeared to be
paying any attention to her. All eyes were glued to consoles, heads and ears covered with headsets. She turned
the secure crypto-key in the STU-3 secure phone and
pulled it free, slipping it into her breast pocket. She went
to find Carlisle. And Elwell.

She found Elwell first. As she walked toward him, she
would have sworn that he had not seen her. He appeared
deep in conversation with the bosun's mate, and was
explaining some of the finer points of rigging the netting
posts to hold the net out at different angles. However,
as she came within fifteen feet of them, the sergeant
stood and turned towards her. He nodded and said,
''Commander, forgive me if I'm appearing discourteous.
However, if you haven't already done so, I would suggest that you tell your troops to lay off the salutes while
we're in this area.'' He motioned with his head back
towards the hills behind them. ''No point in telling them
who the boss is.''

She nodded. ''Good idea. Any other pointers while
you're at it?''

''Now that you mention it.'' He pointed at her bright
collar devices. ''If you didn't bring the subdued camouflage version, then I suggest you dispense with them
entirely. And all other insignia of an officer. It may be
too late—they've probably got you pegged by now. But
there's no point in making the job any easier for them
than it has to be.''

''You sound pretty certain that snipers are watching
us.''

''Wouldn't you be?''

She thought about it for a moment, then said,
''Maybe. I take it as a compliment that you think I

would be. But we're sailors, Sergeant—we've got some experience in land operations, but not nearly as much as you do. And that's exactly what I wanted to talk to you about.''

They walked away from the camouflage netting and towards a supply locker. When she was sure they were safely out of earshot of the rest of the unit, she explained *Jouett*'s request for an assistance visit.

"It comes at a bad time," she said. "I'm not at all comfortable leaving the unit under these circumstances."

"You shouldn't be."

"I know. At this point, I've got two choices—go along with this, or tell the higher-ups that they're putting my entire unit in danger. If I take the second choice, I may be missing the forest for the trees. Whatever is causing that problem with *Jouett* is bound to have some bearing on our situation.'' She shrugged, already knowing which choice she would be forced to take. "I've got some good people, Sergeant, but they're out of their league here. Can I count on you?"

The sergeant didn't answer for a moment. He looked around the compound, studied a couple of seemingly insignificant knots holding the camouflage netting in place, then turned back to her. "Of course you can, Commander. Since the rest of SouthCom bugged out, I've got sole say in what my duties require. Who are you leaving in charge while you're gone?"

"Lieutenant Boston. He's a good man—he and I see eye-to-eye on most things."

The sergeant looked slightly doubtful.

"He is just a lieutenant, though," she said. "Probably the same sort of situation you find yourself in with junior captains in the Army. Don't worry, though. He's got a thorough grounding in the facts of life, and I'll make sure he understands he's to rely on you. I don't expect any problems with that. None at all."

"Like you said, there's some things you expect from

captains—and some things you don't. I'm sure Lieutenant Boston and I will get along just fine.''

She nodded, relieved that at least Elwell would be on hand in camp to keep an eye on things. Nothing could beat his years of experience in ground warfare. Although she suspected that she would never know the true depth of his skill in the deadly arts, she was glad to have him there—and on her side.

"For starters," he said, "you have to figure out what your strengths and weaknesses are in any position. Then you turn your weaknesses into your strengths, and use them both against the enemy."

She smiled. "The gospel according to Master Sergeant Elwell?"

He shook his head. "No. Chinese guy by the name of Sun Tzu. You said you heard of him."

"I have." She studied him for a moment, noting the lines crinkling the corners of his eyes, the ironic twist to his mouth. "I guess I shouldn't be surprised that you have too."

"Surprise is a good thing," he said neutrally.

"More Sun Tzu?"

He nodded. "Now, in your situation here, you've got a couple of problems. First, the terrain. Those hills look down on you, giving anyone a good visibility on your site. That's not what you like in a good camp."

"And how do we turn that into a strength?"

"Well, a couple of ways. Remember this—tracer fire works both ways. If they can see you, you can see them. You've got a helluva lot more area to search, but if they're there, you can see them."

"So I need more lookouts."

He nodded. "The other thing is, you can start interfering with their visibility. That's what I was telling the bosun's mate there," he said, pointing at the sailor busily rerigging the camouflage netting. "You've got this all lined up to prevent a view from ground level into the campsite, but what you need is a way to obstruct a higher-up view. It's mostly a matter of changing locations, putting a couple of extenders on the poles—it won't be a lot, but it'll help some. Second, you need some contingency plans.''

"Like what?''

He pointed down the two-mile-long pier at the scaffolding and gantries staged alongside. "You borrow some things—take them into protective custody before some son of a bitch can steal them.''

"We have a similar custom in the Navy.''

"Figured you did. You take some of that scaffolding and you get a better reach with your camouflage netting. Maybe you don't even use it down near ground level—you use the deuce-and-a-halves further in like you've done to block that field of vision. You get it up high, mask off your location from the best shooting points. You understand how that works?''

She studied the equipment and construction gear lining the pier, seeing it now with new eyes. It looked more like raw material, like something that could usefully be turned to their purposes instead of merely obstructions that impeded the progress of their deuce-and-a-halves. "Roadblocks too,'' she said as she saw the pier in this new light. "We could block off access pretty easily with some of that.''

He smiled approvingly. "Now you're thinking like a mud puppy, ma'am. Give me a couple of weeks with you and I'll have you rigging claymores and concertina wire.''

"I don't suppose you have any,'' she said.

He avoided her gaze. "Now how would a master sergeant in the United States Army know how to get his hands on that sort of stuff this far from home, Commander?''

"In other words, I'm better off not asking. Is that it?''

He smiled and said nothing.

She felt a good deal better now about leaving the camp. Elwell's nasty, suspicious turn of mind was ex-

ceptionally reassuring. "I'll only be gone a day and a
half, if that," she said.

"And you're taking that young fellow with you—
Carlisle, is he?"

She nodded. "He's a pretty handy fellow at a lot of
things."

Elwell studied her for a moment, then said, "I don't
imagine you know how thoroughly we get briefed on
anybody entering the theater, do you?"

"What's that supposed to mean?"

"I probably know a bit more about you and Mr. Carlisle than you think. You especially, but Mr. Carlisle's
no mystery either."

"Then you know that I'm not going to answer any of
your questions," she said calmly. "And you also know
better than to get anyone else asking them."

"That I do. When you get Carlisle out to the ship,
you get that medic out there to look at him. He may
think he's fine, but he still looks a little shaky to me."
Elwell frowned. "The man's got something on his
mind—he's not willing to ask about it, yet, so I didn't
ask too hard. But it's there, I can see it plain as day.
You spend enough time out in the field, you get sort of
the ability to read a fellow's thoughts. And I don't like
the direction Mr. Carlisle's are going."

She puzzled over that, trying to remember if she'd
noticed anything particularly odd about Carlisle. She
hadn't—but then again, she hadn't been looking that
closely. It always threw her for a while, the transfor-
mation from her relationship with Carlisle at NSA to
their relationship within the Reserves. Neither had had
any particular problems with it, but it did tend to skew
her perceptions.

Would she have paid more attention to him if he'd
been injured at NSA? Yes, she was almost ashamed to
admit—she would have. The times, the circumstances
would have been different.

"I'll keep an eye on him while we're out there," she said finally. "Thanks for pointing it out."

Elwell caught the note of embarrassment in her voice. "Don't be too hard on yourself about it," he said. "That's someone else's job out here, not yours."

"He's my friend," she said simply.

"Not right now. As long as you wear that uniform, he's one of your troops. Now," Elwell continued, seeing the expression on her face, "that doesn't mean you don't take care of them. You watch out for those troops as least as much as, if not more than, you do the officers. But it also means that there's other eyes watching him as well—his chief's already picked up on something being wrong, and I think he's already talked to Lieutenant Boston about it. If they think they can't handle it, they'll come to you. Don't you think?"

"Thank you, Sergeant," she said. "I'm glad you're here. I'll leave tomorrow."

He nodded. "We'll get through this, Commander. One way or the other. One way or the other."

25

***

PANAMA CITY, PANAMA:
6 OCTOBER

CALLE DE RORAIME

"I don't like it," Murphy said immediately. "Why is she going to *Jouett*?"

His communications technician shrugged. "That's the problem with eavesdropping, sir. Sometimes not everything makes sense."

"Not good enough," Murphy snapped. He turned to his second in command. "Find out what's going on down there. I want to know—now."

SEAHAWK 101

Bailey peered out of the small window located to her left as the SH-60B helo made its approach on the USS *Jouett*. The ship was smooth and sleek, no acute angles or awkward deck projections marring her clean lines. Aircraft were not the only weapons to benefit from Stealth technology. *Jouett* had the radar cross section of a medium sized tugboat.

Another odd incongruity of naval warfare, she mused. In addition to its low-visibility paint and Stealth technology, *Jouett* also possessed a blip enhancer. This arcane piece of electronic gear was designed to make it look like an aircraft carrier on an enemy radarscope, which would supposedly decoy enemy missiles from the high value unit and its bird farm and into the very capable missile sump of the cruiser.

And another anomaly. She patted the pocket of her flight jacket, feeling the bulky shape of the .45-caliber pistol nestled there. Not particularly covert—the outlines were visible, and had caused a stir of reaction from the pilots. Why exactly Elwell had insisted she take it, she still didn't know. Just some Army reflex, she supposed, but he hadn't stopped harping on it until she'd agreed to carry it.

She turned to Carlisle and shouted, not wanting to use the ICS and be overheard by the two pilots sitting forward. "You ready for this?" She studied him for a moment, concerned about his pale complexion and grimacing mouth. "You okay?"

He nodded, making a resigned gesture with his hands. "Just a little bumpy up here," he shouted back.

She nodded. As they neared the cruiser, the air around them boiled and bubbled, disturbed by the passage of the ship through the air. The helicopter wobbled, steadied, and commenced its final approach to the flight deck of the cruiser.

Near the hangar doors, she saw a small, thin figure in khakis. Blond hair ruffled wildly in the downdraft generated by the helicopter, and the face was in plain view, unobscured by a ball cap or sunglasses that would pose a foreign-object damage hazard to the helicopter.

Collins. She studied the woman as they descended, wondering how the more junior officer felt about seeing her again. Hopefully, the blanket grant of immunity and rehabilitation granted by the White House would go a long way toward soothing any hurt feelings.

  If she doesn't mention it, I won't.

Carlisle fought down the nausea as the helicopter drifted over the flight deck. A few minutes more, that's all. Back on solid ground. At least they hadn't had to horse-collar down—he'd have been puking before he was out the hatch. Still, between the turbulence and the lingering effects of his concussion, he wasn't entirely sure that he could keep his breakfast down.

  "Wave off," a voice said over the ICS. Carlisle groaned. Evidently the flight deck crew below had detected some problem with the approach, and had directed the helicopter to make another circuit before landing. The noise inside the helicopter cabin increased markedly as the pilot applied power and veered off sharply to his right.

  Carlisle crossed his hands over each other and grasped his wrists, searching for the one pressure point just above the wrist bone that sometimes helped prevent nausea. He'd used the trick a couple of times on cruises, even seen other crew members wearing the plastic bands with bumps inside of them that supposedly prevented it. Others swore by it—it was worth a try now.

  Circling, circling. His vision was blurry at the edges, dwindling down to a narrow tunnel in front of him. Circling, circling—what was it about this? He felt like he had when he first regained consciousness in the—

  Suddenly, without warning, the memories flooded back. Hot, sticky sheets clinging to his body at the SEAL headquarters, the vague smell of alcohol and medicine permeating his room. Drifting in and out of consciousness, hearing the babble of voices around him, struggling to open his eyes and being unable to. A vague, ill-defined ache at the crook of his elbow.

  Circling, circling—they'd been cutting doughnuts in the water while laying sonobuoys, wide, lazy circles designed to give the MIUW tracking team a quick refresher course in fast-moving contacts. They'd been just at the point for the second buoy drop, and he'd leaned forward in the RHIB to double-check the sonobuoy channel assignment on the device.

Then a metal ping, a sharp, screaming noise. He remembered looking back, concerned that something in the outboard engine had snapped. A scream, Storey pitching forward in the RHIB. Then the right side of the RHIB disintegrating into a spray of plastic and metal shards. The sea, warm and inviting, flooded into the boat.

He remembered screaming, remembered reaching desperately for Storey, popping the auto-inflation device on the man's life jacket. Then another noise, and the RHIB pitching down suddenly. He had a vague memory of one of the floorboards from the RHIB rocketing towards him, a brief flash of pain, then nothing.

But why was that important? A voice came back to him, one fogged and unclear as he'd heard it through the drug-induced haze.

"Electromagnetic spectral breakout. Tell me about NSA's capabilities."

He sucked in a hard breath, his nausea almost completely forgotten. That was it—he'd overheard the SEALs talking while in a drug-induced state at their compound.

How much did I tell them? The sunspots? Cold fear trickled down his back and invaded his stomach and groin, sending his guts lurching in an unsteady fashion. He groaned again, now aware that motion sickness was just moments away. He reached hastily for the plastic bag tucked into the seat behind him.

"What is it?"

He looked up into the anxious face of Jerusha Bailey.

"Jesus, Carlisle, maybe I shouldn't have—"

"No," he croaked, his voice raw and harsh from the stomach acid that had seared it. "I remembered something. Not good.'' With his stomach empty, he felt noticeably better.

Bailey stared at him, horrified. ''You're going back to the States. Now.''

He shook his head, the movement engendering another wave of nausea. ''Not yet. That's exactly what they'd like, I think. There's something they're worried about and it has to do with what I know. Whether from NSA or from being in the RHIB, I don't know.''

The helicopter swung around the ship again, making a far more stable and determined approach on the flight deck. Jerusha Bailey leaned back against her hard lumbar cushion, barely aware of the final approach. ''You're certain of this?''

Carlisle nodded. ''Completely.'' He grimaced slightly. ''We have the technology back at NSA to completely verify it, of course. I'm not looking forward to that.'' Both of them knew that hypnotic agents produced reliable results, but caused whopping headaches afterwards.

''Well, there's nothing we can do about it now,'' she said firmly. ''Not until I get access to the crypto spaces on *Jouett*. I'll shoot off a personal for message, get NSA alerted.''

''What about SouthCom?'' Carlisle asked.

She was silent for a moment, then said, ''I don't know. We need to think this over before we do anything.'' A vivid picture of Sergeant Elwell's face flashed into her mind. She trusted the man—but should she? For all she knew, SouthCom, or at least a portion of it, was in on this. Who could she turn to with news about the renegade SEALs? Who would be likely to believe two Reservists, one an officer and one enlisted, against the word of an active-duty SEAL commander. The more she thought about it, the less probable it seemed.

''We wait, for now,'' she said finally. ''As soon as we get onboard, we'll talk to NSA.''

''What about the camp?'' Carlisle said.

"And to Lieutenant Boston." She would use the secure phone, going via satellite lookout, to ensure that no one else inside the van was privy to this information. Not that it made any difference—but until she knew just how far this rot had spread throughout SouthCom, Sergeant Elwell would be in the dark.

She hoped.

26

GULF OF PANAMA:
6 OCTOBER

LOTUS GLORY

From six miles off *Jouett*'s port bow, the Chinese merchant ship watched the military helicopter circle, approach, and finally land. The military advisor turned to the master. "You know what to do."

The master nodded. He reached for the 1MC to inform the torpedo crews.

HALLELUJAH CHORUS

Carl Timmons spread his blanket out on the massive foredeck of the tanker. The breeze picked up one corner of it, tugged it away from him. He stamped his foot down on it hard, then followed it with the rest of the body to hold it down on the deck.

It wasn't often that a wiper got a chance to escape the confines of *Chorus*'s Engineering spaces. As the most junior man in the department, Carl had inherited a host of duties from his predecessor that had gone undone for two to three months. Most of them involved lubricating oil and rags—hence the name wiper for a junior engineering technician in the Merchant Marines.

Now, finally, he was caught up. Undone preventative maintenance, routine calibrating and testing—all of it. Finally done. As much of a pain in the ass as this delay outside the Canal had been, at least some good had come of it.

Carl rolled over on his back, shut his eyes, and lifted his chin slightly. A few rays now, maybe a late lunch— with a halfway decent tan and a huge wad of overtime money bulging out of his pocket, he had every intention of making liberty in Miami one of the high points of his young life.

First, the tan. Accumulating overtime hours had put him seriously behind schedule on that. He was quite certain that the money could go a long way to make up for the lack of attractiveness to women. But he felt a need to prove not only his financial but also his physical attractiveness, to the beach bunnies that would abound there. A tan, coupled with an extra twenty minutes a day in the weight room, would do it.

The tropical sun, still potent this late in the year, beat down on his lean, hard body, soaking in and warming him. He sighed, completely and utterly happy for the first time since he'd undertaken this voyage aboard *Chorus*.

Chorus hadn't been his first choice. It wasn't for any of the crew. American ships had so many stringent safety regulations, and paid such low wages, that only the rawest recruits and least proficient crews sought out duty on board them. The foreign ships simply paid so much better that it only made sense. However, with just a basic seaman license to his credit, and no experience, Carl hadn't had much of a choice.

He'd heard the talk, the rumor that the Master was sleeping with his life jacket on, and that the Chief Engineer refused to spend more than a few minutes belowdecks. It worried him when he had time to think about it, which wasn't often. But the ship's owners wouldn't leave them out here if there were really any danger, would they? Risk losing the ship completely just to keep on the transit schedule? No, that didn't make sense. Maybe one of those Panamanian companies might take that sort of gamble, but not an American company.

He rolled over on his stomach, and felt the sun start to work on him immediately. He stretched his hands out on either side of him and let his cheek rasp against the rough woolen blanket. Heat radiating up from the deck, down from the sky, enveloped him in a cocoon of moist tropical air.

The sounds of the ship radiated up through the steel deck, beating an insistent refrain in his bones. His mind automatically sorted the noises out—there, a hydraulics pump. The constant thrum of the main propulsion diesel engines. The intermittent squawk of a high-pressure air compressor blasting 1500 pounds of air into another system. It was the quiet, reassuring hum of a well-maintained and efficient propulsion plant. He took quiet satisfaction in contributing his small part toward that reassuring noise.

Carl Timmons shut his eyes, basked in the sun, and dreamed of Miami.

LOTUS GLORY

T'sing Lin felt sick the moment he heard the announcement over the loudspeaker. He stood slowly, reluctantly, abandoning the ancient game of chance going continuously in the Engineering compartment as he responded to the summons. He walked up two ladders, and made his way forward, his steps growing ever slower as he approached the mess-deck door.

He was the last to arrive. The remaining kamikaze pilots were already assembled, seated quietly around the

table. In the beginning, there'd been too few chairs—
now there was one empty. He slid into it, clasped his
hands politely on his lap, and waited. His stomach was
clutched in a tight knot of dread; his blood was pounding
in his temples.

He felt the perspiration break out on the back of his
neck, trickle in slow, taunting rivulets down his back.
Surreptitiously, he glanced at the other pilots assembled.
Were they feeling the same thing? Surely they must be.
It was simply a matter of courage, of commitment—of
the things that he lacked most in his life. But this would
be his redeeming event, the one thing that made his life
worthwhile and useful. It would be his defining moment
of glory, his assured entry into the heavens.

Or at least he tried to believe so. Yet could any man
truly look death so closely in the eye and not be bothered
by it?

Evidently his companions could. There was not a
flinch, not a nervous look among them. Only he, of the
original ten, lacked that quality of divinity he saw in the
faces of the others in the Divine Wind program.

The master pronounced the name—Li. T'sing heard
a tiny noise in the compartment, and realized to his relief
that he was not the only one who had released a long-
held breath. He glanced at them again, now alert to the
signs of relief on their faces. Maybe he was not as alone
as he'd thought.

The cheers this time sounded even more forced, the
slightest bit tentative. T'sing joined in, striving to outdo
each of the others as they prayed for a contagious enthusiasm that would alleviate the stark dread pounding
in each heart.

They trooped downstairs together, standing closer together than they had when the first torpedoes had been
deployed. Now more than ever, it seemed important to
draw strength from each other, to bolster each other's
spirits and courage through the days that lay ahead.
While they had known what would happen in theory,

the stark reality of it had not yet begun to set in until they'd seen the faces absent at their morning meetings, looked at the empty bunks each night as they went to sleep. It was that more than the actual launch of each torpedo that brought home the true nature of their mission to each one of them.

T'sing hesitated as the dull black cover slid back from the torpedo's passenger compartment. He saw Li take a deep breath, steady his nerves, then step forward resolutely. He paused again at the hatch and shot one look back at his companions. He smiled, an expression T'sing could see was meant to be brave. The corners of his mouth quivered, however.

They got through the normal insertion and lockdown procedures, as usual. Li ran through his prechecklist in front of them, quietly counting off the steps. As he reached the final test, the warm rollover of the electrical motor that powered the torpedo, his hands began to shake. He touched the ignition switch—the assembled men waited for the quick growl that signified successful completion. Nothing. Li tried again, then looked up at the master. "It isn't working."

The master frowned. He motioned to two technicians who operated the cradle. The torpedo was hefted back up out of the water, its shining tail, glistening with seawater, exposed again.

The technicians popped an access cover off, busied themselves for a few moments with screwdrivers and voltage testers. Finally, the elder of them looked up at the master and nodded.

"Try now." Li's finger was shaking so hard as it touched the switch that it almost failed to make contact. He grasped the wrist with his other hand and forced the finger down on the switch. A quick, harsh noise. Then he released it.

The master nodded and smiled. "Go to glory, my son."

Li's shrill scream ripped across the solemn air in the

Engineering compartment. T'sing Lin took a step back, aghast and yet relieved. That men could bear this much without reaction—that *he* could—had never seemed entirely sane.

Li was struggling now, pulling against the harness, his hands scrambling frantically over him as he sought to find the latches. T'sing Lin took one step forward involuntarily—it was too much to watch, this frantic struggle for survival. They would stop it now, they had to. He looked over at the master.

The old Chinese man's face was cold and impassive. "Do not disgrace yourself," he snapped.

The words did nothing to calm Li. His screams grew louder, echoing through the vast underwater maze of steel steam conduits and machinery, seeming to gather and pool in the dark black reaches of the engine room.

Blood was flowing now from one shoulder where the strap had cut into his skin. Li was struggling with all his might against the floor of the submarine, trying to wrest himself free of the grasp of the restraining straps. The release mechanism was located behind the back of his seat, out of the reach of his hands.

"Now." The master's voice was curt. "Launch now."

The technicians, now pale beneath the gleaming sweat on their faces, nodded. Staying out of reach of Li's hands, they moved to either side of the torpedo and slid the hatch forward. Li's hands stuck up in the gap, a last, frantic attempt to prevent it from clicking shut. The technicians paused with the hatch almost closed, prevented from shutting further by Li's hands.

The master sighed. He picked up a spanner wrench and walked to the side of the torpedo. Li's hands were now groping frantically around the outside of the torpedo that he now could not see, and the master brought the spanner wrench down sharply on the backs of the hands.

By reflex, Li snatched his hands back from the gap.

Moving as a well-trained team, the technicians slammed the hatch shut.

Satisfied, the master stepped back. He shifted his gaze to the remaining pilots assembled on the catwalk next to the cradle. "He may still yet redeem himself." With a nod, he directed the technicians to continue.

The torpedo slid back into the water and the cradle arms were retracted. Li's screams were now muffled by the thick canopy that encased him, but still clearly audible over the pounding of the machinery. Even after the watertight doors slid over the exposed torpedo well deck, T'sing Lin thought he could still hear his friend screaming. A minute later, the sound ceased completely as the well deck flooded and the torpedo was deployed.

As they walked back up to their compartment, silent and shaking, T'sing Lin could not help dwelling on Li's last moments. Would he find a new reservoir of courage inside himself somewhere to complete the mission? Or would he lose his last fragile grip on sanity and sink screaming into the water, to lie amid the muck and the goo on the ocean floor, never deploying his engine, until his air expired.

Or—a radical thought struck Lin, one that he would never have dared contemplate before. There was another way—one other way. No, it would not result in life, but it would make one's death seem avenged.

If Li could regain enough of his sanity to keep his bearings, he might be able to redirect the torpedo around off its programmed course and back towards the *Lotus Glory.*

Would he do it? Would T'sing Lin himself do it? Would he forgo the assurance of heaven and glory for completing his mission as assigned in exchange for the personal vengeance of destroying the man who had sent him to that death?

T'sing Lin felt the heat rise in his cheeks, and was terribly afraid that he knew which one he would choose.

HALLELUJAH CHORUS

Carl felt the noise radiating up through the steel deck
before he ever heard it. It was not worrisome at first,
just a dull thud followed by an odd change in the vibration patterns of his machinery. He frowned, propped
himself on his elbows, wondering if he should go back
down into the Engineering hold to investigate it. No,
there was an Engineering Officer on duty—if he needed
Carl, he knew where to find him. And that wouldn't be
unless there was something particularly dirty and nox-
ious to do.

He had just decided to lie back down when the first
violent explosion ripped through the ship. The deck
shuddered below his feet, then gave a violent jounce
upward. The motion catapulted Carl off his warm blanket, away from his dreams of Miami, and onto the rough,
gray-painted nonskid that coated the weather decks. Carl
landed on his right shoulder, felt the rough surface rip
away layers of skin, then hit his head. He felt skin grate
off his right cheekbone, then the sudden, sickening feel
of a metal file running across the exposed bone. He
screamed, his vision of a perfect tan vanishing.

The ship continued to rock violently from side to side,
tossing him back and forth across the nonskid repeatedly. Carl scrambled for a purchase on something, anything, finally snagging a small loop of metal embedded
in the deck and intended for tie-down chains. He curled
his hands around it, and hung on for dear life as the
motion continued.

The violent rocking damped out, to be replaced by a
far more ominous sensation. *Chorus* was listing, and
quite badly. He estimated the slant on deck to be at least
twenty degrees, far too radical a tilt for the merchant
ship under any circumstances except a hurricane.

When he was sure the motion had stopped, Carl
scrambled to his feet and started aft towards the pilot

house and Engineering spaces. He had just reached the pilot house when the ship heaved itself up under his feet, and tossed him toward the starboard railing. Carl screamed, made a frantic grab for a winch located near the railing, and missed. He rolled, tumbling, as the ship shook herself like a wet dog. Finally, he fetched up against the safety railing. His hands clamped around a stanchion. His body slipped under the line, and he dangled free in the space down the side of the giant ship.

His injured shoulder was hurting now, becoming increasingly weak and shaky. Loss of blood, one part of his mind noted dispassionately. It was pulsing out of his shoulder faster now, running in itching, ominous rivulets down his side and back. He tried to focus, tried to clamp his hands around the stanchion as though they were cement. But blood coated his right hand and was spreading to his left. The ship continued to buck, throwing him against the steel hull, then swinging him back up in the air. If he let loose now, he'd never be found. There was no chance that a damage-control party fighting whatever catastrophe had occurred would have any time to spare for thoughts of their missing wiper.

Finally, gravity and friction conspired to overcome his will. His hands slipped free of the stanchion just as the ship took a deep dip to port. The motion catapulted him off the railing as he lost his grip and plunged into the waiting sea.

Warm, black water closed over his head as he plummeted beneath the surface. The surface seemed so very far away, as though the bright sun that had warmed him only minutes earlier had receded another million miles from the earth. Sheer survival instinct took over, and he clawed his way frantically through the roiling water to the surface.

His head broke the waves, and he sucked down a deep gasp of air. His right arm was completely useless, dangling limply at his side. With one hand, and both legs, he treaded water, screaming, hoping someone on board would hear him.

The water was full of sound now, violent explosions beneath the waterline of the ship radiating into the ocean. It was like being next to a destroyer with her sonar operating at full power, a painful, harsh, vibration that sank into the skin and settled in the bones. He could feel it gnawing at him as though it would separate muscle from bone and skin from body.

Chorus was barely moving now, slipping past him with a forward motion that seemed to be composed entirely of her momentum. He watched her pass, her sides rising ninety feet up out of the water to the flat weather deck he'd stretched out on so recently. She was drifting closer now, and a new danger occurred to him. Instead of treading water now, he devoted his efforts to putting as much distance between the ship and himself as he could.

He could hear it now, the danger he'd just remembered. It was a slow, sucking sound, the noise of the sea chest pulling in water from the ocean for cooling and saltwater firefighting. A fire—the saltwater pumps would be operating at maximum speed as they sought frantically to extinguish the flames in Engineering. He paddled harder, desperately aware of how slow his pace was with only one arm.

Finally, he felt it. At first, a gentle tug that ruffled the swimming trunks he wore, then an insistent pull. He fought against it, swearing and screaming, praying that he could remain far enough away from the ship until the dangerous seawater-chest suction had passed. He dared not even risk a glance back at the ship to see whether or not he was succeeding.

His foot touched metal. The side of the ship—he shoved violently away from it, trying to pull himself aft and toward the now slowly windmilling propellers. His other foot touched, and he was aware of just how much strength he'd lost in the last three minutes.

The force pulled him down, sucking his head under the water, taking the sun away.

The seawater chest was equipped with a grate that kept kelp, fish, and the other flotsam and jetsam of the ocean out of the intricate maze of saltwater piping and strainers. It kept Carl Timmons out too. He died plastered against the grating, its wire mesh marking his face.

27

GULF OF PANAMA:
6 OCTOBER

Bailey glared at the ship's radioman. "What do you mean you can't get through? That line is never busy."

The offending technician held a new modular patch cord in his hands, and glanced from his crypto gear to the officer standing in front of him. "Like I said, Commander. A busy signal."

"Not possible. Try realigning the satellite—"

"Ahem." The noise cut into the middle of Bailey's instructions to the radioman. Bailey turned to find Collins staring at her coldly.

Bailey suddenly realized what she'd been about to do. This was not her ship—she had no business giving equipment-alignment instructions to the radioman. Politely, gently, but firmly, Collins had reminded her of that fact.

"XO, what would you suggest?" Bailey said immediately. "I've had some experience with satellite communications with my own gear, but of course each setup is different."

"I believe you were about to make a practical suggestion, Commander," Collins said formally. It was an unexpectedly gracious statement on Collins's part, since sparks had been flying between the two women ever since Bailey and Carlisle had touched down. "Go ahead and try a realignment," she said to the radioman.

He nodded. "I will, but it won't help. It's a busy signal, not a satellite-alignment problem."

Five minutes later, the technician proved the truth of his statement. The unmistakable tones of a telephone busy signal came out of the overhead speaker.

"I don't understand." Bailey stared up at the speaker as if she could force it to reveal its secrets. "That particular line—" She broke off, glanced over at Carlisle. He shook his head.

"Maybe you could try a little later, Commander," Collins said.

The insistent gonging of the General Quarters alarm cut through whatever Collins had intended to say next. The women looked at each other by reflex, transported immediately back to the last time they'd both been on the same ship with a General Quarters alarm sounding. Without a word, Collins turned and ran for the bridge.

Bailey turned to Carlisle. "You stay here—keep trying to get through. As their circumstances allow," she added, glancing at the radioman, who was quickly donning his nuclear, biological, and chemical gear. "I'll be in Combat."

Bailey stepped into Combat just in time to see Captain Renninger settle into his chair. He glanced up at her as she walked over, but immediately shifted his attention back to the large-screen display. Without interrupting his concentration, she took up a station at his side.

The large-screen display told the entire story, coupled with a small camera mounted on the mast that relayed pictures back to a TV screen in Combat.

The jagged symbol representing a torpedo snaked its way across the screen with its track terminating on another symbol—the one for friendly merchant traffic.

As sailors pounded in and out of the compartment, she took a look at the TV screen. On it, a massive tanker listed badly in the sea, black smoke fouling the air around it. Its deck was canted precariously. The water around it shone with an unnaturally green oily glare. She walked back towards Sonar, intending to get a first-hand look at the weapon that had caused the damage. A sailor shoved an extra set of flash gear and an NBC mask at her.

Inside Sonar, the watch team was a flurry of activity. The bold, ominous spiral of the torpedo cut across the passive acoustics screen, ending four minutes earlier. Now the sonar supervisor coordinated a new search pattern. The bell-like tones of the active sonar radiated into the compartment from the water around them.

Four hours later, the United States' intent was clear. A message was issued to all merchant traffic in the area offering protection from the attacks in the vicinity of the Panama Canal. Those wishing to participate should steam north immediately, to rendezvous with the battle group that was en route to the Canal Zone. Once in visual contact with each another, the carrier would direct the ships into a convoy formation, in an evolution not practiced on such a massive scale since World War II. Ringed with destroyers, cruisers, and a protective air umbrella, the merchant ships would be safe.

Forty-three waiting tankers, oilers, and mass cargo ships took advantage of the United States' offer. Among them was the *Lotus Glory*.

The response from the Panamanian government was not long in coming.

MIUW 106

"I don't like the way this is looking." Lieutenant Boston dropped the night-vision goggles and passed them

to Sergeant Elwell. ''That crowd doesn't look like a wel-
coming committee.''

Elwell took the glasses, raised them to his eyes, and
studied the group of people assembled two miles away
at the base of the pier. The lieutenant was right—he
upped his estimation of the other man's capabilities
slightly. Detecting the subtle signs of problems before
they became realities was the hallmark of any good warrior.

No, there was nothing particularly overtly menacing
about this crowd. It looked, in fact, like a group of dockworkers getting off of their normal shift, stopping at the
end of the pier through mere chance. It would have been
easy to dismiss the assembly as little more than a group
of chance encounters, the kind of coincidence that often
appears in large groups of people.

But there was something more here, something that
Elwell himself couldn't have immediately defined. It
was in the way the people moved, the eddies and currents of their flow from group to group. There was no
sign of weapons—not yet. But there didn't have to be
for him to sense that something was seriously wrong at
the foot of the pier.

He passed the glasses back to Boston. ''Give these to
one of your lookouts—they'll need them.''

''I'm open to suggestions, Sergeant.''

Elwell waited for a moment before answering, assessing exactly how much confidence he should place in
Lieutenant Boston's understanding of the situation. The
remark he'd made while looking through the night-
vision goggles decided him—it would be easier, at any
rate, if they were all operating with the same understanding.

''We're going to have problems.'' He stopped for a
moment and assessed the lieutenant's reaction. Concern,
some degree of annoyance—no fear. He nodded. That
would come later. ''We need to set up some defensive

positions. You remember the stuff we talked about the other night?''

The lieutenant nodded. ''Barricades.''

''Exactly. Now comes the delicate part. If we wait until we really need it, it will be too late. We won't be able to get down pier to the gantries, drag them back into position, then topple them over. They'll have firearms by then, maybe those snipers we ran into earlier.''

''So we do it now.''

Elwell shrugged. ''Then on the other hand, if our suspicions are incorrect, we may push them into acting when they hadn't really planned to.'' He gestured towards the mob assembled two miles away. ''Groups of people—it's hard to tell sometimes what they'll actually do. This whole thing might blow over. Port authorities might appear shortly and disperse them. But they see us hauling off their equipment, tipping it over, and tearing it apart, we may instigate the very thing we're trying to prevent. So there are no guarantees on this, Lieutenant. None at all.''

''If we build the barricade, how long can we hold them off?''

''How much ammunition have you got?''

Lieutenant Boston thought for a moment, then said, ''I'd have to check with the bosun's mate to make sure, but we should have about sixty rounds for the shotguns. Maybe two hundred for the .45's.''

Elwell winced slightly. ''Not a whole lot of firepower.''

''We're not supposed to need it.'' Boston's voice was impatient. ''This is an MIUW unit, not a combat unit. We're geared up for self-protection—we should be able to handle a small-team assault, but nothing any bigger than that. That's why the SEALs are supposed to be here.''

''SEALs aren't much on defending fixed positions either. What we really need is a platoon of Marines or

Army grunts. Well, that can't be helped. We'll make do with what we have."

"So how long?" Boston repeated.

"That depends, Lieutenant," Elwell said carefully. It was important that they go down this track, but equally important that he not destroy the lieutenant's confidence. "That's not a lot of ammunition. Still, it will buy us some time, depending on how big a force they attack with. If they attack."

Elwell let that sink in for a moment, then continued. "What we really need is a way out of here. I wish I could believe otherwise, but I think we are ultimately going to get overrun. Whether we run out of ammo, they come in by the sea, or they simply break through the barricades, we can't stay here forever. Not against a determined attack."

Lieutenant Boston looked stunned. Elwell could tell that this was far out of his range of experience within the Navy. "We can't leave by the pier. That's obvious."

Elwell nodded. "Not unless the Panamanian police show up and give us an armed escort. I don't think that's going to happen—I thought I saw a couple of official-looking cars parked at the edge of that group. My guess is the government's going to let a group of rowdies and terrorists make a political statement for them, then disavow all responsibility for it."

Boston turned and looked out toward the ocean. The night sky was clear, and stars spattered across the heavens like paint. The ocean was so smooth and calm, they could see the reflection of the stars momentarily before the surface of the ocean rippled into gentle waves. There was a quarter moon—eighteen-percent illumination, Elwell remembered from his infantry days.

"We'll have to go out by sea," Boston said. He turned back to Elwell. "And the van—it will have to be destroyed before we leave. We can burn the classified material, destroy most of the equipment with a sledgehammer. That's why we have one in there, after all."

Elwell was grimly pleased to note that the lieutenant looked shaken but determined. The young officer's pale face caught the moonlight, which gave it a smooth, young look. It was always like this when they went into their first engagement—a mixture of fear and bravado that would either carry the men through or lead them to disaster.

"I suggest we start now," Elwell said finally. "Give it a couple of hours, work out a plan, and as soon as the moon sets we start hauling gear down here."

"They'll see us, won't they?"

Elwell nodded. "Hear us too. That shit's going to be a bitch to move. And no doubt they have night-vision goggles themselves."

"At least the darkness will give us a little bit of cover," Boston said. He stood up, brushing the grime from the pier off his pants. "I'd better go get on the radio circuit—we need to work something out with *Jouett*. She's the only friendly asset within immediate reach."

Elwell stood as well, heard his knees complain at the sudden movement. "There's one thing we haven't discussed, Lieutenant. I sort of hate to bring this up, seeing as it's another Navy unit—the SEALs."

Boston nodded. "Whose side are they on, you mean."

Elwell nodded. "Exactly. At this point, I don't think we can afford to make any assumptions."

Boston stared at him, his face a pale mask of determination. "Until the captain returns, the responsibility for this unit is mine. I'm not relying on them or anyone else."

"I'll stay here a bit, keep an eye on the crowd down there," Elwell offered. "Go ahead and make your arrangements, sir. The sooner the better. In two hours, we move."

As Elwell watched the young lieutenant walk back towards the van, the question of the SEAL platoon kept hammering in his brain. Why had they kept the young petty officer after the RHIB accident? What were they after?

And more importantly, where did their loyalties lie?

USS JOUETT

Bailey glared at the tall, beefy Navy Captain. "I have to get back to my unit. You heard what he said."

Renninger shook his head. "Not on my helo. Nor in my boats."

"What am I supposed to do—swim?"

"Frankly, I don't care what you do. As long as it doesn't involve endangering my ship or my helo." Renninger turned away from her and back towards the tactical display. Bailey moved around to the other side of his console to confront him.

"We're going to need to evacuate them—that at least ought to be clear. The motor whaleboat, maybe one of your launches—"

Renninger interrupted her. "As I said—I'm not going to do it. There's a SEAL team assigned for defense of your unit. Let them deal with the problem."

"You'd leave my unit there to die?"

Renninger turned towards her and fixed her with a steely glare. "This discussion is ended."

"It's not. Don't you understand that—"

Collins stepped forward, interposing her body between the two larger officers. She turned to face Bailey. "I believe the Captain said he was through discussing this," she said calmly.

Bailey reached out as though to shove her away. Collins caught her hand. "I wouldn't try that," Collins said quietly. "Not on my ship, Commander."

Bailey pulled back, and was suddenly aware of the spectacle that they presented to the rest of the crew. Collins was right—*Jouett* was their ship, not hers. Had she made any aggressive move toward the Executive Officer or the Commanding Officer, she would have immediately found herself buried under a pile of sailors. This wasn't her unit—these weren't her people.

Bailey took a step back and let her arms fall to her side. "I apologize, sir," she said, directing her comments to the Captain. "No disrespect was intended. I am simply concerned about the safety of my people. As you would be under the same circumstances."

"As I said, this discussion is concluded." Renninger turned his attention back to the tactical display. On the screen, a flurry of merchant ships had suddenly gotten under way and were headed north, the American battle group still well north of them, but steaming south at twenty-five knots. According to Combat's calculations, the two groups should meet up in about eighteen hours.

"I need to talk to my people, at least," Bailey said finally, aware that the fate of her unit was only one small part of the problem that Renninger was trying to manage. She could see his point—didn't agree, but saw it. "At least let them know what's going on."

Renninger motioned roughly to Collins. The Executive Officer said, "Of course. Secure tactical circuit is yours."

As Bailey headed back toward Radio to use the circuit, she felt her anxiety grow. Her people were stranded ashore, supposedly in the care of a unit that she deeply distrusted. Murphy and his SEALs—of what use had they been so far? None, as far as she could tell. But surely they understood the obligation imposed on them to protect the MIUW unit. And they would understand about the evacuation. Hell, practicing the evacuation of civilian populations was something that they trained in every month.

But these weren't civilians, were they? They were sailors who had been chosen to go into harm's way, who'd been stationed on the end of the pier by SouthCom and left in position even after the unexpected

attacks began. There must be some plan for their evacuation—there must be.

PIER 36

The SEAL observer shifted his position slightly, trying
to avoid a rock that seemed determined to remain immediately under his right knee. He focused the night-
vision goggles in, trying to make some sense of the
pattern of movement he saw down below. Five miles
away, the MIUW pier was a flurry of activity. Panamanians were still massed at the foot of it, while MIUW
sailors were nowhere in sight. He'd seen them go into
the command tent an hour earlier. As yet, none had
emerged except for a few security patrols.

Finally, some movement. A few MIUW sailors
stepped out of the tent, followed shortly thereafter by
the rest of them. The SEAL watched as they broke into
smaller teams and approached the camouflage netting
barrier that separated their camp from the rest of the pier.
The sailors pulled the netting off one truck, and even at
this distance the SEAL could hear the harsh hammering
of the two-and-a-half-ton truck's diesel engine turning
over. Six sailors piled into the back of it. The truck
jerked uneasily back from its blocking location, and
headed down the pier towards the Panamanians.

The SEAL shifted his gaze towards the civilians. They
appeared as puzzled as he was, but were maintaining
their position. A few minutes later, the truck pulled up
to one of the steel gantries that edged the pier. The truck
pulled in front of it, placing its bulk between the observer, the crowd, and the gantry. A few minutes later,
the truck pulled out again. The gantry jerked, wobbled,
then fell obediently in tow behind the truck.

The truck hauled it down the pier, stopping just a few
feet in front of the current barricade. It left the gantry
there, and repeated the entire evolution with another one.

Finally, after four of the massive structures had been hauled down to the MIUW position, the truck slid back into position. The MIUW sailors carefully redraped the camouflage netting before proceeding back out to the gantries.

The SEAL watched as one by one the frameworks of metal struts and gratings were toppled and shoved into place. In the end, they formed an eight-foot-high barrier immediately in front of the trucks. The sailors then produced additional camouflage netting and strung it over them.

Finally satisfied that he understood what they were doing, the SEAL radioed in and described their activities. He concluded with, "It won't stop bullets. Not for long."

Three miles away, from a considerably closer vantage point, the Chinese watched from the end of their own pier. Their assessment was much the same as that of the SEALs. The gantry barricade might provide a brief delaying action against an assault, but in the end it offered little protection.

28

PIER 36:
6 OCTOBER

MIUW 106

Master Sergeant Elwell walked the perimeter of the camp, noting the well-placed positions of the gantries. It wouldn't hold off a determined attacker—then again, nothing much would. But in the game they were playing, buying a little bit of additional time might make all the difference in the world.

"Sergeant?" Elwell turned and saw Boston walking up towards him, his face pale and gleaming in the moonlight. "We may have more problems than we thought."

Elwell frowned. "More forces gathering down at the end of the pier?"

Boston shook his head. "No, this is something we know a little bit more about." He tried for a wry laugh, which didn't quite come off. "The submarine contact we were holding earlier—it's back."

USS JOUETT

"You were the one who was so opposed to any interaction between NSA and your military duties," Atchinson pointed out, his voice even more emotionless and
pedantic than normal over the Top Secret circuit. "And
now you seem ready to reverse that position, yes?"

Bailey seethed, wondering whether Atchinson could
really understand the reality of what her unit was facing.
"They're cut off, surrounded, and I've got no way to
get to them," she said again. "Jim, I'm not asking for
much—just find out what the hell's going on with those
SEALs. Surely NSA can do at least that."

"I don't know," Atchinson said, his voice musing.
"After all, it might be viewed as entirely inappropriate."

"Inappropriate is letting my sailors get killed when
there's something you can do about it," Bailey said
harshly. "You people owe me, Jim—you've already
screwed around with me by sending me down here to
start with. I know you were behind it, no matter that
Terry signed the orders. I can recognize your hands at
work. It's the stink, I think—a sort of unhealthy odor
that arises from anything you touch."

"No need to get personal," Atchinson said. "And if
that's how you feel about it, I'm even less inclined to
pass on your request to Terry."

Terry, Bailey thought, her heart sinking. Since when
had Intanglio become Terry to that asshole?

"Just tell him," Bailey said desperately. "That's all,
Jim—just tell him."

"Terry Intanglio is a very busy man," Atchinson said.
"I'll think about it."

As Bailey replaced the microphone in the holder, she
heard a small noise behind her. She turned to find Collins standing in the door. "I hope you enjoyed that,"
Bailey said.

Collins shook her head. "I need to talk to you. In
private."

"Why? There's only one thing that you have to say of interest to me, and that's a plan for getting my sailors off that pier. Or in the alternative, getting me back to them. Anything other than that is just—"

"In your stateroom, Commander." Collins's voice was firm and unmistakably determined.

Bailey paused to consider the smaller officer. There was something new in her demeanor, something she hadn't seen since Germany. Intrigued in spite of her growing anger, Bailey finally nodded. "All right. In my stateroom." She glanced back at the radio crew. "If your Executive Officer has no objection, I would appreciate it if you'd leave this circuit open for further traffic."

"Do it," Collins ordered immediately. She stepped back from the doorway, and allowed Bailey to precede her down the passageway.

"There's something else going on here," Collins said bluntly. "It started with the airbus."

"You shot it down—what's the mystery?" Bailey said.

"I should hope I shot it down," Collins retorted. "I was aiming at it."

"So what's the problem? Other than precipitating an international incident, I don't know what else you expected."

Collins was silent for a moment. Her feet, Bailey noted, barely reached the floor as she sat in the chair. She'd noticed Collins was short, but never realized exactly how short.

"I've been through every tape a thousand times," Collins said finally. "There was every justification for shooting down that contact—no question about it."

"So?" Bailey asked.

"So this is the question," Collins said. "Who set me up? And why?"

"What makes you so sure it was a setup?"

"What else could it be?" Collins shot back. "Sure, I know it sounds crazy, but that's actually the most logical explanation I can come up with. There was a reason I got that radar paint, a reason I held those contacts. And you've seen it happen since then—these ghost contacts aren't like anything else I've ever seen. They come across on the radar looking exactly like hostile contacts, and then vanish. You can't tell me this is accidental. And I know it's not an equipment malfunction on our end." She shook her head vigorously as she saw the look of doubt on Bailey's face. "No—it's not. I've been through every tracking algorithm, every piece of gear connected to the Aegis system. We've run every test possible, and it's just not reasonable. The problem's not on the ship— it's out there."

"Out there? What, there's a bogeyman?"

Collins kept shaking her head. "Somebody else is behind this, Jerusha," she said.

The unexpected use of her first name made Bailey pause. She'd never known the other officer to be anything except completely competent when it came to tactical acumen. And, it was true, she'd given Bailey little reason to suspect otherwise. "What makes you so certain someone's out to get you?" Bailey asked finally. "Maybe you just made a mistake."

"I made a mistake—but it was the one I was supposed to make." Collins's voice was firm, convinced.

In spite of herself, Bailey began to have doubts. Was it possible? Could there have been an operational electronic deception of some sort executed against *Jouett*?

"I thought your ESM gear was supposed to prevent this sort of thing."

"It does—to a certain extent. But we've never had anyone sophisticated enough to execute an operation against us. Not like this. All I want you to do is to bring it up to NSA the next time you talk to them." Collins smiled slightly as she saw the look on Bailey's face. "Don't play coy with me—I know you've been talking to them."

"And what about my unit?" Bailey asked. "Your Captain's going to leave them on the end of the pier to die."

To her horror, she felt her voice start to catch and break. She stifled down the emotions, grimly determined to show no sign of weakness in front of the one woman whose help she needed.

"I'll be talking to the Captain," Collins said calmly. "I'm not promising anything—hell, I haven't been on the best of terms with him myself." She laughed, a harsh, bitter sound. "You can guess how excited he was to have me ordered in as his Executive Officer."

Bailey nodded. "I can see it hasn't been easy for you."

"Well, no use crying over spilt milk. Or downed airbuses." Collins's smile turned bitter. "It's just that this time, I don't intend to be used as the whipping boy. Someone's out to get me, Jerusha—and I want to know why."

MIUW 106

"Problems, Lieutenant." The lookout's voice was slightly unsteady. "There's a group of people coming down towards us from the end of the pier."

Boston and Elwell bolted up from their seats within the command tent, where they'd been downing a couple of MREs. "How many?" Boston asked into the radio.

"Ten. They're carrying cartons, sir. No guns that I can see."

Boston looked at Elwell. "It may be starting now."

Elwell looked doubtful. "No guns, only ten men—I don't think so, sir. They'd come at us in force with some armored vehicles, I suspect. Maybe an earlier softening up with mortars or something.''

Boston looked pale. ''Mortars. I hadn't even thought—''

''Sort of small for mortars unless they've got the Czech ones. Look, we need to get out there, Lieutenant,'' Elwell said, gently breaking into Boston's train of thought, ''try to get some idea of what they're doing. While I don't think this is an attack, you'd better mobilize that security-alert team of yours.''

Boston nodded. ''Covert, since they're not outwardly taking aggressive action.''

''That's right. Now you're thinking,'' Elwell said approvingly, as much to bolster the lieutenant's spirits as any real evaluation of his tactics. It was the right thing to do, however.

Boston spoke quietly into the radio as they walked out of the tent. Sailors tumbled out of racks, grabbed arms, and made their way to their assigned positions around them, moving quietly through the darkened shadows of the night. All the camp lights had been secured, with the idea of minimizing the target profile they would present to any enemy.

''Use your cover.'' Elwell demonstrated, moving from the shadow of one truck to the next as they made their way forward. ''No point in giving them a free shot.''

Boston followed him, his unease mounting steadily. ''We don't know how to do this,'' he said as they approached the lookout. ''Dammit, Sergeant, we—''

Elwell turned and grabbed him by the arm just above the elbow. He pulled the lieutenant to a sudden halt and spun him around to face him. ''Cut it out, sir. Right now.'' He gestured at the camp around him. ''Right now we've got them believing that there's something they can do about this. You can't let anything shake their confidence right now—not now. Regardless of the tactical realities, they're all looking to you to see how they

ought to feel about this. If they see you uncertain—
substitute the word frightened for that if you want, sir,
and they'd be damned accurate—they'll lose confidence
in themselves. It won't make it any easier."

Boston took a deep breath, let it out slowly. "You're
right. Thanks, Sergeant."

They proceeded slowly toward the lookout, Boston
moving quietly now. They approached the lookout's
concealed position. Elwell held a quick, hurried conversation with him, and came down from the top of the
truck with a pair of night-vision goggles.

"Let's see what they're up to."

He focused in, and saw the bright blobs moving in
the greenish darkness of the night-vision goggles. Ten,
that was right—and he didn't see any sign of weapons
either. Not unless you counted the crates that each two-
man team was lugging.

The intruders came to a halt approximately one quarter of a mile from the MIUW. They set down their
crates, popped open the tops with crowbars. As the first
one took an object out of the crate, the veteran sergeant's
blood went cold.

"Claymores," he said. "Or whatever local variety
they're using—but probably our own claymores."

"Mines?" Boston looked momentarily confused.
"But what do they—oh."

Elwell nodded. "If you were still harboring any
thoughts about getting out of here in those deuce-and-a-
halves of yours, I think the Panamanians just put paid
to that notion."

"Lieutenant, if you've got a moment, we need you in
the van." The watch chief's voice was low and urgent.
"It's that submarine."

"Not now, Chief," Boston said quietly.

"Well, we've got problems back here too," the chief
said. "That submarine—it's been trolling back and forth
along the approaches to the Canal. We keep hearing torpedo tubes opening, some massive air bubble noise, then

nothing. It's like a torpedo launch—only there ain't any torpedo. You know what that means."

"More mines," Boston said. The energy and determination seemed to drain out of him. He turned to the sergeant. "I think our chances of leaving by sea just disappeared as well."

29

PANAMA CITY:
7 OCTOBER

PANAMANIAN PRESIDENTIAL PALACE

Won Su studied the intricate rococo carvings that adorned the ceiling of the Presidential Palace. The gold, the intricacy, the sheer excess of it all made him slightly nauseous. Was there any way to understand a people who viewed such architecture as desirable? He suppressed the expression of distaste.

"The President will see you now, sir," one of Aguillar's multiple aides said.

Won Su ignored the quiet insolence of the man, suddenly weary of the demands of his profession. He'd been away from home so long, gone from the peace and tranquility that characterized his estates in China. His spirit longed for them, and every day he felt more unclean, contaminated by the excesses of this hot, filthy, and uncivilized nation.

Yet how much choice did he have? How much choice did any of them have?

He pondered the question as he rose from the gilded chair and paced slowly across to the massive ornate doors that opened into the President's official offices.

He must remember that—even if Aguillar did not yet realize it—political power was a fleeting thing in the affairs of humans. It had come, brought on unexpectedly and suddenly by the death of his predecessor, and it could vanish just as quickly as the morning mist in sunshine. That brought on another pang as he remembered the morning fog that filled his gardens at home, melting away as the sun rose upon it like gossamer.

As he entered, the President rose to greet him. They exchanged pleasantries for a few moments, Won Su carefully adding some appreciative comments on the President's recent redecoration of the palace. He stroked and flattered subtly, never once approaching the line over which the President might find him insincere. If there were indeed such a line—he suspected not. Aguillar appeared more than ready to believe any flattery, any approving comment from any source.

"I hesitate to bring the matter to your attention, but my superiors feel that I must." Won Su let the words sink in for a few moments before continuing. "The Americans—they continue to pose a problem here, both for your country and for mine."

Aguillar shook his head and sighed. "Most especially for us. It is not only the transit fees through the Canal, you understand. The revenue that the ships bring in is even more considerable than that. Dockworkers, provisioners—all of those businesses depend as well on a steady flow of traffic. Without the ships, we suffer." He sighed heavily. "And who knows when the Americans will allow them to transit again."

Won Su shook his head gravely. "Such a misuse of power—such a raw exercise of military force," he murmured consolingly. "I have no wish to add to your burdens, but there is another factor that you must consider as well. Again, the Americans." Won Su made a dismissing gesture with his hand. "Of course, I have no doubt that you already know these facts. I explained to my superiors the excellent workings of your intelligence service, the eagerness of every Panamanian citizen to participate in your regime, but they do not truly understand Panama. Not the way I do, after having been stationed here for so long." He eyed Aguillar gravely, assessing whether or not the President was buying it at all. "We have become such good friends, Panama and China. And you and I as well, I would hope."

"Of course." Aguilar nodded vigorously. "Let no man ever doubt the deep and true ties between China and Panama. There is so much in common—and the experience you have shared with us on the turnover of Hong Kong from the British has been most helpful. Most helpful indeed." Aguilar scowled briefly, as though remembering something distasteful. "The Canal should have been ours for decades. To ever allow American domination on our soil was a travesty."

Won Su nodded. "Of course, this we understand. Our experience has been with the British—and the British, of course, are the predecessors of the Americans. Can it be any wonder that the similarities between the nations are so great? Or that the problems of those who have dealt with them in good faith in the past are so severe? I think not."

"You mentioned some intelligence," Aguillar said.

Won Su smiled. Of course the Panamanian President would come back to the point eventually.

"As I said, it is no doubt something of which you are already aware. Indeed I must admit that I'm somewhat puzzled that you have not shared the information with me so far. After all, it affects our leasehold on the docks as well. But the mines—Mr. President, how could you not allow us to participate in resolving this matter?"

"The mines?" Aguillar looked surprised, then quickly smoothed his face over into a neutral expression. "There are questions of national security, of course," he said uncertainly, his voice betraying what his face did not.

"The mines." For a moment, Won Su was tempted
to let Aguillar twist a bit, let him try to guess what it
was that the Chinese knew about mines that he himself
did not. In the end, however, embarrassing the President
would only make his job more difficult. "My people
would consider it an honor if you would allow us to
assist you in clearing the mines," Won Su continued
smoothly. "I doubted the reports when I received them
myself, as you must have. The sheer audacity of it all,
to conduct minelaying operations on the approaches to
the Canal. But my sources say that you are absolutely
certain this is what has occurred—that the Americans
have mined the entire harbor with command-activated
devices in order to control the source of your livelihood.
As you have said, the Canal is a significant asset—a
national treasure, if you will."

Aguillar's face was tight and closed. "We should
share information more often," he agreed. "Perhaps you
could share with me everything that you know about
this. I may be able to correct some misunderstandings,
perhaps add a depth of detail. Naturally, my military
officials will wish to coordinate with yours as well. Your
assistance would be most welcome." He eyed the Chinese minister, evidently confident that he had outbluffed
the inscrutable Won Su for once.

"Of course. According to our sources, the Americans
commenced minelaying operations inside Panama Bay
eight hours ago. Two submarines, working together,
transiting the entire line along the approaches to the
Canal. It is our understanding that control of these mines
has been transferred to the American destroyer just outside the twelve-mile limit—the USS *Jouett*. Of course,
your information is undoubtedly better than mine." Won
Su shrugged. "One must depend on sources, and they
are fragile sometimes."

Aguillar was almost beside himself with rage. His face
was red, and his breath was coming in short gasps. Small
beads of perspiration popped out on his forehead. "Min-

ing our harbor? Of course we knew the operations were afoot. Of course we did.'' Aguillar stood suddenly and motioned to an aide. ''Have the Minister of Defense join us immediately.''

Won Su held up one hand. ''Of course, if you think that is necessary . . .''

Aguillar looked uncertain. ''But what else—?''

Won Su sighed, interrupting the Panamanian President. ''Military problems demand military solutions. But this is indeed a problem of a far greater magnitude, is it not? Of course, if you wish to approach it as solely a military operation, then we would not question your decision. However, it might be to your advantage to turn this into a more powerful expression of Panamanian national will. You understand, of course.''

With a sharp gesture, Aguillar dismissed his aide. ''Matters such as this are best discussed in private,'' he confided as he watched the heavy door close behind the aide. ''Let us speak frankly, my friend.''

''Of course.'' Won Su took a deep breath and ran through his plan quickly in his mind again. How much would the old fool buy? Most of it—all of it, most probably. And for good reason. The plan had been carefully devised by master Chinese strategists to play carefully upon the fears and weaknesses of Aguillar. Two experts had spent decades studying the man, watching his rise to power, assessing his every character flaw. In a nation of almost two billion people, there were many experts hungry for just such projects. ''They have not yet acknowledged your assumption of office, have they?'' he said delicately. ''The United Nations—''

''No, they have not.''

''Just so. Nor will they acknowledge Panama's right to absolute control over three hundred miles of the ocean surrounding her coastline. A standard economic enterprise zone, yet the Americans persist in treating it as their own. It must be a daily annoyance to you.''

''It is, it is. You mentioned the destroyer?''

"Yes. Our theory seems sound—in this case at least. Knowing of the friendship between China and Panama, as well as your leadership among the other nations of both Central and South America, the American submarines have no doubt already left the area. That leaves primary control of the minefield vested in the destroyer. Which continues, I might add, to cruise through your waters as though they were her very own. Even after destroying your aircraft, taking your predecessor's life, they remain boldly here as a continual challenge. In short, there can be but one solution. The crux of this matter revolves around that ship."

"It seems so logical," Aguillar murmured, "the way you explain it. . . ."

Won Su nodded, completely aware that Aguillar had taken the bait and swallowed it deep. Now, just set the hook as delicately as he would in any sport fish. "The Panama Canal is yours. It is the symbol of your Administration, as is this conflict. If you do not take a stand this time, the insults will continue. Therefore, it is imperative that you destroy the American ship."

Aguillar's jaw dropped. "Surely you don't mean that—"

"Destroy the ship and you destroy the Americans' ability to activate the minefield. And is it not true that they shot down your airbus without a single thought of warning?"

Aguillar nodded. Now he appeared slightly uncertain. "They claimed that it was an accident—it appeared to be a hostile contact."

"And this is how they deal with nations with whom they desire friendship?" Won Su shook his head sadly.

"I'm not certain we can do it," Aguillar said after a long silence. "Destroy the ship."

The statement took Won Su aback. Nothing in his dealings with Aguillar or in his intelligence reports had suggested that the man was capable of admitting any weakness in his military. This required some additional thought.

"This is what friends are for," Won Su said slowly. "In fact, if you do not allow us to assist, we would be quite hurt." Won Su let a grave expression slip across his face. "Friends do not treat each other this way."

Aguillar nodded slowly. "But an attack on an American ship?"

"They shot first. The tenets of international law are firmly behind you. Mining your harbor is an act of war. I am certain that your military advisors can confirm all of this for you. You have been done a grave injustice, one which we wish to help you to rectify.

"After all, we both want the same thing. Peace."

Won Su sat back in his chair and watched Aguillar swallow the hook.

30

THE PACIFIC OCEAN:
7 OCTOBER

LOTUS GLORY

T'sing Lin sought out the quiet solitude of the ship's massive forward deck. Even with the small crew on board, the pilot house and the living quarters had become too cramped. Not because of the number of people, but because of the lack of sleep for everyone.

Steaming northward with the rest of the gaggle of merchant ships, *Lotus Glory* was far closer to other ships than she ever was likely to be on open ocean. The ship was manned for the solitude of open ocean, not the crowded confines of a convoy. For safety's sake, the master had increased the number of officers on watch on the bridge. He himself had barely slept in the past twenty-four hours. The strain was already beginning to tell. Dark circles ringed the eyes of every crew member, and tempers flared suddenly at the slightest provocation.

The torpedo pilots were faring no better. While they had no underway watch station, the knowledge that they too must shortly execute the mission for which they'd been trained was wearing on them.

Or at least, it was on T'sing Lin. After one last vicious
squabble in their quarters over a bar of soap, he'd left
and sought some peace and quiet on the deck.

Overhead, the evening stars shone brilliantly clear.
This far from land, there was no pollution to obscure
them, and they seemed closer and brighter than they ever
had, even at home. The shapes were vaguely reassuring,
slightly distorted because he was so far from his home,
but recognizable nonetheless. He picked out the constellations he'd learned from his father—the Rat, the
Jeweled Lotus, the Bamboo Field. Comforting, but
somehow disconcerting with their outlines slightly
warped by distance.

How many more times would he be able to do this?
Stand outside and stare up at the stars, remembering the
old stories about the constellations' origins? Stories he'd
hoped to teach his son, along with the other sagas and
myths that made up their history.

T'sing Lin sighed, a deep shuddering sound that broke
loose from somewhere deep inside him. Life was short,
so very short. The awe and exhilaration that he'd felt so
long ago at being chosen for this training program had
long since faded. Now all that was left was worry, fear,
and the dawning realization of what executing his mission would require. While his mind still insisted that he
would bring glory to his family by his acts, some stub-
born remnant of flesh resisted the idea of self-
immolation. To die alone, trapped in the steel tube, his
body ripped apart in a shred of fire and water—he shuddered, his mind skittering away from what would eventually be his fate.

In the last twenty-four hours, he'd finally begun to
see the strain in his compatriots' faces. The impassive,
proud expressions had been gradually replaced by an
odd nervousness, tentativeness, and irritability. They
were not so very different in the end, he realized. Despite the demeanor they presented to the master and the

rest of the crew, none of them wanted to die. Not this way. Not for this war.

North—they were steaming north. As usual, there'd been no explanation from the master, just a muttered oath and an abrupt order to remain out of the way.

"Your time will come soon," the master had snarled when one of T'sing Lin's compatriots had ventured a question about their change of course. "Sooner than you know."

Suddenly, the stars' light dimmed. The hard speckled points of light blurred into vague, glowing orbs. T'sing Lin touched his eyes and felt the tears streaming down his face.

MIUW 106

The Panamanian patrol boat proceeded out from the shore at a slow speed. It headed straight for open ocean, cutting to port only after it drew even with the MIUW. It approached the pier and slowed to bare steerageway. The soldiers and sailors on its deck were armed, obviously alert, but made no threatening gestures towards the American unit.

"What do you suppose they're doing?" Boston asked the sergeant. He pointed at the large drums located aft on the sixty-five-foot craft. "I don't imagine that's fresh water. Though God knows we could use it."

The sergeant studied the oil drums, an uneasy feeling creeping through his stomach. "I don't like the looks of this."

"We can't shoot." Boston's voice was determined. "They haven't made a move towards us."

On the boat, two sailors popped the top off one oil drum and lifted it up to a brace located on the stern. They tipped it into the brace. A thick, sludgy material flowed out, quickly coating the surrounding water with a foul-looking substance. It shimmered and gleamed on top of the water, reflecting back an odd phosphorescence.

"They're trying to keep us from drinking the seawater?" Boston asked. He frowned.

Elwell shook his head. "No," he said slowly as a familiar smell reached his nostrils. It brought back memories of Korea, of days he would much rather have forgotten. "No, not at all. Unless I'm very much mistaken, that's napalm."

Five minutes later, the boat headed back to shore. It had circuited the end of the pier, dumping the contents of ten oil drums over the side. The viscous substance now completely covered the ocean around the MIUW. Without retracing its path, the boat headed to shore on the opposite side of the pier.

Elwell turned to Lieutenant Boston. "I think the odds of getting out of here by sea just got a lot smaller."

USS JOUETT

The bitch box crackled to life with an angry snarl. "Combat, this is Outboard." The technician from the highly classified Signal Exploitation Unit on board the ship sounded worried. "We have launch indications from Panama—they've got twenty fighters on the deck, all nationalities, from the multinational force."

"When?" Renninger asked.

"Can't tell, sir. But it could be any moment."

Renninger shook his head and motioned Collins to come over to him. "I don't like the sound of this. Let's set General Quarters. If they're carrying antiship missiles, we're within their weapons envelope almost as soon as they launch."

Collins nodded. The fighters from the group of Central and South American nations were capable of carrying a full load of antisurface and antiair weapons.

In response, *Eisenhower*, now within comfortable

Carrier Air Patrol range, had anted up a brace of fighters for outer air perimeter defense. The first two had arrived on station just fifteen minutes before, checked in with the ship, and assumed their assigned stations seaward of the ship.

"Let's go to full auto," Renninger added. "Alone out here, if we hit a massed attack from a full group of fighters, we'll never be able to keep up."

The Aegis ship was capable of operating in a fully automatic mode in which the computer on board would independently target, track, and release weapons on up to two hundred incoming targets. In a quick-reaction scenario, it was the only way of doing business.

"There's the first one." Renninger watched as the first hostile symbol tracked away from the coast of Panama. "The rest of the flight will be—there they are, there they are."

The coast of Panama was cluttered with enemy fighter-aircraft symbols. With *Jouett* just outside the twelve-mile limit, the fighters would be within range to release their weapons inside one minute. The target symbols appeared, were quickly tagged with assigned priorities by the Aegis system, and moved steadily toward the ship.

"Missile separation, missile separation," the track supe howled immediately. "Vampire inbound!"

On the screen in front of them, a horde of tiny new tracks separated from the fighter-aircraft symbols. The speed leaders all converged on a single point—their ship.

"Any second now," Renninger murmured. Collins glanced at him. He sounded almost bored. His eyes were fixed on the large-screen display. "We should hear—there it is."

A low rumble filled the compartment, quickly crescendoing to an unbearable scream. The first antiair missile launched, and the large-screen display showed its extended track towards its first target. In short order, the ship independently launched six missiles at incoming targets.

"Where are they coming from?" Collins shouted. She wheeled towards the Electronic Warfare Center. "Dammit, this isn't real—it can't be." On the large-screen display in front of her, twenty-four enemy air targets had just popped into being, all located within six nautical miles of the ship. "There's nothing there—we would have seen them inbound. This isn't happening."

"No jamming, XO," the technician shouted. His fingers were flying over the keys as he struggled to keep up with the changing scenario. "I can't find any source. There's nothing to—fire-control radar lighting us up now."

The noise from the missile bay crescendoed until it was an unbearable cacophony of firepower. Collins wheeled on the Captain. "You have to take us out of auto—those aren't targets. They're ghosts."

"There's no way to tell a ghost from a real target right now," he said tersely. "We can't take the chance of one getting through. One missile, that's all it would take."

"The carrier," Collins said, desperate for some answer. "Where's our combat air?"

The captain stabbed at a button on his console and expanded the range of the screen. The symbols indicating friendly fighter air were just forty miles to the north. "Get 'em down here—now."

Just then, a new voice came in over Tactical. "*Jouett*, this is Black Knight 101, inbound for Carrier Air Patrol," the Tomcat pilot said. "What the hell's going on down there?"

Collins grabbed the mike. "We're holding massive contact on a massive inbound raid. What are you holding on the AWG-9?" she asked, referring to the Tomcat's radar.

"Nothing around you, *Jouett*, except a bunch of missiles you put in the air."

"Get it out of auto," Renninger snapped. "And auto-destruct the missiles."

Collins collapsed in her chair, her hands shaking. What had they done? Launched a large chunk of their antiair inventory at what? Ghosts. That much was clear so far. But where had they come from? And more importantly, who was behind it?

MIUW 106

Sergeant Elwell pulled Lieutenant Boston back behind the shielding bulk of the MIUW van. "Not a good idea, sir. You lose your night vision."

"Holy shit." Boston stared up at the sky overhead. A loud boom, then a brilliant blast of white light. Elwell grabbed him by the collar with one hand and jerked open the heavy steel door to the surveillance van. He shoved Boston inside ahead of him and pulled the door shut.

There was a heavy spatter of noise as debris rained down on the metal trailer. The van rocked slightly from side to side, the generator kicked off-line, and the red emergency battery-operated lights came on. The thin, shrill of warning indicators filled the van.

"What the hell was that?" one technician asked. He turned to look at Boston, his face aghast. "Sir?"

Sergeant Elwell gave Boston a moment to gather his thoughts, then said, "Looks like that cruiser off the coast has been mighty busy, son."

From the little Elwell had seen, the air battle made no sense. There'd been no roiling yellow clouds of aviation gas—indeed not even any sounds of aircraft launching. Just what the hell had the cruiser been shooting at?

"I have to get back out there," Boston said, undogging the door. "We had people in the tents, people around the trucks—Jesus, the casualties."

"Let's take a pair of these, then, sir." Elwell picked up a padded black case, opened it, and extracted a pair of night-vision goggles. He looked thoughtfully at the lieutenant for a moment. ''I'll wear these—might be helpful in finding any casualties.''

Boston nodded, and pushed the hatch open. They moved silently around the MIUW compound, searching for casualties. The well-trained sailors had already assembled in their muster area and were breaking into alert teams. Twice in fifty yards, Elwell and Boston were challenged by men carrying shotguns. One woman, virtually invisible behind a pile of sandbags, drew a bead on them with a .45 before she recognized them.

Ten minutes later, they'd completed their nose count. Miraculously, there were no casualties. The command tent, however, was a complete loss, along with their backup unclassified radio gear.

''Could have been a lot worse,'' Elwell said.

''I suspect it will be before long.'' Boston shot Elwell a telling glance. ''I'd give a lot to know right now what happened out there.''

As he studied the burning wreckage of the command tent, Sergeant Elwell nodded. ''That would make two of us, Lieutenant.''

The small metal fishing boat motored out quietly from the shore to the end of the MIUW pier. The engine noise would carry a long way in the night, so there was little chance that his approach wouldn't be detected. As soon as it cleared the shallow area, it cut underneath the pier and wove its way between the pilings toward the end. It stopped immediately under the end of the pier and the van.

Two men dressed completely in black wetsuits gently guided the boat towards the endmost pier stanchion. Working quickly, quietly, communicating by hand gestures, they affixed large packets of C-4 explosive to the cement pillars. After placing the charge on the fore end supports, they moved back to the center of the pier.

The man in charge motioned to his subordinate. He

picked up a flare gun and aimed it out at the open ocean past the end of the pier. The thick, gooey sludge still floated on the surface.

He fired. The flare arced out, and landed burning on the substance spread there earlier. The brilliant glow of the white phosphorous flare was quickly replaced by a burst of yellow flame.

The motor boat was already turning as it started. It sped back towards the shore, outracing the hungry flames.

The MIUW camp was a chorus of surprised yelps and shouted instructions. While they'd developed contingency plans against almost any form of land attack, including assault up the shaky ladder that led down to the floating dock, almost no one had considered the possibility that the sea would turn into a raging inferno.

No one except Sergeant Elwell. Shouting to be heard over the noise of the flames, he assembled the MIUW crew members. They moved to the center of the pier and away from the end, communicating with the van by radio. The van secured all outside ventilation.

"They can't last in there," Boston said. "Can they?"

Elwell nodded. "Plenty of oxygen in there for a while. This stuff will burn hard for a while, then go out. All it does is destroy our night vision and make the odds of getting out of here by sea less probable."

Boston swore silently. "This is way past what we're trained for. We're supposed to be in a rear support area—with troops, some form of protection." He looked up at Elwell almost pleadingly. "They're good people, Sergeant. You have to believe that. But this—"

Elwell laid one hand comfortingly on his shoulder. "We're going to get out of here, sir. Trust me on that. But right now, you gotta use your head. Get to the van— the mission is what matters. I'll handle everything out here."

31

PIER 36:
7 OCTOBER

USS JOUETT

Jerusha Bailey whirled around to face the speaker as Lieutenant Boston's scratchy, high-pitched voice came over it. She listened in horror as he described the flaming water around the end of the pier, the small boat that had approached covertly, and the thick black choking smoke that was enveloping them.

Bailey turned to Renninger. "We have to go get them out."

Renninger shook his head. "It's too dangerous. Especially when we can't even rely on our own air-search radar to tell us if we're about to be targeted."

"Isn't that why we have carrier air cover?" she argued.

A peevish look crossed Renninger's face. "I've got my orders too. To stay outside the twelve-mile limit."

"And that's going to be your testimony when you have to explain why you let my people die?"

The question hung in the air between them, unanswered. Finally, Renninger broke the silence. "My XO

was right about you,'' he said gruffly. ''All right, we're
going in.'' He turned to the operations specialist. ''Call
those Tomcats—tell them what we're up to. Make sure
we have air cover, especially radar cover, the entire way
in. And when they start going snakeshit on you, just
mention Commander Bailey's name.'' He turned back
to her with a sardonic gleam in his eyes. ''Let's see how
much weight you swing around here, lady.''

MIUW 106

The air inside the van was already stifling hot. He was
certain it was his imagination, but Boston felt as though
he was already breathing faster. How long would it take
carbon dioxide to build up inside the van anyway? And
did it really matter? Whatever his situation was inside
the van, the fate of the people outside clustered in tents
and inside trucks was even less certain.

''We've gotta keep the smoke out,'' his sonar tech
said quietly, ''if nothing else. That shit'll gum up the
gear faster than anything.''

Boston nodded. He took a deep breath and said, ''Listen, people, this is for real now. We forget about everything else and do our job. That's what the Navy pays us
for. Any questions?''

He glanced around the van, and saw everyone shake
their head no. He felt a brief rush of grim pride in their
dedication. ''Okay, let's get to work.'' He turned back
to the status board on the jobs console.

''Sir. We just gained contact on a submarine. A nuke,
by the looks of the signature.'' The sonarman pointed
out a set of thin lines tracing their way down the CRT
screen on the SQR-17 sonar. ''I make her submerged—
yes, definitely a nuke,'' he added, pointing out a sudden
change in one of the lines.

''Where is she?'' Boston asked.

''About two miles from the entrance to the Canal.

She's headed outbound, doing about three knots. Routine patrol status, it looks like."

Boston frowned. What was the submarine doing now? For the past week, the subs had been the eternal goblins of this operation, injecting a factor of uncertainty into every evolution.

He turned back to the chief. "I want us operational until the last possible second. You heard Commander Bailey—you know what the plan is. Get our people ready."

The chief nodded. "I've already sent the new submarine contact to *Jouett* over the link. It may slow up the rescue operation, Lieutenant."

"There's not much we can do about that, is there?" Boston turned back to the sonarman. "At the first hint that she's getting ready to fire, let me know. Not that you wouldn't anyway," he added hastily as a look of annoyance crossed the sonarman's face. "We'll go to voice reports only. With *Jouett* inbound, she needs to know what she's coming into."

"Standing in harm's way," the chief said quietly. "That's what it's all about, isn't it?"

Boston nodded. "Let's see what we can do to even up the odds."

USS JOUETT

Bailey gathered the bosun's mate and damage-control personnel around her on the empty bow of the ship. The smoke from the MIUW fire was clearly visible now, an ugly, ominous black cloud billowing up from the surface of the ocean. The pier was already obscured, wreathed in tendrils of the foul substance. She turned to the chief bosun's mate. "You've got the fire hoses rigged?"

The tall, taciturn man nodded. "All forward, ma'am, just the way you wanted." He frowned slightly as though not convinced it would work. "We're going to need a hell of a repainting after this."

"My people will need more than that if this doesn't work." She gazed at him steadily for a long moment. "This stuff floats on water. This is just like your basic safety drills in boot camp. You all remember—the ones where you practiced surfacing after abandoning ship and splashing your hands in front of you to clear the oil away?" She saw a chorus of nods from the assembled sailors. "Same principle." She pointed forward. "If you keep up the pressure to the fire hoses, we ought to be able to blow a clean water path through all this shit. It doesn't burn that long—you know how flammable gas is. I want everybody in a respirator as well. No point in taking any chances."

Her sailors on the end of the pier wouldn't have the luxury of respirators, though. How many of them were still alive? Boston's voice still came over the circuit in Tactical, and his messages were relayed to her via a walkie-talkie. But the fate of the men and women outside the van was still uncertain. Still, she had a nagging conviction that somehow they'd survived. Boston had told her that Sergeant Elwell was out there with them. If any man could get them through it, it was Elwell.

Well, there was nothing she could do about them at this moment. Not anything more than she was currently doing. She shoved the thought to the back of her mind and resumed her lecture. "Hoses two and four, you'll stand by to douse any problems on board. I suspect what we'll really get out of this is some fouled paint and filthy air, but if the flames try to creep up, you guys knock them down. Clear?"

Two hose teams nodded their heads.

"And you men up forward—keep your streams of water intersecting. You don't have to blow a huge path through the water. Our bow wave will take care of most of it. Just get us somewhere to start and then watch the edges of the path. This ought to work—it will work."

"The high-line rig is set up," another bosun's mate put in. "It's moored and tied off on this end well enough, and I've got the cage ready to go."

"How fast can we transfer passengers?" she asked.

"Maybe four at a time—that's stretching it. And that's assuming they have a secure tie-off point on that end."

"Oh, it'll be secure. You got enough men to haul it in?"

He nodded. "We can use the winch if we need to. Regulations call for manual line-handling when pax transfer is involved, but I think we can make an exception in this case."

"All right." She scanned the assembled faces again, saw the grim determination on each of them. "Let's do it then." She raised the walkie-talkie to her lips. "Bridge, Damage Control One. We're ready to proceed."

The deck shifted under her feet as the gas-turbine-powered ship quickly built up speed. Within moments, water was curling away from the bow in the smooth clean spirals associated with calm water. Sailors manning the fire hoses stood along the rail, some with their arms hooked over the lines running through the supports to steady themselves. Within moments, *Jouett* was at flank speed.

"Full ensemble," the chief bosun's mate ordered as the first hints of acrid smoke drifted across the fo'csle. "Nobody goes down, people. We can't afford it this time."

Bailey reached down to the deck and picked up the hood to her firefighting ensemble. She popped it over her head and felt the cool, sweet-stale rush of canned air on her face.

"Now." The bosun's mate gestured abruptly.

Long arcs of pressurized seawater streamed out from the hoses, playing across the water in front of them.

Bailey shouted to be heard through her fire ensemble.

"Bridge, DC One. Too fast—recommend fifteen knots."

"Fifteen knots, aye," she heard Renninger respond. His voice was barely audible. As the ship slowed, she was no longer overrunning the four arcs of saltwater spraying ahead of her. By adjusting the speed by a few knots here and there, Bailey finally managed to match their forward speed with the rate at which the firefighting teams could blast a small path of clean water through the still-smoldering napalm. The bow wave took care of the rest of it, pushing it away from the ship. Back aft, one fire team stood ready to keep it away from the stern.

One thousand yards away from the end of the pier, *Jouett* slowed to three knots and executed a sharp turn to port. The fire teams staggered slightly, but kept their balance and their hoses trained forward. The arc of the turn took them to within two hundred feet of the pier. By using the bow thrusters, Renninger turned the ship so that she was beam-on to the pier. Over the radio, Bailey could hear the stern firefighting team snapping out crisp orders as they cleared the burning napalm away from the ship.

"Ready with the shot line," the chief bosun's mate said. Seconds later, the sharp crack of a pistol rang out. The line attached to it lofted up and over to the MIUW camp, and dangled across the van. Through the black smoke and obscured visibility, she tried to see if anyone was responding. Too much smoke, too distant—as far as she could tell, there was no one at the other end of the line.

Her heart sank. Were they too late? Had the smoke already killed all of her sailors? The possibility that she would have to live with that knowledge, that everyone in her command had died while she was gone, struck her full force.

"They got it!" Even through his ensemble, Bailey could see the smile on the bosun's mate's face. "They're pulling the line over now." The manila line looped on the deck began feeding out from the ship and to the van.

The shot line was a series of increasing thicknesses of cord. Attached to the weight at the very end was a length of light nylon followed by heavier manila. Finally, the thick manila high line was paid out.

"They've got it secured," Renninger's voice said over her walkie-talkie. "Sending over the messenger tow line."

A second coil of line began unfurling as the sailors on the pier hauled it across. "Deploying the passenger cage." The rickety metal frame that would carry the sailors back and forth between the ship and the pier disappeared into the oily smoke.

How many of them had made it? The question seemed desperate, all the more so because she could not change the results. If they were in time, they were in time, and nothing she could do or say now would make a difference for the sailors on the pier. They either survived, or they hadn't. She clung to the hope that Sergeant Elwell and Lieutenant Boston had been able to keep them safe in her absence.

"Here we go." The bosun's mate chief shouted to a team of sailors, who began hauling in on a second line. A few minutes later, a transfer cage reappeared out of the smoke. In it were five hacking, coughing sailors.

She rushed to the cage and surveyed the faces. They were pale, gasping, and wheezing, but alive. The corpsmen took charge of them quickly and hustled them inside the skin of the ship, clamping portable oxygen bottles over each face.

They repeated the process eight times, hauling in far more than the maximum allowed number of passengers on each trip. The sailors hauling on the transfer line were growing visibly tired. On the last trip, she okayed the use of the winch, and let the sailors steady the motion in with the manual lines. Each time the cage came aboard, she checked the faces, mentally checking off names against her roster of personnel. The last load carried Lieutenant Boston and three chiefs.

"Elwell?" she demanded as she met Boston on the deck. "Where is he?"

Boston shook his head and coughed weakly. His face was pale, an unhealthy bluish tint underlying his normally rosy cheeks. "He didn't come—said he had something else to do."

Bailey swore silently. "What the hell was he doing?" she said as they stepped inside the skin of the ship.

"Ma'am—not now," the corpsman said firmly. "This man can't even breathe, much less talk."

"I have to know. Where's Elwell?"

Boston hacked again, a low, protracted sound, before he finally gasped out a sentence. "Said he was going ashore—the RHIB—the SEALs." As he choked the last word out, Boston turned deathly pale and crumpled to the deck.

"Commander Bailey, get your ass up here." Renninger's voice over her walkie-talkie was unmistakable. "We need you on the bridge."

"Take care of him," she said to the corpsman.

"I will, ma'am. That's my job. Now, why don't you go do yours?"

Bailey ran up the ladder to the bridge and stepped out into the compartment. The hatches leading out to the bridge wings had been firmly dogged down, but the ship had been designed to withstand nuclear, biological, and chemical attacks, and not a trace of smoke fouled the air.

"Get the deck clear," Renninger ordered. "If that line snaps . . ." He left the sentence unfinished.

They all knew what would have happened if the manila line attached to the MIUW van snapped. It would snake across the deck with the force of a whiplash, cutting through human flesh like a knife through hot butter.

Renninger glanced at her. "It's not built to withstand that much strain."

"There's not time to get the wire line across."

He nodded. "Let's see what we can do then. All back one third." The vibration throughout the ship changed subtly as the controllable pitch propellers began backing the ship down. Bailey watched through the forward window as the manila line stretched and gave. The bow was empty of sailors, but she could hear the thin, high-pitched whine as the manila took the strain.

On the pier, the van moved slightly. A rough, grating sound. Then it lurched, moving steadily towards the end of the pier until the forward edge of it was suspended over the water.

"Now for the tricky part. You say when."

She watched the van edge further and further over the water until it teetered on the very edge of the pier. At the first sign that it was beginning to topple, she said, "Now."

Three decks below, just inside a weather deck hatch, a chief bosun's mate tripped a quick-release trigger. The manila line sang as it slipped through the pulleys on the ship, suddenly free of restraint on this end. The line between the van and the ship went slack. Carried by its weight and momentum, the van toppled forward and into the ocean.

"That ought to take care of any security problems," Bailey said grimly. She turned back to Captain Renninger. "That was perhaps the finest example of deck seamanship I've ever seen. Thank you."

He brushed aside her thanks. "Now let's see if the rest of your plan works as well. You're Officer of the Deck, Commander. Make it happen."

Bailey nodded. She picked up a sound-powered headphone set and slapped it over her ears. "Man all gunnery stations."

32

Elwell felt his way down the rusted iron ladder to the floating dock below. The RHIB that the SEALS had been using to lay sonobuoys had been pulled up on to it for some minor maintenance. Most of the flames immediately around the dock had died down, but the thick, choking smoke reduced visibility to less than two feet.

Prior to departing, the corpsman had given him his last emergency oxygen canister. Intended for on-scene treatment of smoke-inhalation victims, it was now preventing the evil it was designed to treat.

Elwell sucked deeply on it, tasting the peculiar tang of canned air. He pulled the mask away from his face, tried one experimental breath of the air, and almost lost his grip on the ladder in the subsequent fit of coughing.

Fifty-two rungs later, he stepped down on the grated metal dock. The smoke was even thicker here, and he moved carefully. To fall off the side into the fouled water was unthinkable.

As he reached the bottom of the ladder, he dropped to his hands and knees and carefully crawled across the platform. With his hands stretched out in front of him, he felt the rugged, rubberized side of the RHIB. The skin was stretched taut. Evidently the flames around the dock had heated up the air inside the tubes. Now if he could just launch it.

He felt his way forward, and found the line still attached to the bow. He looped that around a stanchion, then shoved and tugged on the boat until it was at the edge of the dock. With one final jerk, the boat slid smoothly off and dropped one foot into the fouled water.

Moving quickly now before the remaining flames in the water could ruin his plans, Elwell got into the boat. The engine started on the first try.

To his left, flames broke out again on the water as the motion of the boat disturbed the upper crusted layer of napalm and exposed fresh fuel to air. The resulting turbulence fanned the flames even more, and they now stretched five feet into the air.

With his K-bar knife, Elwell cut the line that tethered him to the dock. The flames were nearly at the boat now, lapping hungrily at the rubberized sides. The sides were under pressure from the expanded air inside, and he was afraid that they could not stand much more strain, particularly not if they were weakened by heat. As the rope parted, he slammed the throttle forward to its maximum position. The lightweight craft went bow-high and blocked his view of the shore. He steered outward from the pier, trying to give himself a measure of safety in the poor visibility. Where had that smaller merchant ship been tied up? About five hundred yards forward, he decided. He moved further out into the open ocean.

The flames were creeping higher now, licking hungrily at the sides. Still bow-high, the RHIB acted as a flame barrier as he shot through the water to the shore.

In the end, the landing was almost anticlimactic. As he neared the shore, the smoke thinned slightly. He saw the quay wall loom up suddenly, and slammed the engine in reverse. The RHIB hit, and skittered across the concrete sideways. The engine and stern slammed into the cement with an unholy shrieking sound.

The impact almost threw him out of the boat. He clutched desperately at the lines that ran along the side and held on, staring at the water outside the RHIB. This close in to shore, the napalm coating was patchy and intermittent. Debris from normal pierside operations fed the fire, however. Panamanian ecological precautions were not nearly as stringent as in the United States.

Finally, the boat stabilized. Elwell puttered slowly along the wall until he reached a metal access ladder. He tied the boat to it and climbed the fourteen rungs to the edge of the wall.

As his feet hit dry land, he heaved a sigh of relief. This was his element, the ground and the dock, and the environs surrounding it. Not on the water, where feature-less terrain baffled his tactical instincts. Out there, de-spite Commander Bailey's high opinion of him, he was at a disadvantage.

But here, on dry land, he was in his element. He smiled grimly. Whether or not the SEALs knew it, the odds had just shifted in his favor.

Just as he turned towards the port facility itself, the ocean behind him erupted into a roaring fireball. He whirled and stared out at the end of the pier. Even through the dark haze he could see the flames shooting up to well over one hundred feet, hungry and demand-ing. An unholy shrieking and grinding sound filled the air. As he stared, stunned, the last two hundred feet of the pier, including all of the MIUW vehicles and re-maining equipment, shuddered and collapsed into the ocean.

USS JOUETT

The sonarman recovered first. As soon as he was able to speak, he began demanding to speak to Bailey. When the corpsman finally reached her, she was on the bridge, supervising the next phase of their evolution.

The corpsman strode onto the bridge, accompanied by the sonarman. He carried a portable bottle of oxygen with him, and stayed close to his patient.

"Had to tell you, Captain," the sonarman said weakly. He stopped, drawing in a deep gasp of breath. The corpsman slapped the oxygen mask over his face. The sonarman breathed in deeply, took several deep breaths, then shoved the mask away. "Just before we evacuated, we had a submarine contact. Nuke, I'm sure. We were just starting to put out the voice call when we had to get the hell out of there."

He quickly summarized the tactical details, concluding with: "He could be anywhere by now, ma'am. But it was a nuke—I'm sure of it. And he was laying mines."

"It's gotta be that Chinese one," Collins muttered. She shot Bailey a rueful look. "We should've taken it out when we had the chance."

Bailey shook her head. "No, there was no justification then. But now—I think the situation may have changed."

Between the evacuation of the MIUW and the subsequent explosion that engulfed their end of the pier, there was no doubt in her mind that the Panamanians were involved in hostile actions. But she was certain the Chinese were behind them. Especially now, with the submarine deployed in their vicinity. She turned to Renninger.

"What are your intentions?" she asked.

"Shoot first and ask questions later," Renninger said gruffly. "I've already taken too many chances today."

"Do you really think this will work?" Collins asked. *Jouett* was now proceeding along the coast, violating almost every traffic regulation in force in Panama Bay, but taking the shortest route toward the Canal. "Even if it does, we're going to be in a hell of a lot of trouble."

"Better to be judged by twelve than carried by six," Bailey answered. "Between the submarine and the air power, it's only a matter of time. Especially with this funky avionics problem you're having. The carrier can't keep up air cover the entire time, and who knows when that multinational squadron of fighters is going to take some action." Bailey shook her head, contemplating their possibilities for survival. "No, there's only one place that will be absolutely safe. At least for the time being, until the rest of the Navy gets here."

"It's a good idea," Renninger said unexpectedly. He nodded approvingly. "Tactically sound, but perhaps impossible to execute."

"Not to mention the reparations the U.S. will have to pay."

"To hell with reparations," Bailey responded. "It was our Canal for a hundred years. We put those doors on it, built the lock, lost countless lives cutting this channel across the continent. If anybody has the right to claim force majeure, we do."

Collins turned back to study the approach to the Canal. "It's worth a try."

"XO! All gunnery stations manned." The bosun's mate had his hand on the 1MC as he made his report.

Collins nodded. "Put it out over the 1MC, Boats. We're in for a hell of a gunnery exercise."

AMERICAN EMBASSY

Doug Turner studied the man standing before him. Had he not known it was Hank Flashert, he would have been convinced that the man was a native Panamanian. The clothes, the haircut, the subtle look of disarray—it all fit. Turner realized with a sinking heart that Flashert had succumbed to the one mortal sin in the religion of the State Department. He'd gone native.

That, more than anything, decided him. Despite his

earlier gaffe in allowing the Panamanians to believe that
the U.S. supported them while subtly trying to play on
their insecurities with the airbus shoot-down, Turner was
over his head. The violence directed towards the MIUW
unit, the attacks on civilian merchant ships—it had all
escalated to a level that was far beyond his experience.
There could be no way to use this profitably, not in the
United States' best interests. Inevitably, both his culpability and the true state of affairs in Panama would be
exposed.

Thus would end his career. He thought back to Bradley Jeets, who had only a little while to go until retirement. He himself would never make it that far, he was
convinced.

"The situation is untenable," Turner began, uncomfortably aware of how gross an understatement that was.
"We're fast approaching the point where the only solution will be a military one. I'm sure that's not what
any of us want." He paused, giving Flashert a chance
to respond, hopefully with more accurate in-area information that he would have gleaned from his Panamanian
contacts.

Oddly enough, Flashert started to laugh. "You old
fool. It was always out of our hands from the moment
the Chinese bought those bases. Did you really think we
could maintain an area of presence down here after that?
Ever since the Panamanians gained control of the Canal,
this situation has been ready to explode." Flashert shook
his head, still evidently amused at the naiveté of his
superior. "You people back there don't understand anything. Not anything at all. It's a bright, shiny world when
you look at it from D.C. All anyone needs is a chance—
a little military foreign aid, some leftover MREs, and
you're convinced the world is your friend. But things
don't work like that down here, Turner. They never
did."

Turner's rage knew no bounds. How dare the man
stand there and laugh at him? His career might be falling

down in ruins around him, but he was still a senior State Department official. He would not be treated so—not by someone who'd gone native.

"There's always a solution," Turner said crisply. He struggled to keep a calm, professional expression on his face. There was no point in showing Flashert how strong a reaction he'd caused. "You just haven't seen it yet."

Flashert slumped into the chair before Turner's desk. He chuckled again, then propped his feet up on the highly polished surface. "Doug, Doug, Doug. When are you going to get over it, man?" Flashert gestured with one hand, taking in not only the office but the entire country of Panama. "The military—that's how we do business down here."

"What do you mean?" Turner asked, uneasily curious despite his resolution to take charge of the situation.

Flashert snorted. "The only thing these people understand is force. I ought to know—I'm the one who's been living in this shithole for the last ten years. You want the Panamanians off balance? Looking to the good old U.S. of A. for assistance? There's only one way to do it. And besides," he continued, ignoring the shocked expression on Turner's face, "you've always given us a large amount of latitude. You told me to solve the problem—so I solved it. So don't start carping about the results."

Doug Turner felt the blood drain from his face. In twenty years of distinguished service with the State Department, he'd never faced a situation that felt so completely out of his control.

"What happened with that unit out on the pier?" Turner demanded, suddenly certain that he knew the answer. "The one that was attacked? And the attacks on the merchant ships? The airbus, for that matter?"

Flashert laughed. "I don't know a damned thing about the merchant ships," he said. His failure to deny knowledge of the other two incidents shook Turner even more.

"The airbus?"

Flashert shrugged. "Personally, my money is on the Chinese. Oh," he continued at once, noting the look of astonishment on Turner's face, "don't any mistake about it. We shot the little bastard down. Not a bad thing, as far as I'm concerned, if it took out Garcia. That bastard needed to die."

"But we shot the missile," Turner said, still confused. "How does that—?"

Flashert cut off his sentence by standing up suddenly and taking two steps towards him. "The Chinese, Doug. Haven't you ever wondered about them? In the last two decades, they've made incredible progress. You see their submarine parked out there—hell, you see them all over the world these days. Between industrial espionage and military spies, is there anything they don't know? Do you really think the inner workings of the Aegis radar are that far beyond them?"

"They took control of the ship?"

Flashert shook his head. "No. Not of the ship itself. Just of the environment in which it operates. Think about it, Doug. These ships today operate on more than water. It's the whole electronic environment—all the airspace around them, the electromagnetic radiation, even the international data-relay circuits. Do you really think it would be that difficult to insert a false target into the Aegis radar picture?"

Numbly, Turner sat down in his chair. He hit hard, felt the jolt rocket up his spine. "The Chinese are behind this." He felt a sudden, bitter hopelessness. He looked over at Flashert. "You could have warned me."

Flashert shook his head. "Not a chance, old buddy. You got yourself deeper into this than I could ever have managed."

"But the airbus—"

"Like I said, a casualty of war. Or of politics. Take your choice. It wasn't until this century that the two were ever separated anyway. The Chinese understand that a hell of a lot better than we do."

"I've got to talk to the Secretary," Turner said suddenly. "There's a way to stop this—if we act now. This whole thing is out of control."

Flashert studied him for a moment. "I wouldn't be so eager to do that, Dougie. There are a whole lot of people involved in this that wouldn't like that at all. Not one little bit. Other people have careers to think about too. You ought to think about that before you run squealing to the Secretary of State."

A sudden, vivid picture flashed into Turner's mind. Flashert, down here alone, a loose cannon out of control. After ten years of living in Panama, working closely with the military and the other people who chose to make this their permanent home, he must have dozens of contacts. Particularly within the military, who seemed to circle in and out of Panamanian tours with surprising frequency, homesteading in the area just as whole divisions used to call Germany their permanent station. The scope of the problem expanded, sprouting ugly tendrils and heads like a hydra. For the first time in his career, he saw just how far out of his depth he was.

"Let me introduce you to some of them," Flashert said easily. He stood and walked over to the door, opened it, and made a motion with his hand. He turned and looked back at Turner, triumph in his face. "I suppose you've already met Commander Murphy."

Turner stared aghast at the SEAL commander as the pieces started to fall into place. "What are you going to do with me?" he said quietly, grimly pleased that his voice sounded steady.

Flashert gestured towards his chair. "I suggest you have a seat. All we have to do now is wait."

33

GULF OF PANAMA:
7 OCTOBER

USS JOUETT

"There's no other way." Bailey took a deep breath and dove into her explanation once again. "Whatever's going on here, one thing is clear. The whole thing is about the Panama Canal and who controls it. It's the center of gravity, sir. We control the Canal and we control the entire course of the battle. They won't dare attack *Jouett* once she's inside the first lock. Not and risk jamming the Canal with debris for years to come."

"But you heard that fellow—the harbor's mined." Renninger made a dismissive gesture. "There's no way I'm taking *Jouett* into mined water. Not until it's been swept, and we're damned short on minesweepers right now, in case you hadn't noticed."

"Captain, you agree that the Canal's the center of gravity?" Bailey persisted.

"Of course, but—"

"Sir, if you would, just tell me. If you were going to mine the approaches to the Canal, how would you do it?"

"Moored mines," Renninger said immediately. "Command-activated, set at a depth of around thirty feet."

"Where?"

"I'd put a staggered line in right here." Renninger sketched out a line five miles long outside the immediate approaches to the Canal. "You keep traffic out of the entire entrance area, don't have as much problem with somebody bumping into them before they're armed."

"Maybe. It's a hell of a long line, though. The only platform that's mining is supposedly this one sub, and for every mine they carry, they give up a torpedo. Not many sub skippers will give up their entire load of torps for mines." Bailey took the pencil from Renninger and moved it further in toward the entrance. "And if they're command-activated, you don't have to worry about premature actuation. Until they get the signal, they're just chunks of metal. A tanker wouldn't even notice one unless the mooring line to the sea bottom fouled a propeller. No," Bailey continued, laying the pencil down, "I'd put my minefield in a good deal closer. Real close to the entrance, in fact, in water just deep enough to keep any wreck from completely blocking the entrance."

"And your point?"

"Just a few more questions, Captain. How hard is it to keep a minefield in place in a strong current?" Bailey asked.

"Damned hard. Even two to three knots is a problem."

Bailey straightened up from the chart table she'd been leaning over, and felt the bones in her lower back creak. "That's what I thought. So what do you think a current of fifteen to twenty knots would do?"

"Flush them," Renninger said. "Even the bottom mines would be dislocated."

"So we're going to reroute a couple of ocean currents into the Bay?" Collins asked. "Or were you just planning on using some NSA magic to make one materialize for us? Please, I do want to know.''

"No magic to it," Bailey said, unperturbed. She pointed at the massive lock doors towering seventy-six feet above the water five miles off their bow. "There's at least twenty feet of water piled up behind those doors. What kind of current do you think that'll create if it's released suddenly?"

"She's right," Collins said unexpectedly. Bailey glanced over and saw an acid expression on the XO's face. "Dammit, I hate to admit it, but she's right."

Bailey nodded. "We blow the doors and we create a small tidal wave that sweeps the approach clean for us. It's not a hundred-percent solution, but it's as good as we're going to get."

Renninger studied them both for a moment. "I see the logic in your solution, but the danger to the ship . . ." He shook his head gravely. "We're not going to come under air attack as long as the Tomcats are overhead."

"And how much longer are they going to be?" Collins said. "There's no tanker support in the area—they'll have to meet the tanker halfway back to the carrier. That leaves us with large gaps in antiair coverage. Captain, with the submarine out here and us in shallow water, we've got to get the ship to safety. At least until the rest of the fleet arrives with the convoy."

"And how does it help any if we blow the first lock open?" Renninger said. "Then you destroy the ability of the Canal to operate at all."

"The locks are not that difficult to replace," Bailey countered. "Besides, they have enough lift capability built into the other three locks to handle the traffic. Captain, if there was any other way—"

"That's always your argument, isn't it?" he snapped.

"Captain—Tomcats off station in twenty mikes," the CIC watch officer broke in. Collins glanced over at him. Odd that after all the trouble he'd caused her, it was Lieutenant Williams who came to the rescue. "They say it'll be another two hours before the next flight is in area.''

Renninger swore vehemently and slammed his hand down on the plotting table. He turned to glare at the two women. "There's not a damned thing I liked about this mission from the start. However, without air cover, I don't feel like we have many options. It's either this, or cut and run. I'd prefer the latter, but we'd have to get by that submarine. And we'd still have the problem of the radar ghosts.''

He scowled for a moment longer. Then his face faded into an expression of calm professionalism. "All right,'' he continued briskly, "batteries free.'' He turned to Collins. "You run this, XO. And don't screw it up.''

The preparations for gunnery stations went quickly, and Bailey stayed on the bridge, listening to the familiar flow of reports and commands on the sound-powered phones. She felt a light tap on her shoulder, and turned to stare into the grizzled face of Chief Templeton.

"Commander? You got a minute?'' the chief asked. "I've got something on my mind.''

Bailey motioned the chief to follow her to the small compartment the quartermasters used to stow their gear. When he'd closed the door behind them, she asked, "What's up?''

"We wouldn't have gotten out of there without Elwell,'' he said without preamble. "But it seems to me that he's on his own back there now. Doesn't seem right. *Jouett*'s got a full crew—she doesn't need another couple of gunner's mates or boatswain's mates.''

She studied him for a moment, aware from his tone of voice that Chief Templeton had already reached his own decision about the scenario. "And you think you'd be more help ashore than on the ship, is that it?''

Chief Templeton nodded. "I spent some time talking with the sergeant. He wanted someone to know where he was going. Just in case.''

"Just in case he didn't come back, I take it?"

"That'd be about the size of it."

So Chief Templeton knew where Billy Elwell was headed and what he intended. She felt a flash of irritation at that, the close-knit camaraderie that developed so quickly between the senior enlisted personnel of different services, a fellowship that permitted them to keep secrets from their officers. She was about to say no, to remind Chief Templeton that his primary duty had to be to the safety and well-being of his own unit, when the chief spoke again. "I've got five volunteers—no, I didn't ask for them. They each came to me of their own mind. Ma'am, you don't have to like it, but you know it's the right thing to do. We owe him—and if the situation were reversed, he'd be coming after us."

"So what do you want?" Bailey asked.

"Weapons and the Captain's gig. It's fast and it's covered, and we won't look as out of place in it as we would in the other boats."

Bailey sighed. "Okay, I'll ask Captain Renninger. But Chief, one thing—you bring my sailors back alive, understand?"

The chief nodded. "That's part of the plan, Skipper. We all come back together."

As Bailey stepped back out on the bridge, she heard Collins say, "All stations, report."

"How close are we?" Bailey asked.

"Ten thousand yards. A good distance. It'll just take a couple of minutes," Collins said.

They waited in silence as the flurry of status and readiness reports came in on the circuit. Collins coordinated the actions of the ship effortlessly, seemingly always one step ahead of the gunnery crew. The Combat watchstanders quickly fell into the calm yet brisk manner of operating that signified complete confidence in the officer directing their actions. Finally, Collins looked up at her Captain. "All stations report ready, sir."

Renninger nodded. "I already gave you batteries free," he pointed out.

"Gun Plot, this is the Weapons Officer. Fire one round for effect."

"Gunnery Plot, aye, fire one round for effect."

There was a slight whir as the gunnery fire-control radars mounted immediately above them shifted into position. "Solid contact, Gunnery Officer," came the report.

Bailey nodded. While electronics and weapons loads might change throughout the decades, the ancient art of naval gunfire support—no, naval surface-weapons support, she corrected herself—remained much the same as it always had. A gun, a radar or lookout report, and then the first shot.

A loud boom reverberated throughout the ship.

Collins smiled.

"All stations report."

"One round fired for effect, no apparent casualties." One by one, each gunnery station reported in.

"Damage?" Collins asked. She frowned as she listened to the lookout's report. She turned to the Captain. "Two hundred yards short."

"Another round."

Once again, they went through the ritual of order and response, each one repeated back word for word to assure there were no misunderstandings.

"I'll go to the bridge and watch from there," Bailey said quietly to the captain.

He nodded. "I think I'll join you." A small smile crossed his face. "Everything looks like it's under control here."

They had just reached the door leading from Combat out when a startled exclamation caught their attention. "Air contacts—twenty-eight of them." The operations specialist's voice was high-pitched and worried. "Captain, they're all inbound—they just appeared—they weren't there before."

Bailey heard the familiar whine of the Aegis system focusing its air-search radar tower on the incoming targets. She darted back into Combat and grabbed Collins just above the elbow. "Train the fifty-five on them. These are the ghosts again—I'm sure of it."

Collins paused uncertainly. "The faster we get in the Canal, the faster we're out of danger."

Bailey shook her head firmly. "Those contacts aren't there. They're the same ghosts we saw before. They may fool the Aegis SPY system, but let's see how they work against the old-fashioned fire-control radar. Just try it— the lock doors will still be there if I'm wrong."

"Combat, Sonar. Submarine contact, inbound. Range, ten thousand yards. Recommend deliberate attack at this time."

Over the open microphone, they could hear a flurry of noise from Sonar. "She's closing us, XO. We don't have much time."

Collins smoothly and quickly transitioned into a different tactical scenario. Cupping the sound-powered microphone to her mouth, she said, "Dieten, we're sending you a target"—she looked across at the chief operations specialist—"now. You got it?"

"Affirmative," the gunner's mate said. "What do you want me to do with it?"

"Lock it up with the fifty-five. See if it's really there." Collins left that problem, and turned immediately to the submarine issue. "Set up for deliberate attack. Weapons tight, but be ready. What's she doing now?"

"Fifteen knots—bearing constant, range decreasing."

"Estimated range of her torpedoes?"

"I don't know, XO," the sonarman said. "I'm not even certain what kind of boat it is."

"Give me your best guess."

"Six thousand yards—maybe."

"Fine," Collins answered. "Weapons free. Take her out at sixty-five hundred yards."

"That'll be at the edge of our own capability."

"Do it," she snapped. "Dammit, don't let her get within range. Weapons free."

"Aye, aye, ma'am," the sonarman answered, a new note of confidence in his voice. "We'll get her."

"Combat, Gun Plot. There's no contact there."

Collins stopped midstream in the rapid flow of tactical orders. "Are you certain? Give me a firm answer, Dieten. There's a lot riding on this."

"I'm certain, XO. There's not a damned thing in the sky up there."

Collins's eyes met Bailey's. They'd both heard the lookout's report confirming that he had no visual contact on the aircraft that were supposedly in the area. "We're being spoofed, aren't we?" Collins asked. "You know anything from NSA that would explain this?"

Bailey shook her head. "No. But it just made sense. The AWG-9 Tomcat radar didn't see it. I figured the high-frequency fire-control radar might not be susceptible to it either."

Collins shook her head. "We've still got a submarine left to deal with." She glanced sardonically at Bailey. "I assume you agree with me that that's real?"

"Absolutely. And I agree with you—sixty-five hundred yards."

"Nice of you to say so." Collins paused for a moment, evidently remembering the English Channel. "There was a time when we didn't agree. It's nice to have it different this time."

"I'll be on the bridge," Bailey said. As she left Combat, she heard another flurry of gunnery orders. Apparently satisfied that the air contacts were not there, Collins had returned her attention to the gunnery problem.

Another loud blast shook the ship, followed in rapid succession by three more. The noise reached down into the very bowels of the ship, and Bailey could feel the strakes and structural members of the hull resonating with the noise. As the final shot still echoed in the compartment, the collision alarm sounded. Bailey grabbed a stanchion and braced herself.

The second shot cleared the lock with just inches to spare, hit the water beyond, then evidently skipped several times. She saw the tall spurts of water that indicated an impact, followed by the skip spouts as well.

The third shot, seconds later, nailed the right-hand door. A giant hole exploded inward in the massive steel panel, followed immediately afterwards by a solid stream of water shooting out a hundred feet before arcing down to the ocean.

The fourth and fifth shots went dead on. The first one pierced the upper edge of the junction between the two doors, shoving the right-hand one back and shattering its edges. Instead of the smooth mass of metal that had stood there for over sixty years, the door's edge was now lined with wicked-looking spikes of twisted, deadly metal.

The pressure of the water built up between the two doors was too much for them. They burst open, releasing a tidal wave forty feet high that shrank to a strong swell as it crossed the ten thousand yards between *Jouett* and the lock.

Bailey ignored the flurry of activity around her and stared at the damage the ship had wrought. The two massive doors to the first lock of the Panama Canal now hung askew on their hinges. One was canted perilously towards the center of the Canal, held in place evidently only by the lower hinge. The other was slammed back against the approach wall.

"Can we get by it?" Renninger asked.

Bailey shook her head. "I don't know. If we can, it's going to be tight."

"More damage to my paint job."

Bailey looked up, surprised at the Captain's sardonic remark. "Do you want to try it?"

316   C. A. MOBLEY

He nodded. "We've blown the hell out of the Canal—
now let's go in and prove who owns it."

The quartermaster's voice coming over the speaker
from the chart house was tense. "Thirty-five feet beneath the keel. Captain, not much room to spare."

Renninger nodded. "We don't have a choice."

Normally, with the Canal flooded and the lock holding
back the water, there would have been considerable
clearance between *Jouett*'s keel and the bottom below.
As it was, there was still sufficient water, since the ship
drew only twenty-eight feet. However, navigating within
the confines of the Canal sometimes led to peculiar problems. In particular, as the ship accelerated, the stern of
the ship had a tendency to settle down lower, a phenom-
enon called squatting. There were other considerations
as well: the currents and water flows that ran along the
banks, the possibility of obstructions below. Generally,
the Canal was superbly maintained.

Renninger turned to Bailey. "So where do you suggest we go? Stay here and wait for the cavalry to arrive,
or move deeper into the lock?"

Bailey considered the question. "Further inland," she
said finally. "First, we might want to turn around. Better
to have the bow facing the ocean than the stern. That
way, we can make a quicker exit if we need to."

"I assume there's another reason as well?" Renninger
said.

She nodded. "Preliminary indications show that the
origins of the false targets may be here." She pointed
at the Chinese port facility with one finger. "If it came
down to it, we'd have to use guns against it. And we're
too close where we are right now—the elevation would
be so depressed we might cause collateral damage. But
if we move off some, get it at the four to five mile point,
we'd have better odds."

"Surely you're not suggesting we attack the facility?"
Renninger demanded. "My God, even for you—"

She cut him off firmly but politely. "I'm not sug-

gesting anything at this point, Captain. I'm merely saying we should keep our options open. And like it or not,
that's got to be one of them.''

Renninger turned back to the chart table and studied
the blank of the Canal now stretching before *Jouett*. Finally, he nodded. ''Okay, lady. We'll do this your way.''

34

THE PACIFIC OCEAN:
7 OCTOBER

LOTUS GLORY

T'sing Lin moved around the ship like a ghost. Before, when there'd been other pilots with him, at least he'd had their companionship. The crew had always been a bit standoffish, perhaps superstitious over the nature of their mission, or even envious of the divinity awaiting them. They had never been the most companionable collection of beings, but at least they'd had their training and prospects in common. That had knitted them together far more tightly than he'd realized.

Now, he was alone. The last of the small group. He no longer interpreted the avoidance by the rest of the crew as a form of awe, but rather as superstitious fear. It was as though death hung so close over him that it threatened their lives as well.

And for what? Finally, he realized with a start that he no longer believed. The others—they were shredded bits of flesh scattered across the ocean floor far away from home, not martyrs for the great nation. Nor had their targets been military. He ran over the last launches in his mind, matching that up with his frequent forays on deck. No, not military targets—other civilian vessels. Sailors such as those who crewed his own ship. That perhaps was the real genesis of the crew's distaste for him.

They avoided him, except for these two. He glanced down the passageway and saw the two hulking figures concealed in the shadows. Had the master said something? Had his own failure to cheer at his comrades' death somehow betrayed him? For whatever reason, ever since the last one had deployed, he'd been sighting these two all over the ship. Especially on his frequent ramblings up on the upper deck.

It was as though they suspected—no, how could they? Until this very moment, he'd not been certain himself.

T'sing Lin took one last look around his small compartment. The shadows of his comrades lingered there still, their faces and peculiarities still strong in his memory. If nothing else, he would keep them alive that way—as he would himself.

He was careful to show no outward sign of his intentions. Rather, he ate the usual sparse meal alone, and retired to his cabin at the normal hour. It had been his custom to spend a period of time in silent prayer and meditation before seeking out the open deck of the ship for his nightly walk. He stuck to that routine.

Finally, at the usual time, he stretched and let out a loud sigh. He walked to the door, opened it, and moved into the passageway, taking no precautions to avoid being seen. Let them think that he was merely about his normal routine.

From fifty feet above, he gazed down on the sea. It looked almost smooth, its surface barely broken by the long, slow swells coming in from the west. A few seagulls circled aimlessly just abaft the pilot house. One hung in the air almost motionless, riding a wind current he could neither see nor feel. Except for the noise and sound of the ship, and the distant lights on the horizon from the other vessels, he could have been alone in the world.

Alone. As he already was within the ship.

T'sing Lin breathed deeply, raising his hands up over his head to expand his lung capacity. He lowered them slowly, feeling the long rush of air cleanse his lungs of impurities. Again he repeated the maneuver, one he'd been taught from his earliest childhood as a method of centering the soul. He felt the calm creep into him, washing away the anger and terrible loneliness of the last two days. Out here, on the deck of the ship and under the stars, his connection with the rest of the universe was clear. It transcended him as an individual, his loyalty to his country, and even his connection to every living being on the planet.

Completely at peace for the first time in three weeks, in one swift motion, T'sing Lin vaulted lightly over the side of the ship.

The water approached slowly at first, as though somehow his connection with the ship was slowing his fall. Then time accelerated, and he had just a few microseconds in which to realize that the gentle swells were far greater close up than they appeared from the deck of the ship.

He hit the water at an awkward angle, slamming the right side of his body into the ocean first. The force snapped his neck painfully back, and he felt the small muscles corded there screaming in agony.

The fall continued through the water, down past the light, frothy surface layers and into the deeper blackness. With his neck canted back at an uncomfortable angle, he watched the light from the stars vanish, to be replaced by an inky, completely encompassing blackness. Still he fell, until he wondered whether or not the floor of the ocean could be that far from him. With no light, he was quickly disoriented. Up, down, even sideways were all one, all one direction in the complete and utter darkness.

He began to panic. He could feel the pressure grinding

in on him, forcing the air out of his lungs. He flailed violently, trying to remember which way he'd fallen, why this had seemed such a fine idea. The last vestige of his calmness deserted him completely, and he started to scream.

As he opened his mouth, a flurry of bubbles boiled around him.

Bubbles. Something of his early training at the torpedo school sunk in. Bubbles. Follow them to the surface if you're uncertain.

Now his motions had a focus. He followed his bubbles up, flailing at the water as though it were a martial arts opponent, beating the black into submission.

Eons later when his head broke through the surface, his surroundings were just barely lighter than they'd been beneath the sea. The one difference was the light, sweet kiss of the sea air on his face. He choked, coughed, sucked air violently down while maintaining his head above water with the same violent swimming motions.

Finally, when the hypoxia started to clear, he calmed somewhat. His motions were calmer now, just sufficient to keep his head above the water.

The ship. He whirled in a circle, still treading water, and searched for the giant shape. It seemed impossibly far away, as though he'd spent far longer beneath the water than he thought possible.

Would they search for him? Of course they would—the last pilot on board, the last one who knew how to pilot the deadly vehicle to its prey. His desertion—for that's what it was—could not have gone unnoticed. The two massive, hulking figures that had followed him on deck would surely have seen him go over the side, have raised the alarm immediately. Indeed, any second the ship would be turning, beginning a search pattern. He wondered if the other ships in the group would be brought in as well—perhaps their search helicopters.

The thought drove him to panic. He knew what the

punishment would be for desertion, the one that had been drummed into him from the first day of his training. Yet would it be enforced now? Probably not. No, the longer he thought about it, the less sense it made. They would simply lock him in his room, feed him there, keep him under constant guard until his moment came. Then he'd be carried, kicking and screaming if necessary, down into the bowels of the ship and jammed into the torpedo. After the incident with Li, he had no doubt that that was what would happen.

Not that his death would be much different now. He rolled back and tried floating for a while, staring up at the stars overhead. The swells made it difficult, but eventually he arrived at the correct arch of his back to keep his body afloat and his face still above the swells. He rode that way for a while, staring at the night sky and gently sculling with his hands to keep his feet into the waves.

How long could he last out here? The answer, in the end, was simple. Longer than he could in the torpedo.

Alone and in the ocean, T'sing Lin composed his mind for death.

USS JOUETT

The hideous squealing of tortured metal was their first indication of trouble. Renninger and Bailey exchanged a horrified look, then darted out onto the bridge wing. Behind the ship, the damaged lock doors were closing.

"They can't possibly be watertight," Renninger blurted. "Why in the hell—we're trapped." A look of grave concern settled on his face. "The Miraflores Locks are just a little over a mile and a half long, and Miraflores Lake isn't much bigger. They've got us confined now. They can do anything they want to us."

"There's another option," Bailey said suddenly. "One that makes this just as good a decision as it was before. Come on.'' She touched Renninger lightly on the shoulder. ''We need to get a look at the second Miraflores Lock.''

She followed Renninger back onto the bridge, and they went down two ladders to the main deck. Once there, they exited the ship to the weather decks, and quickly trotted forward.

The two sets of locks on the Pacific side of the Canal were each about the same size, about a half a mile in length. The doors to the second lock were closed.

''Wonder what the water level is behind that?'' Bailey asked.

Renninger turned to study her. ''You can't be serious.''

She nodded. ''Oh, but I am. And so are you, if you think about it.'' Out of earshot of their subordinates, her voice no longer held the deference due to the commander of the ship. She spoke to him as an equal.

''Do you know how much damage this could do to the ship?'' Renninger snapped. ''I won't allow it—I can't. There has to be another way.''

''Then you tell me what it is. Because as far as I can tell, there's only one way out of this trap. Either the way we came in—and the lock gate behind is in the gun's blind cutout—or to go deeper into the Canal until we get to Gatun Lake and get some room to maneuver.''

Renninger took two steps closer to the fantail and stared out at the massive gray lock in front of him. In most respects, it was identical to the one they'd already blasted through. He turned back to Bailey. ''It depends on how high the water level is right now,'' he said. ''Too much water could swamp the ship when it rushes out.''

''Get the quartermaster on it. The locks on this end of the Canal are bigger than they are on the Atlantic because of the wide tidal range in the Pacific. A thirty-one-foot drop at the Pedro Miguel Lock, all in one step, then the remainder of the distance in two steps at Mir-

aflores. I think we were at high tide—there should be
no more than thirty-six feet of difference between the
two locks and Gatun Lake. Eighteen feet of swell on
either side.''

''It was high tide.'' He shot her a look intended to
convey that the Captain would of course know that.
While a mere passenger wouldn't. ''You're talking
about a wall of water eighteen feet tall rushing at the
ship.''

She sighed. ''Look, this ship is built to have water
over the bridge and still survive at sea, isn't it? It won't
be pleasant—we'll get knocked around a bit again—but
she can do it. You know she can.''

''Then why not just stay where we are?'' Renninger
asked. ''We've done what we intended to do—put us in
a place where they wouldn't dare take a shot at us.''

The quick crack of an automatic weapon chattered out
through the enclosed space, answering that question.
Bailey grabbed Renninger and pulled him behind the
five-inch-gun mount. ''That's why.'' She pointed up at
the wall of the lock eighteen feet above them. ''They
won't risk sinking the ship, but they can damn well do
some damage to us. Enough to board us, maybe.''

The ship wobbled uneasily, a strange sensation in enclosed waters. Bailey frowned for a moment, trying to
place the sensation.

It was Renninger who gave her the answer. ''They're
flooding the lock. Those doors aren't watertight, but if
they flood fast enough, they may be able to keep up with
the leakage. If they bring us up to level with the quay
wall, they can board us.'' He opened the hatch on the
side of the five-inch-gun mount. ''How well can you
climb?''

She stared at him, wondering for a moment if he'd
snapped under the strain. All at once, it made sense.
''Down into the magazine, you mean?''

He nodded. ''I haven't done this since I was an en-sign, but I'm up for it. Come on—it's our safest way back into the skin of the ship."

The gun mount was built to house one operator, a secondary method of firing the gun manually should the combat systems fail for some reason. Shells fed up into the mechanism from the magazine below. By grabbing onto handholds, they made it over to the ladder, then crawled down to the magazine. A startled gunner's mate looked up. "Captain?" He stared, as though seeing a ghost, at his Captain, who was now streaked with grease.

"Don't worry," Renninger said. For some reason, that struck Bailey as the most senseless thing anyone had said so far.

Forty seconds later, they were back in Combat. Renninger set General Quarters, explaining to Collins what he intended to do, stilling her protests with a harsh glare.

The crew, already at gunnery stations, was ready quickly. Renninger handled the evolution himself, depressing the five-inch gun to minimum elevation and ordering the gunner's mate they'd startled to manually sight in on the two locks with reduced-charged shells to further flatten the rounds' trajectory. Just before Renninger gave the firing order, he turned to Bailey and smiled slightly. "If we damage the first one, the flood'll be slower. More survivable than an eighteen-foot tsunami."

"Of course." Collins glared at Bailey as though the entire situation were her fault. And indeed, in a way it was. Bailey mulled that one over as the Captain gave the order.

"Batteries free."

A blast reverberated inside the enclosed lock, throwing the ship violently around. Two more shots followed in quick succession.

Bailey grabbed hold of the radar repeater and clung to it as the wall of water towered over them. The hatches to the bridge were already dogged down, and the rest of the watch-standers were similarly braced. The lookouts had been called in just seconds before.

The wall of water approached them, black shot with blue, churned into air bubbles at the leading edge. It decreased in height slightly as it approached them, but still towered thirty feet above the normally calm surface of the ocean. Time seemed to slow as it engulfed first the bow of the ship and then moved inexorably towards them. It hit the bridge full force, immediately submerging them in water. One pane of Plexiglas shattered under the impact. A torrent of water flooded into the deck and knocked a junior officer off his feet. It flung him across the bridge and smashed him against the opposite bulkhead. It seemed to go on forever, the bridge quickly filling with water. She glanced down at the radar repeater and hoped that the casing was as watertight as the manufacturer had promised. If not, she would have only seconds to live before a high-voltage circuit shorted out and electrocuted her. Five seconds, six seconds, seven. Bailey found herself holding her breath as the water crept higher and higher.

Finally, just before it reached the top of the radar console, the wave passed over them. The windows of the bridge were suddenly exposed, wiped glistening clean by the torrent of water. The water inside the bridge itself was still four feet high.

Renninger fought his way over to the port bridge wing and jammed down the dogging lever. The hatch shot open under the pressure of the water and poured out over the bridge wing, trying to drag everything not nailed down, including people, out with it. Bailey fought against the pull, tightening her grip on the console.

"Any casualties?" Renninger asked when the flood had finally subsided. The lieutenant who had been completely submerged under the water moaned softly. The bosun's mate was at his side in seconds, kneeling down beside him.

He looked up at the Captain. "He's alive. Doesn't seem to be any serious damage."

"Damage Control reports," Renninger snapped. He

pointed to the bosun's mate. "Get the corpsman up here."

Finally, the report came. "Three shots fired for effect, no apparent casualties."

Thirty minutes after the first shot, they broke free of the Miraflores Locks and into the mile-wide man-made Miraflores Lake.

Renninger turned to Bailey. "Now what?"

"Pedro Miguel Lock. One more set of doors and we're into Gatun Lake. With some room to maneuver."

Renninger nodded. "What the hell have we got to lose at this point?"

"Our ship," Bailey said.

35

PANAMA CITY:
7 OCTOBER

U.S. EMBASSY

Master Sergeant Elwell was halfway up the stairs to
Doug Turner's office when a dull thud rattled the windows in the Ambassador's building. He paused on a
landing, instinctively pressing his back against the wall
in the shadow of a potted plant. The noise struck again,
rippling through the old building like an earthquake.
Plates chattered in shelves, and the chandelier gracing
the foyer swung precariously.

Gunfire. And not the small stuff either. He was far
more familiar with this particular noise than almost anyone in the building. Even the Marine captain heading up
the security force would have had less experience with
the distinctive sound of naval gunfire support.

It had to be *Jouett*. And just what the hell was she
shooting at? He ran through the logical targets quickly,
dismissing each one. Finally, he arrived at the one possible explanation. One corner of his mouth twitched. An
eminently logical, elegant solution to *Jouett*'s tactical
position. He wondered just how much of the plan was

Commander Bailey's idea, and then decided that most of it must be.

There was one way he could get the definitive answer. Do what he'd set out to do in the first place. After thinking long and hard the previous night, Billy Elwell had arrived at the one answer that he felt fit all the facts of his situation. What lay at the head of the stairs would merely be validation of that premise.

He started up the stairs again, moving more slowly. His pistol was drawn, held easily in a one-handed grip as though it were an extension of his arm. He heard voices above, coming from behind one of the closed doors along the passageway. He stopped, listened for a moment, and matched them with the players in motion.

Doug Turner—it had to be. Those resonant, plummy tones could have come from nowhere but the State Department.

The muffled, sharp commands—his gut twisted slightly as he confirmed his worst fears. Those voices were military, and not just any kind. Marines, maybe. But more likely, given the volume, the SEALs.

Finally, a thin, whiny snarl. Flashert, the wild card in the entire equation. Elwell shook his head, marveling at the process of going native. He'd seen it too many times in the last thirty years.

The prospect of taking on a squad of armed and annoyed SEALs was not an appealing one. Yet what were his alternatives? Go to the security force, to the Marines charged with the safety of this building and the embassy? He shook his head and dismissed the thought. Even if he could convince the Marine captain to believe him—never an easy process with a junior officer—mobilizing the security-alert team would simply put the SEALs in Turner's office on guard. The results could turn ugly. Elwell had no great liking for either Flashert or Turner, but something in him balked at getting innocent civilians killed.

That left two possibilities. The first was only slightly less appealing than calling a security alert.

He could walk away. Now that was a thought—not a good one, but still an option. He even had a justification of sorts. As part of the Special Forces advisory group with SouthCom, he really had no business interfering with the State Department. Indeed, if he were wrong, his actions might seriously destabilize an already precarious situation. Yes—walk away, leave Flashert and Turner to sort out their own messes. Come back later, help with the body count, and go about his business.

Reluctantly, he concluded that was not an option. While tactically it was a possibility, morally it was not.

So what was left? Take on four armed SEALs by himself? Yes, but perhaps not in the way that they were accustomed to.

Elwell moved silently towards the door from which the voices were coming. He paused outside for a moment, verifying his initial conclusions as to who was in the room. Finally, when he heard a lull in the noise, he knocked politely on the door.

Sudden silence, as deadly as the noise of a shotgun pumping. He slid his own weapon into the holster and held his hands out in plain view.

There was no warning, no footsteps to betray the SEAL. The knob turned and the door was jerked open so quickly that it startled even him. He stilled the reflexive motion of his hand towards the gun.

"Good evening, sir," Elwell said politely. He sketched a salute at the SEAL commander. "If it wouldn't be too much problem, I have a couple of questions I believe you could answer."

Without waiting for an answer, Elwell stepped into the room. The scenario was as he'd envisioned it— Turner pale and shaken behind his desk, hands trembling and eyes flickering around the room. Flashert pacing back and forth, a half-consumed cigarette clutched in one hand. The SEALs arrayed out in a tactical formation, silent and deadly. Any one of them would have choked before showing surprise at his arrival.

"Bad timing, Sergeant," Murphy said. He motioned towards a chair with his Uzi. "You want to have a seat?"

Elwell walked across the room and sat down in the chair, careful to keep his hands away from his own weapon.

"Take his weapon," Murphy said to one of the SEALs. Elwell was divested of his pistol within moments. "So what are these questions you want to ask?" Murphy said, relaxing slightly now that Elwell was no longer armed.

"I think you answered most of them," Elwell said quietly. He turned to Doug Turner. "You weren't involved in this, were you?"

Turner shook his head slightly. Elwell nodded approvingly. "Better not to say anything, sir. Good move." He turned back to Murphy. "So, the question remains, what do we do now? I assume you've heard the five-inch guns."

Murphy smiled sardonically. "I know what they were."

"Can you see anything from that window?" Elwell asked, lifting his chin to indicate the expanse of glass behind Turner's desk.

"Enough."

"*Jouett*'s in the Canal, isn't she?" Elwell asked.

Murphy was motionless for a moment, then dipped his head in acknowledgment. "For all the good it will do her."

"I think I've figured most of this out, sir. You and Mister Flashert there—been down here a long time, have you?" Somehow Elwell made it sound more like a polite question than an accusation. "I know about that sort of thing—got a German wife and kids myself." His eyes took on a faraway look.

Murphy laughed. "Not hardly. Any of these guys look like good fatherhood candidates to you? No, I'm afraid it's a little simpler than that, Sergeant. Just a question of money.''

"Drugs?'' Elwell asked softly, something cold and hard in his eyes washing away the expression the thought of his family had invoked.

"I don't ask.''

"Just little packages are they?''

One of the other SEALs finally spoke up. "Not so little.''

Murphy turned on him. "Shut the fuck up.''

Elwell looked thoughtful. "I can think of a lot of different ways to do it. The actual smuggling, I mean. Makes it pretty easy if you've got access to cargo that doesn't go through customs here or there.''

Without warning, Murphy lowered his pistol and shot Elwell in the right thigh. The Army noncom let out a sharp yelp. The force of the impact spun him around in a circle and slammed him into the far wall. He lay dazed on the elegant carpet, his hands clamped over the wound. Dark black-red stains erupted around them, blending in with the camouflage pattern on his pants.

"What the fuck—'' Flashert spat out. "You said there wouldn't be—''

"We're going to kill him, of course,'' Murphy said calmly. "There were never really any options, not after he found our safe house. I guess you did keep your word to my petty officer, Elwell—nobody's come looking for us. Still, you understand—it's not a chance I can continue to take.''

Elwell groaned as shattered bone dug viciously into stunned nerves. The pain was coming now, as it always did after a gunshot wound. A few minutes of numbness, then the all-encompassing red agony that would soon be his world.

He gritted his teeth, forced himself to pull his right hand away from his wound, and dipped into his right blouse pocket, moving slowly so as not to provoke Murphy. He extracted a small metallic button and held it out to the SEAL commander. "I wouldn't be in such a hurry. A little toy I picked up from a fellow from NSA—you might remember him. Mr. Carlisle?"

Murphy stared at the button for a moment, then motioned at one of the other SEALs. "Get it."

The younger SEAL was careful to stay out of Murphy's field of fire. He moved in sideways and snatched the device away from Elwell, then handed it to Murphy. The commander examined it for a moment, then shrugged. "So what? We just leave a little sooner than we thought we would." He raised the pistol again.

A blast blew out the windows behind Murphy. The commander shot through the air with a gaping hole in his chest. As the fragments of glass and curtain spiraled to the floor, the grim face of Chief Templeton appeared in the opening.

"Good job," Elwell managed to say before the black started closing in.

36

THE PACIFIC OCEAN:
8 OCTOBER

A helicopter off the USS *Shiloh*, a guided-missile cruiser, was the first to spot the anomaly in the water. At first, the pilot thought it was a piece of debris from the massive Chinese merchant ship, reflecting the moonlight and circled in for a closer look. As he descended to two hundred feet, he noticed the widening circle of the downdraft that beat out its distinctive pattern on the ocean. The rotors generated an effective wind of over sixty knots against the surface of the water. At one hundred feet, the pilot turned pale. What he thought was an old garbage bag in the water raised one hand and waved.

An SAR-equipped helicopter was on the scene fifteen minutes later. With the original SH-60 marking the spot, the rescue helo vectored in, deploying two rescue divers into the water with a horse collar. Within minutes they were at the man's side, determined that he was still alive, and affixed the horse collar to him. Three minutes later, T'sing Lin was winched up into the belly of the helicopter.

•   •   •

He'd been ready to die. Ready, and even looking forward to it with a calm resignation that he'd always heard
preceded death. It had been a good life—a short one,
but a good one, as least until the last year. He felt a
minor ripple of anguish that his son would grow up
without him, that his parents and wife would never speak
his name again in public. But even that had been no
more than a minor ripple in the sea of calm that had
enveloped him, the certainty that he'd at least expiated
his own shame.

To be wrenched away from certain destiny so suddenly, in such a noisy and ungainly fashion, offended
something deep in his soul. Anger boiled up that he'd
put himself through the agony of preparing for death
only to have it snatched away at the last moment.

He raised a hand to the white man hovering anxiously
over him, somewhat surprised at how weak he was. How
long had he been in the water? His mind, fuzzed by
sensory deprivation and overwhelmed by the sudden
change in his fate, refused to yield up the answer.

"I am from the *Lotus Glory*," he said slowly. Even
as he spoke, he almost laughed at his own foolishness.
None of these men would understand his language—
there was no chance at all of it. Then why try to explain
to them what had happened, how he'd come to be floating in the sea so far behind his ship?

It seemed only fitting that they should know about the
Lotus Glory. The gods worked in strange ways, and evidently it had been their decision that the battle would
go in another direction. Otherwise, why would they have
chosen such a weak vessel as himself for such an important program? No, his own weakness had a place in
the scheme of this. He'd been spared from the torpedo
for some purpose, and it was only now, after hours of
floating in the endless ocean, at one with the water and
sky, that it finally came to him. He was to stop a war,

prevent other young men from dying as his friends had done.

But how to communicate that to these men? While the remaining weapons on board *Lotus Glory* might be useless without pilots, there was no way of being certain that someone on the ship didn't know how to operate them. Or perhaps they could even be fired without the operator—God knows, they'd discussed that very matter in the long, silent hours in their compartment before dawn. No, these men must know. He racked his brain, trying to think of some way to communicate. He made a scribbling motion as though writing something out. After a brief flurry of shouted orders, the white man shoved a pad of paper and a pencil at him. He took it gingerly, paused, and concentrated on how to draw out the complicated scheme now in motion. Finally, he had it.

He started to sketch out the ship. As he drew out the symbols that represented the ship's name across the stern in order that they might identify it, another thought struck him. A brilliant one, one that obviously came from the gods. The little schooling that he'd had made one thing perfectly clear—the Americans remembered the waves of suicide aircraft that had swept over them during World War II, the Divine Wind from Japan that had decimated so many of their forces.

The Japanese were barely civilized, heathens of the worst sort. But brutality had to be fought with brutality, as the Admiral had made clear. The concept had been noted, improved upon, and melded into the Chinese war-fighting ethos.

The Americans were only now learning of the Niru Tao, the Arrow's Way. Someday, they would know *niru.* But for now . . .

One word stood out in his mind, blazing through as though wreathed in glory itself. A wide smile split his face. He turned to the American rescuer and said the one word that might make sense to them, the name of the precious Divine Wind forces that had so ravaged their forces in the last world war.

"Kamikaze." The hated Japanese word felt ugly in his mouth. T'sing Lin pointed at the sea.

The hospital corpsman checking him over for signs of injury turned pale. He turned to the flight crewman standing beside him. "Tell the pilot there's been a change of plans. We need to get this fellow on board the carrier immediately."

"He needs a hospital?" the crewman asked.

The corpsman shook his head. "No. An interpreter."

As the helicopter descended to the large, flat deck of the aircraft carrier, T'sing Lin shook his head at the wonder of it. The deck was packed with a wide variety of aircraft, each more potent and deadly than the last. He'd been half afraid, when he said the word, that the Americans would immediately eject him from the helicopter in retribution for his part in the scheme. But no, if anything, they'd been even more solicitous than before. He could still taste the warm, dark flavor of chocolate in his mouth, the sweet, tangy liquid that they'd forced on him afterwards. With those little bits of sustenance, strength already seemed to be returning to his body.

The helicopter landed, and as the blades were still turning, the hospital corpsman helped him to the deck. T'sing Lin staggered, his feet swollen and aching and barely able to bear the weight of his body. The corpsman studied him for a moment, then motioned for a stretcher. They placed him in it, stretched a blanket across him, then carried him across the hot, noisy tarmac. A few minutes later, he was inside the ship.

More white men—and then one of his own. A smooth Chinese face, broad through the cheeks, with the thin lips of the Szechwan Province.

"I am Charlie," the other man said in carefully phrased words. T'sing Lin noted the odd accent.

He gave his own name in return, then stared in wonder at the turmoil raging around him. "Where am I?"

"You are on the—" The interpreter paused for a moment, struggling to find the right word. Then he finally settled for, "The big ship. The one with yours. What ship are you from? They will be worried about you."

"The *Lotus Glory*," T'sing Lin said immediately. "And yes, they will be worried—but for reasons that you do not know yet." Briefly, he summarized the exact nature of his duties on board the Chinese grain ship.

Five minutes later, a helicopter lifted off the deck again, this time carrying a platoon of SEALs. It headed for the *Lotus Glory*.

37

THE PANAMA CANAL:
8 OCTOBER

USS JOUETT

Gatun Lake was crowded with merchant vessels in the early morning light. The man-made lake that stretched almost the entire width of the country held not only the foreign-flag traffic that was transiting through the Canal, but all of the American merchants that had been stopped when the embargo was first imposed. The Panamanian government, while not actually declaring the ships hostage, insisted that suspension of the right of free passage meant just that—that American ships, no matter what their location in the Canal when the embargo was imposed, would be required to remain exactly where they were. As a consequence, the forty-three grain ships that had been en route to the Pacific from the Atlantic were still captive inside the lake.

Bailey stepped out onto the bridge wing, and studied the small Panamanian patrol craft that was hovering officiously two hundred yards off their port bow. Fifty-caliber guns mounted on the forward portion of the boat

were conspicuously trained on *Jouett*. While the Panamanians had not yet made any overtly aggressive moves
from their patrol ship, it would only be a matter of time
before they followed the lead of the land-based troops.

"Loan me your binoculars," Bailey said, reaching out
a hand to the lieutenant standing next to her. He slipped
the strap over his neck and handed them to her. She
lifted them to her eyes and studied the Panamanian craft.

"You notice anything odd about the crew?" she
asked. She dropped the binoculars long enough to
exchange a knowing glance with Renninger.

The Captain nodded. "They seem to have a Chinese
contingent on board as well. Is that what you're talking
about?"

"Yes. These new bonds of friendship between Panama and China go a little deeper than I'd like."

"Like cancer." Renninger squinted against the harsh
tropical sun and motioned toward the patrol craft. "Do
they really think they can stop us with that?"

Bailey passed the binoculars back to the lieutenant
and thanked him. "Oh, they might. I guarantee, though,
that's not the only weapon they have at their disposal.
Did you check the stern of the vessel carefully?"

Renninger lifted his own binoculars. "A bunch of
crates. You're thinking mines?"

"Aren't you?"

Renninger turned to face her. "Unfortunately, yes.
But your prior reasoning applies here as well. The Canal
is Panama's only real asset—why would they mine their
own waterway?"

"If you use moored mines and only set them in a
small area, it might be a useful way to cordon off a
group of ships." She gestured toward a cluster of ships
across the lake. "Like there. It's starting to look like a
real international community here. All of the American
ships have been directed to moor in the same area. And
all the Chinese ships at the other end of the lake."

"They wouldn't dare." Renninger's voice was fierce. "Mining an international waterway is an act of war."

"Like they're really concerned. No, I think we have to consider the possibility that they're equipped to lay mines. Are your lookouts familiar with minelaying activities?"

"I'll have Collins brief them again," Renninger said, tacitly admitting the validity of her point. "We need a contingency plan, though. If they start minelaying activities . . ." His voice trailed off as he considered the possibilities.

"Then we have to move out of the area immediately," Bailey said briskly. "My bet is that the safest place will be near the Chinese ships."

"There aren't any good answers here, are there?" Renninger looked as though he didn't really expect an answer.

"Captain. Flash traffic." A radioman stepped out onto the bridge wing and handed Renninger a sheet of paper. "It's from the battle group." Renninger scanned the message quickly, and turned pale. Without comment, he passed it over to Bailey.

FROM: CTG 34.1
TO: CTE 32.1.4

SECRET NOFORN

1. HUMINT CONFIRMS CAPABILITY OF CHINESE MERCHANT VESSELS TO DEPLOY OFFENSIVE SUBSURFACE WEAPONS AGAINST U.S. FORCES. WEAPONS DEPLOYED THROUGH LOCKOUT COMPARTMENT LOCATED ALONG KEEL OF MERCHANT VESSELS. SOURCES CONFIRM CHINESE MERCHANT VESSEL LOTUS GLORY EQUIPPED WITH SYSTEM. THERE ARE INDICATIONS OTHER MERCHANT VESSELS MAY BE EQUIPPED WITH SIMILAR DELIVERY SYSTEMS.

2. EXERCISE EXTREME CAUTION IN THE VICINITY OF CHINESE MERCHANT VESSELS. TO DATE, EXISTENCE OF SYSTEM ON RO-RO VESSELS ONLY CONFIRMED INSTALLATION.

3. VESSELS ESTIMATED CAPABLE OF DEPLOYING 28-FOOT TORPEDO ARMED WITH HIGH EXPLOSIVE. INDICATIONS ARE THAT THE DESIGN IS ROUGHLY SIMILAR TO LATEST RUSSIAN MODELS. POTENTIAL OFFENSIVE CAPABILITY INCLUDES DESTRUCTION OF AIRCRAFT CARRIER WITH ONE SHOT. REPEAT: EXERCISE EXTREME CAUTION.

4. NORMAL ANTI-TORPEDO TACTICS MAY BE INEFFECTIVE AGAINST THESE WEAPONS. EXPECT A HIGH DEGREE OF MANEUVERABILITY AND FLEXIBILITY IN APPROACH/ATTACK PROFILES.

5. SOURCE INDICATES THAT TORPEDOES ARE EQUIPPED WITH TERMINAL GUIDANCE, COMPUTER AIDED NAVIGATION SOURCES, PASSIVE AND ACTIVE SONAR RANGING. ADDITIONALLY, EACH TORPEDO IS ESTIMATED TO BE MANNED BY ONE HIGHLY TRAINED PILOT.

6. AVOID APPROACHING CHINESE MERCHANT TRAFFIC AT ALL COSTS.

Bailey looked up from the message and stared at Renninger's pale, stricken face. It was a mirror of her own, she was certain.

"The Japanese," she said softly. "World War II." She passed the message back to the waiting radioman and scribbled her initial on the top of it.

"The Japanese used kamikaze pilots in aircraft and torpedoes. But the Chinese?" Renninger's voice was, for the first time since she'd known him, uncertain. He shuddered. "My God, to think of it . . ."

"They deploy them from Chinese merchant vessels," she said crisply, refocusing on the problem at hand. "I think that effectively does away with my plan for hiding out among them."

"They'd probably love it if we got that close," Renninger said bitterly. He slammed his hand down on the sunbaked wooden railing surrounding the bridge wing. "Dammit."

"Every culture has its own ways of making war," Bailey said, her voice somber. "We train for the European variety—direct force, the blitzkrieg, a sudden onslaught." She shook her head ruefully. "Always fighting the last war, we are. That's what'll get us killed this time."

"What are you suggesting?"

"Just this." She gestured out towards the large lake around them. "I think we're in agreement that the Chinese are behind this, right?" She waited for the confirming nod of head, then continued. "So, even if we are in Central America, we're fighting a Chinese war. We've never gone directly head-to-toe with China—not this far from their mainland. Sure, they've supported other forces, like in Vietnam. But this is still something new for us. They've spent a lot more time studying us than we have studying them."

"This is hardly a time for academics," Renninger snapped. "You got anything useful to say?"

"There's never been a better time," she shot back. "Think about how the Chinese plan their wars—think about it. You've read Sun Tzu, haven't you?"

He nodded. "Completely irrelevant. What does an ancient Chinese military theorist have to do with us now?"

"The same thing Bismarck has to do with European wars. This lake—the area around it—all of it is terrain for the Chinese. Remember, they're a good deal more used to fighting wars on the ground than they are on the water. And they have few compunctions about wasting human life. In a nation of two billion people, you can afford to expend some troops. Even as armament.''

"This is a lake, not terrain. Water, lady.''

Bailey shook her head. "Think about it. When we talk about hunting submarines, we look at the sound-velocity profile of the water. The ocean floor has mountains, cliffs—even canyons and volcanoes. It's all an environment, it's all terrain. It just depends on how you see it.''

He looked at her suspiciously. "You've been thinking about this too much.''

"The Panama Canal is the center of gravity of this entire war,'' she continued. "Terrain is a factor in holding onto it. Therefore, we need to pay some more attention to how our environment affects the war. Like those torpedoes. If we can't hide amongst those Chinese merchant ships, just how are we going to deal with an unconventional torpedo in these waters?''

Renninger sighed and stared out at the American ships on the other side of the lake. "I'm open to suggestions.''

Briefly, Bailey outlined her plan. At first, Renninger's face was a mask of outrage. Then it mellowed into interest, then into enthusiasm. "It might work.''

"It's got to.''

The cell phone holstered in a small leather catchment on her belt shrilled, startling both of them. She picked it up and flipped it open. "It's as you thought, Commander,'' she heard the gravelly voice of Sergeant Elwell say. "But the situation is resolved.''

Careful to avoid discussing classified information over the cell phone, Bailey said, "Is he going to contact them?''

"He sounded quite cooperative,'' Elwell said, a trace of amusement in his voice. "Under the circumstances, understandable.''

"Good, get back to me. There's some other intel—'' She broke off suddenly, unable to find a way to convey the essence of the message to Elwell over the unclassified circuit. Finally, she decided it didn't matter. Tor-

pedoes in the water were not his concern. "Just let me
know when it's finalized," she finished. "We'll be
here."

"I imagine you will." Elwell broke the connection.

Bailey turned back to Renninger. "So what do you
think?"

"I think we need to go to gunnery stations," Renninger said. "And spin up a couple of torpedoes as well."

Jouett trolled slowly up the coast, only fifty feet off the
banks that sloped down to the lake. Bailey and Renninger crowded into the chart house, standing on either side
of the senior quartermaster. Finally, the enlisted man
spoke. "Here it is." He pointed to a return from the
fathometer. "Not much of one, but it's the closest I can
see."

"They're fairly diligent about dredging," Renninger
said. "But it looks like the current crisis might have
slowed them down some."

"Good for us." Bailey turned to the gunner's mate
standing at her side. "Can you do it?"

The chief gunner's mate nodded. "We can. But you'll
need to move us further out into the center of the lake.
It's too slow as is." He frowned. "Helluva steep angle."

"Can you do it?" Bailey repeated.

He nodded. "Four shots ought to be enough. That will
blast the hell out of the bottom."

Ten minutes later, the first shot rang out. *Jouett*'s five-
inch gun was pointed almost straight into the sky. The
five-inch shell arced high above their heads, out of sight,
then descended back down to the lake on a nearly
straight trajectory. In quick succession, the other three
shots followed. Renninger smiled approvingly. True to
his word, the gunner's mate had found his range on the
very first shot. Good thing too, with civilian structures
only half a mile away.

The four shells dove down through twenty feet of water before hitting the sandy, well-swept bottom. As they hit the Canal's floor, they exploded, gouting up huge plumes of water and debris that rained out in a wide pattern around the impact point. Just to the south of the explosion was a newly formed sandbar, swept into a shaft protruding out into the Canal by the currents along the bank. Renninger and Bailey were counting on the explosion to heap even more debris up on top of it.

"Did it work?" Renninger asked.

Bailey studied the coastline. The water was dark and clouded with silt, the bank along the edge shredded and jagged. If everything worked as planned, the five-inch shells would have dug out a narrow trench between two piles of debris. The question was—how narrow? Wide enough to get *Jouett* in? And high enough on the sides to offer her some protection?

"We could approach it slowly," she said finally. "Keep the fathometer going—try to map the contours of it."

Renninger joined her on the bridge rail and stared out at the murky water. "We could. But we run the danger of going aground. And of letting them know what our plans are."

The sonar warning buzzer cut short their discussion. "Conn, Sonar, torpedo inbound. Range two thousand yards, speed twenty knots. Bearing constant, range decreasing."

"Right full rudder, all engines ahead flank," Collins ordered immediately. She turned to Renninger. "Captain? How lucky do you feel?"

He grimaced and shrugged. "Not very. Maybe we won't need it." He turned to Bailey. "You take the conn, Commander Bailey. Take us in."

Bailey started to protest, then realized the reasoning behind it. If the ship went aground, or if the torpedo hit its mark, she and Renninger would bear the sole responsibility.

"I'll do it," Collins said. She stepped forward and

stood in front of Renninger, a small blond figure in front of the towering Captain. "Captain, it's my job. My ship."

He shook his head. "Not this time, XO," he said, his voice unexpectedly gentle. "Not this time. Well, Miss Bailey?"

Bailey nodded and took a deep breath. "Engineering, stand by for backing bells."

Jouett responded quickly, sluing around 180 degrees. Bailey stood on the bridge wing, keeping one eye on the Panamanian patrol boats and the other on the point of land she'd picked out as her guide point. Five hundred yards away, she eased off to one third ahead, then finally to full stop.

"Range, five hundred yards and closing. Captain, the contact is accelerating. Now passing thirty knots." The concern in the sonarman's voice was evident.

"Ahead one third," Bailey ordered. Close, too close. She would prefer to gently drift into position, interposing the sandbar they'd created between the ship and the torpedo, but the Chinese weren't going to give her time. It was now or never.

Jouett bucked slightly, and a sick grating noise filled the ship. "Emergency back full," Bailey shouted. The ship responded instantly, as though waiting for her command. A huge gout of water streamed up behind the ship as the propellers fought to bite into the churning water.

The noise stopped suddenly as *Jouett* shuddered to a halt. The ship canted at five-degrees list.

Bailey looked over at Renninger. "I think we're there." The jagged and torn bank was still twenty yards away.

"We're aground. You realize that, don't you?"

"Yes, Captain."

"One hundred yards and accelerating. Captain, it's headed straight for our starboard beam." The sonarman's voice was shrill now.

"Sound the collision alarm," Renninger ordered. "All hands brace for shock."

They counted down the seconds, each lost in their own thoughts.

Twenty seconds later, a huge explosion rocked the ship as the torpedo slammed into the sandbar. *Jouett* canted violently to port and stayed there, still wedged on the shallow ground near shore. A waterspout gouted up from the starboard side of the ship, drenching them all.

Amid the muffled screams and oaths, a ragged cheer broke out in Combat.

"Did you get a bearing off the torpedo?" Bailey asked the TAO.

He pointed along a circuitous track approaching the ship. "It wasn't a normal torpedo—I can tell you that much. The course changes, the maneuvering—I've never seen anything like it. But as close as I can tell, it came from here." The tip of his laser pointer rested on one Chinese vessel moored out slightly from the others.

"Has it got a name?" Bailey asked.

"The *Lotus Vengeance*," the TAO said.

Bailey felt a thrill of vindication. It was the same ship she'd seen the oddly shaped helicopter landing on before, the one with the unique tail rotor.

At the first shot, the Panamanian patrol boat had spattered the ship with gunfire. When *Jouett*'s own fifty-cals were swiveled around and trained on them from behind the shielded turrets, they beat a hasty retreat. They were now milling about aimlessly across the lake in the vicinity of the American ships moored there.

Renninger pointed over at the patrol boats. "Think they'll give them any problems?"

"Not any more than they've got already."

The harsh gonging of General Quarters alarm made them both start. Renninger darted back onto the bridge and down the ladder into Combat, Bailey hot on his heels. They burst into the darkened compartment.

"Sonar alarm," the TAO said. "It could be one of those torpedoes you briefed us on, Captain." He pointed up at the symbol on the large-screen display. "It's only doing fifteen knots—damned unusual for a weapon."

Renninger and Bailey exchanged a telling look. There was no telling if the barricade would hold up to another attack.

The large-screen display exploded into a flurry of air contacts. The TAO let out a muffled yelp.

"Which radar is primary input?" Bailey demanded.

"The Aegis—hold on, I'm taking it off-line." The TAO's fingers flew over his console buttons. "There."

The contacts faded abruptly off the screen, to be replaced by a spattering of noise. "The fifty-five is still working," Bailey said approvingly. She turned to Renninger. "With your permission, Captain, I'll call SESS and get a bearing. Then we can get a cross fix from our last detections."

Renninger nodded silently.

Moments later, Bailey had the answer she needed. She reached over and tapped the portion of land just next to the entrance to the Canal. "Right there. The cross fix is solid."

"Generating ghost radar contacts—that sounds like a hostile act to me." Renninger's voice left no doubt as to his decision. "If the electromagnetic spectrum is part of the terrain of this war, then the Chinese have been conducting mining."

Bailey nodded and waited. All she could do was put forth a theory and demonstrate the science behind it. The final decision, however, had to be Renninger's.

Collins spoke up unexpectedly. "Shall I set gunnery stations, Captain?"

Finally, Renninger nodded. "Set gunnery stations." To the TAO, he said, "And assign this target to the five-inch-gun targeting system. I want two shots, fire for effect."

The TAO nodded. "Aye, aye, Captain."

• • •

The guns boomed once, twice. Bailey and Renninger were crouched behind the metal on the bridge wing, and stood and looked out at the Chinese naval base. Two large flumes of dust and debris were rising up from the central warehouse building.

"Captain, SSES reports the signals have vanished."

"Switch to Aegis radar input to the display," Renninger ordered. "Tell me what you see."

The relief in the TAO's voice was palpable. "No contacts, Captain. They're off-line."

"She's turning," Bailey said, pointing across the lake at *Lotus Vengeance*. She had been beam onto them earlier, and was now showing a stern aspect. A small wash of churned water fanned out a short distance behind her. "Captain, your orders?"

"Gunnery stations," Renninger ordered. "Stand by for batteries free."

"Wait," Collins interrupted. "Are we certain that she's the one that attacked us?"

"I am," Bailey said.

Renninger nodded in agreement. "I'm satisfied as well, XO."

"Captain, she's headed for the other end of the lake. Look at her, sir. I think she's withdrawing from this engagement," Collins said.

"Not good enough," Renninger said.

Collins lifted her binoculars and focused in on the merchant ship. A light was blinking amidships, pulsing out in a regular pattern of short and long flashes. "Captain, she's trying to signal us. Flashing light."

"I don't give a god damn what she wants. That bastard fired on me." Renninger wheeled on her, furious.

"XO, all gunnery stations report manned and ready. Request batteries free," the officer of the deck said.

Renninger took two steps toward Collins and yanked her binoculars away from her face. "XO, what's your problem? Two rounds, fire for effect. *Now.*"

"Captain, I—"

"*Now*, XO. You disobey me now, I'll see you at court martial."

Time seemed to stop on the bridge wing. A light breeze snapped the flag overhead, but there was no other sound. Collins and Renninger faced each other, Renninger's face a study in anger, Collins's hardening into steel. Bailey stood behind Collins, her eyes fixed on the officer who'd once before refused to obey Bailey's orders.

"Why?" Bailey's voice, low and urgent, broke the impasse. "Why, June?"

"She's signaling, ma'am. I think I recognize the letters. It's in the international code book. But I've got to have the signalman confirm it. I've never seen this one used before." Collins's voice was firm. "Captain, if we could just—"

"If there's a torpedo in the water right now, XO, I'll see you in hell," Renninger snarled. *Jouett* had pulled away from the sandbar and was in open water, a clear target for a shallow-running torpedo. "A court martial will be the least of your worries. In hell—I mean it."

"Captain!" A signalman skidded to a halt as he rounded the corner of the superstructure. "International Q-code, sir, from that merchant. She's signaling surrender, sir. Surrender."

"Weapons tight," Renninger snapped, his gaze still locked on Collins's eyes. "She could be lying. She could have more torpedoes."

"And she could be surrendering, sir," Collins said.

Bailey stepped forward. "Captain, I'm available if you decide to send a boarding party. Or as gunnery officer if you want to fire." She turned slightly to face Collins. "It's not your decision, not this time. It was with the airbus, but not now. Not with the Captain here."

Collins seemed to deflate. Renninger turned away

from both of them, lifted his binoculars and stared across the lake at the merchant ship. He was silent for a long moment, then said, ''No, Commander Bailey. My XO will lead the boarding party.''

38

NATIONAL SECURITY AGENCY

Terry Intanglio was waiting in her office. She nodded curtly, thumped the cardboard box down on her desk, and began moving personal memorabilia from her credenza into the box. A coffee cup, its interior surfaces grimy and well-seasoned. A small picture of her parents, a paperweight given to her from her first ship, and a few other items that had no intrinsic value but had served to define that space as hers.

"Could we talk?" Terry asked mildly. "After all, you have been gone for nearly two weeks."

"Nearly two weeks is only the beginning. I'm out of here." Bailey opened the lower doors of the government-issue desk and began rooting around through her files. "Do whatever it is that you have to do—call security or somebody to come make sure I'm not stealing secrets."

"Come on, Jerusha. It was just—"

She slammed the top desk draw shut, cutting him off. "It was just business, right? NSA business. Well, no longer. Not for me. I'm tired of playing your tame commander, your spook on the scene.''

"That was the last time. Division Heads don't go out in the field."

"I am Division Head for Western European affairs—or was."

"Not anymore."

"Exactly what I've been trying to tell you."

"You own all of Europe. As of yesterday."

A long pause, broken only by the soft shuffling of paper. "What do you mean?"

"Jim Atchinson is taking early retirement." Nothing in Intanglio's voice gave away his role in Atchinson's decision. "I need a replacement. I want you."

"Get somebody else."

"Nope. Gotta be you. Besides, there's something else as well. Here." He tossed a small red-and-white cardboard box to her. "You'll be needing these."

The box hit her desk top with a small thud. She reached out, turned it over, and stared down at two silver eagles mounted on a cardboard backing. "I'm not up for captain yet." The eagles caught the fluorescent light and flashed at her. "Not for another year."

Intanglio smiled. "You got deep-selected. Evidently the board heard about you. And your buddy, June Collins—she got picked up for a command tour." He glanced at his watch. "She should be getting the notification just about now. The evidence she gathered onboard *Lotus Vengeance* made her CO—not to mention the Navy—look very good. It proved the Chinese were behind the airbus shoot-down."

"And all this is contingent on my staying at NSA?"

He studied her for a moment, then shook his head. "No. I wish it were. But I didn't have anything to do with it. Nor would I make that a condition of your promotion, even if I could. You earned it, Jerusha."

She collapsed into her chair, suddenly out of energy. The final arrival of the USS *Eisenhower*, the garbled radio reports as the SEALs boarded *Lotus Glory*, and the slow, careful transit back out of the Canal past shattered lock doors and the lifeless *Lotus Vengeance*—too much, too fast. As they'd outchopped back to the clean, open Pacific waters, she'd seen crews scurrying around behind them at the two locks, already wheeling replacement doors into position along the sides of the Canal.

"What happened to Billy Elwell?" she asked suddenly. That had been the one loose end she hadn't resolved prior to leaving, although Carlisle had made a full confession on the employment of his last two bugs.

"He got shot."

"And he's recovering quite well," Intanglio answered immediately. "Yesterday I heard he was headed back to Germany to see his family. I think the Army's going to leave him there until he retires. He said something about going native."

Bailey shook her head. "Not Elwell."

"So will you stay? Come on, Jerusha. Give it a couple of weeks, at least. Just a chance?" Intanglio's face contorted for a moment. Then he said, "Please?"

She laughed at the expression of discomfort on his face. "OK. Just promise me one thing."

"I know, I know—no more using you and the MIUW."

"That too. But if you ever do—Pete Carlisle gets to take anything he wants."